# A CELTIC READER

A selection of lost classics from Celtic literature.

They prayed to CHRIST
with much fervour
Their inward foes to quell:
Sans fear they rode in
high ardour
Good issue to compel.
GLORY TO HOLY TRINITY
That be of most avail!
Honour to heaven's
sweet ladye
That prays for us, saun fayle
To Joseph, hight Arimathie,
And to the HOLY GREAL!

Frontispiece: 'The quest for the Graal' by *Evelyn Paul*.

# A CELTIC READER

## Selections from Celtic Legend, Scholarship and Story

Compiled and edited by
# John Matthews

**Foreword by P. L. Travers**

Aquarian/Thorsons
*An Imprint of* HarperCollins*Publishers*

The Aquarian Press
An Imprint of HarperCollins*Publishers*
77–85 Fulham Palace Road,
Hammersmith, London W6 8JB

First published by The Aquarian Press 1991
This paperback edition 1992
3  5  7  9  10  8  6  4  2

A catalogue record for this book
is available from the British Library

ISBN 1 85538 228 8

Typeset by Harper Phototypesetters Limited,
Northampton, England
Printed in Great Britain by
Mackays of Chatham, Kent

# Dedication

To David Deutsch and Debra Niehoff
and to Jennifer and Haley.

And to all the great Company of Story-tellers
who keep the Celtic Tradition alive.

# Acknowledgements

Once again I must thank all those people, friends and strangers, who either sent or wrote to tell me of certain out-of-the-way books and articles which I might otherwise never have found. And to the tireless interloans staff at Kensington Central Library (colleagues in every sense of the word) who good-naturedly sought out others at my request. Thanks also to Philip Carr-Gomm, present head of the Order of Bards, Ovates and Druids, for allowing me to reprint material by their former Chief, the late Ross Nichols. Love and thanks as always to my wife, Caitlín, who helped with the chores of proof-reading and wielded a nifty glue-stick on more than one occasion. And lastly to Pamela Travers, for her kind and generous Foreword — as a great keeper of the Celtic Tradition herself it was a privilege to have her words grace this book.

# Foreword

## by P. L. Travers

A welcome before you!

I use this old Celtic greeting to John Matthews and his latest collection of myth, fable, legend and poetry. With it he has added one more to his literary progeny of love and learning.

As he informs us in the introduction, 'the page is in a sense being turned back from the Arthurian era', his earlier work, and we find ourselves here involved with Druids, Taliesin of the Shining Brow, Angus Oge and a host of cosmic gods and goddesses.

He speaks of these as 'other-worldly images' but he is clearly aware that such images can only become evident in a 'this-worldly' ambience, just as the supernatural has no other home than in the natural. The worlds are woven together as closely as the braids of the Goddess of Wisdom's hair.

I was particularly pleased to see an A.E. (George William Russell) story fished up from the Irish stream. That myriad-minded man, as he has been called, would have been familiar with the way in which those braids are intertwined. Friend and colleague of W. B. Yeats since their boyhood days and the poet's most valued critic, he has perhaps been put a little in the shade by his great contemporary. But it is a question as to which luminary shone with a more luminous glow in that famous twilight that never fades into night.

John Matthews and his kind have seen to that. Like faithful servants they labour to keep the essence of tradition alive and vibrant, no matter how uncaringly the modern mind, taking myth as lie (or at least fiction) and accepting as real only what is material, allows it to fall into Lethe.

Novalis wrote in the eighteenth century, at a time when people needed the reminder far less than they do today, that 'poems, myths and fairy tales, are the true history of the world'. And we in Celtic Britain have an adage, known to any old wife — if indeed any old wives still exist or admit to being old wives — 'Ask the wild bee what the Druids knew.'

But the bee, of course — its very name is cognate in most world languages with the verb 'to be' — goes back infinitely further than the Druids, to the first of all things, whenever that was. In fact, man himself is, in a sense, a bee, for from our birth, and indeed from our conception, bee-stuff is alive in us, running in our bloodstream as it does in that of Gaia, the Earth, through all her streams and rivers — Thames, Tigris, Ganges, Nile, Liffey, the wide Missouri. When we neglect this essential life-giving, heart-healing psychic element we do so at our peril and also at hers.

Books such as *A Celtic Reader* and others of its kind should be thought of as a modern form of the old art of 'telling'. In older times, told round a turf fire or beside a sacred spring or even, by Raftery, under a hedge, were always celebrations. And celebrations bring about renewal. If modern man would allow himself to be reminded of the 'true history of the world' and to live once more in intimate relation to the song-lines of tradition, he would serve a double purpose — ease his own sense of separateness and, despite the ravages to her person, prevent any discontinuity in Gaia's pulse-beat which is nothing other than the Perennial Memory. The author seems wordlessly to underline this possibility when, with a benediction, A Celtic Blessing from the *Carmina Gaedelica*, he closes his book.

P. L. Travers

# Contents

# Introduction

Making a selection from the incredible richness of material which makes up the Celtic Tradition can be no easy task, and certainly not one to be approached with lightness. However, as in *An Arthurian Reader* (Aquarian Press, 1988), I have once again chosen to look for the out-of-the-way and the unusual, rather than repeating the many variations of Celtic lore, life and literature already available. As before, the mixture is of original text, scholarly and speculative commentary, and more recent stories and poems which draw upon the more ancient sources. I much regret that one of the most important aspects of Celtic culture, their significant and individual art work, has been only briefly illustrated by the selection of black and white pictures scattered throughout this volume. However, in this as in the mass of material *not* included here, I have comforted myself in the knowledge that there is a huge number of specializing books — some of which are listed in the Bibliography — which make it possible for the reader to follow his or her own particular path of interest once it has been aroused.

For it is once again my intention to excite and stimulate a fascination with the subject, a fascination I have personally felt for more than 20 years, and to this end I have cast my net widely — to history, religion, myth, and story — each of which was, as it remains today, a vital part of Celtic culture.

The sheer richness of the material has made this a heady brew. In a certain sense we are turning the page back from the Arthurian era dealt with in the earlier volume; but there are overlaps here also, as will become apparent. The same brilliantly coloured kaleidoscope of Otherworldly images is present, the same sense of magic hovering just on the horizon.

I hope that if you are excited and moved by the material collected here, you will be encouraged to look deeper, to explore the Celtic world still further. If you do so you cannot help but be enchanted — as the Celts themselves are — with a tradition that, far from fading with the passage of time, grows stronger as the years go by.

John Matthews
London, 1989

# PART ONE:
# THE DRUID PRIESTHOOD

Undoubtedly the single aspect of Celtic life and culture which springs most readily to mind when the subject is discussed is the existence of the mysterious priesthood known as the Druids. Little or nothing is known about them beyond the descriptions found in the writings of Julius Caesar, who founded most of his knowledge on the Gaulish Celts rather than the native Britons. Beyond this we know that the word 'Druid' probably stems from the word *duir*, 'oak', which has given rise to the assumption that the Druids were priests of the sacred oak groves believed to have once proliferated in this country and Ireland. Other fragments of information suggest that there were a number of Druid Schools which taught the precepts of their religion, and trained their formidable memories (they were required to memorize vast genealogies for the scattered tribes of the island). Beyond this, all is speculation — or nearly all. While we still do not possess any valid documentation on the Druids, there are hints and clues scattered throughout Celtic literature and archaeology which enable us to piece together a sketchy picture (see Anne Ross and Don Robins: *Life and Death of a Druid Prince*, Rider, 1989, for the very latest speculations).

Speculations there certainly are, in plenty. Numberless volumes have been published since the eighteenth century which have claimed to give the inside on the Druids. Most are worthless, though also fascinating, both for their ingenuity and for the occasional hares they start.

Since the eighteenth century a number of revival Druidic groups have come into being, several of which still exist, practising a form of neo-naturalism mixed with a yearning for the lost bardic mysteries of the kind promulgated by Iolo Morgannwg (see Part Four), and Edward Davies (see Chapter 3 of this section). Both these men were worthy and desired only the continuance of the Celtic Traditions, and, though their ideas were frequently wild and had little or no foundation in reality, their works are included here both for the sake of completeness and because there are genuinely exciting passages contained within them.

Of the three writers who appear in this first section only one, Eugene O'Curry, is a bona fide scholar. The others, enthusiastic amateurs, breathe life into what they have to say, and put out an at times breathtaking amount of exciting and challenging material. W.B. Crow writes illuminatingly of the association of Druids with mistletoe, and of their festivals in general. Lastly the Revd Davies follows a fantastic train of reasoning whereby he endeavours to prove the popular nineteenth-century theory that some of the lost tribes of Israel may have settled in Celtic lands, and that the Ark of Noah brought the wisdom of the ancients to these shores. This theory, though it must appear eccentric in the extreme today, nonetheless gave rise to some extraordinarily interesting material, among which Edward Davies' researches are included.

They are placed here in this collection, in a lengthy extract, because they are worth looking at again with fresh eyes for the insights they offer to all who feel the fascination of the Druidic and mythic lore of the Celts.

Chapter 1

# Druids and Druidism in Ancient Ireland[1]

## by Eugene O'Curry

Of all the systems of religion or worship, mixed with philosophy and science, of which the fertile mind of man was the parent, from the earliest period to the present day, there is not one perhaps which has obtained more early and lasting celebrity than that which has passed under the somewhat indefinite name of 'magic', as the description of the very imperfectly investigated religion or philosophy of the more ancient nations of the East. And there is, unfortunately, no system of which fewer satisfactory vestiges, or authentic historical details, have come down to our times.

The compilers of modern encyclopaedias have, I suppose, exhausted all the ancient classical writers in an effort to present to the world some intelligible view of the religion or philosophy of 'magic' under one of its most interesting forms, and one that seemed the least unfavourable for historical investigation, that, namely, of Druidism; to which, as that form of the Eastern philosophy or religion which prevailed in early ages in our own as well as other western nations, I have now to direct attention. The best English article I have found on the subject, because free from the gross fabrications of Vallancey and Toland, touching Irish Druids, is to be found in *Rees's Encyclopaedia*. Yet, after all the labour of the learned writer, and although he has devoted many closely printed pages to the subject, liberally quoting his authorities, still when we come to look for some specific description of Druids and Druidic rites we find nothing but the most vague and general assertions: that the Druids were priests who sacrificed human and other victims; but how, or to whom, we are not satisfactorily told; that they were teachers of occult sciences, and the favourite tutors of the children of the higher classes, but no instances are given; that they were absolute judges in cases of life and property, but by whom constituted, or under what laws, we are not told; that they practised magic and augury; but we are not given any particulars — not even furnished with so much as the name of any one great master of those arts among them, nor with any remarkable instance of their application.

As to the origin and history of Druidism, where and how it originally sprang, such books of reference as those I have alluded to, are equally unsatisfactory. Yet perhaps the best general introduction by which I can preface what I have to say on the subject of Druidism in Erinn would be to quote the substance of the account given by the essayist in *Rees's Encyclopaedia*, for we shall then see to what extent our Gaedhelic authorities will enable us to define what this learned writer has been unable to make clear, and to supply what he has failed to discover from classical authorities.

'The Druids' (says this writer) 'are said by some to have been a tribe of the ancient Celts or Celtae, who emigrated, as Herodotus assures us, from the Danube towards the more westerly parts of Europe, and to have settled in Gaul and in Britain at a very early period. Accordingly, they have traced their origin, as well as that of the Celts, to the Gomerians or the descendants of Gomer, the eldest son of Japhet. But little certain is known concerning them before the time of Caesar, who says that they were one of the two orders of persons that subsisted in Gaul, the other being the Nobles. The case was the same in Britain, where it was supposed the principles and rites of Druidism originated, and from which they were transferred to Gaul. This seems to have been the custom according to the account of the historian: Such of the Gauls as were desirous of being thoroughly instructed in the principles of their religion, which was the same with that of the Britons, usually took a journey into Britain for that purpose. It is universally acknowledged that the British Druids were at this time very famous, both at home and abroad, for their wisdom and learning as well as for their probity, and that they were held in high estimation as the teachers both of religion and philosophy. But it has been disputed whether they were the original inventors of the opinions and system which they taught, or received them from others.

'Some have imagined that the Gauls and other nations in the west of Europe derived the first principles of learning and philosophy from a Phoenician colony which left Greece and built Marseilles in Gaul, about BC 540. Others have suggested that the Druids derived their philosophy from Pythagoras, who flourished about five hundred years before Christ, and taught his doctrines at Crotona in Italy.

'It does not appear how widely the Druids were dispersed through Britain and the adjacent isles; but it is well known that their chief settlement was in the isle of Anglesey, the ancient Mona, which they probably selected for this purpose, as it was well stored with spacious groves of their favourite oak.

'As one principal part of their office was to direct the worship and religious rites of the people, the service of each temple required a considerable number of them, and all these lived together near the temple where they served. The Arch-Druid of Britain is thought to have his stated residence in the island of Anglesey above mentioned, where he lived in great splendour and magnificence, according to the custom of the times, surrounded by a great number of the most eminent persons of his order.

'The Druids were also divided into several classes or branches, viz, the *Vacerri, Bardi, Eubages, Semnothii* or *Semnothei*, and *Saronidae*. The *Vacerri* are held to have been the priests; the *Bardi*, the poets; the *Eubages*, the augurs; and the *Saronidae*, the civil judges and instructors of youth.

'Strabo only distinguishes three kinds: *bardi, eubages*, or *vates*, and Druids, though the last name was frequently given to the whole order.

'As several monuments were erected by the Druids for religious and other purposes, to say nothing of Stonehenge, we cannot question their having made great progress in the science of mechanics, and in the mode of applying mechanical power, so as to produce very astonishing effects.

'Medicine, or the art of healing, must also have been the object of attention and study among the Druids, for they were the physicians as well as the priests both of Gaul and Britain. To this purpose, being much addicted to superstition, those who were afflicted with a dangerous disease sacrificed a man, or promised that they would sacrifice one, for their recovery.

'The British Druids were great magicians, and much addicted to divination, by which they pretended to work a kind of miracle, and exhibited astonishing appearances in nature, to penetrate into the counsels of Heaven, to foretell future events, and to discover the success or miscarriage of public or private undertakings.

'"In Britain", says Pliny (N. H. 1.30, c. 1.) "the magic arts are cultivated with such astonishing success and so many ceremonies at this day (AD 60), that the Britons seem to be capable of instructing even the Persians themselves in these arts."

'Of the British Academies the most considerable were situated in the Isle of Anglesey, near the mansion of the Arch-Druid. Here is a place that is called *Myfyrion*, that is, the place of meditation or study; another called *Caer-Edris*, that is, the city of astronomers; and another *Cerrig-Brudyn*, or the astronomer's circle.

'Their great solemnity and festival was that of the cutting the mistletoe from the oak. This festival is said to have been kept as near as the age of the moon would permit to the 10th of March, which was their New Year's Day. The first of May was also a great festival, in honour of Bellinus or the sun.

'Of the Druidical creed it was an article that it was unlawful to build temples to the gods, or to worship them within walls, or under roofs. (Tacit. *De Mor. Germ.*, C. 9.)

'The Druids, says Pliny, have so high an esteem for the oak, that they do not perform the least religious ceremonies without being adorned with a garland of its leaves.

'The Druids had no image, but they worshipped a great oak tree as a symbol of Jupiter.

'They were selected from the best families. They were chief judges, and held their high court in Anglesey, in a cirque. One of these is called *Brein Gwyn*, that is, the supreme tribunal, in the townland of Fér Dryid.'

So far the article in *Rees's Encyclopaedia* on the Druids; but let us see what Rowlands, another and older Welshman, a native, too, of Mona itself, or Anglesey, says of the sort of authority which existed for these glowing accounts of the Druids of that island.

'I think I may take it for granted', says this very candid writer, 'that it is the generally received account, among all sorts of people in Wales who pretend to anything of antiquity, that the Isle of Mona or Anglesey was anciently the seat of the British Druids: nay, there is not a book of late written of history or geography which touches the Isle of Anglesey but gives the same account; though the opinion, for all I could yet see, rather seems to have been taken upon trust, passing from hand to hand, among the authors who had lately mentioned it, than well settled upon its due foundation and evidence. 'T is to no purpose to recite instances which are too many, and which only serve to prove a consent, and that it has not been till of late years contradicted, which is all I propose in this part of the proof.'[2]

So far, then, Rees and Rowlands upon the general character of the British Druids, their reputed learning and religion, and their establishment in the island of Anglesey; and I have here introduced so much on the subject, in order that we may be able to judge by comparison how far, and where the few notices of our Irish Druids which I have been able to collect, will agree with them.

We see from these English articles that nothing precise is known in England of the origin of Druids and Druidism in Britain; no native authorities of any kind quoted; in fact, nothing but a few opinions derived from foreign writers, and elaborately stated on trust by modern English authors, as Rowlands so honestly admits.

It must occur to everyone who has read of Zoroaster, of the Magi of Persia, and of the sorceries of Egypt mentioned in the seventh chapter of Exodus, that Druids and Druidism did not originate in Britain any more than in Gaul or Erinn. It is indeed probable that, notwithstanding Pliny's high opinion of the powers of the British Druids, the European Druidical system was but the offspring of the Eastern augury, somewhat less complete, perhaps, when transplanted to a new soil than in its ancient home.

I shall not, however, here attempt to trace the first origin of Druidism in Europe; nor shall I even endeavour, at present, to suggest any theory of what exactly constituted our own Druidism in ancient Erinn. Perhaps the time is not come for satisfactory inquiry, either into the nature of the druidical philosophy, (or 'religion', if it be proper so to call it), or into the details of the rites and ceremonies used by the Druids. For my own part I feel that I have at present more to do with the *materials* upon which hereafter to found a theory concerning this difficult subject of history, than with the imagination of one for myself. And so, merely calling attention to the rashness of such speculators upon Druidism as the writers I have just referred to, I shall confine myself here to a simple narration of what is to be found, upon Druids and Druidism, scattered over our own annals and earlier historic pieces; and that entirely apart from any comparison of the results of such an inquiry with what is to be found in the classic or other foreign authorities. Be it for others to undertake the task of a final and exhaustive examination of the subject of Druidism in Europe generally.

Let us begin with the earliest mention of Druids as preserved in our annals and historical traditions.

The origin of Druids in Erinn is carried back by our ancient writings (and I am convinced with great probability), to the earliest colonizers of the country, who were all, it is to be remembered, referred to the race of Japhet; and whether there was or was not in the more ancient times anything more than traditional authority for this belief, it is, I think, sufficient to show that the ancient Gaedhils never assumed the origin of the Druidic system themselves, nor acknowledged to have received it, any more than any other part of their social system, from any neighbouring country.

*Parthalon* is by our most ancient authorities recorded to have come into Erinn about three hundred years after the Deluge. He is said to have come from '*Migdonia*', or Middle Greece, with a small company; but among these we are told that there were three Druids, whose names are given: *Fios*, *Eolus*, and *Fochmare*; that is, if we seek the etymological meaning of the words, Intelligence, Knowledge, and Inquiry. We have no record of any performance of these Druids of *Parthalon*.

The next colony, led by *Nemid* and his sons, is said to have come from '*Scythia*', about three hundred and thirty years after the coming of *Parthalon*. *Nemid*'s sons were: *Starn*, *Iarbonel* 'the Prophet', *Fergus* 'the Half-Red', and *Aininn*. And this colony soon, according to our oldest records, came in contact with the power of hostile Druidism, to which they opposed their own. *Nemid*, it appears, had not remained long in peace in the country, before he was disturbed by the incursions of the sea rovers, who are known in our old writings under the name of the Fomorians. These adventurers, under a valiant leader named *Conaing*, son of *Faebhar*, took possession of Tory Island (on the north-west of the coast of Donegal), which they fortified, and converted into a sort of citadel or depot, and by this means made themselves most formidable and oppressive to the Nemidians on the mainland. The Nemidians, driven to despair at last, assembled all their forces, men and women, from all parts of the country, on the shore opposite Tory Island; which the Fomorians perceiving, sent their Druids and Druidesses, we are told, to confound them by their Druidic spells: but these were met by the Nemidian Druids and Druidesses under the leadership of *Reilbeó*, 'daughter of the king of Greece', *Nemid*'s wife, and chief of the Druidesses. A fierce contest of spells as well as of blows ensued between them, in which the Fomorian party were defeated. A general battle ensued then, which resulted in the utter rout of the Fomorians, whose tower or fortress on Tory Island was demolished, and their chief leader, *Conaing*, and his sons, were killed.

The Nemidians did not long enjoy the peace and freedom which this victory brought them; for *More* the son of *Dela*, another famous rover or Fomorian chief, came, with sixty ships, took possession again of Tory Island, and renewed the oppressions practised by his predecessor upon the Nemidians. This led to another great battle, in which the destruction of the parties was mutual; *More* and a few of his followers only, escaping to the island, and but one ship of the Nemidians, with only thirty warriors and three leaders on board, escaping to the land. These three leaders were: *Beothach*, the son of *Iarbonel* 'the prophet', son of *Nemid*; *Simeon Breac* (or 'the speckled'), son of *Starn*, son of *Nemid*; and *Britan Mael* (or 'the bald'), son of *Fergus* the Half-Red, son of *Nemid*. And it is to these three cousins that the races of the *Tuatha Dé Denaan*, the *Firbolgs*, and the Britons, are traced by our early genealogists, from whom we learn that the three soon afterwards left Erinn, and proceeded to seek a better fortune elsewhere. *Beothach*, we are told, with his clan, went to the northern parts of Europe, where they made themselves perfect in all the arts of Divination, Druidism, and Philosophy, and returned, after some generations, to Erinn, under the name of the *Tuatha Dé Danaan*. *Simeon Breac* with his clan wandered southward into Greece, and in many generations after returned to Erinn under the name of the *Firbolgs*. And we learn that *Britan Mael*, with his father *Fergus*, and his clan, went to *Moinn* or *Mainn Chonaing*, the present Island of Mona (or Anglesey); 'from which', says the *Book of Ballymote* (folio 15), 'their children filled the great Island of Britain, which they inhabited until the coming in of the Saxons, who drove the descendants of Brutus to the one border of the country, and the descendants of *Britan Mael* back to *Moinn Chonaing* [or Anglesey] on the other border'.

And here, let me observe that it seems strange that Rowlands and the other Welsh writers of modern times have not attempted to make any guess at the etymology of the name of Mona. This name is indifferently written in our ancient Irish manuscripts as *Moin*, *Main*, *Moein*, and *Maein*, and never but in connection with the name of *Conaing*, the great *Fomorian* chief already mentioned, who had occupied and fortified Tory Island on the coast of Donegal, from which he ravaged the mainland of Erinn, and perhaps other countries also. And it was from the tower or fortress erected by him there, and which has been always called *Tor Chonaing*, or *Conaing's* Tower, that the island received the name of *Tor Inis*, or Tower Island, a name modified by the Danes, to Tor-eye (eye being the Danish name for an island), and adopted in sound, and nearly in orthography, by English writers and speakers.

When we remember, then, that Tory was called *Tor Inis Chonaing*, or *Conaing's* Tower Island (and also, for brevity, *Tor Chonaing* or Conaing's Tower), and that in like manner we find the Island of Anglesey invariably written *Moin* or *Moen Chonaing*, we have established an analogy between the origins of both names, which to understand fully requires but to explain the word *Moin* or *Moen* through the medium of some recognized language. This we can well do, for, in an ancient Gaedhelic glossary (preserved in MS H.3.18,T.C.D.), we find the following words and explanation:

'*Moen*': from [the Latin] Moenia [signifying] a structure of walls [or ramparts]. [3]

Now, if *Tor Chonaing* meant, as it is well known it did, *Conaing's* Tower or Fortress, *Moen Chonaing*, or *Conaing's* 'Moen', must have had simply a corresponding meaning; and that such it had, I have, I trust, sufficiently shown, from an authority that cannot be questioned. *Moen Chonaing*, then means simply, *Conaing's* Fortress, or fortified island; in the same way that *Tor Chonaing* meant *Conaing's* Tower, or Tower Island.

It is also but rational to suppose that the strait or channel which divides this Island of Mona from the mainland of Britain, and which is now called the 'Menai Strait', did not derive that name from any independent source, but that it borrowed it from *Maen*, the name of the island. And in fact it was anciently called *Sruth Moena*, or *Muir Moena*; that is, the River or Sea of *Moen*; the nominative *moen* taking a final *a* in the genitive case, and forming *Moena* or *Moenai*, the correct form of the present name of Menai. That channels of this sort were named after the islands which they cut off from the mainland, and not from the land itself, could be shown by many examples if it were necessary; but it is too well known a fact to require illustration here.

It appears then that it was from Erinn that the Isle of Mona (or Anglesey) received its earliest colony, and that that colony was of a Druidical people.

Now going back to the ancient legendary history of the Gaedhils, it is to be remembered that on the flight of *Nemid's* three grandsons from Erinn, one of them, *Simeon Breac*, the son of *Starn*, is said to have gone with his clan into Thrace, that is into Greece. There, we are told, they remained and multiplied during more than two hundred years, when at last they fled from the oppression which, it seems, held them there in a state of slavery, and after many wanderings returned to Erinn again, and with little trouble made themselves masters of the country. These were the *Firbolgs*. These again, in their turn, were soon after invaded by the *Tuatha Dé Danann*, the descendants of *Iobath*, the third grandson or great-grandson of *Nemid*; and their power and rule were overthrown in the great battle of *Magh Tuireadh*, of which some account has been given in a former lecture. [4]

The *Tuatha Dé Danann*, or *Dadanann* tribes, as we have already seen, during the long period of their exile from Erinn, devoted themselves much to the cultivation of Divination, Druidism, and the Philosophy of the northern and eastern parts of Europe; so that they appear to have returned perfectly accomplished in all the secrets and mysteries of the occult sciences of those times. They had a Druidical chief or demigod, the great *Daghda*, as he was called, who was also their military leader. They had, besides him, three chief

Druids: *Brian*, *Inchar*, and *Iucharba*; and two chief professional Druidesses: *Beonill* and *Danann* — besides a great number of private Druids and Druidesses, mentioned by name in the early accounts of the coming of this race.

On the first arrival of the *Tuatha Dé Danann*, they took up their position in the fastnesses of Middle Connacht, but soon discovered that the country was inhabited by the Firbolgs; they then moved farther south and west, to the plain called *Magh Tuireadh*, near Cong, in the present county of Galway, as described on a former occasion. The ancient tales record that while they were making this important movement three of their noble non-professional Druidesses, namely, *Bodhbh*, *Macha*, and *Mór Rigan*, went to Tara, where the Firbolg hosts were assembled in a council of war; and that there, by their Druidical arts, they caused clouds of impenetrable darkness and mist to envelop the assembled multitudes, and showers of fire and blood to pour down upon them from the heavens, so that for three days all business was suspended; that at last the spell was broken by the Firbolg Druids, *Cesarn*, *Gnathach*, and *Ingnathach*, but that during this time the *Tuatha dé Danann* had already established themselves without opposition in a new defensive position at a safer distance from their enemies. This may serve as one instance of the ancient tradition of the practical use of Druidical magic at a very early period in Erinn.

Again we are told, in the oldest accounts, that previous to the invasion of the *Tuatha Dé Danann*, the king of the Firbolgs, *Eochaidh Mac Erc*, had an unusual dream, which he submitted for interpretation to his chief Druid, *Cesarn*. The Druid is said to have had recourse to the secret agencies of his art, and to have discovered from a vision the approach of a powerful enemy; and this he is said to have communicated to the king in a series of short simple sentences, of which a few are preserved in the account of the great battle of *Magh Tuireadh*, of which so much was extracted on a former occasion. [5] The great battle came at last; and it is stated that the men of science and 'knowledge' of both parties took up their positions on rocks and stages on the battle-field, practising their Druidic arts in favour of their friends and against their foes respectively; until at last the *Tuatha Dé Danann* prevailed, and the Firbolgs were defeated.

I need not describe here the curious Druidic medical fountain or bath prepared by the *Tuatha Dé Danann* physicians on this occasion, having gone fully into the whole subject of the battle of *Magh Tuireadh* in a former lecture. [6]

So much for what is found in the few records we possess of our very early colonists.

We now come to the Milesian colony. According to our ancient traditions, these people, who were also Japhetians, passed in their migrations back from Scythia into Greece, out of which they had previously come; then into Egypt; then into Spain; and so, from Spain into Erinn, which they reached about two hundred years after the conquest of the *Tuatha Dé Danann*, that is, in the year of the world 3,500 or above 1,530 years before Christ, according to the chronology of the Annals of the Four Masters.

In the entire course of the migrations of this people, the Druids hold a conspicuous place. Among the most remarkable was *Caicher*, who is said to have foretold to them, on their way to Spain, that Erinn was their ultimate destination.

The chief Druids of the Milesians, on their arrival in Erinn, were *Uar* and *Eithear* (who were both killed in the battle of *Slibh Mis*, in Kerry), and *Amergin*, one of the Milesian brothers, who was the Poet and Judge of the expedition, and a famous Druid, though not by profession.

A remarkable instance of Druidism is stated to have happened even on the very occasion of the landing of the first Milesian colony. Having landed in Kerry, they marched direct to the seat of sovereignty, now called Tara, a place which at the time we are speaking of was called *Cathair Crofinn*, or *Crofinn*'s Court, from a *Tuatha Dé Danann* lady of that name, who had previously resided there.[7] On arriving at Tara, the Milesians demanded the sovereignty of the country from the three joint kings of the *Tuatha Dé Danann*, the brothers *MacCuill*, *MacCecht* and *MacGreine*. These complained of their having been taken by surprise, alleging that if they had had notice of the coming invasion they would have prevented it, and offering to leave it with *Amergin* to give judgment between them. To this proposition the Milesians are said to have consented; and *Amergin* is recorded to have made the very singular decision that himself and his friends should re-enter their ships, and should move to the distance of 'nine waves' (as the authorities agree in stating), out from the land; and then that if they were able to land despite of the *Dé Danann*, the sovereignty of Erinn should be surrendered to them.

This decision, according to this most ancient tradition, was accepted by both parties; and the Milesians re-entered their ships, and went out the prescribed distance upon the sea. No sooner, however, had they done so, that the *Dé Danann* Druids raised such a tempest as drove the fleet out to sea, and dispersed them. One part of the fleet was driven to the south — and so round the island, to the north-east again — under *Eremon*, son of Milesius. The other part was suffering dreadfully from the tempest, when it occurred to them that the storm was raised by Druidical agency. *Donn*, the eldest of the Milesian brothers, then sent a man to the topmast of his ship to discover if the power of the wind extended as high as that point. The man ascended, and announced that it was quite calm at that elevation, upon hearing which *Donn* cried out: 'It is treachery in our men of science not to allay this wind.' [By this expression, 'men of science', the Druids are referred to here, as well as in many other places]. 'It is not treachery', said his brother *Amergin*; and he arose and pronounced a Druidical oration — of the ancient gloss on which the following is a literal translation, taken from the *Book of Invasions* of the O'Clerys, in the Royal Irish Academy:

'I pray that they reach the land of Erinn, those who are riding upon the great, productive, vast sea.

'That they be distributed upon her plains, her mountains, and her valleys; upon her forests that shed showers of nuts and all other fruits; upon her rivers and her cataracts; upon her lakes and her great waters; upon her abounding springs [or, upon her spring-abounding hills].

'That we may hold our fairs and equestrian sports upon her territories.

'That there may be a king from us in Tara; and that it (Tara) be the territory of our many kings.

'That the sons of Milesius be manifestly seen upon her territories.

'That noble Erinn be the home of the ships and boats of the sons of Milesius.

'Erinn which is now in darkness, it is for her that this oration is pronounced.

'Let the learned wives of *Breas* and *Buaigné* pray that we may reach the noble woman, great *Erinn*.

'Let *Ereman* pray, and let *Ir* and *Eber* implore that we may reach Erinn'.

At the conclusion of this oration the tempest ceased, according to our authority, and the survivors landed again. And then *Amergin*, upon putting his foot on dry land, pronounced another propitiatory oration (couched in the same obscure and general language), on the land, and on the waters, to render them more prolific.

In this example we have a curious instance of the very form of words in which it was anciently believed that, in still more remote ages, the Druids framed their incantations. We cannot, however, perceive anything of druidic or magical power, or character, in this oration — nothing, in short, to distinguish it from the prayer of any Christian of the present day, so far as the expression of the speaker's wants and desire. It does not clearly appear to whom the prayer was addressed, or that any ceremony or rite accompanied the delivery of it. I do not, of course, quote it as the certainly genuine prayer of *Amergin*, but it is, without any doubt, a very ancient piece of composition, and it must, I am persuaded, have been written either by some ancient Druid, or by some person conversant with the style of Druidic practices, and probably at a time long before Druidism became extinct in this country. And as regards the intrinsic innocence of the words used, it is curious enough that the Irish people to this day have an old tradition, that in the most profane and forbidden performances of sorcery and witchcraft, harmless and blessed words have been always used. The common proverb still is: 'Blessed words and cursed deeds'.

All that I have set down here is taken directly from our most ancient manuscripts, or those compiled from them; and they show clearly as the historical tradition of the country that each of the older colonies in Ireland was accompanied by its Druids; so that the suggestion of modern British writers that Druidism came first from Britain, or from Anglesey, into Erinn, is totally unfounded. I now proceed to select from the long list of Druidic references found in our old books, such as may serve to characterize the profession, so far, at least, as the limits of these lectures will allow. Very many other references there are, no doubt, which ought all to be gathered, all to be arranged and compared, if the subject of Irish Druidism, or indeed of Druidism at all, is to be completely investigated. But in these lectures I can hardly be expected to do more than give the general results, and to show where further information in detail may be obtained.

The allusions and instances to which I shall refer are very much scattered, and I cannot promise much arrangement in my treatment of the subject. I only propose to myself to give a few specimens of what was called Druidism by way of example, and I shall commence by citing from the earliest authority. The ancient tract called *Dinnseanchas*, (on the etymology of the names of several remarkable places in Erinn) gives the following singular legendary account of the origin of the names of *Midhe* (now Meath), and of *Uisnech*, in Meath.

*Midhe* the son of *Brath*, son of *Detha* (says this legend), was the first that lighted a fire for the sons of the Milesians in Erinn, on the Hill of *Uisnech* in Westmeath; and it continued to burn for seven years, and it was from this fire that every chief fire in Erinn used to be lighted. And his successor was entitled to a sack of corn and a pig from every house in Erinn, every year. The Druids of Erinn, however, said that it was an insult to them to have this fire ignited in the country; and all the Druids of Erinn came into one house to take council; but *Midhe* had all their tongues cut out, and he buried the tongues in the earth of *Uisnech*, and then sat over them; upon which his mother exclaimed: 'It is

*Uaisnech* [i.e. proudly] you sit up there this night' — and hence the names of *Uisnech*, and of *Midhe* (or Meath).

This, I believe, is the first reference to a Druidical fire to be found in our old books.

The next remarkable allusion to this subject that is to be found is the account of King *Eochaidh Airemh*.

It was a century before the Incarnation that *Eochaidh Airemh* was monarch of Erinn; and his queen was the celebrated *Edain*, a lady remarkable not only for her beauty but for her learning and accomplishments. One day that *Eochaidh* was in his palace at *Teamair*, according to this ancient story, a stranger of remarkable appearance presented himself before him. 'Who is this man who is not known to us, and what is his business?' said the king. 'He is not a man of any distinction, but he has come to play a game at chess with you,' said the stranger. 'Are you a good chess player?' said the king. 'A trial will tell,' said the stranger. 'Our chess-board is in the queen's apartment, and we cannot disturb her at present,' said the king. 'It matters not, for I have a chess-board of no inferior kind here with me,' said the stranger. 'What do we play for?' said the king. 'Whatever the winner demands,' said the stranger. [They played then a game which was won by the stranger.] 'What is your demand now?' said the king. '*Edain*, you queen,' said the stranger, 'but I will not demand her till the end of a year.' The king was astonished and confounded; and the stranger, without more words, speedily disappeared.

On that night twelvemonths, the story goes on to tell us, the king held a great feast at *Teamair*, surrounding himself and his queen with the great nobles and choicest warriors of his realm, and placing around his palace on the outside a line of experienced and vigilant guards, with strict orders to let no stranger pass them in. And thus secured, as he thought, he awaited with anxiety the coming night, while revelry reigned all round. As the middle of the night advanced, however, the king was horrified to see the former stranger standing in the middle of the floor, apparently unperceived by anyone else. Soon he advanced to the queen, and addressed her by the name of *Bé Finn* (Fair Woman) in a poem of seven stanzas, of which the following is a literal translation:

> 'O *Béfinn!* Will you come with me
>   To a wonderful country which is mine,
>   Where the people's hair is of golden hue,
>   And their bodies the colour of virgin snow?
> 'There no grief or care is known;
>   White are their teeth, black their eyelashes;
>   Delight of the eye is the rank of our hosts,
>   With the hue of the foxglove on every cheek.
> 'Crimson are the flowers of every mead,
>   Gracefully speckled as the blackbird's egg;
>   Though beautiful to see be the plains of *Inisfail*,
>   They are but commons compared to our great plains.
> 'Though intoxicating to you be the aledrink of *Inisfail*,
>   More intoxicating the ales of the great country;
>   The only land to praise is the land of which I speak,
>   Where no one ever dies of decrepit age.
> 'Soft sweet streams traverse the land;
>   The choicest of mead and wine;

Beautiful people without any blemish;
Love without sin, without wickedness.
'We can see the people upon all sides,
But by no one can we be seen;
The cloud of Adam's transgression it is,
That prevents them from seeing us.
'O woman! Should you come to my brave land,
It is golden hair that will be on your head;
Fresh pork, beer, new milk, and ale,
You there with me shall have, O *Béfinn!*'

At the conclusion of this poem, the stranger put his arm around the queen's body, raised her from her royal chair, and walked out with her, unobserved by anyone but the king, who felt so overcome by some supernatural influence that he was unable to offer any opposition, or even to apprise the company of what was going on. When the monarch recovered himself, he knew at once that it was someone of the invisible beings who inhabited the hills and lakes of Erinn that played one of their accustomed tricks upon him. When daylight came, accordingly, he ordered his chief Druid, *Dallan*, to his presence, and he commanded him to go forth immediately, and never to return until he had discovered the fate of the queen.

The Druid set out, and traversed the country for a whole year, without any success, notwithstanding that he had drawn upon all the ordinary resources of his art. Vexed and disappointed at the close of the year he reached the mountain (on the borders of the present counties of Meath and Longford) subsequently named after him *Sliabh Dallain*. Here he cut four wands of yew, and wrote or cut an *Ogam* in them; and it was revealed to him, 'through his keys of science and his *ogam*', that the queen *Edain* was concealed in the palace of the fairy chief, *Midir*, in the hill of *Bri Leith* (a hill lying to the west of Ardagh, in the present county of Longford). The Druid joyfully returned to Tara with the intelligence; and the monarch *Eochaidh* mustered a large force, marched to the fairy mansion of *Bri Leith*, and had the hill dug up until the diggers approached the sacred precincts of the subterranean dwelling; whereupon, the wily fairy sent out to the hillside fifty beautiful women, all of the same age, same size, same appearance in form, face, and dress, and all of them so closely resembling the abducted lady *Edain* that the monarch *Eochaidh* himself, her husband, failed to identify her among them, until at length she made herself known to him by unmistakable tokens — upon which he returned with her to Tara.

This tale exhibits two curious and characteristic features of Irish Druidism; the first, that the Irish Druid's wand of divination was formed from the yew, and not from the oak, as in other countries; the second, that the Irish Druid called in the aid of actual characters, letters, or symbols — those, namely, the forms of which have come down to our own times cut in the imperishable monuments of stone, so well known as *Ogam* stones (many of which may be seen in the National Museum of the Royal Irish Academy).

The antiquity of this story of *Eochaidh Airemh* is unquestionable. There is a fragment of it in *Leabhar na-h-Uidhré*, in the Royal Irish Academy, a manuscript which was actually written before the year 1106; and it is there quoted from the Book of *Dromsnechta*, which was undoubtedly written before or about the year 430. There is a better copy, but still not perfect nor so old, in the collection formerly in the possession of the late Mr William Monk Mason, in England.

From the reign of *Eochaidh Airemh* we now pass down about a century to our next remarkable instance in poetic tradition of these early examples of Druidical magic, namely, to the commencement of the Christian era, at which time *Cuchulainn* the great Ulster champion flourished. This *Cuchulainn*[or *Cuchulaind*], of whom so much has been said in former lectures, [8] was as much celebrated for the beauty and symmetry of his person as for his bravery and military accomplishments. It is not to be wondered at, therefore, that, in the ages of romance, so renowned a warrior should have had many personal admirers among the fair dames of his own and other countries, and that attempts should be made to attract his attention, and to secure his devotion, by those secret arts of sorcery, in the efficacy of which everyone believed in those times. I gave, in a former lecture, [9] a free analysis of the ancient historic tale of *Cuchulainn*'s successful courtship of the lady *Emer*, the daughter of *Forgall Monach* of Lusk, (in the present county of Dublin). The following occurrence is reported in one of the same series of historic tales [10] to have taken place subsequently to his marriage with that lady.

At one time, says this ancient story, that the men of Ulster were celebrating a fair in the plain of *Muirtheimné* (*Cuchulainn*'s patrimonial territory, which was in the present county of Louth, and comprised the district in which the present town of Drogheda is situated), a flock of beautiful birds appeared on the *loch* (or expansion of the Boyne) before them. *Cuchulainn* gave the birds a peculiar blow with the flat of his sword, called *taithbéim*, so that their feet and their wings adhered to the water, and they were all caught. *Cuchulainn* then distributed them among the noble ladies at the fair, two to each, until he came to *Eithné*, his own lady-love at this time, when he found that he had none left to give her. So *Eithné* complained bitterly of her lover's neglect, in thus preferring the other ladies to her. 'Don't be cast down,' said *Cuchulainn* 'should any more beautiful birds visit the plain of *Muirtheimné*, or the river *Bóind* [or *Boinn*] you shall have the two most beautiful among them.' Shortly after they perceived two beautiful birds upon the lake, linked together by a chain of red gold. They sang low music, which cast all such of the assembly as heard them into a profound sleep. *Cuchulainn*, however, went towards them, and putting a stone into his *crann tabhaill*, or sling, cast it at them; but it passed them by. He threw again, and the stone went over and beyond them. 'Alas!' said he, 'since I first received the arms of a champion, I did not ever make a false throw before this day.' He then threw his spear at the birds, and it passed through the wing of one of them; upon which they immediately dived under the water.

*Cuchulainn*, proceeds this singular tale, went away dispirited at his failure, and after some time, resting his back against a rock, he fell asleep. Immediately afterwards, two fairy women approached him, of whom one wore a green, and the other a crimson cloak, of five folds. The woman with the green cloak came up and smiled at him, and struck him a little blow with a horse-switch; then the other went up to him and smiled at him, and struck him in the same way; and they continued to do this for a long time, each striking him in turn, until he was nearly dead. All the Ultonians saw what happened, and they proposed to awaken him. 'Not so,' said Fergus, 'let him not be touched till we see what shall happen.' He soon after started up through his sleep. 'What has happened you?' inquired the Ultonians. 'Take me to the *Teti Breac* [i.e. the speckled or painted court] at Emania,' was all that he was able to say to them. He was therefore taken thither, and he remained there a whole year without speaking to anyone.

One day, at last (the tale goes on), before the next November eve, the Ultonians were assembled about him in the house: *Fergus* between him and the wall; *Conall Cearnach* between him and the door; *Lugaidh Reo-derg* (or 'the red-striped') at the head of his bed; and *Eithnē in-gubai* (or 'the sorrowful'), his mistress, at the foot. While they were thus placed, a strange man came into the chamber, and sat on the side of the bed or couch on which *Cuchulainn* lay. 'What has brought you there?' said *Conall Cearnach*. 'Now,' said the stranger, 'if this man were in health, he would be a protection to all Ulster, and even in the illness and debility in which he lies, he is still a greater consolation to them. I have come to converse with him,' said the stranger. 'You are welcome then,' said the Ultonians. The stranger then stood up, and addressed *Cuchulainn* in the following stanzas:

> 'O *Cuchulainn*! in thy illness,
>   Thy stay should not be long;
>   If they were with thee — and they would come —
>   The daughters of *Aedh Abrat*.
> '*Libán*, in the plain of Cruaich, has said —
>   She who sits at the right of *labraid* the quick —
>   That it would give heartfelt joy to *Fand*,
>   To be united to *Cuchulainn*.
> 'Happy that day, of a truth,
>   On which *Cuchulainn* would reach my land;
>   He should have silver and gold,
>   He should have abundance of wine to drink.
> 'If my friend on this day should be
>   *Cuchulainn*, the son of *Soaltē*,
>   All that he has seen in his sleep,
>   Shall he obtain without his army.
> 'In the plain of *Muirtheimnē*, here in the south,
>   On the night of Samhuin [November eve], without ill luck,
>   From me shall be sent *Libán*,
>   O *Cuchulainn*! to cure thy illness.' [11]

This, it will be perceived, was no other than a poetical invitation to *Cuchulainn* from *Aedh Abrat*, a great fairy chief, requesting him to visit his court, at the approaching November eve, and to take his daughter *Fand* [or *Fann*] in marriage, promising that he would be then cured of his illness.

'Who are you?' asked the Ultonians. 'I am *Aengus*, the son of *Aedh Abrat*,' said he. The man then left them; and they knew not whence he came nor where he went to, says the tale. *Cuchulainn* then stood up and spoke. 'It is time, indeed,' said the Ultonians; 'let us know what happened to you.' 'I saw,' said he, 'a wonderful vision about November eve, last year' — and he then told them all that happened, as related already.

The tale proceeds. 'What shall I do now, my master, *Conchobar*?' said *Cuchulainn* to the king [*Conchobar Mac Nessa*]. 'You will go,' said *Conchobar*, 'to the same rock again.' *Cuchulainn*, therefore, went till he reached the same rock again, where he saw the woman with the green cloak coming towards him. 'That is well, O *Cuchulainn*!' said she. 'It is not well,' said he. 'What was your business with me last year?' said *Cuchulainn*. 'It was not to injure you we came,' said she, 'but to seek your friendship, I have come now,' said she, 'from *Fand*, the daughter of *Aedh Abrat*, who has been abandoned by *Manannan Mac Lir*, and who has fallen in love with you; *Liban* is my own name, and I salute you from my husband, *Labraid* of the quick hand at sword, who will give you the woman in marriage for your assistance to him in one day's battle against *Senarch* the distorted, *Eochaidh n-Iuil*, and *Eoghan I bhir*.' 'I am not well able to fight this day,' said *Cuchulainn*. 'Short is the time until you are,' said *Liban*. 'You will be quite restored; and what you have lost of your strength will be increased to you. You ought to do this for my husband *Labraid*,' said she, 'because he is one of the best champions amongst the warriors of the world.' 'Where is he?' said *Cuchulainn*. 'He is in *Magh Mell* [i.e. the Plains of Happiness],' said she. 'It is better that I depart now,' said *Liban*. 'Be it so,' said *Cuchulainn*; 'and let my charidteer, *Laegh*, go along with you to see the country.' *Laegh* was accordingly conducted to a certain island, where he was well received by *Labraid* 'of the quick hand at sword'. He then returned to *Cuchulainn*, and (in a very curious poem of twenty-eight stanzas) he describes to him his journey and *Labraid*'s court. *Cuchulainn* himself then goes to visit the lady *Fand*, and to fight the battle for her brother *Labraid*, which they won.

Meanwhile, continues the story, the lady *Emer*, *Cuchulainn*'s most cherished of women, was pining in grief and jealousy at her court at *Dun-delea* (now Dundalk), but, unable to brook her miseries in silence any longer, she at last repaired to Emania, to King *Conchobar*, to crave his assistance for the recovery of her husband, who was now living with the lady *Fand* in Fairyland. Just at this time *Manannan Mac Lir*, the famous *Tuatha Dé Danann* (fairy)-chief, the former husband, as we have seen, of the lady *Fand*, repented his repudiation of her, and came and invited her to accompany him back to his court in the isle of *Manainn* (now Man, which bears his name), to which she consented. *Cuchulainn*, upon her desertion, seems to have lost his senses, and fled in a delirious rage to the mountains, where he remained for a long time without eating or drinking. *Emer*, therefore, informed King *Conchobar* of his condition, and *Conchobar*, we are told, sent the poets, scholars and Druids of Ulster to seek out the champion, and bring him to Emania. He thereupon attempted to kill them, but they pronounced 'Druidic orations' against him, until he was caught by the hands and feet, when at length a glimpse of his senses returned to him. He was then taken to Emania, where, as he was begging for a drink, the Druids gave him a 'drink of oblivion', and the moment he drank it he forgot *Fand* and all that had happened. The Druids then gave *Emer* also a drink, 'to cause oblivion of her jealousy'; for she was in a state of madness hardly less extravagant than that of her husband. And finally, when *Manannan* was going off with his wife *Fand*, it is stated that he 'shook his cloak between her and *Cuchulainn*', so that they should never again meet. 'And this,' continues the tract from which I quote, 'was the vision of bewitching *Cuchulainn*, by the *Aes Sidhe*, or dwellers in the hills; for the demoniac power was great before the introduction of the Christian faith, and so great was it that they (that is, the demons) used to tempt the people in human bodies, and that they used to show them secrets and places of happiness, where they should be immortal, and it was in that way they were believed. And it is these phantoms that the unlearned people call *Sidhe* or fairies, and *Aes Sidhé* or fairy people.'

This curious and very ancient medley of Druidism and fairyism I have abridged from the ancient *Leabhar na-h-Uidhré*, so often referred to in these lectures. I have given it at greater length than the plan of the present lecture would, perhaps, strictly warrant, but as it affords a fair specimen of true ancient fairy doctrine, as well as an instance of Druidism, as described in a very ancient writing, I trust the digression will not be thought too long.

The next example of a Druidical performance that presents itself has reference also to *Cuchulainn*'s time; for the young prince *Lugaidh Reo-derg* (*Lugaidh* 'the red-striped'), grandson of the monarch *Eochaidh Feidhlech*, was educated in literature and the science of arms by *Cuchulainn*. This Druidical story (one of the most curious in detail which remains to us) runs as follows:

'A meeting of the four great provinces of Erinn was held at this time (at *Teamair*), to see if they could find a person whom they could select, to whom they would give the sovereignty of Erinn; for they thought it ill that the Hill of Sovereignty of Erinn, that is *Teamair*, should be without the rule of a king in it; and they thought it ill that the people should be without the government of a king, to administer justice to them in all their territories. For the men of Erinn had been without the government of a monarch upon them during the space of seven years, after the death of *Conairé Mór*, at *Bruighin Da Derga* [*Bruidin Da Derca*] until this great meeting of the four great provinces of Erinn. at *Teamair* of the kings, in the court of *Erc*, son of *Cairbré* [or *Coirpre*] *Niadh-fear*.

'These were the (provincial) kings who were present in this meeting, namely, *Medhbh* (or Meave), queen of Connacht, and *Ailill*, her consort; *Curoi* (*mac Dairé*), king of South Munster; *Tighernach Tetbannach*, son of *Luchta*, king of North Munster; and *Find* or *Finn Mac Rossa*, king of Leinster. These men would not hold kingly counsel with the men of Ulster at all, because they were unitedly opposed to the Ulstermen.

'There was a Bull-feast made by them there, in order that they might learn through it who the person was to whom they would give the sovereignty. This is the way in which that bull-feast was made, namely, a bull was killed, and one man eat enough of its flesh and of its broth; and he slept under that meal; and a true oration was pronounced by four Druids upon him: and he saw in his dream the appearance of the man who would be made king of them, his countenance and description, and he was occupied. The man screamed out of his sleep, and told what he had seen to the kings, namely, a soft youth, noble, and powerfully made, with two red stripes on his skin around his body, and he standing at the pillow of a man who was lying in a decline at *Emain Macha*, (the royal palace of Ulster).

'The kings then sent messengers immediately to Emania, where the Ultonians were assembled round *Conchobar* (their king), at this time; and *Cuchulainn* was lying in a decline there', (as stated in the story the substance of which was given in the last lecture). The messengers told their tale to *Conchobar* and to the nobles of Ulster. 'There is indeed with us,' said *Conchobar*, 'a noble, well-descended youth of that description, namely, *Lugaidh Reo-derg*, "the son of the three twins", *Cuchulainn*'s pupil, who now sits over his pillow yonder, as you see, cheering his tutor.'

The tale goes on to say that *Cuchulainn* then arose, and delivered a valedictory address to his pupil (a very curious piece), chiefly on the conduct which should distinguish him in his new character of monarch; after which *Lugaidh* repaired to *Teamair*, where he was fully recognized as the person described in the vision, and proclaimed as monarch; after which the assembly broke up.

This *Lugaidh* was the father of the monarch *Crimhthann Niadhnair*, who had a famous court at *Beinn Edair* (now the Hill of Howth, the site of the court being that of the present 'Baily', according to Doctor Petrie), where he died and was buried; and it was in the ninth year of his reign that our Saviour is supposed to have been born.

At the time of which we are speaking, that is, about the time of the Incarnation of our Lord, *Cathbadh*, of the province of Ulster, and chief or royal Druid to King *Conchobar*, at Emania, was perhaps the most celebrated professor of the Druidic order in Erinn. There are a great many references to this *Cathbadh* in his Druidic character, but of these I shall content myself with one only, and translate from the ancient history of the *Táin Bo Chuailgné* (cattle spoil of *Cuailgné*) a short extract:

> One day that *Cathbadh* was outside Emania, on the north-east, lecturing his pupils, who numbered one hundred (that being the number which *Cathbadh* taught), he was questioned by one of them as to the signs and omens of the day, whether they were for good or for evil, and for what undertaking that day would be propitious. The Druid answered that the fame and renown of the youth who should take arms upon that day should last in Erinn *go brath* — that is, in Erinn 'for ever'. *Cuchulainn*, the great hero of the cow-spoil, of whom so much has been said, and who was one of the pupils, immediately begged of his master to recommend him to the king as a candidate for championship, or knighthood, as we should now call it, to which *Cathbadh* assented. *Cuchulainn* then repaired to the king, and in the proper manner solicited him for the arms of a champion. 'Who instructed you to seek them?' said *Conchobar*. '*Cathbadh*,' said the youth. 'You shall have them,' said the king; and *Conchobar* then presented him with a sword, a shield, and two spears — a form which constituted him thenceforth a knight or champion at arms.

From this extract we may see what the character of *Cathbadh*'s school was — it was evidently one of those institutions so often referred to in our ancient writings, an academy for instruction, not only in poetry and Druidism, but also in military accomplishments.

That the Druids shared largely in the instruction of the youth of Erinn, of all classes, in ancient times, could be shown from innumerable passages in our old writings (to which I shall make further allusion before I leave the subject); but one remarkable instance, from the ancient *Tripartite Life of St Patrick*, will be sufficient for the present. According to this most ancient authority, St Patrick, having overcome and confounded the monarch *Laeghairé*'s chief Druids at Tara, passed over the Shannon into Connacht, to prosecute his apostolic labours. Now, at this period, it happened that at *Magh Ai* (a district of which the modern county of Roscommon forms part), in the royal palace of *Cruachain*, there resided two other of king *Laeghairé*'s Druids, the brothers *Mael* and *Coplait*; and that, to their joint tuition the monarch had committed his two beautiful daughters — *Eithne*, 'the fair', and *Fedelim*, 'the rosy'. When the Druids, in whose charge the king's daughters were brought up, heard of St Patrick's coming into their country, and of his success against the Druids at Tara and elsewhere, they resorted to their magical arts to defeat him, and by an exertion of their demoniac power, brought a dense darkness over the whole of *Magh Ai* during the space of three days and three nights. Patrick, however, prayed to God, and blessed the plain; and it so befell that the Druids alone remained involved in the darkness, while all the rest of the people had the light restored to them.

Shortly after this, the saint, we are told, came to the palace of *Cruachain*; and the following incident, which is related to have occurred on the occasion, throws a curious light on the sort of theological education which the young princesses received from their Druidic preceptors. Thus says the *Life*:

'Patrick then repaired to the fountain called *Clibech*, at the side of *Cruachain*, at the rising of the sun. The clergy sat at the fountain; and while they were there the two princesses, the daughters of *Laeghairé Mac Neill*, came at an early hour to the fountain, to wash, as was their custom; and encountering the assembly of the clergy at the fountain in their white vestments, and with their books before them, they wondered much at their appearance. They thought that they might be men from the hills, i.e. fairy-men, or phantoms. They questioned Patrick, therefore, saying: "Whence have ye come? Whither do ye go? Are ye men of the hills? Or are ye gods?" To which Patrick answered: "It would be better for you to believe in God than to ask of what race we are?" The elder daughter asked: "Who is your God, and where is he? Is he in the Heavens, or is he in the Earth, or under the Earth, or upon the Earth, or in the seas, or in the streams, or in the mountains, or in the valleys? Has he sons and daughters? Has he gold and silver? Is there abundance of all sorts of wealth in his kingdom?" ' To these questions Patrick made, of course, suitable answers; and the end of the conversation was that not only the two princesses but even their tutors, the two Druids, were soon afterwards converted to the true faith.

Here we have an example of the active influence of Druids in St Patrick's time. But it is to be observed that Druidism by no means ceased, even with the introduction and establishment of Christianity in Erinn, as we have ample proof in the old books. For instance: in an ancient *Life of Saint Colum-Cillé*, preserved in the *Leabhar Mór Duna Doighré* (commonly called the *Leabhar Breac*), in the Royal Irish Academy, it is stated, that his mother even consulted a Druid as to the proper time to put him to the work of his education, and that this Druid was in fact his first tutor.

In the last lecture — after having shown from the most ancient historical MSS the existence of Druids as a profession in the early ages, and among all the races which successively inhabited Erinn — I collected a few instances of their professional interposition so as to show by example what was the nature of their knowledge or their power as far as we find it recorded. I proceed now to make a selection of some characteristic examples of Druidism as it is referred to in the old books. I have already observed that no definite account of the rites, any more than of the belief or of the magical or other powers of this mysterious order, has come down to us; it is only from a number of isolated examples and mere allusions in the historical tales and poems that we can form any conception, even the most general, of what Druidism really was.

One of the most remarkable of the Druidical rites thus recorded was that, for instance, of the charmed handful of straw, or hay, to which allusion is made in more than one place as having been made use of with the most powerful effect by these magicians of the early ages. We learn from several authorities that the ancient Druids here had a curious practice of pronouncing an incantation or charm on a wisp of straw, hay, or grass, which, thus charmed, they used to throw into a person's face, and so (as it was believed) cause him to become a lunatic and unsettled wanderer. This wisp or handful was called *Dlui Fulla*, or 'fluttering wisp';

The first reference that I find to the exercise of this piece of Druidism goes as far back as the time of *Nuadha Fullon*, one of the early kings of Leinster, who flourished so long since as about 600 years BC. It is stated in an ancient tract on the etymology of ancient Gaedhelic surnames that this *Nuadha Fullon* had received the addition of *Fullon* to his first name on account of his having been educated by a celebrated Druid named *Fullon*, who was the first person that practised the art of pronouncing Druidical incantations on a wisp of straw or hay, of such a character as that, when thrown in anyone's face, it caused him to run, jump, or flutter about like a lunatic. And this was the origin of the *Dlui Fulla*, or *Fullon*'s 'fluttering wisp'.

The second reference is to the affecting case of the young prince *Comgan*, son of *Maelochtair*, king of the Decies — the king who bestowed the site of the great ecclesiastical establishment of Lismore, in the county of Waterford, on St *Mochuda*, who died in the year 636.

*Comgan* was the son of *Maelochtair* by his first wife, and was remarkable for beauty of person, grace, and manly accomplishments. His stepmother (for *Maelochtair* remarried when advanced in life), who was much younger than his father, conceived a criminal passion for him, and made advances which he rejected with horror; upon which her love was converted into the most deadly hatred, and she sought anxiously for an opportunity to be revenged upon him. Now it so happened that, on one occasion, a fair and assembly having been held by the men of Munster, in South Tipperary, Prince *Comgan* carried off the victory in all the sports and exercises of the day, and won the applause of all spectators. His father's Druid was especially delighted with his prowess, and celebrated his praises above all the rest. The malicious stepmother, seeing this, accosted the Druid, and said to him, 'You are the last person who ought to praise *Comgan*, for he is in love with your wife, and has access to her at his pleasure. Observe him when he rides around to receive the congratulations of the fair ladies, and you will see that your wife regards him with peculiar favour.' 'If this be so,' said the Druid, 'his power of acquiring favour with her, or any other woman, shall soon cease for ever.'

Soon after, *Comgan* came up at the head of a troop of cavalry and rode around the assembly, according to custom, to receive the congratulations of the fair ladies who were witnesses of his success; and he addressed to each some courteous words, and to the Druid's wife among the rest. Although the unsuspicious *Comgam* in reality paid no more court to her than to others, yet to the Druid's eyes, already filled with jealousy, his passing compliment seemed an undoubted confirmation of all the suspicions with which his mind had been poisoned; and when *Comgan* retired to wash his horses and himself in a neighbouring stream, the Druid followed him, and suddenly, we are told, struck him with a Druidic wand, or, according to one version, flung at him a tuft of grass over which he had pronounced a Druidical incantation. The result, according to the story, was that when *Comgan* arose from bathing his flesh burst forth in boils and ulcers, and his attendants were forced to carry him to his father's house. At the end of the year he had wasted away; his hair fell off, his intellect decayed, and he became a bald, senseless, and wandering idiot, keeping company only with the fools and mountebanks of his father's court.

Such was said to have been the fate of Prince *Comgan*, brought about by apparently a very simple Druidic process. This *Comgan* was brother, by his mother's side, to the holy bishop St *Cummain Fada* ('*Cummain* the Tall'), of Clonferta, in the county of Galway, who died AD 661, and of whose history and life the full particulars will be found collected in Dr Todd's Notes to the first part of the *Liber Hymnorum*, lately published by the Archaeological Society.

There is yet another curious instance of the use of the magic wisp, recorded as having occurred shortly before the period just referred to; one which I cannot omit as an illustration of this form of Druidism, because the account is one given with so much detail.

The simple incident itself could be told in a few words, but it would scarcely be intelligible without some account (which shall be as condensed as I can make it), of the circumstances which led to it. And first a few words as to the *Deisi* clans, — for this tale also is connected with their eventful history.

The *Deisis* (Decies or Deasys) of Munster, just mentioned, were originally a tribe located in the present barony of Deisi, or Decce, in Meath, which derives its name from them. They were the descendants of *Fiacha Suidhé* (brother to the monarch *Conn* of the Hundred Battles) and his followers. One of the chiefs of this people was *Ængus Gae-buaifnech* (*Æengus* 'of the poisoned spear'), a valiant and high-minded man, and the champion of his tribe at the time their cousin *Cormac Mac Airt* was monarch of Erinn. *Cormac* had, besides *Cairbré Lifeachair*, his successor in the monarchy, another son named *Ceallach*, or 'the diviner'. This *Ceallach* took away, by force or fraud, a young lady of *Æengus*'s people, who was also a near relative of his own. *Æengus*, enraged, followed the offender to Tara itself, entered the royal palace, and killed *Ceallach* in the very presence of his father the king, after which the champion escaped unhurt. King *Cormac*, however, immediately prepared for vengeance, and raised a force sufficient to drive the Decies out of Meath southward into Leinster, in which province they sojourned for some time, and from which they afterwards passed into Munster to king *Oilioll Olum*, who was married to *Sadhbh*, one of the three daughters of *Conn* of the Hundred Battles, and consequently cousin to the Decian chief. *Oilioll Olum* gave them the territory which still bears their name, in the present county of Waterford; and here and in other parts of Munster they remained for about two hundred years, until the reign of *Ængus*, son of *Nadfraech*, king of Munster, who was converted and baptized by St Patrick. It is to about this latter period that the events recorded in the following story are referred.

About this time the Decies felt the need of a more extensive territory, to meet the wants of their growing numbers. They accordingly consulted, we are told, their Druid, who told them that the wife of *Crimhthann*, king of Leinster, was then pregnant; that she should bring forth a daughter; that they should contrive to procure that daughter in fosterage; and that when she should get married, her husband would extend their territory. All was done according to the Druid's directions. The Decies received the young princess, whose name was *Eithné*, in fosterage; and under their assiduous care she grew up to become eminent for ability as well as beauty. Some of our old romances assert that her growth was promoted by her being fed on the flesh of infants, from which she got the nickname of *Eithné Uathach*, or 'the Hateful'; the only allusion that I am aware of to any instance of similar barbarity — for as to the existence of cannibalism to any extent whatever among the Gaedhils, even in the most remote ages, I am bound to declare at once that there is no vestige of authority whatever. However, be this shocking story of the princess *Eithné* as it may, having now grown to womanhood, she attracted the notice of *Ængus*, king of Munster, who sought her hand in marriage. His suit was promoted by the Decies, and gladly accepted by her father, and they were forthwith married; after which *Ængus* did grant The Decies an addition of territory, lying north of the river Suir, in the present county of Tipperary, provided they drove out some tribes from the neighbouring district of Ossory, who had some time previously settled themselves in it.

Now, these Ossorians had a famous blind Druid named *Dill*, the son of *Ui Creaga*. And *Dill* had a daughter who attached herself to the person of the newly-married *Eithné*, queen of Cashel, who in return provided her with a husband of the Decies, and a settlement at her court. 'Good, now,' said the queen to her one day, 'your father is not kind to our people the Decies.' 'I have not the power to change him,' said the Druid's daughter. 'Go from me,' said the queen, 'with rich presents to him, to know if he will consent to turn away his enmity from us; and you shall also have an additional reward for yourself.'

The daughter (the tale tells us) accordingly proceeded southwards from Cashel, and so reached her father's residence. 'Whence have you come, my daughter?' said the Druid. 'From Cashel,' said she. 'Is it true that you are attached to that hateful queen, *Eithné*?' said he. 'It is true,' said she. 'Good, now, *Dill*,' said she 'I am come to offer you wealth.' 'I will not accept it,' said he. 'I will light a fire for you,' said she, 'that you may eat, and that I may obtain your blessing.' He raised his voice then, and said: 'These (meaning the *Deisi*) are a bad swarm, who have planted themselves on the borders of the territory of Cashel; but,' said he, 'they shall depart at midday tomorrow. I am preparing incantations,' said he. 'The *Inneoin* (the name of a town at a certain hill near Clonmel) shall be burned on tomorrow; I shall be on the west side of the hill, and I shall see the smoke; a hornless red cow shall be sent past them, to the west; they shall raise a universal shout, after which they shall fly away; and they shall never occupy the land again.' 'Good,' said the daughter; 'sleep now, when you please.' He then slept, and the daughter stole the wisp of straw out of his shoes, and fled with it to Cashel, and gave it to queen *Eithné*, who immediately set out with it to the south, and stopped not until she reached the Decies, at their town of *Inneoin*. 'Here,' said she to the Decies, 'burn this wisp, and procure for us a hornless red cow.' Such a cow could not be procured. Upon which one of the Druids of the Decies said: 'I will put myself into the form of the cow to be slain, on condition that my children be made free for ever.' This was done; and the red cow passed westwards.

The Druid *Dill*, who at some distance was watching the effect, as he thought, of his own spells, now addressed his attendant: 'What is doing now?' said he. 'A fire is being lighted,' said the attendant, 'and a hornless red cow has been sent over the ford from the east side.' 'That is not desirable,' said Dill. 'Is the wisp here?' said he. 'It is not,' said the attendant. 'Bad,' said the Druid, 'do the men wound the cow?' 'They have let her pass, but the horseboys are wounding her' said the attendant. 'What shout is this I hear?' said the Druid. 'The shout of the horseboys killing the cow,' said the attendant. 'Yoke my chariot for me,' said the Druid, 'the town cannot be damaged, nor can we withstand it.' The Decies rushed past him eastwards; the Ossorians were attacked and routed; they fled like wild deer, and they were followed till they reached a place called *Luininn*, where the close of the day put an end to the pursuit; and this place became the boundary for ever after between Munster and Leinster. And the Ossorians, concludes the tale, who were previously called the descendants of *Bresal Belach*, after a remote ancestor of theirs, were from this time down called *Ossairghé*, from *Os*, a wild deer, and the wild-deer-like precipitance of their retreat.

The next instance of Druidism in the selection I have made is that of a peculiar rite of divination, which it seems might be performed by either a Druid or a Poet; it is described in the *Glossary* of the holy Cormac MacCullinan, King and Bishop of Cashel, compiled about the year 890. The article is an explanation of the words *Imbas Forosnai*, or (literally) 'Illumination by the Palms of the Hands'. At this word (*Imbas Forosnai*) he says. 'This describes to the Poet what thing soever he wishes to discover; and this is the manner in which it is performed. The Poet chews a bit of the raw red flesh of a pig, a dog, or a cat, and then retires with it to his bed, behind the door, where he pronounces an oration upon it, and offers it to his idol gods. He then invokes his idols; and if he has not received the ''illumination'' before the next day, he pronounces incantations upon his two palms, and takes his idol gods unto him (into his bed), in order that he may not be interrupted in his sleep. He then places his two hands upon his two cheeks, and falls asleep. He is then watched, so that he be not stirred or interrupted by any one, until everything that he seeks is revealed to him, at the end of a day, or two, or three, or as long as he continues at his offering; and hence it is that this ceremony is called Palm Illumination, that is, his two hands upon him, crosswise, that is, a hand over and a hand hither upon his cheeks. And St Patrick prohibited this ceremony, because it is a species of *Teinm Laeghdha*; that is, he declared anyone who performed it should have no place in Heaven, nor on Earth'. Such was the *Imbas Forosnai*.

The *Fileadh* ('poets', or rather 'philosophers', as they ought more properly to be called) had another very curious secret and Druidical rite for the identification of dead persons, such as those who had been beheaded or dismembered. This art was called *Teinm Laeghdha*, that is, the 'Illumination' of Rhymes. When the performance of this art was accompanied by a sacrifice to, or an invocation of idols, it was called *Teinm Laeghdha*, or the Illumination of Rhymes, and came under St Patrick's prohibition; but when not so accompanied, it was called *Dichetal do Chennaibh*, or the Great Extempore Recital, and was not prohibited.

Of the *Teinm Laeghdha* we have at least two instances on record, of nearly equal date, and referred back to the second and third centuries of the Christian era.

In one of those instances the celebrated *Finn Mac Cumhaill* was the performer; for *Finn*, as was shown in a former lecture, was a poet and a philosopher, as well as a champion or knight-at-arms. *Finn*, from his infancy, was intended for the military profession, and in compliance with the Fenian rules must have studied philosophy, and letters also, to a certain extent; but after having made his profession of arms, and received a high appointment at the court of Tara, from the monarch *Conn* of the Hundred Battles, the young champion became involved in an affair of some delicacy with one of the king's daughters, which made it prudent for him to retire awhile from court. Abandoning, then, for a time, his military course, he placed himself under the tuition of *Cethern Mac Fintain*, a celebrated poet, philosopher, and Druid, under whose instructions he is said to have soon made himself perfect in occult studies. This curious statement is preserved in a very ancient poem, a copy of which is to be found in the *Book of Leinster*.

The account, however, in which *Finn*'s performance of the *Teinm Laeghdha* is recorded, is preserved in Cormac's *Glossary*, at the word *Orc Treith*, and may be shortly told as follows:

*Finn*, at the time that we are speaking of, had to wife a lady of the tribe of *Luighné* (now Lune, in Meath); and he had in his household a favourite wit or buffoon, named *Lomna*. Now *Finn* chanced to go on one occasion on a hunting excursion into Teaffia (in Westmeath), accompanied by his wife, and attended by his domestics and his buffoon, whom he left in a temporary house or hut in that country, while he himself and the chief part of his warriors followed the chase. One day, during *Finn*'s absence, *Lomna* the buffoon discovered *Cairbré*, one of *Finn*'s warriors, holding a rather suspicious conversation with *Finn*'s wife. The lady prayed him earnestly to conceal her indiscretion, and *Lomna* reluctantly promised her to do so. *Finn* returned after some time, and *Lomna* felt much troubled at being obliged to conceal a secret of such importance; and at last, unable any longer to do so, he shaped himself a quadrangular wand, and cut the following words, in *ogham* characters, in it: 'An alder stake in a palisade of silver; a sprig of hellebore in a bunch of cresses; the willing husband of an unfaithful wife among a select band of tried warriors; heath upon the bare hill of *Ualann* in *Luighne*.' *Lomna* then placed the wand in a place where *Finn* was sure to find it. *Finn* soon did find it, and immediately understood its metaphorical contents, which gave him no small uneasiness. Nor did his wife long remain ignorant of the discovery, which she immediately attributed to *Lomna*; so she forthwith sent privately for her favourite to come and kill the buffoon; and *Cairbré* came, accordingly, and cut of *Lomna*'s head, and carried it away with him. Afterwards *Finn* came, in the evening, to *Lomna*'s hut, where he found the headless body. 'Here is a body without a head,' said *Finn*. 'Discover for us,' said the Fians, his warriors, 'whose it is.' And then, says the legend, *Finn* put his thumb into his mouth, and spoke through the power of the *Teinm Laeghdha*, and said:

> 'He has not been killed by people;
>   He has not been killed by the people of *Laighné*;
>   He has not been killed by a wild boar;
>   He has not been killed by a fall;
>   He has not died on his bed — *Lomna*.'

'This is *Lomna*'s body,' said *Finn*, 'and enemies have carried away his head.'

This piece of sorcery differs in one instance from any other that we know of, namely, that instead of a bit of any other kind of flesh, *Finn* chews his own thumb, which, of course, he thus makes his sacrifice to his idols.

Another instance of the *Teinm Laeghdha* occurs also in Cormac's *Glossary*, at the word *Megh Eimhé* ('the Slave of the Haft'); and though this story will seem in this place a little longer than I should wish, still, as it contains other curious and important historical facts, I am tempted to give a translation of it at length.

'*Mogh Eimhé*,' says *Cormac*, 'was the name of the first *oircné*, or lap-dog, that was known in Erinn. *Cairbré Musc* was the man who first brought it into Erinn, out of the country of Britain. For at this time the power of the Gaedhils was great over the Britons; and they divided Albion among them in farms, and each of them had his neighbour and friend among the people; and they dwelt no less on the east side of the sea than in Scotia [that is, the land of the Scots or Gaedhils, a term then only applied to Erinn]. And they built their residences and their royal Duns (or courts) there; as, for instance, *Dun Tradin*, or *Dun Tredin* [the three-walled court] of *Criomhthann Mór Mac Fiodhaidh*, monarch of Erinn and *Albain* [Scotland], as far as the Ietian sea; and also *Glastimberi* [Glastonbury], now a church on the brink of the Ietian sea, in the forest of which dwelt *Glas Mac Cais*, swineherd to the king of *Irfnaté*, to feed his pigs on the mast — the same who was resuscitated by St Patrick six score years after he had been slain by *Mac Con*'s huntsmen. And one of these divisions [of land] is *Dun Mac Lethan*, at this day [AD 890], in the country of the Britons of Cornwall, that is *Dun Mac Liathain*. And so, every tribe of them [i.e. of the Scots, or Gaedhils of Erinn] divided the lands into portions on the east side of the channel; and so it continued for a long time after the coming of St Patrick into Erinn.

'It was on this account, therefore, that *Cairbré Musc* was in the habit of going over frequently to visit his family and his friends. Down to this time no lapdog had come into the country of Erinn, and the Britons commanded that none should ever be given, either for satire, or for friendship, or for price, to the Gaedhils.

'The law which was then in force in Britain was that every transgressor became forfeited for his transgression, if discovered.

'At this time a friend of *Cairbré Musc*, was possessed of a celebrated lapdog in the country of Britain; and *Cairbré* procured it from him in the following manner. *Cairbré* went on a visit to this man's house, and was received with a welcome to everything but the lapdog. Now *Cairbré* had a costly knife, the handle of which was ornamented with gold and silver, a most precious jewel. In the course of the night he rubbed the knife and its haft thickly over with fat bacon and fat beef, and laid it at the lapdog's mouth, and then went to sleep. The dog continued to gnaw the knife until morning; and when *Cairbré* arose in the morning, and found the knife disfigured, he made loud complaints, appeared very sorrowful, and demanded justice for it from his friend; namely, "the transgressor in forfeit for his transgression". The dog was accordingly given up to him, then, in satisfaction for its crime; and thus it received the name of *Mogh Eimhé*, or "the Slave of the Haft", for *mogh*, a slave, and *eimh*, a haft.

'It so happened that the dog was a female, and was with young at the time of its being brought over. *Ailill Flann Beg* was the king of Munster at the time, and *Cormac Mac Airt* monarch of Tara. Each of these claimed the dog, but it was agreed that she should remain for a certain time, alternately, in the houses of *Cairbré* himself, and of each of the two kings. In the meantime the dog brought forth her whelps; and each of the royal personages took one of them; and it was from this little dog that sprang all the breed of lapdogs in Erinn. The lapdog died in a long time after; and in many years after that, again, *Connla* the son of *Tadg*, son of *Cian*, son of *Oiloll Oluim*, king of Munster, found the bare skull of the lapdog, and brought it for identification to *Maen Mac Etnae*, a distinguished poet, who had come with a laudatory poem to his father.

'The poet had recourse to his *Teinm Laeghdha*; and he said:

> Sweet was your drink in the house of *Eogan*'s grandson;
>   Sweet was your flesh in the house of *Conn*'s grandson
>     each day;
>   Fair was your bread in the house of *Cairbré Musc*,
>     O *Mogh Eimbé*!

'"This," said the Poet, "is the skull of *Mogh Eimbé*, the first lapdog that was ever brought into Erinn."'

*Cairbré Musc*, by whom, by no very fair means, this first *oircné* or lapdog was brought into Erinn, was son of *Conairé*, monarch of Erinn. He fought at the battle of *Ceann Abrat*, AD 186; and he was ancestor to the O'Connells, the O'Falveys, the O'Sheas, and other families of ancient distinction in West Munster, as well as of others in East Munster.

So much for the *Teinm Laeghda*, which seems to have been a charm of rhyme, by which it was supposed that the rhymer would be led to name the name of that which he sought by a sort of magic inspiration, the nature of which is not indicated to us save by such examples as that contained in this short legend.

To this period may be also referred another occurrence of ancient historic interest, namely, the Siege or Encampment of *Drom Damhghairé*, of which some account was given in a former lecture,[12] and in the Historic Tale concerning which some wild Druidical performances are described in some detail. To this Tale, therefore, as containing another series of examples of what was called Druidical Art, I have next to refer.

The Encampment of *Drom Damhghairé* took place under the following circumstances. The celebrated *Cormac Mac Airt* commenced his reign as monarch of Erinn at Tara, AD 213. It would appear that his hospitality and munificence soon exhausted the royal revenues, so that in a short time he found it necessary not only to curtail his expenditure, but to seek immediate means of replenishing his coffers. In this difficulty he was advised to make a claim on the province of Munster for a double tribute, on the plea that although there were properly two provinces of Munster, yet they had never paid more than the tribute of one. *Cormac*, therefore, on these very questionable grounds, sent his messengers into Munster to demand a second tribute for the same year. *Fiacha Muilleathan* (the son of *Eoghan Mór*, son of *Oilioll Oluim*) was king of Munster at the time, and he received the messengers of the monarch (at *Cnoc Raffann*, in Tipperary) with all the usual honours and attention. He denied the justness of *Cormac*'s demands, but offered to send a sufficient supply of provisions to him as a present, for that occasion. The messengers returned to Tara with this answer, but *Cormac* would not listen to it, and he consulted his Druids on the probable success of an expedition into Munster. They, however, after having recourse (as we are told) to their divinations, gave him an unfavourable answer. Still, he would not be persuaded by them, but insisted on undertaking the expedition. He therefore mustered a large force, and marched directly to the hill of *Damhghairé* (now *Cnoc Luingé*, or Knocklong, in the south-east part of the county of Limerick, bordering on Tipperary). Here *Cormac* fixed his camp; and from this, with the aid of his Druids, by drying up the springs and streams of the province, he is said to have brought that great distress on the people of Munster which was described in a former lecture. Ultimately, the monarch and his Druids were overmastered by the superior power of the great Munster Druid, *Mogh Ruith*. This celebrated sage, one of the most renowned of those ages, is recorded to have completed his Druidical studies in the East, in the school of no less a master than Simon Magus; and it is even stated in this tract that Simon Magus himself was of the race of the Gaedhils of Erinn.

After *Mogh Ruith* had relieved the men of Munster from the drought and famine which *Cormac*'s Druids had brought upon them, *Cormac* again took into council his chief and oldest Druid, *Ciothruadh*, and inquired of him what was best to be done. *Ciothruadh* answered that their last and only resource was to make a Druidic fire against the enemy. 'How is that to be made?' said Cormac. 'In this way,' said *Ciothruadh*. 'Let our men go into the forest, and let them cut down and carry out loads of the quickbeam (i.e. the Mountain-ash, or roan-tree), of which large fires must be made; and when the fires are lighted, if the smoke goes southwards, then it will be well for you to press after it on the men of Munster; and if it is hither or northward the smoke comes, then, indeed, it will be full time for us to retreat with all our speed.' So, *Cormac*'s men forthwith entered the forest, cut down the wood indicated, brought it out, and set it on fire.

Whilst this was going on, *Mogh Ruith*, perceiving what the northern Druids were preparing for, immediately ordered the men of Munster to go into the wood of *Lethard*, and each man to bring out a faggot of the roan-tree in his hand; and that the king only should bring out a shoulder-bundle from the side of the mountain, where it had grown under three shelters, namely, shelter from the (north-east) March wind, shelter from the sea wind, and shelter from the conflagration winds. The men soon returned with the wood to their camp; and the Druid *Ceannmhair*, *Mogh Ruith*'s favourite pupil, built the wood up in the shape of a small triangular kitchen, with seven doors; whereas the northern fire (that prepared by *Ciothruadh*), on the other side, was but rudely heaped up, and had but three doors. 'The fire is ready now,' said *Ceannmhair*, 'all but to light it.' *Mogh Ruith* then ordered each man of the host to give him a shaving from the haft of his spear, which, when he had got, he mixed with butter and rolled up into a large ball, at the same time pronouncing those words in rhythmical lines:

   'I mix a roaring powerful fire;
     It will clear the woods; it will blight the grass;
     An angry flame of powerful speed;
     It will rush up to the skies above.
     It will subdue the wrath of all burning wood,
     It will break a battle on the clans of *Conn*' —

and with that he threw the ball into the fire, where it exploded with a tremendous noise.

'I shall bring the rout on them now,' said *Mogh Ruith*. 'Let my chariot be ready, and let each man of you have his horse by the bridle; for, if our fires incline but ever so little northwards, follow and charge the enemy.' He then blew his Druidical breath (says this strange tale) up into the sky, and it immediately became a threatening black cloud, which came down in a shower of blood upon the plain of *Cláiré* before him, and moved onwards from that to Tara, the Druid all the time pronouncing his rhythmical incantations. When the rushing of the bloody shower was heard in the northern camp, *Cormac* asked his Druid, *Ciothruadh*, what noise it was. 'A shower of blood,' said the Druid, 'which has been produced by a violent effort of Druidism. It is upon us its entire evil will fall.'

After this (the tale proceeds), *Mogh Ruith* said to his people: 'What is the condition of the flames from the two fires now?' [for *Mogh Ruith* was blind]. 'They are,' said they, 'chasing each other over the brow of the mountain, west and north, down to *Druim Asail* [now Tory Hill, near Croom, in the county of Limerick] and to the Shannon, and back again to the same place.' He asked again the state of the flames. 'They are in the same condition,' said they, 'but they have not left a tree in the plain of middle Munster that they have not burned.' *Mogh* asked again how the flames were., His people answered that 'they had risen up to the clouds of Heaven, and were like two fierce angry warriors chasing each other'. Then *Mogh Ruith* called for his 'dark-grey hornless bull-hide', and 'his white-speckled bird-headpiece, with its fluttering wings', and also 'his Druidic instruments', and he flew up into the air to the verge of the fires, and commenced to beat and turn them northwards. When *Cormac*'s Druid, *Ciothruadh*, saw this, he also ascended to oppose *Mogh Ruith*; but the power of the latter prevailed, and he turned the fires northwards, and into *Cormac*'s camp, where they fell, as well as [*i.e.* where also fell] the Druid *Ciothruadh*. *Cormac*, on this, ordered a quick retreat out of the province.

They were hotly pursued (we are then told), by the Munster men, led by *Mogh Ruith* in his chariot drawn by wild oxen, and with his Druidic bull-hide beside him. The pursuit continued beyond the border of the province, and into *Magh Raighné*, in Ossory. And here *Mogh Ruith* asked, though he well knew, who were the nearest parties to them of the retreating foe. 'They are three tall grey headed men,' said they. 'They are *Cormac*'s three Druids, *Cicht*, *Ciotha*, and *Ciothruadh*,' said he, 'and my gods have promised me to transform them into stones, when I should overtake them, if I could but blow my breath upon them.' And then he 'blew a Druidic breath' upon them, so that they were turned into stones; and these are the stones that are called the Flags of *Raigné* at this day — and so on.

This extraordinary tale contains more of the wilder feats of Druidism than any other Irish piece known to me. But not only is the main fact recorded in it true, but some of the principal personages, at least, are historical; for it is a curious fact that the great Druid, so celebrated in this piece, *Mogh Ruith*, for this or some other singular piece of Druidic service rendered to the men of Munster, is recorded, in truly historic documents, to have received from them the extensive territory anciently known as *Mogh Meiné*, or the 'Mineral Plain' (now the district of Fermoy, in the county of Cork); a territory which the race of *Mogh Ruith*, moreover, continue to inhabit even to this day, in the families of O'Dugan, O'Cronin, etc., of that and the neighbouring districts.

The use of the quicken or roan-tree in Druidical rites is a circumstance by no means incidental to this tale alone, since many of its uses for superstitious purposes may be found in our old writings, and some of them have come down even to the present day, in connection, for example, with the superstitions peculiar to the dairy. I have myself known some housewives in Munster who would not have a churn for their dairies without at least one roan-tree hoop on it — or without having a twig of that sacred tree twisted into a gad, and formed into a ring placed upon the churn-staff while churning — for the purpose of putting it out of the power (as they conceived) of some gifted neighbour, to deprive them of the proper quantity of butter, by any trick of witchery.

The following short article from an ancient manuscript (H. 3 17, T.C.D.) is conclusive, on the use of the roan-tree in Druidical rites. It is the case of a woman clearing her character from charges affecting it, by an ordeal, when she had failed to find living compurgators. The ordeal she was to go through was to rub her tongue to a red-hot adze of bronze, or to melted lead (but not, it appears, to iron), and the adze should be heated in a fire of blackthorn, 'or of roan-tree'; and this says the book, was a Druidical ordeal.

When St Patrick had purified the laws and the course of education in Erinn, in the ninth year of his mission (about the year 443), he, of course, prohibited all Druidical rites and performances, but particularly those which required sacrifices to idols. He left, however, to the lawfully elected territorial poet, liberty to write satires, according to ancient custom, upon the kings or chiefs in whose service he was retained, whenever the poet wrote an historical, a genealogical, or a laudatory poem for his patron, and was not paid for it the reward which custom or the law of the land had provided in such cases. How far the spirit of Druidism may have pervaded these compositions it is now out of our power to ascertain; but, considering the prevailing belief in the effects ascribed to them, it is very probable, to say the least, that in such incantations the satirical poet must have dealt largely in Druidism as known or practised in times not yet far removed from his own.

Some curious, though apparently simple examples of this species of poetry have come down to us; and the following account of the ceremony of its composition (from the Book of Ballymote), stands, perhaps, unique in the annals of satire. The composition was called *Glam Dichinn*, or *Satire from the Hill-tops*; and was made in this way. The poet was to fast upon the lands of the king for whom the poem was to be made; and the consent of thirty laymen, thirty ecclesiastics (bishops, the tract says), and thirty poets, should be had to compose the satire; and it was a crime for them to prevent it when the reward for the poem was withheld. The poet, then, in a company of seven (that is, six along with himself), upon whom had been conferred literary or poetic degrees, namely, a '*Fochlac*', a '*MacFiurmedh*', a '*Doss*', a '*Cana*', a '*Cli*', and an '*Anrad*', with an '*Ollamh*' as the seventh, went at the rising of the sun to a hill, which should be situated on the boundary of seven farms, (or lands), and each of them was to turn his face to a different land; and the *Ollamh*'s face was to be turned towards the land of the king who was to be satirized; and their backs were to be turned to a hawthorn which should be growing upon the top of the hill; and the wind should be blowing from the north; and each man was to hold a perforated stone and a thorn of the hawthorn in his hand; and each man was to sing a verse of this composition for the king, the *Ollamh* or chief poet to take the lead with his own verse, and the others in concert after him with theirs;

and each, then, should place his stone and his thorn under the stem of the hawthorn; and if it was they that were in the wrong in the case, the ground of the hill would swallow them; and if it was the king that was in the wrong, the ground would swallow 'him, and his wife, and his son, and his steed, and his robes, and his hound'. The satire of *Mac Fiurmedh* fell on the hound; the satire of the *Fochlac*, on the robes; the satire of the *Doss*, on the arms; the satire of the *Cana*, on the wife; the satire of the *Cli*, on the son; the satire of the *Anrad*, on the steed; and the satire of the *Ollamh*, on the king.

This is a very singular instance of Druidism, as it was believed to have prevailed in Erinn even after the introduction of Christianity.

It is now too late in the world's age to canvass the power and nature of satire; all that I can say on the subject is this: that from the remotest times down to our own, its power was dreaded in Erinn; and that we have numerous instances on record of its having driven men out of their senses, and even to death itself.

Of the antiquity of satire in Erinn, and of the belief in its venomous power, we have the very important authority of *Cormac's Glossary*, in which the word *Gairē* is explained and illustrated in the following manner:

'*Gairē*; that is, *Gair-seclé* [short life]; that is, *Gair-rē*; that is, *re-ghair*; ut est, in the satire which the poet *Neidhē*, son of *Adhna*, son of *Guthar*, composed for the king of Connacht, who was his own father's brother, namely *Caier*, the son of *Guthor*;for *Caier* had adopted *Neidhē* as his son, because he had no sons of his own.

'*Caier*'s wife' (continues *Cormac*) 'conceived a criminal passion for *Neidhē*, and offered him a ball of silver to purchase his love. *Neidhē* did not accept this, nor agree to her proposals, until she offered to make him king of Connacht after his uncle *Caier*. ''How can you accomplish that?'' said *Neidhē*. ''It is not difficult,'' said she; ''make you a satire for him, until it produces a blemish upon him, and you know that a man with a blemish cannot retain the kingly rule.'' ''It is not easy for me to do what you advise,'' said *Neidhē*, ''because the man would not refuse me anything; for there is not in his possession anything that he would not give me.''' [The poets only fulminated their satires in case their privileges were violated, or their requests refused.] '''I know,'' said the woman, ''one thing that he would not give you, namely, the knife which was presented to him in the country of *Alboin*. [Scotland]; and that he would not give you because it is prohibited to him [*i.e.* because he is under a vow or pledge not] to give it away from himself.'' *Neidhē* went then and asked *Caier* for the knife. ''Woe and alas,'' said *Caier*, ''it is prohibited to me to give it away from me.''' *Neidhē* then, continues Cormac's authority, 'composed a *Glam Diebian*, or extempore satire for him; and immediately three blisters appeared upon his cheek.' This is the satire:

> 'Evil, death, and short life to *Caier*;
>   May spears of battle slay *Caier*;
>   The rejected of the land and the earth is *Caier*;
>   Beneath the mounds and the rocks be *Caier*'.

*Caier*, we are then told, went early the next morning to the fountain to wash; and in passing his hands over his face, he found three blisters on it, which the satire had raised: namely (says the story), 'disgrace', 'blemish', and 'defect', in colours of crimson, green, and white. On discovering his misfortune, he immediately fled, in order that no one who knew him should see his disgrace; and he did not stop until he reached *Dun Cearmna* (now the Old Head of Kinsale, in the county of Cork), the residence of *Caichear*, son of *Eidirsgul* chief of that district, where he was well received, as a stranger, though his quality was not known. *Neidhé*, the satirist, then assumed the sovereignty of Connacht, and continued to rule it for a year.

The conclusion of this strange story (the historical meaning or foundation of which is now lost to us), is worth telling. After a year's enjoyment of his ill-gotten rank, *Neidhé*, it is said, began to repent of having unjustly caused so much misery to *Caier*, and having after some time discovered his retreat, he resolved to visit him. He set out accordingly in the favourite chariot of *Caier*, and accompanied by the king's treacherous wife; and he arrived in due time at *Dun Cearmna*. When the beautiful chariot arrived on the lawn of the *Dun*, its appearance was curiously examined by *Caichear* and his people. 'I wonder who they are,' said everyone. Upon which *Caier* rose up and answered: 'it is we that used to be driven in its champion's seat, in front of the driver's seat.' 'Those are the words of a king,' said *Caichear*, the son of *Eidersgul*, who had not recognized *Caier* until then. 'Not so, alas!' said *Caier* — and he rushed through the house, and presently disappeared in a large rock which stood behind it, in a cleft of which he hid himself. *Neidhé* followed him through the house; and *Caier*'s greyhound, which accompanied him, soon discovered its master in the cleft of the rock behind the house. *Neidhé* approached him, but when *Caier* saw him he dropped dead of shame. The rock then 'boiled', we are told, 'blazed', and 'burst', at the death of *Caier*; and a splinter of it entered one of *Neidhé*'s eyes and broke it in his head; whereupon *Neidhé* composed an expiatory poem — which is, however, omitted by *Cormac*, and by all the authorities that I am acquainted with.

This extravagant legend is valuable as exhibiting one of the earliest illustrations of that peculiar belief, in Erinn, concerning the satire of a poem, of which I have before given more than one less singular and more modern instance. This belief also may be taken to have preserved to us one of the traditions of that Druidism into whose mysteries we are unable to prosecute inquiries exact in detail.

I have now given instances of almost all the kinds of Druidism to which we find allusion in any of our tales or any of our historical pieces. And I shall add but one other example, which, as usual, I shall give in the form of an abridgment of the account itself, as it has been handed down to us. It is an instance of the mention of a Druid and some Druidical operations of his, preserved in the history of the Daleassian race of Thomond. The story is shortly as follows.

*Cas* (from whom the Dalcassians derive their distinctive race-name) was the son of *Conall* 'of the swift steeds', who was contemporary with the monarch *Crimhthann*, who died AD 379. *Cas* had twelve sons, from whom descend all the Dalcassian tribes; and of these twelve *Lugaidh Delbaeth*, (or *Lugaidh* 'the fire-producer') was the twelfth. This *Lugaidh* had six sons, and one daughter whose name was *Aeifé*. The sons were named: *Gno Beg, Gno Mór, Bac lan, Samtan, Aindelbadh*, and *Sighi. Lugaidh* the fire-producer had received a large territory from his father; and in time gave his daughter *Aeifé* in marriage to *Trad*, son of *Tassach*, who was a kingly chief and Druid, but without much land.

After some time *Trad* found himself the father of a numerous family, with but little provision for their support and advancement in life. Accordingly he said to his wife, *Aeifé*: 'Go thou and ask a favour from thy father; it would be well for us and for our children to get more land.' *Aeifé*, therefore, went and asked her father to grant her a favour. 'Then *Lagaidh* consulted his oracles,' says the writer of this account, 'and said to his daughter: "If thou shouldst order any one to leave his country now, he must depart without delay." "Depart thou, then," said she, "and leave us the land which thou inheritest, that it may be ours in perpetuity."' Whereupon, we are told, *Lugaidh* her father immediately complied, and with his six sons left the inheritance assigned to him by his father to his daughter *Aeifé* and her husband *Trad*. And I may add that this territory, even to the present day, retains the name of *Trad*, forming, as it does, the deanery of *Tradraidhé*, in the present barony of Bunratty, county of Clare (a tract which comprises the parishes of *Tuaimfinnlocha*, *Cill-ogh-na-Suloch*, *Cill Mailuighré*, *Cill Coirné*, *Cluain Lochain*, *Drom Lighin*, *Fiodhnach*, Bunratty, and *Cill Eoin*, and the island of *Inis-da-dhrom*, in the river Fergus).

The story proceeds to inform us that the Druid *Lugaidh*, having been thus deprived of his inheritance by his selfish daughter, crossed the Shannon with his sons and his cattle, and passed into the south-western district of Westmeath, to *Carn Fiachach*; where *Fiacha* was buried, the son of the monarch *Niall* of the Nine Hostages (ancestor of the families of *Mac Eochagan*, O'Mulloy, etc.). On arriving at this *Carn* he built up a large fire; and this, we are told, he ignited by his Druidic power — from which circumstance he acquired the title of *Delbaeth* or 'the fire-producer', a name that to this day is preserved both in that of the territory and in the Tribe name of his principal descendants, the family of *Mac Cochlann* of *Dealbhna* (now called Delvin), in Westmeath. The legend, however, does not stop here. From this fire we are told there burst forth five streams of flame, in five different directions; and the Druid commanded his five elder sons to follow one each of the fiery streams, assuring them that they would lead them to their future inheritances. The two elder sons, *Gno Beg* and *Gno Mór*, accordingly followed their streams across the Shannon into Connacht, where they stopped in two territories, which retained these names down to the sixteenth century, when they were united under that of the Barony of Moycullen, in the county of Galway, a district of which *Mac Conrai* (a name now anglicized King) was the chief in ancient times. The three other sons were led by their streams of fire to various parts of Westmeath, where they settled, and after whom those territories took the name of *Dealbhna* (anglicized the Delvins), from their father *Delbaeth* the Druid. Of these 'Delvins', *Dealbhna Ethra* was the most important, of which *Mac Cochlann* was the chief, whose residence was at the town now called Castletown-Delvin, in Westmeath; a house that preserved a considerable degree of rank and importance down even to our own times. *Sighi*, the sixth son of *Lughaidh Delbaeth*, remained in his father's neighbourhood; and it was to his son *Nós* that belonged the place in which the celebrated church of St *Ciaran* of *Cluain-mac-Nois* was built. The field in which the church was built had been appropriated to the use of the hogs of *Nós*, son of *Sighi*, and was therefore called *Cluain Muc Nóis*, or the field of the hogs of *Nós*; and the present name of Clonmacnoise is but a slightly Anglicized corruption of the old name. In fine, the old Druid *Lughaidh Delbaeth* himself settled on the brink of a lake near *Carn Fiacha* — which lake was thenceforward from him called *Loch Lugh-phorta*, or the lake of *Lughaidh*'s Mansion — and after his death his people buried him on the brink of this lake, and raised over him a great heap of stones which was called *Sidh-an-Caradh*, or the Friendly Hill.

In this story of *Lughaidh* we have allusion to two separate arts of professional Druidism; the one, that of ascertaining Fate by consultation of 'oracles', that is, Soothsaying, I suppose; and the other, the production of the magical Fire, of which we have already had so many other examples in these ancient legends.

From these various instances recorded or alluded to, either in the ancient annals, on the one hand, or in ancient tales which at least preserve what men believed of the Druids, on the other, we can gather much information as to the rank and authority, and something, at least, as to the ceremonies of the Druids of ancient Erinn. We have, indeed, no precise record of their specific rights, powers, or privileges; nor of the forms in which they exercised their magical arts; nor of the nature of the superstitions or religious belief which they taught. But the examples I have collected (mere examples out of a great number of similar cases to be found in ancient MSS) will at least prove that the historical student has a vast quantity of materials to investigate before he can pronounce with any confidence upon any of the details connected with this subject, much less theorize upon it with any safety as a whole.

It is a matter worthy of remark, that in no tale or legend of the Irish Druids which has come down to our time, is there any mention, as far as I know, of their ever having offered, or recommended to be offered, human sacrifices, either to appease or to propitiate the divine powers which they acknowledged. Not so, however, as to the British Druids, of whose acts so very few also have come down to us, voluminous as are the essays of modern 'antiquaries' on their history. One reference, reliable for its antiquity at least, and well worthy of notice, is found in the *Historia Britonum* of Nennius, a work believed to have been written about the year 800. Of this ancient British history the oldest version now known, I believe, is the Irish translation of it made by the learned poet and historian, *Giolla Caeimhghin*, who died in the year 1072. This translation has been published, with an English translation and notes, by the Irish Archaeological Society, in the year 1848, under the able editorship of the Revd Doctor Todd, assisted by the labours of the late learned, but sometimes very fanciful, Revd Algernon Herbert. At page 91 of this volume, where the distress of the British king, Gortigern, pressed by the treachery of the Saxon invaders, is related, the old author speaks as follows.

'Gortigern, with his hosts and with his Druids, traversed all the south of the island of Britain, until they arrived at Guined; and they searched all the mountain of Herer, and there found a hill over the sea, and a very strong locality fit to build on, and his Druids said to him: "Build here thy fortress," said they, "for nothing shall ever prevail against it." Builders were then brought thither, and they collected materials for the fortress, both stone and wood; but all these materials were carried away in one night, and materials were thus gathered thrice, and were thrice carried away. And he asked of the Druids, "Whence is this evil?" said he. And the Druids said, "*Seek a youth whose father is unknown, kill him, and let his blood be sprinkled on the fort, for by this means only it can be built*" ' — The youth thus indicated proved afterwards, as we know, the celebrated philosopher Merlin, of whom so many poetical legends are current among the traditions of Celtic Britain. The Druids' recommendation was not carried into effect; and this is, I think, the only instance of ancient allusion to human sacrifice even in Britain. In Erinn, as I have already said, there appears never to have been an instance even of a proposition made to take such means of propitiating the Fates, or the Deity.

I have now, I think, given specimens of all the magical arts referred distinctly to the Druids, as such, in our old books. Whether the interpretation of dreams and of auguries drawn from the croaking of ravens, the chirping of wrens, and such like omens, (of which we find, of course, a great many instances alluded to), formed any part of the professional office of the Druid of ancient Erinn, I have not been able to ascertain. But whoever it was, or whatever class of persons, that could read such auguries, there is no doubt that they were observed, and apparently much in the manner of other ancient nations. There is indeed a small tract devoted specially to this subject, among the valuable MSS preserved in the library of Trinity College, Dublin, to which I may direct attention in connection with the general subject. This tract is divided into three sections, which contain the three classes of Omens I have just alluded to; that concerning dreams and visions, being, however, much more copious than either of the others. As it would not be possible, perhaps, to investigate the subject of the Druids and their rites without reference to whatever can be traced of the superstitious beliefs and observances of the people of their time, I cannot wholly pass by this matter in concluding what I had to say, though I shall not do more than to mention generally what it contains.

And first, as to visions or dreams: the list of them is in extent very copious, though the subjects are very meagrely treated; and though the connection between the several articles mentioned and the vision of the dreamer to whom they may occur does not seem very clear, it may however, perhaps, become so when all the various examples of such visions preserved in the tales, etc., are critically considered. For the present purpose I need do no more than give a literal translation of some few of the entries or memoranda in the tract, as specimens of this interesting record. Those on dreams run as follows.

'A dead King denotes shortness of life. A King dying denotes loss. A King captured alive denotes evil. A brilliant Sun denotes blood. A dark Sun denotes danger. Two Suns in one night, disgrace. The Sun and Moon in the same course, battles. To hear Thunder denotes protection. Darkness denotes disease. To cut the Nails denotes tribulation. A golden Girdle around you denotes envy. To sow Tares denotes combats. To catch Birds by night denotes spoils by day. Birds flying from you by night denote the banishment of your enemies. To carry or to see Arms denotes honour' — and so on.

The divisions of the tract concerning auguries from the croaking of ravens and the chirping of wrens are in the same style, but more specific, because the subject is so. Some of the distinctions taken respecting the sounds made by birds are very curious, almost suggesting the recognition of some species of language among them. I should observe that both the ravens and the wrens, whose croaking and chirping was the subject of the augury, seem to have been domesticated birds (probably domesticated for the very purpose of these auguries), as will be perceived at once, even in the few examples I am about to select. These, as before, shall be literally translated.

Of the raven the writer says: 'If the Raven croaks over a closed bed within the house, this denotes that a distinguished guest, whether lay or clerical, is coming to you. But there is a difference between them. If he be a layman that is to come, it is "*bacach! bacach!*" the Raven says. But if it be a man in holy orders, it is "*gradh! gradh!*" it says; and it is far in the day that it croaks. If it be a soldier or a satirist that is coming, it is "*grog! grog!*" that it croaks; and it is behind you that it speaks, and it is from that direction the guests are to come.' And again: 'If it be in a small voice that the Raven speaks,' says this tract, 'namely, "*err! err!*" or "*ur! ur!*"', there is sickness to come on some person in the house, or on some of its cattle. If it is wolves that are to come to the sheep, it is from the sheep-pens, or else from beside the woman of the house, that he croaks, and what he says is "*carna! carna!*" "*grob! grob!*" "*coin! coin!*" (that is, wolves, wolves).' and again: 'If the Raven should accompany or precede you on an expedition, and that he is joyous, your journey will be prosperous. If it is to the left he goes, and croaks at you in front, it is at a coward he croaks in that manner, or his croaking denotes disgrace to some one of the party' — and so on.

Of the chirping of the wren a similar list of observations is recorded, and in the same manner; but I need not give details of further specimens of this class.

As may be imagined, the practice of augury, or Soothsaying, was not confined to these observations, and one instance may be remembered of another class of auguries as already described in a former lecture,[13] I mean that of the auguries taken from observation of the stars and clouds by night, by the Druids of *Dathi*, the last of our pagan monarchs. In that instance the divination is stated to have been conducted by the Druids by name. And I suppose it is but probable that all such auguries as those of which I have just been speaking were generally practised by the same influential order. I have, however (as already remarked), no positive proof that these divinations were confined to the class of Druids. Indeed, this class of learned men is not anywhere suffi- ciently defined to us in the old MSS, either as to their privileges, their doctrines, or their system of education; and we have, as may be observed, many instances of kings and chiefs who happened to have been also Druids, though no instance of a Druid, as such, arriving at or exercising any civil or military authority.

In this too short account of what is really known from authentic histories of this mysterious class or order of men, I have, as I already observed, by no means exhausted the subject; on the contrary, there are vast numbers of allusions to the Druids, and of specific instances of the exercise of their vocation — be it magical, religious, philosophical, or educational — to be found in our older MSS, which in a course of lectures like the present it would be quite impossible to unfold at full length. For these examples generally occur in the midst of the recital of long stories, or passages of history; and they could not be made properly intelligible without giving the context at so much length as often to lead us entirely away from the more immediate subject. And yet, considering the meagreness of facts and of any specific statements in all that has been yet published concerning the Druids of Britain and of Gaul (who, I may observe, appear to have differed materially from those of our island in many of their most important observances), I believe I have already described so many instances of Druidism as recorded in Gaedhelic MSS as will be found to throw a great deal of light upon the path of the investigator of this difficult and curious subject.

From the records of the earlier stages of our history instances have been adduced of the contests in Druidical spells between the Nemidians and Fomorians; of Druidical clouds raised by the incantations of the Druidesses before the celebrated battle of *Magh Tuireadh*; of showers or fire and of blood said to have been produced by the same agency on that occasion; of the spells, broken, after three days, by the counter arts in magic of the Firbolg Druids; of the Healing Fountain gifted by Druidical spells, at the same battle; and of the Explanation of the Dream of the Firbolg King *Eachaidh Mac Erc*, through the means of a vision raised by the 'prophetic art' of his Druid *Cesarn*.

After this period we have, on the coming of the Milesian colony, the Tempest raised by the Druids of the *Tuatha Dé Danann*, when they had persuaded their invaders to take to their ships again; and the discovery of the magical nature of this tempest by that observation from the topmast of one of the vessels, which proved that it only extended a few feet above the level of the water. And I quoted from an ancient authority the very words attributed to *Amergin* the Druid, one of the sons of Milesius, in the Druidical oration by which he allayed this magical tempest.

Passing on in the course of time we had an instance of the Druidical Fire, in the story of *Midhé*, the son of *Brath*, son of *Detha*; and in the singular tale of *Edain (Bé-finn)*, the queen of *Eochaidh Airemh*, (in the first century before Christ), an example of Druidical incantation; of the early science of *Ogam* letters; and of the use of the yew-wand, which, and not the oak, nor the mistletoe, seems to have been the sacred Druidical tree in Erinn.

In the stories of *Cuchulainn*, again, we had an instance of a trance produced by magical arts; of the mad rage of the hero, and of how, in the midst of that rage, he was caught as it were by the hands and feet, through Druidical incantations; and another kind of Druidical charm instanced by the drink of oblivion, finally given to the hero and to *Eimir*, his wife.

In the account of the means taken to discover the destined successor of King *Conairé Mór*, we had then in some detail the description of a vision produced by Druidical incantations; and of the omens of a day, an instance in those observed by *Cathbadh*, the Druid, on the day of the admission of *Cuchulainn* to the arms of knighthood; while of the general observation of the stars and clouds, those made by the Druids of King *Dathi*, before his foreign expedition, and described in a former lecture, afford a very distinct example. Of Druidical oracles, that which I have just referred to in the story of *Lughaidh Delbaeth*, and *Aiefé*, his daughter, is a fair specimen. The singular sorcery of the 'wisp of straw', occurring in the curious stories of *Nuadha Fullon* and of the prince *Comgan*, son of *Maelochtar*, is another remarkable case of Druidical ceremony, very minutely described. And in addition to this example, we had that, in full detail, of the use of the wisp in connection with the Druidical fire, in the story of the Ossorian Druid *Dill* and queen *Eithné* of Cashel, so lately as the fifth century. Lastly, the very extraordinary account of the siege of *Drom Damhghairé*, or Knocklong, with the Druidical contests of *Mogh Ruith* and *Ciothruadh*, proved even still more specific in the details of the same kind which it preserves to us. And the stories of St Patrick's contests with the Druids again afforded instances of Druidical darkness magically produced, even in his time.

Closely connected with the Druidical rites and belief were the systems of poetical divination, such as the *Imbas Forosnai*, and the *Teinm Laeghdha*, prohibited by St Patrick, as connected with idol worship; and this species of

Druidism we found practised by the famous *Finn MacCumhaill* in the third century. Another curious instance of it was preserved in that story of the recognition of the skull of *Mogh Eimhé*, the lapdog, two centuries after its death, by the poet *Maen Mac Etne*. Lastly, of the effects of the poetical satires I gave some further instances, as they were evidently the remains of the more ancient magical usages.

It is unfortunate that we have no certain account of the religion of the time of the Druids. We only know that they worshipped idols, from such examples as that of the Idol Gods taken into the Druid's bed, so as to influence his visions, as described in *Cormac's Glossary*, and that of the invocation of idols in the case of the *Tienm Laeghdha*; and we know that in certain ceremonies they made use of the yew tree, of the quicken or roan-tree, and of the blackthorn, as in the instance of the ordeal or test of a woman's character by means of fire made of these sacred woods. That the people of ancient Erinn were idolaters is certain, for they certainly adored the great idol called *Crom Cruach*, in the plain called *Magh Slecht*, as I showed on a former occasion.[14] But it is remarkable that we find no mention of any connection between this Idol and the Druids, or any other Class of Priests, or special Idol-servers. We have only record of the people, generally, assembling at times, to do honour to the Idol creation.

As little, unfortunately, do we know of the organization of the Order of the Druids, if they were indeed an Order. They certainly were not connected as such with the orders of learned men or profession of teachers, such as before explained. The Druids were often, however, engaged in teaching, as has been seen; and it would appear that kings and chiefs, as well as learned men, were also frequently Druids, though how or why I am not in a position to explain with certainty at present.

I have, therefore, simply endeavoured to bring together such a number of examples as may give some general idea of the position and powers of the Druids, so far as special instances are preserved in our early writings, of their mode of action and position in society. And I have refrained from suggesting any theory of my own upon the subject. This negative conclusion, nevertheless, I will venture to draw from the whole: that notwithstanding the singularly positive assertions of many of our own as well as of English writers upon the subject, there is no ground whatever for believing the Druids to have been the priests of any special positive worship — none whatever for imputing to them human sacrifice — none whatever for believing that the early people of Erinn adored the sun, moon, or stars — nor that they worshipped fire — and still less foundation for the ridiculous inventions of modern times (inventions of pure ignorance), concerning honours paid to brown bulls, red cows, or any other cows, or any of the lower animals.

There are in our MSS, as I have already observed, a great number of instances of Druidism mentioned besides those I have selected. I have merely taken a specimen of each class of Druidical rites recorded. I only hope I have so dealt with the subject as to assist the student, at all events, in attaining some general idea of our ancient life in respect of the superstitious observances of the people, though I cannot satisfactorily specify the forms and doctrines of our ancient system of paganism.

There are some curious allusions to an educational connection with Asiatic magi, in some of the stories of the very early Gaedhelic champions, many of whom seem to have travelled by the north of Europe to the Black Sea, and across into Asia. But these will, perhaps, more properly come under our consideration in connection with the subject of military education, and especially that of the professed champions.

1. Originally appeared as part of *Manners and Customs of the Ancient Irish* (Dublin, 1873) [Ed.]
2. Rowlands's *Mona Antiqua*, p.; 80 (Dublin: 1766).
3. Original: *Moen: moenia, mupopum aedificia.*
4. O'Curry, *Lectures on the Manuscript Materials of Ancient Irish History*, (Dublin, 1861), p. 243 *et seq.* [Ed.]
5. Ibid.
6. Ibid.
7. The Hill of Tara had five names. The first was *Druim Decsuin*, or the Conspicuous Hill; the second was *Liath Druim*, or *Liath*'s Hill from a *Firbolg* chief of that name who was the first to clear it of wood; the third was *Druim Cain*, or the Beautiful Hill; the fourth was *Cathair Crofinn*; and the fifth name was *Teamair* (now Anglicized Tara, from the genitive case *Teambrach* of the word), a name which it got from being the burial place of *Tēa*, the wife of *Eremon*, the son of Milesius.
8. See *Lectures on the MS, Materials of Ancient Irish History*, p. 37 *et seq.*
9. Ibid. p. 281 *et seq.*
10. See 'The Tale of Seirglige Conchulainn, or 'The Sick-bed of Cuchulainn and only jealousy of Eimer', in the *Atlantis*, vol. i, p. 362, *et seq.*; and vol. ii, p. 96.
11. See original in *Atlantis*, vol. i, p. 278.
12. *Lectures on MS Materials of the Ancient Irish History*, p. 271.
13. Ibid. pp.281–5.
14. Ibid. p. 103; and App. pp. 538, 631–2.

# Chapter 2
# The Mistletoe Sacrament
## by W. B. Crow

**DRUIDIC FESTIVALS.** That the Druids regulated all religious ceremonies and festivals goes without saying. Like other ancient priesthoods they studied the movement of the sun, moon and stars and regulated the calendar accordingly. As with many other nations they had festivals at the equinoxes and solstices. The year was personified at these festivals[1] at the spring by a youth, at the summer by a middle aged man, at the autumn by an elderly man and at the winter by an old man. These distributed gifts. The memory of one of these, the last, has persisted to the present time having become fused with the personality of St Nicholas, Santa Claus, or Father Christmas.

It is probable that the lighting of bonfires at certain times, which is a very ancient British custom and has continued until recent times, is of Druidic origin. Besides lighting these at the solstices and probably also at the equinoxes there were two other festivals which were of especial importance. These are Beltaine on the 1st May, and Samhaine on the 1st November. In view of the rivalry between the Druids (or rather their successors the Culdees) and the Roman Catholic hierarchy it is interesting to note that the celebrations at the beginning of November were continued, after the Gunpowder Plot, in the form of the Guy Fawkes celebrations, which still commemorates the ancient Catholic festival of the dead under an anti-Catholic guise!

And in view of the rivalry between the paganism of the Druids and the official Christianity which afterwards ousted them (in spite of fundamental resemblances and continuity) it is remarkable that the Labour Party still makes May Day its main festival, although, to the official Church, May Day is altogether of minor importance.

Like most Christian festivals the aforementioned were determined by the sun's position. In the Christian Church the most important group of festivals, however, are determined both by sun and moon. These include the Lent, Easter and Whitsun series. The Druids attached even more importance to the moon, and there were festivals on the day of the new moon, on the sixth day of the moon and on the day of full moon. It is not believed, however, that they celebrated any nocturnal ceremonies; all their services are said to have taken place in daylight.

**THE TEMPLES OF DRUIDISM.** It is popularly supposed that the rough stone monuments, of the architectural type known technically as the Cyclopean, of which the most imposing is that known as Stonehenge, were the temples or places of worship of the Druids. There are many good authorities who accept this popular view. It is based on the fact that these remains are the chief pre-Christian structures in these islands, that they were undoubtedly places of worship of an astronomical priesthood, that no other Druidical places of worship are known, other than natural groves, and that no other religion, to which these temples could have belonged, existed in Britain.

I am quite aware that T. D. Kendrick denies that there was any connection of Druidism with the Cyclopean monuments, but the very argument that he advances, *viz.*, that the Druids seem to be without temples and Cyclopean structures are without known priests, and that the attraction of the one for the other is irresistable, appears to be proof for the connection rather than the reverse. Again, Lewis Spence thinks that these stone monuments are pre-Druidic, but that the Druids used them (a view also held by other authors), yet he makes Druidism as ancient as any other cult in the world and connects it with the Stone Age times.

The sequence of events appears to have been as follows: in the most primitive stage known to archaeologists the worship took place in groves, under an open sky. Then upright stones took the place of trees, which was better, because the columns for the purposes of the ritual had to be arranged in a particular way. There was no roof to these Cyclopean buildings. Then, because of the weather, a roofed building was used, but the roof was taken off for certain ceremonies in which the sky had to appear. Finally it was found more effective to make the roof represent the sky, and representations of the heavens with its stars were painted inside the roof, so that the ritual could take place independently of the weather, and this, the most generally useful arrangement, is that found in Roman Catholic churches and Masonic lodges to this day.

All the ancient religions were sacrificial in nature, and we have already alluded to the allegation that the Druids offered human sacrifices. We are even told the way they did it. They constructed high hollow wickerwork figures, put their victims inside, and then set fire to them. According to some accounts the victims were animals.

A recent exponent of Druidism, however,[2] repudiates the idea that human victims were ever sacrificed, but admits that sheep, oxen, deer and goats were burnt, their charred remains having been found at Avebury, Stonehenge and even under St Paul's, which was built over a Druidical place of worship. Professor Canney says, 'It is doubtful whether human sacrifice was common. It would seem to have sufficed to take a few drops of blood from the victim and to burn only the wickerwork dummy.' White bulls were, however, offered, according to Welsh bards. This reminds one of Ancient Egypt.

**MISTLETOE AND SERPENTS' EGGS.** The most mysterious feature of Druidism, and one that has excited the utmost curiosity, is their veneration for the mistletoe. The oak was sacred to the Druids, but the mistletoe, growing on the oak, even more so. I have never seen any satisfactory explanation of this remarkable cult but I think in the light of comparative religion it is possible to reconstruct the meaning. One clue, I think, is to be found in a remark by Elder,[3] who, after mentioning that the Hebrew Messiah was referred to as the branch, refers to the fact that the Druids, equally with the Jews, expected the Messiah, and that the mistletoe was the symbol of the Messiah. The tree of Jesse was one of the most profound symbols of sacred tradition. It signifies the ancestral tree of the Messiah, who springs from this tree; and yet is planted on it by the descent of the Holy Ghost. The bird is always the symbol of the Holy Ghost, and the bird plants the seed of the still more sacred mistletoe on the sacred oak tree. What more accurate, one might almost say diagramatic, symbology of the coming of the Messiah could be devised? When we say that the Druids cut off branches of mistletoe and distributed them to believers in a sacramental manner, and when we see that sacred plants were used as sacraments in other religious ceremonies the parallel becomes perfect. For does not the Catholic priest take the juice of the grape and after consecrating it as the blood of Christ consume it from a golden vessel, just as the Druid cuts off mistletoe with a golden sickle because no other metal than gold is worthy to touch the most holy sacrament? The symbolism of the world tree and the mistletoe is also found among the Teutonic peoples, as we have seen, but they do not appear to have used it in their ceremonies.

One of the most peculiar ritual objects of the Druids was known as the *serpent's egg*. This is mentioned by Pliny in his *Natural History*. He describes it, from personal observation, as about the size of a small apple, with cartilaginous shell and pitted surface. Pliny says it is obtained in the following manner. In summer numbers of snakes entwine themselves together into a mass, held together by a secretion of their bodies and the saliva. When the creatures hiss some of the secretion is thrown into the air. This had to be caught on a cloth before it reached the ground and instantly carried away on horseback, as the serpents would pursue, until one had crossed a stream. The material, it was alleged, had the remarkable property of floating against the current of a river. Furthermore these eggs can only be taken on a certain day of the moon.

The Druids themselves were known to the Welsh bards by a word that means adders, and Lewis Spence is of the opinion that the ridiculous statements of Pliny really refer to the manner in which the Druids manufacture these eggs. Later bards also refer to a ceremony in which a ball was snatched and carried across water.

The Druidic custom just mentioned, we cannot help thinking, may have been the origin of the curious mediaeval rite of *pelota*, which took place in certain Catholic churches in France and Italy on Easter Monday. The ceremony consisted in bringing a ball of considerable size into the church and after solemnly presenting it before the altar, certain of the clergy beginning to dance and throwing the ball about in a special manner. The ceremony symbolises both the passage of the sun and the planets through the heavens and also the vicissitudes of the soul of man (the causal body of the theosophists). In Egyptian mythology the trial of the soul after death is associated with the passage of the sun through the underworld. The whipping of a spinning top, representing Alleluia on the Saturday before Septuagesima, a ceremony not uncommon in this country in former times, is related to this practice.

Madame Blavatsky has some interesting remarks on the connection with the serpent cult, which was at one time widespread and which is still widely practised in South India. The serpent is a symbol of regeneration. Not only does it lay eggs from which new life arises after having been preserved in the dormant state, but the reptile itself sloughs its skin at regular intervals. The initiate, in the ancient mystery religions, went through certain occult processes whereby his vehicles were actually renewed, and in symbolism thereof cast off his old clothing and was clad in new vestures. What better symbolism than the serpent could be chosen to represent this change in the personality? Besides this, the regeneration by sloughing refers to the regeneration of the physical body by reincarnation and the regeneration of races and worlds of the theosophic cosmogony. Some primitive peoples, after a death has occurred, perform a ritual in which the performers are divided into two groups and a struggle for the body takes place between the parties. This refers to the struggle between the powers of light and darkness for the spirit of the deceased, an eschatological myth of many ancient peoples. In the course of the evolution of this ritual it became a game in which the skull alone was the object of combat or had to be kicked into a goal. The various forms of the game of football and polo, and perhaps other ball games, are supposed to have originated from this, the original religious significance having become lost. The Druidic ritual of snatching an egg and running away until one got over a stream (which acts as the goal) suggests a similar game and connects up with funeral games. The egg or ball is an excellent symbol of the causal body, if one can believe clairvoyants, who see it as a kind of rounded or egg-shaped structure, in fine matter of the higher mental plane. After death, according to accounts of occultists, there is a kind of play of forces, good and evil, which do seem to struggle for the possession of the causal body and to determine whether it goes to a good or bad incarnation when next it descends to clothe itself with coarser matter.

The Druid's egg, says Pliny, was unknown to the Greeks. But other kinds of eggs are mentioned in Greek and Hindu mythology, and the consecration of an egg was one of the most important acts in the secret ritual of the Eleusinian mysteries. The Christian Church continued the use of the same symbol, as we see in the so-called Easter eggs, and in the ostrich eggs which are still to be seen hanging in Orthodox Catholic Churches in the East. In fact a whole lecture might be devoted to the symbolism of the cosmic egg.

**THE CAULDRON OF CERIDWEN.** The Greeks and to a less extent, the Romans had two special features of their culture which are absolutely characteristic of the Druidic. The one is the great prominence given to the cultivation of poetry (*bardism*) and the other is the importance of the cult of the dead (*lares* and *penates*).

The chief god of the Graeco-Roman pantheon, Jupiter, had the oak as his sacred tree and his sacrifices were offered every month. The oak was the chief ritual tree of the Druidic vegetation cult and the Druidic calendar was, as we have seen, largely lunar.

The Pagan Romans describe the gods of Druidism as being the same as their own, under different names. This in itself does not indicate any close connection of the Roman religion and Druidism, for the Romans were in the habit of describing the gods of all the peoples of antiquity as the same as their own. They not only identified their own gods with those of the Greeks, an identification that has been accepted by Western literature generally (so that for example we make no distinction now between the Roman Jupiter and the Greek Zeus or between the Roman Minerva and the Greek Athena), but the Romans also identified most of the gods of the Egyptian and Teutonic pantheons with their own. What we have to indicate is that the *details* of Celtic mythology and ritual are *identical with* or *almost* so with that of the Greeks. And this has been proved by Lewis Spence, although in his research he fancied himself employed in quite a different task. The Druidic mythology and culture consists mainly of Greek traditions which, however, are not those that are the best known. Druidism is not, in the main, the worship of Jupiter, Apollo and Mars, although these gods were recognizable, as we have seen, in the Druidic pantheon. It was the worship of the mysterious Cabiri. In this was retained an ancient sacramental and initiatory system, inherited from the Pelasgi. The centre of this worship was not in the mainland of Greece, but in the island of Samothrace. To the priests of the Cabiri repaired all the great heroes and princes of Greece and surrounding countries, to be initiated into the mysteries. The Eleusinian mysteries were something similar, instituted at a place called Eleusis in Attica on the mainland of Greece. These mysteries centred on the figures of Ceres, Pluto, Proserpina and Bacchus. Pluto, it will be remembered, was the god of the dead and he carried off Proserpina to the nether regions, whereupon she was sought for by her mother Ceres. It was ultimately agreed that she should spend half of each year below and half above ground. Ceres is the goddess of agriculture and the myth refers to the seasons. Bacchus was the wine god, Ceres the wheat goddess. They are the wine and bread of the Christian religion, but in a crude and natural form. And here we have the fertility cult connected with death and resurrection, as in other religions, which Sir James Frazer has told us so much about in his *Golden Bough*. The Druidic religion is clearly one branch of this cult of the golden bough, but further than this the Druidic mysteries, as far as can be made out from the survivals of the same, and from reconstruction of the originals, resemble the Cabiric and Eleusinian mysteries.

For instance, in their rites the Welsh bards made a decoction of berries and herbs and sea foam in a vessel, which is the cauldron of the goddess Ceridwen of Celtic mythology. In the Greek mysteries of the goddess Ceres a decoction of flowers, barley, salt and sea water was used. In both rites, after a little of this had been taken by the initiates, the residue was regarded as poisonous and accursed having symbolically taken the sins and pollutions which had been cast out of the candidates.

The cauldron was prepared by a ritual in which nine maidens warmed it with their breath. In the Greek mysteries nine maidens representing the nine muses (connected with Orpheus) were thought to be imbued with similar special powers. Strabo connects the Druidesses with the priestesses of Bacchus (Dionysos).

**THE MYSTERIES IN BRITAIN.** The consecration of an egg was an important part of the Greek mysteries. As we have seen the egg of a serpent was used by the Druids.

The Gauls, according to Julius Caesar, claimed to be descended from a common forefather, Dis or Pluto, and they said that this was the tradition of the Druids. Dis or Pluto is the god of the Greek underworld, and is the husband of Proserpina of the mysteries.

But some say that Vulcan, the smith-god or skilful artisan and worker in metals and god of fire, was the chief of the Cabiri. The Cabiri are also described as workers in metals. Vulcan, as artificer, is connected with Freemasonry; as worker in metals, with alchemy. But even this goes back to the Druids. An old British chronicle, quoted by Dr Thomas Williams, states that the Pheryllt had a college at Oxford prior to the foundation of the University. These Pheryllt were teachers of all that required the agency of fire. Chemistry and metallurgy were called the arts of the Pheryllt. Lewis Spence says that the Pheryllt appear to have been a section of the Druidic brotherhood.

The Druids, like the Greeks, also celebrated funeral games. The Olympic

Games were perhaps derived from this. At the Olympic Games, by the way, prizes were awarded, not only for running, wrestling, etc., but also for poetry, eloquence and the fine arts. The modern Welsh Eisteddfod is reminiscent of this.

The island of Britain was sacred to the Greeks and Romans and some said it was the actual abode of the dead. Dis or Pluto was regarded as king of the dead, and if the chief god of the Druids had been identified with Pluto we can see how this story might have arisen. The cult of the dead no doubt formed part of the primeval religion of Britain. The Greek religion was at first very deep and mysterious, but became more and more superficial as the people became more and more sceptical and argumentative under the influence of superficial thinkers.

Under the Romans, of course, religion became very debased, as they copied the worst features of the Greeks, becoming by turns highly rationalistic and then highly superstitious. But in Britain the primeval faith of the Celtic sub-race was retained in all its purity, and it is interesting to note that there is an almost complete gradation from the Druidic religion to the Christian, many Druids in fact becoming Christian priests without giving up much of their original religion. The social system of Britain today in fact, as Elder[4] has shown, is founded on the Druidic law and customs

I do not know how far the teaching of history has changed since I was at school, but at that time we began with the Roman invasion of Britain, and the ancient Britons were represented as naked savages. Archaeological investigations have long shown the incorrectness of this view and, as theosophical writers have always maintained, there were great civilizations among the Celtic peoples long before the Roman conquest. The stories of King Arthur and his round table are founded on fact. In the medieval Arthurian romances it was customary to describe the heroes as knights in armour, with all the customs of the age of chivalry. It has been thought by many critics that this was due to the medieval romance writers clothing their heroes in the costume of their own times or of a slightly earlier decade. I do not think this is the whole story. The Romans of the times of the Caesars had, for instance, quite complex coat armour and if the Britons were still more highly civilized than the Romans the pictures of the knights of the round table, going about in shining armour on horseback, and indulging in tournaments and picturesque combats, may not be very exaggerated. According to some legends, not too well known, but equally authentic as any other history of that period, Arthur had an extensive empire, and even conquered Rome. The figure of Merlin has been shown to be very reminiscent of that of a Druid.

The coming of the Saxons, says Kendrick, caused the obliteration of Druidism, but long before that it had merged into Christianity, and its hierarchy had become absorbed into that branch of the Church (the Celtic) that had existed in this country from Apostolic times.

1. S. C. Cox, 'The Bards of Ancient Britain', *Geo-Sophic* III, 1929.
2. Elder, *Celt, Druid and Culdee*, (London, 1938).
3. *Loc. cit.*
4. *Loc. cit.*

# Chapter 3

# The Mythology and Rites of the British Druids[1]

## by Edward Davies

*Traditions relating to the progress, revolutions, and suppression of the British superstition*

A successful investigation of the progress and revolutions of Druidism might be expected to attract the notice of the public. It would certainly be curious to trace the changes, whether improvements or corruptions, which took place in the religion of our early progenitors, and to have an opportunity of discriminating between those rites and superstitions, which they originally brought with them into Britain, and those which, in the course of ages, they adopted from other nations, or devised from their own fancy.

But for the basis of such an investigation, we want an authentic historical document, enlighted by accurate chronology, and divested of allegorical obscurity. Upon this subject, no such aid is to be found. The religion of the Britons, like that of other heathens, grew up in the dark. All that we have left is a mass of mythological notices, which were certainly written in ages when Druidism was in high esteem and had many votaries; and from those, the genuine opinion and tradition of the Britons, during those ages, may be in some measure collected. From these enigmatical tablets, I shall attempt to make a few slight sketches, with the hope of gratifying the curious, and affording some little light to the antiquary; though from the nature of my materials, I almost despair of amusing the general reader.

In the first place, it may be inferred from the tone of the evidence already produced that the primitive religion of the Cymry (long before the age of the oldest bard who is now extant) was a kind of apostasy from the patriarchal religion, or a mere corruption of it.

In the tradition of this people, I have remarked the local account of a vessel, from which they assert that their progenitors sprung after a general deluge; I have noticed their *exclusive* claim to the universal patriarch of all nations; I have observed that their superstition strongly verged from all points, towards the history of the Deluge, and towards that system of theology which Mr Bryant denominates *Arkite*;[2] I have shown that they worshipped the patriarch as a deity, though they had not forgotten that he was a just and pious man; and I think I have proved that the *Ceridwen* of the Druids was as much the *genius* of the Ark, as the *Ceres* and *Isis* of our great mythologist.

If the bards exhibit, together with this Arkite superstition, that mixture of *Sabian* idolatry, or worship of the host of heaven, which the second volume of the *Analysis* traces, as blended with the same mythology, over great part of the ancient world, yet we observe that the *solar* divinity is always represented as the *third* or youngest of the great objects of adoration. Hence it may be inferred, that the worship of the patriarch, in conjunction with the sun, was an innovation, rather than an original and fundamental principle, of the Druidical religion.

That this opinion was inculcated by our old mythologists appears from a very singular triad, which I propose to analyse. But the reader of taste may require some apology, for the homeliness of its characters.

Mythologists have never been very scrupulous in the selection of their figures. Gods and their priests have been presented to us under the form of every animal character, from the elephant and the lion to the insect and the reptile. And it is not to be expected that our ancestors should have been more delicate in their choice than other nations more enlightened and more refined.

Without any such affectation of superior taste, they bring forward three distinct states of the British hierarchy, but all of them more or less Arkite, under the characters of three mighty *swineherds*.

Their disciples, of course, consisted of a multitude of swine. I am not calling them names — these are the titles they thought proper to assume; and no doubt, they regarded them as very respectable and becoming.

Though this representation be partly peculiar to the Britons, it has still some analogy with the notions and the mythology of other heathens.

Thus, we are told that the priests of the Cabiri were styled *Sues* — swine. Greece and Rome consecrated the sow to Ceres, and gave it the name of the *mystical animal*. The learned and ingenius M. De Gebelin says that this selection was made not only because the sow is a very prolific animal but also because she ploughs the ground, and because the plough has a figure similar to that of her snout, and produces the same effect.[3]

The Cymry proceeded somewhat further, but still upon the same road. In Britain, Ceres herself assumes the character of *Hwch*, a sow; she addresses her child, or devotee, by the title of *Porchellan*, little pig; her congregation are *Moch*, swine; her chief priest is Turch, a boar, or Gwydd Hwch, boar of the wood, or grove; and her hierarchy is Meichiad, a swineherd.

The Triad which I have mentioned, upon the subject of the three mighty swineherds, is preserved in several copies,[4] from a collation of which I shall subjoin an English version and add some remarks upon each particular.

'The first of the mighty swineherds of the island of Britain was Pryderi, the son of Pwyll, chief of Annwn, who kept the swine of his foster-father, Pendaran Dyved, in the vale of Cwch, in Emlyn, whilst his own father, Pwyll, was in Annwn.'

In order to understand the meaning of this mythology, it will be necessary first of all to take some notice of the persons and places here introduced.

*Pryderi*, called also *Gwynvardd Dyved*, was the son of *Pwyll, Lord of Dyved*, the son of *Meirig*, the son of *Arcol*, with the long hand, the son of *Pyr*, or *Pur* of the East, the son of *Llion* the ancient.[5]

Though the vanity of certain Welsh families has inscribed these princes in the first page of their pedigrees, it would be absurd to connect their history with any known chronological period. It is purely mythological, as appears from the very import of their names.

*Pryderi* is *deep thought*, or *mature consideration*; and the general subject of this thought may be collected from his other title — *Gwynvardd Dyved* — Druid of Demetia.

*Pwyll*, his father, is *reason*, *discretion*, *prudence*, or *patience*. That both the father and the son were characters wholly mystical or personifications of abstract ideas is shown in Taliesin's *Spoils of the Deep*, where we are told that the Diluvian patriarch first entered the Ark by the counsel of Pwyll and Pryderi.

*Meirig* is a *guardian*. In this series, the word ought to be translated, though it has been the proper name of several Britons.

*Ar-col* may imply the man of the *lofty mount*, but as Arcol with the long hand was avowedly of Eastern extraction, it is probable his name may have been of Eastern derivation, and if so, he may have been no less a personage than the great Hercules, who was known in the East by similar titles, as we are informed by Mr Bryant; who tells us that in the neighbourhood of Tyre and Sidon, the chief deity went by the name of Ourchol, the same as Archel and Arcles of Egypt, whence came the Heracles and Hercules of Greece and Rome. [6]

But the history of Hercules, as we learn from the same author, alludes to a mixture of Arkite and Sabian idolatry.

It is said of Hercules that he traversed a vast sea in a cup, or skiff, which Nereus, or Oceanus sent him for his preservation; the same history is given to Helius (the sun) who is said to have traversed the ocean in the same vehicle. [7]

If the critics can pardon an attempt to identify Arcol, in the character of Hercules, I need not dread their censure for supposing that his father Pyr, or Pur of the East, is to be found amongst the known connections of that demigod.

Pyr is the Greek name of *fire*, and mythologically of the *sun*, who was the same as Hercules. And the great analyser of mythology assures us that Pur was the ancient name of Latian Jupiter, the father of Hercules; that he was the deity of fire; that his name was particularly retained amongst the people of Praeneste, who had been addicted to the rites of fire; that they called their chief god Pur, and dealt particularly in divination by lots, termed of old, Purim. [8]

From hence it may be conjectured, with some degree of probability, that this mystical family, which was of Eastern origin, had a certain connection with the history of Jupiter and Hercules.

But lest we should lose sight of the *fundamental* principles of Arkite theology, our mythological herald takes care to inform us that Pyr, of the East, was the son of Llion the Ancient, that is, the Deluge, or the Diluvian god: for the waters of Llion are the great abyss, which is contained under the earth, and which once burst forth, and overwhelmed the whole world.

This mythological pedigree, therefore, only declares the Arkite origin of a certain mystical system, which was introduced into Britain through the medium of some Eastern people.

The characters here introduced are represented as princes of Demetia, the country of Seithenin Saidi, who is Saturn or Noah. This region was so greatly addicted to mystical rites that it was called, by way of eminence, *Bro yr Hûd*, the *land of mystery*, and said to have been formerly enveloped in *Llengêl*, *a veil of concealment*.

But we are not immediately to conclude that Pryderi conducted his swine, according to the rules of his Eastern ancestors. These were not the property of his father and grandfather, but the herd of Pendaran, lord of thunder, otherwise called *Arawn*, the *Arkite*, and managed under his supreme administration. *His* authority was already established in the West, and, as we shall presently see, it was different from that of Arcol, and Pyr of the East.

Pryderi kept the swine of his foster-father, Pendaran, in the vale of *Cwch*, the *boat*, or *ark*, in *Emlyn*, the *clear lake*, whilst his own father, Pwyll, was in *Annwyn*, the deep — the Deluge.

I must leave the great swineherd to the management of his charge, whilst I seek an elucidation of this mythology from a curious tale upon the subject of Pwyll's adventures. [9]

This tale manifestly alludes to Arkite theology, and I think, also, to the reformation of some foreign abuses, or innovations, which were intermixing with the doctrines and rites of the natives, and to the rejection of Sabian idolatry, or solar worship.

The reader may judge for himself, by the following abstract:

Pwyll, lord of the seven provinces of Dyved, being at *Arberth, high grove*, one of his chief mansions, appoints a hunting party — that is, the *celebration of mysteries*. Thus Ceridwen is said to have *hunted* the aspirant.

The place which he chose for this exercise was *Glyn-Cwch*, the vale of the *boat*, or *ark*. Accordingly, he set out from Arberth, and came to the head of the *grove of Diarwyd*, the *solemn preparation of the egg*.

Pliny's account of the preparation of the *Anguinum*, by the Druids, in the character of serpents, is well known. Mr Bryant also observes that an egg was a very ancient emblem of the Ark; and that in the Dionusiaca, and in other mysteries, one part of the nocturnal ceremony consisted in the consecration of an egg. [10]

In this grove of the preparation of the egg, Pwyll continued that night; and early in the morning he proceeded to the vale of the boat, and turned out his dogs — *priests*, who were called Κυνεφ, [11] dogs — under the wood, or *grove*.

He blew his horn — that is, the herald's horn. Thus Taliesin says: 'I have been Mynawg, wearing a collar, with my horn in my hand; he is not entitled to the presidency, who does not keep my word.'

Pwyll, entering fully upon the chase, and listening to the cry of the pack, began to hear distinctly the cry of another pack, which was of a different tone from that of his own dogs, and was coming in the opposite direction. This alludes to some mystic rites, which essentially differed from those of his Eastern ancestors, Arcol and Pyr.

The strange pack pursued a stag — the *aspirant* — into a level open spot — the *adytum* — in the centre of the grove, and there threw him upon the ground. Pwyll, without regarding the stag, fixed his eyes with admiration upon the dogs, which were all of a shining white hue, with red ears. Such is the popular notion of the Welsh, respecting the colour of Cwn Annwn, the dogs of the deep — a mystical transformation of the Druids, with their white robes and red tiaras.

The prince drives away the pack which had killed the stag, and calls his own dogs upon him — thus, initiating the aspirant into his own Eastern mysteries.

Whilst he is thus engaged, the master of the white pack comes up, reproves him for his uncourtly behaviour, informs him that he is a king, wearing a crown, as sovereign lord of Annwn, the deep, and that his name is Arawn, the

Arkite[12] — this is the personage who is also styled Pendaran, lord of thunder.

Pwyll having expressed a wish to atone for his imprudent offence, and to obtain the friendship of this august stranger:

'Behold,' says Arawn, 'how thou mayest succeed in thy wishes. There is a person whose dominion is opposite to mine, who makes war upon me continually. This is *Havgan, summershine*, a king also of Annwn; by delivering me from his invasions, which thou canst easily do, thou shall obtain my friendship.'

This *summershine*, who invades the dominions of the Diluvian patriarch, can be no other than the *solar divinity*, whose rites had begun to intermix with and partly to supersede the more simple Arkite memorials. Here then, we have a direct censure of that monstrous absurdity, of venerating the patriarch, in conjunction with the sun. Pwyll, or *reason*, is represented as having destroyed this Apollo.

It may be conjectured, however, from the works of the British bards, that he soon revived again, and claimed all his honours.

But to go on with the story. It was proposed that Pwyll should assume the form of Arawn, that he should immediately leave his own dominions and proceed to Annwn, the deep, where he was to preside, in the character and person of the king, for a complete year. This must mean that he was to be initiated into Arkite mysteries, or to pass through a representation of the same scenes, which the patriarch had experienced. Thus Noah had presided in the Ark, for precisely the same period, over the great deep, or the deluged world.

On the day that should complete the year, Pwyll was to kill the usurper, Summershine, or the Solar Idol, with a single stroke; and in the meantime, Arawn assumes the form of Pwyll and engages to take his dominions under his special charge.

It was during this year, of the mystical Deluge, that Pryderi guarded the swine of his foster-father, Arawn, or Pendaran, in the vale of the boat. His herd, therefore, was purely Arkite.

Pwyll, having determined to engage in this great enterprise, is conducted by the king to the palace of the deep — as Noah was conducted to the Ark. Being received by the whole court without suspicion, he is attended in due form by Arawn's ministers, and lodged in the royal bed — the Παροϱ or cell of initiation — where he preserves an *involate silence*, and as a man eminently just and upright, shows a wonderful instance of continence in his deportment towards the queen, who is the fairest woman in the world, and supposes him to be her own husband. Such were the trials of fortitude and self-government to which the aspirants were exposed.

On the appointed day, Pwyll kills the usurper, Summershine, and at the completion of the year returns from the palace of the deep into his own dominions, which he finds in an improved and most flourishing condition under the administration of the great Arawn, with whom he contracts a perpetual friendship.

This part of the tale blends a mystical account of the Deluge with the history of those mysteries which were celebrated in memory of the great preservation.

The prince being now re-established in his palace at Arberth, or high grove, provided a banquet — or solemn sacrifice — for himself and his retinue. After the first repast, the whole company walked forth to the top of the *Gorsedd*, or seat of presidency, which stood above the palace. Such was the quality of this seat, that whoever sat upon it, should either receive a wound, or see a miracle.

Pwyll, regardless of consequences, sat upon the mystical seat, and presently both the prince himself and the whole of his retinue beheld a lady, mounted upon a horse of a pale bright colour, great, and very high.

The lady herself wore a garment, glittering like gold, and advanced along the main road, which led towards the Gorsedd. Her horse, in the opinion of all the spectators, had a slow and even pace, and was coming in the direction of the high seat.

The reader will have no difficulty in comprehending that this splendid lady was the *Iris* riding in her humid cloud; and that she was coming from the court of Arawn, upon a friendly errand. But as she was unknown to all the company now present, Pwyll sent a messenger to meet her and learn who she was. One of his train rose up to execute the prince's order, but no sooner was he come into the road, opposite to the fair stranger, than she passed by him. He pursued her on foot with the utmost speed, but the faster he ran, the more he was distanced by the lady, though she still seemed to continue the same gentle pace with which she had set out at first. She was then followed by a messenger upon a fleet horse, but still without any better success. The same vain experiment was tried the next day.

The prince now perceived that there was a mystery in the appearance, yet being persuaded that the lady had business to communicate to someone in that field, and hoping that the honour of her commands might be reserved for himself, he gets ready his courser and undertakes the enterprise on the third day. The lady appeared; the prince rode to meet her; she passed by him with a steady gentle pace; he followed her at full speed, but to no purpose. Then Pwyll said —

The remainder of the story is lost; consequently, our curiosity as to the adventures of Pwyll and the mystical lady cannot be gratified. [13]

But I have no doubt that this lady in the splendid robe was the *rainbow*, that sacred token of reconciliation, which appeared to Noah after the Deluge, and which was universally commemorated in Gentile mythology.

The mounting of her upon a horse seems to have been a British device. Thus we are told in the mystical poem called *The Chair of Ceridwen* that Gwydion, Hermes, formed for the goddess of the rainbow a stately steed upon the springing grass, and with illustrious trappings.

The circumstance of the vain pursuit of this phenomenon, which seemed to move so calmly and steadily along, may remind several of my readers of a childish adventure of their own. Many a child has attempted to approach the rainbow for the purpose of contemplating its beauty.

Upon the whole it is evident that though the transcriber of this ancient tale may have introduced some touches of the manners of his own age, yet the main incidents faithfully delineate that Arkite mythology which pervades the writings of the primitive bards; at the same time that they pass a severe censure upon solar worship, as a corrupt innovation.

Having taken this view of the great swineherd, Pryderi, or *deep thought*, I proceed to consider the adventures of the next in order, where we shall have some hints of the channel, by which this innovation of Sabian idolatry was introduced.

The learned author of the *Mysteries of the Cabiri* gives me an opportunity of prefixing a few hints, which may serve to keep our British mythologists in countenance.

Having remarked from Tacitus that the Estyi, a people of Germany, worshipped the mother of the gods, and that the symbol which they used was a boar, Mr Faber thus proceeds.

'Rhea, or the mother of the gods, as it has been abundantly shown, was the same as Ceres, Venus, Isis, or Derceto. She was, in short, the Ark of Noah, from which issues all the hero-gods of paganism. With regard to the boar, used by this German tribe as an emblem, we find it introduced very conspicuously into many of those legendary traditions, which relate to the great event of the Deluge. It appears to have been one of the symbols of the Ark, although not adopted so generally as the mare, or the heifer. In the first Hindu *Avatar*, Vishnu assumes the form of a fish; and in the third, that of a boar, when he is represented as emerging from the midst of the ocean and supporting the world upon his tusks. Both these incarnations, as well as the second, are supposed by Sir William Jones to allude to the history of the Flood; whence, as we have already seen that a fish was emblematical of the Ark, it is not unreasonable to conclude that the boar may be so likewise. Accordingly, in the account which Plutarch gives us of the Egyptian Osiris, he mentions that Typhon, or the Deluge, being in pursuit of one of those animals found the Ark, which contained the body of Osiris, and rent it asunder.' [14]

The author subjoins the following note:

'Perhaps, if the matter be expressed with perfect accuracy, we ought rather to say, that a boar was symbolical of Noah, and a sow of the Ark. Hence we find, that as Vishnu was feigned to have metamorphosed himself into a boar, so the nurse of Arkite Jupiter, or in other words, the Noëtic ship, is said by Agathocles to have been a sow.' [15]

'Coll, the son of *Collvrewi — Rod* — the son of *Rod of terrors*, guarded *Henwen — old lady*, the sow of *Dallwyr Dallben — mystagogue, chief of mystics* — in the vale of *Dallwyr — mystics* — in Cornwall. The sow was big with young; and as it had been prophesied that the island of Britain would suffer detriment from her progeny, Arthur collected the forces of the country and went forth for the purpose of destroying it. The sow in the meantime, being about to farrow, proceeded as far as the promontory of Land's End, in Cornwall, where she put to sea, with the swineherd after her. And she first came to land at Abert Tarrogi, in Gwent Is Coed, her guardian still keeping hold of the bristles, wherever she wandered, by land or sea.

'At Wheatfield, in Gwent, she *laid* three *grains of wheat*, and three *bees*. Hence, Gwent is famous to this day for producing the best wheat and honey.

'From Gwent she proceeded to Dyved; and in *Llonnio Llonwen*, the *pleasant spot of the tranquil lady*, laid a grain of *barley*, and a *pig*. And the barley and swine of Dyved are become proverbial.

'After this, she goes towards Arvon, and in Lleyn she laid a *grain of rye*, since which time the best rye is produced in Lleyn and Eivionydd.

'Proceeding from thence, to the vicinity of the cliff of Cyverthwch, in Eryri, she laid the *cub of a wolf*, and an *eaglet*. Coll gave the eagle to Brynach, a northern Gwyddelian prince of Dinas Affaraon, and the present proved detrimental to him. The wolf was given to Menwaed, lord of Arllechwedd.

'These were the wolf of Menwaed and the eagle of Brynach, which in aftertimes became so famous.

'From hence, the sow went to the black stone in Arvon, under which she laid a *kitten*, which Coll threw from the top of the stone into the Menai. The sons of Paluc, in Mona, took it up and nursed it, to their own injury. This became the celebrated Palac cat, one of the three chief molestors of Mona, which were nursed within the island. The second of these molestors was Daronwy, and the third was Edwin, the Northumbrian king.'

I should not have exhibited this fantastical story were I not persuaded that it contains some important tradition respecting the progress of superstition in our country, of which no other account is to be found and that the greatest part of it may be explained.

Before we attend to the mystical sow and her ill-omened progeny, it may be proper to take some notice of her guardian.

Rod, the son of the *rod of terrors*, or of *religious awe*, the hero of this singular tale, cannot be regarded as an individual person. He is an ideal character, implying a principal agent, or the aggregate of agents, in conducting a particular mode of superstition.

*Coll* is repeatedly mentioned in the mythological Triads. He is there classed with the great deified patriarch, Hu Gadarn, as one of three personages who conferred distinguished benefits upon the Cymry nation. He has the credit of having first introduced wheat and barley into Britain, where only rye and oats had been known before his time.[16] Hence it appears that he must have been a great favourite of Ceres, the goddess of cultivation.

He is again brought forwards, as one of the three great presidents of mysteries.[17] And here we must regard his doctrine and institutes as comprehending the mystical theology and rites, which prevailed in a certain age, or over certain districts of these islands.

That of *Menu*, the son of the *three loud calls*, and of *Uthyr Bendragon*, or the *wonderful supreme leader*, was the first of these.

That of Coll, the son of Collvrewi and of Eiddilic Corr, or Gwyddelin Corr, constituted the second; and this agreed with the mode of *Rhuddiwm Gawr*, or the *red, bony giant*.

And that of Math, the son of Mathonwy, Drych eil Cibddar and Gwydion ab Don was the third.

The first of these modes or stages I suppose to have been that corruption of the patriarchal religion, or the more simple Arkite theology, which originally prevailed amongst the Cymry, and of which we have already had some hints, under the characters of Pwyll and Pryderi.

As to the second, when we recollect that Coll first began the superintendence of his mystical sow in Cornwall, which either was one of the Cassiterides of the ancients or else certainly carried on an intercourse with those tin islands, it may be conjectured that the *red bony giant*, the original introducer of this superstition, and who is represented as the uncle and mystical preceptor of Coll, was no other than the Phoenician, or *red merchant*, half Canaanite, and half Edomite, who traded with the tin islands. And as this became the system of Corr, the Coraniad, or Belgian, and also of Gwyddelin, the Gwyddelian, whom our writers regard as of the same family with the other, it appears to be the meaning of the Triads that the Belgae of Britain and Ireland adopted the mode of this stranger. Of the introduction of the same mysticism into Wales, and immediately from Cornwall, we have a more detailed account of the adventures of Coll and his wonderful sow. This superstition contained memorials of the Deluge, but it verged more strongly towards Sabian idolatry.

The third mode, namely, that of Math, Drych, and Gwydion, seems to have been a mixture of the two former; that is, of the superstition of the original Cymry and the more idolatrous rites of the Phoenicians; or that confusion of principles which we find in the old British bards, and which Mr Bryant has detected amongst many ancient nations.

Coll is, then, the great agent in the adventitious branch of the Druidical religion.

Having thus seen what is meant by his character, we will proceed to the history of his sow, and we shall find that however absurd it may be in the literal sense, great part of it will admit of explanation upon mythological principles.

The name of this mystical animal was *Hēnwen, old lady*, a proper title for the *great mother*, Da-Mater, or Ceres, to whom the sow was sacred. But Ceres, or the *great mother*, as Mr Bryant has proved, was the genius of the Ark. Agreeably to this decision, it has occurred to our countrymen that under this allegory of a sow we must understand the history of a *ship*. Upon the story of Coll and his mystical charge, Mr Owen remarks that under this extraordinary recital there seems to be preserved the record of the appearance of a strange ship on the coasts, under the appellation of a sow, and that it was probably a Phoenician ship, which imported into the island the various things here mentioned.[18]

And again in his *Dictionary*, under the word *Hwch*, a sow, the same author tells us 'It has been also used as an epithet for a ship, for the same reason as *Banw* is applied to a *pig*, and to a *coffer*; the abstract meaning of the word being characteristic of the form of both. There is a tradition in Monmouthshire that the first corn sown in Wales was at Maes Gwenith, Wheatfield, in that county, and was brought there by a *ship* which, in a Triad alluding to the same event, is called Hwch' — that is, a *sow*.

That this tale alludes to the history of a ship or vessel, there can be no doubt, and we first hear of its being in Cornwall, that part of Britain which is supposed to have had a peculiar intercourse with the Phoenicians.

But, in a literal sense, wolves and eagles must have been very useless, as well as unnecessary, articles of importation to the ancient Britons. This was a *sacred* ship. Its cargo consisted, not of common merchandise, but of religious symbols and apparatus. And there is every reason to conclude that it was itself a symbol of the Ark.

I have already observed that the name of this mystical vehicle, *old lady*, was a proper epithet for the great mother — the Ark.

The depositing of the various kinds of grain points to the office of Ceres, who was the genius of the Ark; to the British Kēd, who passed through the Deluge, stored with corn; and to the character of Ceridwen, who is styled Ogyrven Amhad, the *goddess of various seeds*, and whose mysteries were Arkite.

The whimsical use of the verb *dodwi*, to *lay*, as a hen lays her eggs, when applied to the parturition of the mystical sow, or ship, cannot be accounted for till we recollect that our Arkite goddess is styled and described as a hen.

And this symbolical sow, like the Argo of antiquity, proceeds by land, as well as by sea, attended by her mystical priest.

The place from whence she began her progress and the persons to whom she belonged with equal clearness point out her mythological character. For this sow, we are told, was the property of Dallwyr, the blind men, or Μυται of Dallben, the mystagogue; and was guarded in Glyn Dallwyn, the glen, or vale, of the mystics, in Cornwall.

To this spot she had been confined during a considerable period; for the Britons were *aware* of her being there, and were jealous of the innovations which she might introduce. Hence the old prophecy that Britain would be injured by her progeny. She was, therefore, of foreign extraction; and the doctrines and rites of her priests differed from the more simple religion of the natives. Wherefore, as soon as she began to propagate, or produce converts in the country, the mythological Arthur, the mystical head of the native and hitherto patriarchal religion, collected the forces of the island in order to exterminate her race; but the design proved abortive — the novel system gained ground.

Let us now consider the various deposits of this mythical vehicle.

The first consisted of three grains of wheat and a Triad of bees. The wheat everyone knows to be the fruit of Ceres, and in Britain the person who aspired to the mysteries of that goddess was transformed into a mystical grain of pure wheat. And as to the bees of mythology, the great analyser of ancient tradition proves, from a multitude of circumstances, that the Melissae, or bees, were certainly female attendants in the Arkite temples. [19]

The appropriation of this title to the priestesses of Ceres, Mr Bryant, as usual, attributes to an error of the Greeks in the interpretation of a foreign term. If this be allowed, the same blunders constantly pervading the sacred vocabularies of the Greeks and Britons might be insisted upon as arguments that the latter borrowed their theology immediately from the former, which I think was not the case in general. The history of the *provident bee*, the architect of her own commodious cell, in which she weathers out the destructive winter, might supply another reason for making her the symbol of an Arkite priestess.

But passing over our author's etymologies, and taking along with us his historical deductions, it will appear, that the sacred ship which brought the bees was a representative of the Ark. For the same distinguished writer, who first proved that Ceres was the genius of the Ark, has also shown that she was styled *Melissa*, or the *bee*, and that the *Melissae* were her priestesses.

So that in this British tale, we have the record of an Arkite temple, founded in Monmouthshire by a colony of priests, which came from Cornwall, with an establishment of three Arkite ministers.

The grain of barley, and the pig, or one of her own species, which the mystical sow deposited in *the pleasant spot of the tranquil lady*, in Demetia, or Pembrokeshire, amounts to nearly the same thing.

The next remarkable deposit consisted in the cub of a wolf, and the eaglet.

The wolf of mythology, according to Mr Bryant, related to the worship of the sun. [20] The eagle also, he tells us, was one of the insignia of Egypt, and was particularly sacred to the sun. It was called *Ait*, or Αετοʒ; and Homer alludes to the original meaning of the word, when he terms the eagle Αιετοʒ αιθων [21]

Hence it appears that the Arkite mysteries of this *old lady* were intimately blended with an idolatrous worship of the sun — that usurper, whom we have seen the great Arawn, king of the deep, so anxious to remove.

The eagle and the wolf were deposited in Eryri, or Snowdon; and Coll is said to have presented the former to a Northern prince, and the latter to a lord of Arllechwedd: which must be understood to mean that these symbols of solar worship were introduced from Cornwall, by a circuitous route, into the regions of Snowdon, and from thence into North Britain, and Arllechwedd.

The place where the eagle and wolf were deposited deserves attention. It was on the top of *Rhiw Gyverthweh*, the *panting cliff*, in Snowdon, and in a structure called *Dinas Affardon*, or *Pharaon*, the *city of the higher powers*. [22] The site was upon the road from the promontory of Lleyn, to that part of the coast which is opposite to Mona, for the mystical sow takes it in her way. Hence it seems to have been the same which is now known by the name of *Y Ddinas, the city*, thus described by the Annotator upon *Camden*. [23]

'On the top of Penmaen stands a lofty and impregnable hill called Braich y Ddinas (the ridge of the city), where we find the ruinous walls of an exceeding strong fortification, encompassed with a triple wall, and within each wall the foundation of at least a hundred towers, all round, and of equal highness, and about six yards diameter within the walls. The walls of the Dinas were, in most places, two yards thick, and in some about three. This castle seems, while it stood, impregnable, there being no way to offer any assault to it, the hill being so very high, steep, and rocky, and the walls of such strength. At the summit of this rock, within the innermost wall, there is a well, which affords plenty of water in the driest summer. The greatness of the work, shews that it was a princely fortification, strengthened by nature and workmanship, seated on the top of one of the highest mountains of that part of Snowdon, which lies towards the sea.' [24]

The temple of Ceres, in the Gyvylchi, is only about the distance of a mile from this place. This stately pile, which has left no other local memorial of its greatness but the emphatical name, 'The city', must have been, as I conjecture, the celebrated Dinas Pharãon, in the rocks of Snowdon, which had also the name of Dinas Emrys, or *the ambrosial city*. This was famous, not only for the wolf and eagle, which were deposited by the mystical sow, but also for certain dragons, [25] which appeared in the time of Beli, the son of Manhogan or, as we are otherwise told, in the time of Prydain, the son of Aedd the Great, [26] that is, in the age of the solar divinity. In this Dinas, the dragons were lodged by a son of Beli, or *child of the sun*; and the destiny of Britain was supposed to depend upon the due concealment of the mystery. [27]

As to these dragons, the reader has seen that they were harnessed in the car of the British, as well as of the Greek Ceres; and more than this, their general connection with solar superstition is acknowledged by the Welsh themselves. [28] Hence it appears that the *old lady*, who wandered from the *mystic vale* in Cornwall to the regions of Snowdon, imported a mixture of Arkite and Sabian idolatry.

But let us come to the last deposit of the mystical sow, namely, the kitten, which was *laid* under the black stone, that is, in a cell, or *Kisvaen*, in Arvon, from whence the mystagogue cast it into the Menai. It was taken up out of this strait, or river, and became the Paluc cat of Mona.

*Isis*, the Arkite goddess, was sometimes represented under the figure of a cat, because that animal, by the voluntary dilatation and contraction of the pupils of its eyes, imitates the phases of the moon, which was also a symbol of Isis; and Mr Bryant thinks that the very names of Menai and Mona have a pointed reference to the worship of the lunar Arkite goddess.

But Paluc cat is spoken of as a large and fierce creature, of the feline kind. Mr Owen thinks it was a tiger. It is often mentioned as one of the molestations of Mona; and as all the symbols imported by the mystical sow were regarded as pernicious innovations by those who adhered to the primitive religion of their country, the destroying of this cat was esteemed a meritorious act. Though it is described as an animal, it seems to have been only an idol, and attended by foreign ministers. Taliesin calls it Cath Vraith, the *spotted* cat, and thus denounces its fate —

> Ys trabluddir y Cath Vraith
> A'i hanghyvieithon [29]

'The spotted cat shall be disturbed, together with her *men of a foreign language*.'

It should seem, from another passage, to have been a symbol of the sun, for Taliesin, who often speaks in the person and character of that luminary, mentions as one of his transformations —

> *Bum Cath Benfrith ar driphren* [30]

'I have been a cat with a spotted head, upon a tripod.'

Upon the whole, we may suppose it to have been the figure of some animal of the cat kind, which was deemed sacred, either to the helio-arkite god, or the lunar-arkite goddess, or to both, as it was a *male* and a *female*, [31] and therefore, at all events, a symbol of the mixed superstition.

But as Coll, the guardian of the *old lady*, learned his mystic lore from the *red giant*, who resided in a nook of Cornwall, a region which had early intercourse with strangers, particularly with the Phoenician, or *red nation*; as the Britons had been jealous of the mystical sow, or sacred ship, which introduced the symbols here enumerated; and as the wolf, the eagle and the cat are mentioned with disapprobation, as things which proved injurious to those who received them, I conclude that these symbols and idolatry which they implied were of foreign growth, and did not pertain to the religion of the primitive British nation.

Having now dismissed Coll and his *old lady*, I proceed to consider the history of the third mighty swineherd, who is better known to the reader of English romance by the name of *Sir Tristram*.

'The third swineherd was *Trystan, proclaimer*, the son of *Tallwch*, the *over-whelming*, who kept the swine of *March*, the *horse*, the son of *Meirchiawn*, the *horses of justice*, whilst the swineherd was carrying a message to *Essyllt*, *spectacle*, to appoint an assignation with her.

'In the meantime, Arthur, March, Cai, and Bedwyr, went forth against him upon a depredatory expedition. But they failed in their design of procuring as much as a single pig, either by donation, by purchase, by stratagem, by force, or by stealth.

'These were called the mighty swineherds, because neither their stratagem nor force could extort from them one of the swine which were under their care, and which they restored, together with the full increase of the herd, to their right owners.' [32]

This story also describes the meddling with some foreign mysteries which had been introduced into Cornwall and from thence extended into other districts, but these mysteries were regarded as unlawful and depraved, for the inter-course of Trystan with his mistress, Essyllt, was both adulterous and inces-tuous. As I have hinted above, it seems to allude to the incorporation of the primitive religion of the Britons with the rites of the Phoenician sow.

By the character of Trystan, we are to understand, as his name imports, a *herald* of mysteries, and hence a representative of the mystical system which prevailed at a certain period or in a certain state of the British hierarchy.

The memorials of this character in the mythological Triads, are many and various.

We are told that of the three heralds of the island of Britain the first was *Greidiawl*, the *ardent*, or, as he is otherwise called, *Gwgon Gwron*, the *severely energetic*, herald of *Envael*, the *acquisition of life*, the son of *Aaran*, *second distribution*. The second herald was *Gwair Gwrhydvawr*, *renovation of great energy*, and the third was *Trystan*, the *proclaimer*, the son of Tallwch, the *overwhelming* — that is, the Deluge. And it is added that such was the privilege of these heralds that none could resist their authority in the island of Britain without becoming outlaws. [33]

The very names and connections of these heralds declare that each of their modes was Arkite, or referable to the history of the Deluge, whatever they may have included besides; and their authority is precisely the same which Caesar assigns to the Druidical chair.

We have, in the next place, some intimation of the dignity with which these characters supported their high office, when we are told that of the three *diademed chiefs* of the island of Britain, the first was Huail, vice-gerent of Hu, the son of *Caw*, the *enclosure*, also called *Gwair*, *renovation*, the son of *Gwestyi*, the *great tempest*. The second was *Cai*, *association*, the son of *Cynyn Cov*, the *origin of memorial*, surnamed *Cainvarvog*, or *with the splendid beard*; and the third was *Trystan*, the son of Tallwch. And *Bedwyr*, *Phallus*, the son of *Pedrog*, the *quadrangle*, wore his diadem as presiding over the three. [34]

After this, we are informed of the constancy and resolution with which the authority and dignity of these characters were asserted. For Eiddilic Corr, the same as Coll, Gwair and Trystan were the three determined personages whom no one could divert from their purpose. [35]

Trystan is again introduced as hierophant; for the three knights, who had the conducting of mysteries in the court of the mythological Arthur, were Menn, son of Tiergwaedd, or the *three loud calls*, Trystan, the son of Tallwch, and Cai, the son of Cynyn, *with the splendid beard*. [36]

From these particulars it may be collected that Trystan is a personification of the great moving power, in the religious establishment of the Britons, during a certain period of their history. And hence it may be inferred that his amorous intercourse with Essyllt, *spectacle*, the wife, otherwise called the daughter, of March, *horse*, the son of Meirchiawn, his uncle, [37] is to be understood in a mystical sense.

We also read of Trystan, the son of this March, who seems to be the same personage, and is ranked with Rhuhawt eil Morgant, the son of Adras, and Dalldav, *mystagogue*, the son of Cynin Cov, *principle of memorial*, as a compeer in the court of the mythological Arthur. [38]

Such being the mystical character of Trystan, let us now look for the owner of the herd which he superintended, and the husband or father of Essyllt, his beautiful paramour.

This personage was a prince of some part of Cornwall; and his singular name Horse, the son of the *horses of justice*, must undoubtedly be referred to the *Hippos*, or horse of the ancient mythologists, which Mr Bryant proves to have meant the Ark. He imputes the name, as usual, to an error of the Greeks, but it is strange that these errors should be constantly and accurately translated into the language of our British forefathers.

But let us hear our learned author.

'I cannot help surmising that the horse of Neptune was a mistaken emblem, and that the ancients, in the original history, did not refer to that animal. What the Ιωωοϛ alluded to in the early mythology was certainly a float, or ship, the same as the Ceto (the Ark); for, in the first place, the Ceto was denominated Hippos, Ιωωον, τον μϛγχν θαλαϛϛισν ιχθυν, i.e. the Ceto, or whale. Secondly, it is remarkable that the Hippos was certainly called Σχαφιοϛ χαι ϛχυφιοϛ [39] I therefore cannot help thinking that the supposed horse of Neptune, as it has so manifest a relation to the Ceto and the Scyphus, must have been an emblem of the like purport, and that it had, originally, a reference to the same history to which the Scyphus and Ceto related (that is, the Ark). The fable of the horse certainly arose from a misprision of terms, though the mistake be as old as Homer. The goddess Hippa is the same as Hippos, and relates to the same history. There were many symbols of a horse. The history of Pegasus, the winged horse, is probably of the same purport. So does Palaephatus, a judicious writer, interpret it — Ονομα ο⁻ ην τω ωλοιω, Πηφασοϛ. This Hippos was, in consequence, said to have been the offspring of Poseidon and Damater.' [40]

The March, or horse of the British mythologists, must evidently be referred to the same Arkite history, which is here intimated by Mr Bryant. And not only so, but also, as I shall prove in the course of this section, the horse was, amongst our ancestors, a favourite symbol of a sacred ship.

The mystical prince of Cornwall is styled the son of the *horses of justice*; probably, with allusion to the *just* patriarch. And, in order the more forcibly to mark his character, he is represented as a *master of ships*, and, in this capacity classed with *Gwenwynwyn*, *thrice fair*, the son of Nâv, the *lord*, a title of the Diluvian patriarch; and with *Geraint ab Erbin*, *vessel of the high chiefs*.[41]

And as March was a mystical character, we must also search the bardic pedigree for the lady, whether his wife or his daughter, of whom Trystan was so greatly enamoured.

We are told that the three unchaste matrons of Druidical mystery were daughters of one father, namely, *Cut Vanawyd Prydain*, which implies *the person occupying the narrow spot, in the waters of Britain*. This very title has an aspect to Arkite mystery. The Diluvian god, or sacred bull, had his residence in such a spot.[42]

The first of these three sisters was Essyllt, *spectacle*, surnamed *Vyngwen*, or *with the white mane*, the concubine of Trystan, the *herald*, the son of Tallwch, the *deluge*.

The second was *Penarwen*, the lady with *the splendid head*, the wife of Owen, the son of Urien.[43]

The third sister was Bûn, the maid Κορη, the wife of the flame-bearer.[44]

It is pretty clear that these three daughters of Manawyd refer to three mystical modes of the same origin, and all Arkite; and I think the reason why they are described as unchaste was either because they were communicated to persons of different nations or because they included some foreign and adulterated rites, which had not been acknowledged by the more simple religion of the primitive bards.

Our present business is only with Essyllt, whose name *spectacle, or subject of steady contemplation* manifestly implies some mystical exhibition. And as she was the wife of the *horse*, so she is described as having a *white mane*. She was, therefore, a mare; but the aspirant, Taliesin, saw the British Ceres in the form of a *proud and wanton mare*; Mr Bryant also acknowledges Hippa, the mare, as one of the most ancient goddesses of the gentile world, and particularly informs us that the Arkite Ceres was distinguished by that title, and that even her priestesses were called *Hippai*, mares.[45]

Hence we perceive that it was of this goddess and her sacred rites that our British *herald* and *mystagogue* was so deeply enamoured; and that the herd, which he superintended, consisted of her priests and votaries.

Here it may be remarked that the character of Trystan seems to refer to a period somewhat more recent than that of Coll, for the former was entrusted with the care of the mystical sow, before she had farrowed, or produced votaries upon British ground. But here, the pigs are already produced and multiplied, though they are still objects of persecution, to the mystical Arthur and his heroes, or the hierarchy of the native Britons. It may also deserve notice that Coll is uniformly described as a foreigner, who introduced something into Britain, but Trystan was a native, and of some mystical eminence, before he tampered with the swine, or the consort of the Cornish horse.

The notices which the Triads have preserved upon the subject of the celebrated Trystan are undoubtedly abstracts of some old mystical tales which were current amongst the early Britons. And although the tales which more immediately regarded the character now before us have disappeared in the Welsh language, it is evident that they must have existed and that they formed the basis of certain romantic histories of the famous knight, *Sir Tristram*, which are still extant in French and English.

Of these, the *Metrical Romance*, written by Thomas of Ereildoune, and lately published by Mr Scott, from the Auchinleck MS, is worthy of special notice as having preserved much genuine British mythology, though blended with the fanciful embellishments of the thirteenth century. I shall, therefore, remark a few particulars of the story.

This author changes the name of Trystan, the *proclaimer*, into Tristrem, and Trem Trist, which in the Welsh language implies a *woeful countenance*; a designation too whimsical to have escaped the notice of the humorous Cervantes, who probably had seen this romance in French or Spanish.

The father of Sir Tristrem is here called Rouland, which seems to be a mere French translation of his British name Tallwch, and the Irish Taileach, a *rolling or overwhelming flood*.

His mother is Blanche Flour, the *white flower*, the sister of King Mark, who is the March or horse of the Triads. This lady is certainly the lovely Flûr of British mythology, of whom the illustrious Cassivellaunus was so deeply enamoured that he undertook an expedition into Gaul, attended by the gods of Britain, in order to redress her wrongs; and by this act, provoked the resentment of Julius Caesar.[46]

The character of Flûr imports that token, or pledge of union, amongst the professors of Druidism which induced the Britons to assist their brethren of Gaul, as related by Caesar, and thus furnished that great commander with a pretext for the invasion of this island.

The emblematical Flûr or *flower*, which this fraternity exhibited, was, I imagine, that of the white trefoil or shamrock. This was a sacred plant amongst the bards[47] displaying the mysterious three in one, the great secret inculcated by the very form of their Triads and *Tribanau*. Hence we are told that wherever their goddess Olwen, the great mother, trod upon the ground, four white trefoils immediately sprung up.[48]

Flûr is the daughter of *Mygnach*, a mystical character, the son of *Mydnaw*, the *mover of the ship*. In a dialogue which he holds with Taliesin, he comes forward like Arawn, the king of the deep, with his white dogs, or ministering Druids; his residence is in Caer Sëon, in the mystical island, and the chief of the bards reveres his *Gorsedd* or throne.

By the birth of Sir Tristrem, from the rolling flood, and the symbol of union, the original narrator seems to have implied that he was a legitimate son of the Arkite religion.

After the untimely death of these, his natural parents, our young hero is committed to the care of a prince, named Rohand, who is a mortal enemy of Duke Morgan, *son of the sea*, a neighbouring potentate. Both these personages are found in the Triads, but with characters somewhat differently drawn. Morgan, surnamed Mwynvowr, or *most courteous*, the son of Adras (Adraste?) was one of the royal knights in the court of the mythological Arthur.[49] And the Rohand of the tale is Rhyhawd, the *man of excess*, styled Eil Morgant, the *successor of Morgant*; and this character, as his name implies, carried his mystical lore beyond legitimate bounds. The Triads rank him with Dalldav, mystagogue and March, the horse, as a compeer, in the court of the same Arthur.

He is also styled *Overvardd*, or one who corrupted the bardic system with a mixture of foreign fable. This is the delineation of a hierophant who made some innovation in the Druidical mode.

This Rohand, anxious for the safety of his charge, directed his wife to feign a second delivery, adopted the infant as his son, and called him by the inverted name of Trem Trist. He took the greatest care of his education, and had him instructed in all the fashionable arts and sciences, amongst which the mysteries of hunting are eminently discriminated.

Under this allegory, which is precisely in the style of the British tales, we have the history of Tristrem's initiation into the mongrel rites of Rhyhawd. Thus the aspirant, Taliesin, was *born again* of Ceridwen, and instructed in her mystical hall; and thus the celebration of mysteries is represented in the story of Pwyll, under the image of hunting. But the new lore, communicated to Tristrem, differed from that of his parents; therefore his name was inverted.

We are afterwards told of a strange ship which appeared upon the coast of Cornwall. The English translator, a rhymer of the thirteenth century, naturally calls it Norwegian, but as the story is mythological, the ship must have belonged to a people who visited Cornwall during the early ages of mythology. This vessel was freighted with hawks, which Tristrem won at chess and distributed amongst his friends. Here it may be remarked that no ship ever sailed with such a cargo. But the British Ceres transformed herself into a hawk, [50] and this bird was a sacred symbol in Eastern mythology. It occurs frequently in Egyptian sculpture as the favourite representative of Isis.

Tristrem is now conducted to the court of Cornwall, and by means of a ring, the *glain*, or insigne of a Druid, which he had received of his mother, is recognized as the nephew of March, knighted, or admitted to the dignities of the bardic order; and advanced to the command of an army, or made high priest, having fifteen attendant knights assigned to him, all of them bearing boar's heads. The meaning of this allegory is evidently the same as that of the Triads, which represent him as a great swineherd.

Invested with this power, Sir Tristrem sallies forth to attack Duke Morgan, the president of the older system of Druidism, kills his adversary, and confers his conquered dominions upon Rohand, or Rhyhawd, the corrupter of bardic mystery. Hence the Triads represent Rhyhawd as *Eil Morgan* or *successor of Morgan*.

We next hear of our hero's combat with a champion of Ireland, whom he kills in the field, but at the same time he is pierced with a poisonous weapon. The wound, proving incurable, renders his person so disgusting that he withdraws from society. In mere despair he goes on board a ship, which he commits to the mercy of the wind and waves, but such is his good fortune that, after tossing about for some time, he finds himself safe arrived in the port of Dublin. Here again, I suspect the rhymer has modernized the geography of his tale. The queen of the country, however, being admirably skilled in medicine, heals the wound of our hero. He is called to court.

The king's daughter, the beautiful Ysonde, the Essyllt, or *spectacle* of the Triads, is committed to his care as a pupil, and instructed in music and poetry, and in every becoming branch of his mystic lore.

Upon his return to Cornwall, Sir Tristrem reports the beauty and accomplishments of his fair pupil to King Mark, who conceives a violent passion for the princess, and commissions his nephew to return to Ireland in his name and demand her in marriage.

Through a series of romantic adventures, the hero of Cornwall arrives at the accomplishment of his commission. The princess is entrusted to his care, and they set sail.

At their departure, the queen mother, anxious to secure the happiness of the married couple, prepared and delivered to *Brengwain*, Ysonde's favourite damsel, a *drink of might*, with directions that it should be divided between the bride and bridegroom on the wedding evening. But fortune decided otherwise. During a contrary wind, when Tristrem was faint with heat and thirst from the fatigue of rowing, Ysonde called for some liquor to refresh him, and Brengwain inadvertently brought the fatal drink of might, of which Tristrem and Ysonde having partaken, they imbibed the sudden and resistless passion, which death alone could overcome. Even a dog, named *Hodain*, who licked the cup after it was set down, felt its invincible power, and became their inseparable companion.

The drink of might which is here mentioned must have been the Κυχεων, or mystical potion of Ceres, agreeing with the preparation of the sacred *cauldron of Ceridwen*, and with the wine and *bragget* of the Welsh bards, which was administered to the aspirants upon their admission to the mysteries, and hence represented as communicating all the benefits of initiation. Brengwain was certainly the Bronwen, or Proserpine of the Britons, whom *Brân*, the *raven*, had carried into Ireland along with the mystical cauldron, and espoused to a sovereign of that country, distinguished by the remarkable name of *Matholwch*, *form of worship*.

Hodain, *corn shooting into the ear*, is the attribute of Ceres, whose priests Taliesin styles *Hodigion*, *bearers of ears of corn*.

The Hodain of this tale seems to have been one of those priests, though he is described as a dog, for heathen priests were called Κυνεζ. The British Ceres transformed herself into a bitch, and in the tale of Pwyll, the priesthood are represented under the character of white dogs.

Ysonde, notwithstanding her intrigue with Sir Tristrem, becomes the queen of Cornwall, but not long afterwards an Irish nobleman, her old admirer, arrives at the court of Mark in the disguise of a minstrel, obtains possession of her person, and conveys her into his ship. I apprehend the import of this incident to be that the Belgae, or other inhabitants of ancient Ireland, were initiated into the mystical rites which prevailed in Cornwall.

But Sir Tristrem recovers the fair Ysonde, and restores her to the king, taking care, however, to devise means of keeping up a private intercourse with her. One of the stratagems to which he had recourse for this purpose is very remarkable. Being separated from his mistress, he contrived to correspond with her by means of small bits of wood, on which were engraved secret characters, and which were floated down a small stream which ran through the orchard of Ysonde's country seat.

This is a clear allusion to the practice of *sortilege*, by which the Druids consulted their gods.

The bits of wood were the *coelbreni*, omen-sticks, or points of sprigs, so often

*Figure 1*: 'An enchantress, having turned a beautiful maiden into a hound, slips a golden collar around her neck' by *Beatrice Elvery*.

mentioned by the bards; or the lots, cut into tallies out of the shoot of a fruit-bearing tree, and distinguished by mysterious characters, as Tacitus has accurately described them. As to the orchard, we may either interpret it as the Druidical grove, in which those fruit-bearing trees must have been cultivated, or else we may restrain the meaning to the lots themselves, which were cut out of that grove. And it is observable that the hierophant, Merddin the Caledonian, describes the whole circle of Druidical mysticism under the allegory of an orchard containing 147 fruit-bearing trees, which were perfect tallies with each other.

Sir Tristrem, after this, is made high constable, or, as the Triads express it, *Priv Hûd*, *president of mystery*, and, as a privilege annexed to this office, sleeps in the queen's apartment. Here he takes some unwarrantable liberties, in consequence of which, he is banished the court of Cornwall and retires into Wales, where he undertakes the defence of *Triamour*, king of the country, against the usurpations of the giant *Urgan*, whom he kills in single combat. Triamour bestows the sovereignty of Wales upon his protector, together with a little dog, which was spotted with red, blue, and green. But our hero immediately restores the crown to Blanche Flour, the king's daughter, and sends the dog as a present to Ysonde.

Triamour seems to be the *Triathmor* of the Irish, in which the *th* are not audible. And the title implies a *great king*, *hog*, *sow*, *wave*, or *hill*,[51] so that it is a term of sufficient mystical latitude to denote either the president of the Welsh Druids, the chief object of their superstition, or their elevated place of worship.

Urgan is probably the *Gwrgi* of the Triads, a mystical cannibal; that is, a priest, or an idol, who delighted in human sacrifices. And here it may be remarked that the character of a mythological giant, for the most part, implies the idea of impiety or heterodoxy. Hence we find that the courteous knight of one tale is not unfrequently the atrocious giant of another. Such circumstances comply with the various opinions of the several narrators.

Tristrem's obtaining and immediately resigning the sovereignty of Wales may imply that his system was introduced into that country but not established there. And it is observable that the daughter of Triamour, as well as the mother of the Cornish champion, was named Blanche Flour, that is, the white trefoil, or shamrock, the mystical pledge of union.

The little dog was a priest; and his spots of red, blue, and green seem to import those insignia, called *Gleiniau*, which were of the colours here specified.

'These *gemmae anguinae* are small glass amulets, commonly about as wide as our finger-rings, but much thicker; of a green colour, usually, though some of them are blue, and others curiously waved with blue, red, and white.'[52]

Mr Owen says they were worn by the different orders of bards, each having his appropriate colour. The blue ones belonged to the presiding bards, the white to the Druids, the green to the Ovates, and the three colours blended to the disciples.[53] It should seem, then, that this parti-coloured dog was either a disciple, or a graduate, in the several orders.

Tristrem, upon his return to Cornwall, renews his intimacy with the queen, in consequence of which they are both banished the court. The lovers retire into a forest, where they discover a cavern that had been constructed in old time by the giants. Here they reside, and subsist upon the venison taken by their mystical dogs. The king, having surprised them when asleep in this cavern with a drawn sword between them, is persuaded of their innocency, and restores them both into favour.

This forest was the Druidical grove; the cavern, a sacred cell, which had been constructed by the giants, or professors of a different mode; the dogs were the priests; the deer their noviciates; and the sword, that weapon which was drawn against the irregular disciple, and religiously sheathed again in the solemn meetings of the bards, upon the stone which covered the sacred cell.

Our unfortunate hero again falling into disgrace, upon the score of his old offence, is obliged to fly. Having traversed several countries, he enters, at last, into the service of Florentin — some relation of Flur, duke of Brittany, who had a daughter named Ysonde, more chaste and scarcely less beautiful than the beloved queen of Cornwall. Tristrem marries this princess, but his ring, or sacred amulet, having reminded him of his former attachment, he treats his lovely bride with absolute neglect.

This Armorican Ysonde, Essyllt, or spectacle, presents a tradition of some more simple religious mysteries which anciently prevailed in Gaul, but which did not satisfy the debauched taste of the Cornish hierophant; and the next incident gives us a hint of the particular defect which he found in it.

As a nuptial present, Tristrem had received a tract of country immediately adjoining the territories of a ferocious giant, named *Beliagog*, but this was accompanied with a strict injunction from Florentin that he should abstain from hunting — celebrating his mysteries — upon the lands of that monster, who was brother to Morgan, Urgan, and Moraunt. The champion of Cornwall, regardless of this injunction, hunts upon the lands of Beliagog, encounters the giant in person, disables him in combat, and makes him his vassal.

As *Beli* was a name of the *sun*, so I think *Beliagod* may imply what would be expressed in Welsh *Beli a gwg*, the *severe* or *frowning Beli*, the *Belenus* of the more recent Druids of Armorica, whom Ausonius expressly identifies with Phoebus, or Apollo. So that the giant, so greatly abhorred by the primitive hierophants of Brittany, though connected with the Cornish superstition, was the solar divinity. And it is observable throughout the Triads and the mythological tales that whenever the corruption of Druidism is described there is always some allusion to the solar worship, or to those symbols by which it is implied. This superstition, indeed, appears in the works of the oldest bards, which are not extant, incorporated with their Arkite mythology. But those who were more peculiarly devoted to it had the opprobrious name of *Beirdd Beli* — the *Bards of Beli*.

When we recollect the Gaulish tradition of Caesar's days, that the discipline of Druidism, such as it then was, had been modelled in Britain and from thence brought over into Gaul, [54] we may deem the following incident worthy of note.

Tristrem ordered his new vassal, Beliagog, to build a hall — temple — in honour of Ysonde and Brengwain — the Ceres and Proserpine of Cornwall. The giant complied with this injunction, and built the hall within his own castle, to which he taught Tristrem a secure and secret approach. He also adorned this hall with sculptures, exactly representing the whole history of his former life, with exact representations of Ysonde, Brengwain, Mark, Meriadok, his minister, Hodain, and Peticrewe, their mystical dogs.

This, surely, as a mythological tablet, describes the introduction of a system of theology and religious rites out of Britain into Gaul; and this appears to have been a mixture of Arkite superstition and Sabian idolatry.

In the chapter which I have just quoted from Caesar, the historian adds the information that in his days those who wished to have a more accurate knowledge of Druidism generally went into Britain for instruction.

This circumstance was not overlooked in the tale of Sir Tristrem. This knight gave his brother-in-law, Ganhardin, prince of Brittany, such an interesting description of the queen of Cornwall that his curiosity was strongly excited. Being conducted by Tristrem to the marvellous castle of Beliagog, which he could scarcely approach without trembling, and having there viewed the portraits of Ysonde and Brengwain, he was so astonished with their beauty that he staggered and fell backward in a swoon. Upon his recovery, he felt a violent passion for the charms of Brengwain, Proserpine, whom he determined to see in person, without loss of time. Accordingly, the Gaulish prince embarks for this island, attended by the British hierophant. They arrive in Cornwall, meet Ysonde and Brengwain, in the forest, or grove, where the enamoured stranger is espoused to the latter.

The Auchinleck MS, being imperfect, breaks off in this place. The conclusion of the tale is supplied by the learned editor from some French fragments. But, if I may judge from British mythology, which certainly constitutes the basis of the history of Sir Tristrem, this part is less authentic than the work of Thomas the Rhymer.

The particulars which I have remarked in this story have the genuine character of that traditional lore, which we find in the Triads, the *Mabinogion*, and several passages of the ancient bards. And they discover one principal source of those romantic narratives, which, for a series of ages, constituted the favourite reading of Europe.

Such tales as the *Mabinogion*, it will be said, do not deserve to be ranked with sober history. This is freely acknowledged. They are only brought forward to diffuse a faint ray over ages, where history refuses its light. In this sense, they may be useful. They contain traditions of remote times, when Druidism had many private and some avowed friends. And they are found to coincide with the most authentic documents which we have upon the subject of British superstition, and with the researches of our best antiquaries.

Thus, under the representation of three mighty swineherds, or hierophants, we have, first of all, an account of the earliest religion of our Celtic ancestors, concerning which any memorials have come to our times. And this appears to have consisted of a depraved copy of the patriarchal religion, with a strong abhorrence of Sabian idolatry.

Coll and his mystical sow present the picture of a novel system, which was introduced into Cornwall, and from thence extended into Wales and into other parts of Britain. This had a general correspondence with the former, in the memorials of Arkite superstition, but it also included an adoration of the heavenly bodies, and viewed the deified patriarch as united with the sun.

The character of Trystan continues the history of a heterogeneous superstition made up of the religion of the native Britons, incorporated with foreign innovation, extending over a great part of Britain, and cultivated in Ireland, but chiefly centering on Cornwall, where it had gained the first establishment upon British ground, and from thence was introduced into Gaul.

As the characters of the three great swineherds, present a general view of the history and revolutions of Druidism, previous to the Roman conquest of Briton, it may not be amiss to consider a few traditions relating to those events which affected the superstition of our ancestors subsequent to that period.

The British documents, in which these traditions are involved are, it must be confessed, like the former, sufficiently uncouth and obscure. But they are the best that we have, and I shall pass over them as slightly as possible.

That the Romans, during their profession of paganism, showed but little countenance to the Celtic priesthood may be inferred from the severe prohibition of their religious rites in Gaul, and from the conduct of Suetonius towards the Druids, the groves and the altars of Mona. And it cannot be supposed that this people, after they became Christian, could view the remains of British idolatry, with more favourable eyes.

The public sacrifices of the Druids, and their open profession of magic, were undoubtedly suppressed in those parts of the provinces which were more immediately under the inspection of the government. But this operation of civil edicts does not necessarily imply the immediate eradication of an inveterate superstition from the minds of the people. From what we know of British infatuation, after the departure of the Romans, it is reasonable to conclude that during their vassalage our progenitors had kept fast hold of their ancient prejudices and customs. We are told, which is probably true, that in many corners of the island the Romans permitted the natives to be governed partly by their own laws, and under princes of their own. In those Asyla, people thus disposed, and who spoke a language which was unintelligible to their political masters, would naturally preserve the memory of their sacred poems and traditional institutes; they would also continue to perform such of their mystical rites as were less obnoxious to observation and public censure.

From the language of the Triads, and some ancient poems, there is reason to infer that they carried their prejudices still further: that during the Roman government there was a seminary of Druids somewhere in the North of Britain, or in an adjacent island, and probably beyond the limits of the empire, where the doctrine and discipline of heathenism were cultivated without control; that those Druids persisted in sacrificing, even human victims; that certain devotees from the Southern provinces repaired to their solemn festivals; that upon the departure of the Romans some abominable rites were brought back from the North into Mona, and into other parts of Wales; and that the Northern seminary was not finally suppressed till the close of the sixth century.

The notices upon which I ground this opinion, I now proceed to state.

Of the introduction of the Cornish mode of Druidism into Carnarvonshire and from thence into North Britain, we have had a hint in the story of Coll, the great mystagogue, who is said to have presented Brynach, prince of the

Northern Gwyddelians, with the eaglet which was deposited by the mystical sow, and which in after times became very famous.

The fame of this eagle and his progeny is now to be recognized only in the history of the two dusky birds of Gwenddoleu, which guarded his treasure, wearing a yoke of gold; and which were in the daily habit of consuming two persons for their dinner, and the like number for their supper.[55] Such is the language of the Triads, and, if this does not imply the sacrificing of human victims to some divinity who acknowledged those birds for his symbols or his attributes, I know not what to make of it.

Gwenddoleu, the master of those *consumers*, is described as a prince who resided on the north of the Strath-Clwyd Britons, but contiguous to them. His destructive birds fell together with himself, by the hand of *Gall Powen*, the son of *Dysg Yvedawg*, the *imbiber of learning*, who is represented as prince of Deira and Bernicia. This catastrophe happened in the battle of *Arderydd ag Eryddon*, the *high eagle, and the eagles*, a fanatical contest on account of a bird's nest,[56] which was decided in the year 593.[57]

These birds which daily consumed their human victims and which were destroyed by the *power* of a prince who had *imbibed learning* or embraced Christianity, in the battle of eagles are certainly to be understood in a mystical sense. And as the eagle was one of the symbols under which an object of Druidical superstition was represented, I presume that these birds of Gwenddoleu must have the same symbolical meaning as the eaglet which was brought forth by the mystical sow, or genius of the Ark, and presented to a prince of the North Britons.

If this be admitted, it must at the same time be supposed that Gwenddoleu himself was either a priest or a divinity in the superstitious establishment of those Britons.

Let us inquire a little into his character and connections.

That there was a celebrated Northern prince in the sixth century, known by the name of Gwenddoleu, and literally opposed to Rhydderch in the battle of Arderydd, I will not take upon me to deny. But as it was a notorious practice of British priests to assume some title of the god they worshipped; and as this name implies *of the luminous oblique courses*, I rather think it was an epithet for the sun. His priest, notwithstanding, may have taken a fancy to it.

Gwenddoleu was the son of *Ceidio*, *preservation*, the son of *Arthwys*, the *encloser*, the Arkite, the son of *Môr*, the *sea*. Amongst his uncles and brothers we have *Paba*, *producer of life*; *Eleuver*, the *luminary*; *Cov*, *memory*, and *Nudd*, *mist*. Those are mystical connections of the Helio-Arkite divinity.

If we look for *Nudd*, we shall find that he draws his pedigree somewhat differently, but from the same vocabulary of superstition. He was the son of *Senyllt*, the *seneschal* or *mystagogue*, the son of *Cedig*, the *beneficent*, a title of the Arkite goddess, recognized by Taliesin. And this Nudd had a son named *Drywon*, the *Druidical teacher*, whose retinue is celebrated for having voluntarily maintained the contest, in the open course of Arderydd, the scene of Gwenddoleu's overthrow.[58]

The fidelity of Gwenddoleu's retinue is equally famous. It is recorded of them that they maintained the conflict for forty-six days after the death of their Lord, and till they had avenged his fall.[59]

Gwenddoleu was also one of the renowned bulls of the contest of mystery, classed with the *primordial great one*, son of the *prior world of former inhabitants*, and with *the parent*, son of the *primitive horse*, Hippos, or sacred ship. He, therefore, personified the great Helio-Arkite god.

From these notices offered by the Triads, let us turn to Merddin, the Caledonian. This dignified priest informs us that his lord Gwenddoleu had presented or privately exhibited to him a hundred and forty-seven apple-trees of equal age, height, length and size, which had sprung from the bosom of Mercy, were enveloped by one mystical veil, and were still left under the protection of Olwen, a mythological character who must be identified with the Arkite goddess. The fruit of these trees were precious things which Gwenddoleu freely bestowed. [60]

Those trees, as I shall show presently, were purely allegorical, and imported the various secrets of Druidism. Consequently, Gwenddoleu, who had the peculiar privilege of exhibiting the mystical orchard and disposing of its produce, must in some sense have presided over the order of Druids. And thus much is implied in the dialogue between Gwyn ab Nudd, the king of the deep, and Gwyddnaw, the great hierophant, or representative of the patriarch, where Gwenddoleu is styled *Colovyn Cerddeu — the pillar of bardic lore*. [61]

Putting these things together, and still recollecting the birds which wore a golden yoke, guarded the treasures of Gwenddoleu and consumed four persons daily, I think we may conclude that Gwenddoleu was the head of an eminent Druidical establishment in North Britain, which admitted of human sacrifices. And whether he is to be deemed a divinity, or an Arch-Druid, the representative of a divinity, his influence at one period must have been very extensive, as we may collect from the language of his votary and chosen priest, Merddin the Caledonian.

'I have seen Gwenddoleu, adorned with the precious gifts of princes, gathering his contributions from every extremity of the land; now, alas the red turf has covered the most gentle chief of the Northern sovereigns.' [62]

As this mystical ruler of sovereigns who had received his offerings from the remotest regions was Merddin's acknowledged lord, it may not be amiss to consider a few particulars of that bard's character, both as drawn by certain ancient writers, who composed in his name, and as exhibited by himself in his genuine works.

To the English reader, I am aware, that the term *bard* suggests only the idea of a person of mean condition, who has distinguished himself by the composition of a few silly rhymes, and this idea is generally accurate when it regards the *modern* Welsh bards. But amongst the ancient Britons, the title was of eminent dignity and importance; it could be conferred only upon men of distinguished rank in society, and who filled a sacred office.

Thus Merddin is styled *supreme judge of the North* (that is, of the regions beyond the little kingdom of Strath-Clwyd), and the *Syw*, or *diviner of every region*. [63] And in virtue of this office, he was *Cerddglud Clyd Lliant, president of Bardic lore about the waters of Clyde*. [64] He was companion of *Canawon Cyntlaith*, [65] the *offspring of the goddess of slaughter*, whom Aneurin thus commemorates in the songs of the *Gododin*;

'If, in the banquet of mead and wine, the Saxons sacrificed to *slaughter* the mother of *spoliation*; the energetic Eidiol also honoured her before the mount, in the presence of the god of *victory*, the king who rises in light, and ascends the sky.' [66]

And this connection between the British divinities of *slaughter* and *victory* is

marked in the character of Merddin, who is styled *Allwedd byddin Bûdd Nêr*[67]
— *the key*, or *interpreter of the army of the god of victory.*

He was the brother of *Gwenddydd Wen, adlam Cerddeu*[68] — *the fair lady of the
day, the refuge of bardic lore* — a mythological character, and this lady addresses
the venerable priest in the following terms:

'Arise from thy secret place, and unfold the books of the Awen (bardic muse,
a name of Ceres), the object of general dread, and the speech of Bún
(Proserpine), and the visions of sleep.'[69]

These are some of the qualifications of Merddin, as recorded by a Northern
but unknown bard who wrote in his name and character about the year 948.[70]
He was a supreme judge, a priest, and a prophet — and he was conversant in
the mysteries of the very same divinities, Cynllaith, Búdd, Awen, and Bún,
which were revered at the great temple of Stonehenge.

His reputation as a prophet has thrown a shade over the few remains of his
genuine productions. It has suggested a hint for their interpolation, by more
recent bards, with political predictions, adapted to the circumstances of the
times or the views of parties. The mystical poem called *Hoianau* certainly
contains some specimens of this kind, which cannot be as old as the time of
Merddin, yet, I think, the bulk of the piece is his genuine composition. At least,
it is not the work of a Welshman, for much of its grammatical idiom, and several
of its terms, are in the language of those Northern people amongst whom it
is acknowledged that Merddin lived.[71]

In this piece, Merddin the Caledonian, like Pryderi, Coll, and Trystan,
supports the character of a swineherd, or mystagogue. He had resided, with
his herd, either in an island or in some remote promontory, where, amongst
other arts, he had practised divination by the flight and voices of sea-fowls.
And it is from this locality of his residence, as I suppose, that he is called the
son of *Morvryn*, the *mount in the sea*.

In this happy retreat, Merddin is exposed, as well as his mystical herd, to a
severe persecution, conducted by a king of Alclud, who is styled *Rhydderch
Hael, Rhwyviadur ffydd* — *Rhydderch the Liberal, the champion of the Christian
faith.*

The flame kindled by this king of the Strath-Clwyd Britons communicates
itself to the neighbouring princes, to a host of bishops and monks, and, in
short, to all the professors of Christianity; and the grunting chorus is in danger
of being roasted alive.

It is upon this occasion that the terrified Druid rouses the attention of his
pigs, and warns them to fly for their lives into some secret place in the
Caledonian forest. His address is worthy of a swineherd, and of his audience.
The reader may be amused with a short specimen or two.

'Attend, little pig — thou initiated pig! Burrow not with thy snout on the top
of the hill. Burrow in a secret hiding place, amongst the forests — a place which
has not been noted by Rhydderch the Liberal, the champion of the faith.'

'Attend, little pig! It was necessary to depart — to avoid the hunters of the
water-dwellings (our insular abodes), if they should attempt to seize us — lest
the persecution should come upon us, and we should be seen. If we can but
escape, we will not deplore our calamitous toil.'[72]

If all this is to be understood in the literal sense, what ideas must we entertain of the Christian princes and bishops, who could condescend to persecute such a grovelling herd!

But the *initiated* or *enlightened swine* were certainly allegorical, and the real objects of persecution are suggested in a little poem, [73] purporting to have been a dialogue between Merddin and a person called *Ys Colan, The Colan.* Here our swineherd appears in the character of an insolent and contumacious pagan.

Merddin, seeing a stranger approach his watery nook, with a black horse and a black cap, and in dark attire, demands if his name was Ys Colan.

The stranger replies, that he really was Ys Colan, a Scottish or Irish scholar, who held the bard in little esteem, and at the same time denounces the vengeance of the king upon those who should refuse to plunge into the water, or be baptized.

As the battle of Arderydd, or the era of the persecution of the bards, is dated in the year 593, [74] and as Merddin and his associates made a precarious stand for some years longer, I think it highly probable that The Colan, an Irish scholar who introduced Christianity amongst the Druidical herd in Caledonia, and enforced the necessity of baptism, was no other than Colomba, the priest and abbot, who came out of Ireland into Britain in the year 605 to instruct the Northern Picts in the Christian religion, and received from his converts the island of Hu, Iona, or I-colm-Kil. [75]

To this mission of the good abbot Merddin seems to have made an obstinate resistance, for in the poem above mentioned he complains of the penalties he had incurred by having burnt the church, obstructed the establishment of a school, and drowned a book with which he had been presented.

He then pleads the merit of having been confined for a whole year upon the pole of a wear, that is, having been initiated, like Taliesin, into the greater mysteries of the wear of Gwyddnaw; and upon this plea he implores the Creator to forgive his offences. [76]

In the conclusion he acknowledges that had he known how perceptibly the wind blew upon the points of the mystical sprigs he would have desisted from an action which he had imprudently committed. As this is an allusion to the bardic mode of writing, it may imply that Merddin had either disclosed or written something in defence of his system which, in the event, proved injurious to it. And the bards have a tradition that Ys Colan threw a heap of British books into the fire.

From these particulars, it is pretty evident that Merddin, the vassal of Gwenddoleu, has been viewed as the hierophant of a herd of heathenish swine.

Let us now consider the character of their great enemy, who instigated the neighbouring princes, together with the bishops and monks, to unite in the persecution of this infatuated race.

Rhydderch the Liberal, the son of Tudwal of Twd-Clyd, or the district of Clyde, was king of the Strath-Clwyd Britons, about the close of the sixth century; and his residence was at Alclud, or Dunbarton. [77] We have seen that he is mentioned by Merddin as the champion of the Christian faith, and the determined persecutor of the mystagogue and his swine.

In the *Cyvoesi*, where Merddin is introduced as prophesying of those events which should take place subsequent to the battle of Arderydd, in which Rhydderch slew the celebrated Gwenddoleu, we are further told —

Dyd Gwynnydd yn rhyd — Tawy,
Rhydderch Hael, dan ysbeid,
Gelyn Dinas Beirdd bro Glyd.

This passage is somewhat obscure, owing to the transposition of the sentences, but the meaning is this —

'Rhydderch the Liberal, the enemy of the community of bards, in the vale of Clyde, after an interval, will put the white-vested ones into the ford of Tay.' [78]

That is, when Rhydderch had routed the idolatrous bards from his own dominions, and the neighbouring districts, they retired into the midst of the Caledonian forest, as related by Merddin. After some time, their retreat is discovered upon the bank of the Tay, and the pagan fugitives are still pursued, by the influence of Rhydderch. But as this 'liberal' prince puts the *white-vested ones*, or Druids, into the ford, and not into the deep parts of the river, we may conclude that his intention was to *baptize*, and not to *drown* them.

Hence we may form a probable idea of what is meant by the celebrated battle of Ard-erydd ag Eryddon, the *high eagle and the eagles*, in which this Christian prince slew Gwenddoleu, who was at the head of the Druidical superstition in which the *imbiber of learning* slew his two mystical birds, which delighted in human sacrifices: in which that cannibal monster, Gwrgi Garwlwyd, *the hideous and grey* human dog, also fell; and in which the united champions of the Christian faith dispersed the adherents to the ancient superstition amongst the rocks and caves of the Caledonian forest.

This battle seems to have been decided not by the sword but by severe edicts, by the oratory of Christian ministers, and the zeal of reformers, manifested in the demolition of idols and heathen temples, and in the punishment of the contumacious, or their expulsion from society.

I have now produced a chain of traditional notices which imply that the symbols of superstition found their way into the North, from Cornwall, and through Wales, in an age of general heathenism, and that the superstition which accompanied these symbols flourished in the West of Scotland till nearly the close of the sixth century.

It is further intimated in a whimsical Triad that the provincial Britons viewed this Northern hierarchy with great respect, and that they not only made pilgrimages to the feasts of the Caledonian priests but also that they reimported some of their mystical furniture and rites into Wales, after the departure of the Romans. This Triad introduces certain sacred ships, under the character of *horses*, like the *hippi* of Greek mythology. The first article runs thus —

'Three horses carried the three loads of the island of Britain. The black horse of the seas, the steed of Heliodorus, the most courteous, carried seven persons and a half from the mount of the flat stone of Heliodorus, in the North, to the mount of the flat stone of Heliodorus, in Mona.

'The seven persons were: *Heliodorus*, the *most courteous*; *Eurgain*, *golden splendour*, his wife, the daughter of *Maelgwn*, the *beneficent chief*; and *Gwyn da Gywoed*, *white*,[79] *good to his contemporaries*, the master of his dogs (his high priest); and *Gwyn da Reiniad*, *white*, *the good darter*; and the monk of *Nawmon*, the *ship of the cow*, his counsellor; and *Pedrylaw*, *four-handed*, his butler; and *Arianvagyl*, *silvercrook*, his servant. And the half person was *Get ben evyn*, *shoot* or *branch*, *with the shackled head*, his cook, who swam with his hands upon the horse's crupper, and his feet in the water.'[80]

It is hoped the general reader will excuse the introduction of this odd paragraph, for the sake of the mythologist or antiquary, who may discover something curious in the several items. I shall only remark that the steed which carried such a load of mysterious beings out of *Scotland into Mona*, and *by sea*, can only be considered as the representative of the sacred ship of mythology, which was the vehicle of the mystical *eight*.

This voyage took place in the interval between the departure of the Romans in the fifth, and the general conversion of the Welsh about the close of the sixth, century. The story, therefore, involves an account of the re-conducting of some Druidical apparatus, with a suite of priests, out of Scotland into Wales. And the name of Heliodorus, the master of the group, has probably a reference to the *sun*, who was a distinguished object in the mysticism of Coll, the Cornish hierophant.

The Triad proceeds thus —

'The second load was that of *Cornan*, *having small horns — crescent —* the horse of the sons *Eliver*, *with the great retinue*, which carried Gwrgi and Perdur, and Dunawd Bwr, the sons of Pabo and Cynvelyn Drwseyl, to see the sacred fire of Gwenddoleu, in Arderydd.'

Here we have pilgrimages to the solemnities of the Northern Druids. This Cornan, or Crescent, was, I suppose, a mere symbol of the sacred ship, an insigne of the same import as the *Cwrwg Gwydin*, or *boat of glass*, mentioned by Taliesin, as exhibited in the hand of the stranger, and procuring his admission to the nocturnal celebrities.[81]

The heroes, whom this Cornan introduced to the Northern solemnities, were near relations of Gwenddoleu, or members of his mystical society. Eliver and Pabo were brothers of Ceidio, Gwenddoleu's father, and grandsons of Môr, the *sea*.[82]

Gwrgi and Peredur, the sons of Pabo, were, at last, deserted by their party, and slain at *Caer Greu*, the *city of blood*[83] or in the battle of Arderydd.[84] Their story is full of mythology. Gwrgi, the human dog, surnamed *Garwlwyd*, *hideous and grey*, like the birds of his cousin Gwenddoleu, delighted in human sacrifices, and, like them, was slain by a son of the *imbiber of learning*.[85]

The third mystical load recorded by our Triad was that of *Erch*, or *Haid*[86] the steed of *Gwrthmwl*, the sovereign, which carried Gwair, and Clais, and Arthanawd, upon an expedition against the cliff of Maelawr, in Cardigan, to avenge their father. It was a sacred law with Maelawr not to close his port against any load that might arrive; in consequence of this, he was slain.[87]

This sea-horse or ship, called a bee in one dialect, and a swarm in another, must be referred to Melissa, and her Melissae, or the Arkite goddess and her priesthood.

Gwrthmwl, the sovereign, was the priest of an idol, or sacred ox, called *Tarw Ellyll* the *bull demon*,[88] but this bull pertained to the Arkite deity.

His residence was at the promontory, or insular mount of Rheonydd, in the North, where he presided as chief elder, or high priest, of one of the regal tribes, under the mythological Arthur.[89] His castle was one of the principal palaces or temples, of that patriarch,[90] and, in a comparatively recent age of Christianity, it became the site of an archiepiscopal church.[91]

Rheonydd is, evidently, the same as Merddin's Caer Rhëon and Rhyd Rhëon, once the chief seat of his superstition, whence he was routed by *Ys Colan*, or St Columba.

Hence it may fairly be conjectured that this celebrated spot, the great asylum of the Northern Druids, was the island of *Hu*, or Iona, which was occupied by the said Columba, and in after-ages contained the metropolitan church of all the western islands. The early Christians did often erect their churches upon the ruins of heathen temples.

Mr Bryant is positively of opinion, from the very names of Columbkil and Iona, that this island was, anciently, sacred to the Arkite divinities. If I may be permitted to go upon similar grounds, I may remind the reader that the Britons did worship the patriarch by the name of Hu; and that Taliesin expressly denominates Mona, the great sanctuary of Arkite superstition, *Ynys gwawd Hu*, *the island of the praise of Hu*; and hence I may infer that Bede's island of Hu, at one period, constituted the centre of Northern Druidism.

From this place, the sons of Gwrthmwl, the sovereign, the master of the bull demon, proceed with their *horse*, or *sacred ship*, and land in South Wales for the purpose of avenging their father, or reinstating him in those honours which he had partly lost during the Roman government.

Amongst the heroes engaged in this expedition, I distinguish the name of *Gwair*, one of the titles of the Diluvian patriarch. This personage and his associates overcome their adversary, or the humbled and more timid superstition, which had hitherto lingered in the Southern provinces; and they succeeded in replanting some mystical rites in the territories of the Welsh, during the short period of British independence.

Thus, the history of the three mythological horses is referred to the tampering of our Cambrian progenitors with some heathenish superstitions, which had been cherished in the North, beyond the line of the Roman empire. And if I may depend upon our Welsh chronologers, for the era of the characters here introduced, these transactions occurred after the departure of the Romans, and a considerable time before Rhydderch, with his princes, bishops and monks, slew Gwenddoleu and his cannibal birds, or ruined the Northern establishment of the Druids.

Of the consequence of the battle of Arderydd, we have some account in the *Avallenau*, or *Apple-trees*, a poem, which Mr Turner has proved to be the genuine production of Merddin, and which contains the expiring groans of the Northern Druids.

However grievous Merddin's afflictions may have been, for the fall of his lord, Gwenddoleu, we find that his own hand added greatly to their weight by the undesigned slaughter of his own sister's son,[92] in the same fatal engagement.

It is difficult to ascertain the precise meaning of this poetical incident, but we may suppose in general that the mystagogue, in the imprudent defence of his fraternity, committed some action which proved detrimental to its cause. We are told, however, that the effect of his error was a derangement of intellect, an abhorrence of society, and a precipitate flight into the forest of Caledonia.

In this frantic mood, and after an interval of many years, he makes the rocks and caves resound with the melody of his strain, in which his derangement appears to have been only assumed for the purpose of repressing curiosity; for though his descriptions are designedly obscure, they have too much method for real madness. It is the madness of a heathen prophet.

The ostensible purport of this poem is a tribute of gratitude for an orchard containing a hundred and forty-seven delicious apple trees, which had been privately exhibited to the bard, by his Lord Gwenddoleu, and which he still carries with him in all his wanderings.

This circumstance at once points out the impropriety of understanding Merddin's orchard, in the literal sense, and leads us to some allegorical meaning.

Many particulars of this allegory may be interpreted from what has gone before in this essay; and it may be admitted as additional evidence, of two curious facts: namely, that the superstitious rites of Druidism were avowedly practised, in certain corners of Britain as late as the close of the sixth century; and that the bards of that age used all the means in their power to conceal their secrets from the knowledge of the populace, to guard them from the persecution of Christian princes and ministers, and at the same time, to transmit them safe and unblemished to future ages.

In support of this assertion, I shall produce abstracts from the several stanzas of the *Avallenau*, translated as literally as the darkness of the subject, and the faults of the copies, will permit, and to these I shall add a few occasional remarks.

'To no one has been exhibited, at one hour of dawn, what was shown to Merddin, before he became aged; namely, seven score and seven delicious apple trees, of equal age, height, length, and size, which sprung from the bosom of Mercy. One bending veil covers them over. They are guarded by one maid, with crisped locks; her name is Olwedd, with the luminous teeth.'[93]

These trees are 147, which was a sacred number amongst the Britons, as we learn from Taliesin.[94]

They were exhibited at the dawn, the hour when the nocturnal celebration of mysteries was completed. The view of these trees, therefore, implies the complete initiation of the priest.

They were in every respect perfect tallies with each other and asserted to have been of divine origin. Hence we may gather that one of the secrets communicated by these trees was the Druidical art of divining by lots; and that Merddin's *Avallen Beren*, in this sense, corresponded with the *Arbor Frugifera* of Tacitus, [95] the shoots of which were cut into lots or tallies, distinguished by energetic marks, thrown into a white garment, or covered with a veil, and thus became the means of interpreting the will of heaven.

These trees still remained under their veil, and in the custody of the divine maid, Olwedd or Olwen — the British Proserpine.

But to proceed —

'The delicious apple tree, with blossoms of pure white, and wide spreading branches, produces sweet apples, for those who can digest them. And they have always grown in the wood, which grows apart. The nymph who appears and disappears, vaticinates — words which will come to pass, etc.

The bard, having described his trees in the first stanza as *exactly similar to each other*, contents himself in the sequel with mentioning one of them. The *white* blossoms seem to imply the *robe* of the Druid, the *spreading* branches his *extensive authority*, the *fruit*, his *doctrine and hopes*, and the sequestered wood *which had always produced this fruit*, his *sacred grove*.

Most of the stanzas conclude with a vaticination of some great event, which is here put into the mouth of Chwibleian, the nymph, or goddess, who is alternately visible and invisible, still meaning Olwen or Proserpine, who guarded the sacred trees, or presided over the mysteries.

In the third stanza, Merddin tells us that he had armed himself with sword and shield, and lodged in the Caledonian wood, guarding the trunk of the tree, in order to gratify Bún, the *maid*, Proserpine, who, by way of acknowledgement, calls to him in the Northern dialect, '*Oian a Phorchetlan*, attend little pig,' and bids him listen to the songs of the birds. The bard complies, and learns the secrets of futurity.

*Stanza 4.* 'The sweet apple tree has pure white sprigs, which grow, as a portion for food. I had rather encounter the wrath of a sovereign than permit rustics in raven hue to ascend its branches. The lady of commanding aspect is splendidly endowed; nor am I destitute either of talents or of emulation.'

The white sprigs could only have furnished mental food for the bards, as constituting their lots and their books. The men in black seem to have been the monks, who strove to expose the secrets of Druidism, whilst Merddin, the fanatical devotee of the mystical goddess, was determined to guard them at the hazard of his life.

*Stanza 5.* 'The fair apple tree grows upon the border of the vale; its yellow apples and its leaves are desirable objects, and even I have been beloved by my Gwnem, and my wolf. But now my complexion is faded by long weeping; I am neglected by my former friends, and wander amongst spectres who know me not.'

Thus pathetically does our mystagogue deplore his forlorn condition, after the ruin of his establishment. Gwnem seems to be a corruption of Gwenyn, *bees*, *priestesses*, which were deposited by the mystical sow, and especially as they are joined with the wolf, another of her productions.

'Thou sweet and beneficient tree! Not scanty is the fruit with which thou art loaded. But upon thy account, I am terrified and anxious, lest the wood-men should come, those profaners of the wood, to dig up thy root, and corrupt thy seed, that not an apple may ever grow upon thee more.'

'I am become a wild distracted object, no longer greeted by the brethren of my order, nor covered with my habit. Upon me Gwenddoleu freely bestowed these precious gifts, but he is, this day, as if he had never been.' — (Stanza 6)

'The proper place of this delicate tree, is within a shelter of great renown, highly beneficent and beautiful. But princes devise false pretences, with lying, gluttonous and vicious monks, and pert youngsters, rash in their designs — these are the aspiring men who will triumph in the course.' — (Stanza 7)

'Now, alas, the tree which avoids rumour grows upon the confluence of streams, without the raised circle.'[96] — (Stanza 8)

In these passages, we perceive the bard's great anxiety to preserve his mystical lore from the effects of persecution, by princes, monks, and their youthful agents, who are employed in polluting and cutting down the sacred groves, and demolishing the circular temples.

'This sweet apple tree abounds with small shoots; but the multitude cannot taste its yellow fruit.'

'I have been associated with select men, to cultivate and cherish its trunk — and when Dyvnant shall be named the city of the stones, the bard shall receive his perquisite.' —

'Incorruptible is the tree which grows in the spot set apart (the sanctuary) under its wide envelope. For four hundred years may it remain in peace! But its root is oftener surrounded by the violating wolf than by the youth who can enjoy its fruit.' —

'This tree they would fain expose to public view; so the drops of water would fain wet the duck's feather.' — (Stanza 9, 10, 11)

Here the fanatical priest cherishes a hope that his Druidism, and his temples will be re-established in some future age, though he has at present more persecutors than disciples. In mentioning the 400 years, he seems to have a retrospect to the period of the Roman government, during which his superstition had already weathered the storm of persecution, and therefore, as the Bard infers, it may survive another calamity of four centuries.

Stanza 13. 'The fair tree grows in the glade of the wood. Its hiding place has no skilful protector from the chiefs of Rhydderch, who trample on its roots, whilst the multitude compass it round. The energetic figures are viewed with grief and envy. The Lady of the Day loves me not, nor will she greet me. I am hated by the minister of Rhydderch's authority — his son and his daughter have

I ruined. Death who removes all, why will he not visit me? After the loss of Gwenddolen,[97] the *lady of the white bow,* by no nymph am I respected. No soother amuses my grief; by no mistress am I visited. Yet, in the conflict of Arderydd, I wore the gold collar. Oh that I were precious, this day, with those who have the hue of the white (the white robed Druids!)'

*Stanza 14.* 'The tree with delicate blossoms grows in concealment amongst the forests. A report is heard at the dawn that the minister has expressed his indignation against the authority of the small sprigs[98] twice, thrice, nay four times, in one day.' —

*Stanza 15.* 'The fair tree grows on the bank of a river. A provost cannot thrive on the splendid fruit which I enjoyed from its trunk, whilst my reason was entire, in company with Bûn, the maid, elegantly pleasing, delicate and most beautiful. But now, for fifty years, have my splendid treasures been outlawed, whilst I have been wandering amongst ghosts and spectres, after having enjoyed abundant affluence and the pleasant society of the tuneful tribe.'

*Stanza 16.* 'The sweet apple tree, with delicate blossoms, grows upon the sod, amongst the trees; and the half appearing maid predicts — words which will come to pass! — *Mental design shall cover, as with a vessel, the green assemblies, from the princes, in the beginning of the tempestuous hour. The Darter of Rays shall vanquish the profane man. Before the child of the sun, bold in his courses, Saxons shall be eradicated; bards shall flourish.'*

This prophecy, which is put into the mouth of Proserpine, unequivocally charges the bards of Merddin's order with the abomination of solar worship. The child of the sun must have been his priest, who, like Taliesin, assumed his title and character —

'The blooming tree grows in Hidlock, in the Caledonian wood. The attempts to discover it, by its seeds, will be all in vain, till Cadwaladyr, the supreme ruler of battle, comes to the conference of Cadvaon, with the eagle of the Towy, and the Teivi — till ranks be formed of the white ones of the lofty mount, and the wearers of long hair be divided into the gentle and the fierce.'

'The sweet fruits of this tree are prisoners of words. The ass will arise, to remove men out of office; but this I know, an eagle from the sky will play with his men, and bitter will be the sound of Ywein's arms. A veil covers the tree with green branches — and I will foretell the harvest when the green corn shall be cropped, when the he eagle and the she eagle shall arrive from France.'[99] — (*Stanza 17, 18, 19*)

'The sweet apple tree is like the bardic mount of assembly: the dogs of the wood will protect the circle of its roots.' —

'Sweet are its branches, budding luxuriant, shooting forth renowned scions.' — (*Stanza 20, 21*)

*Concluding Stanza.* 'The sweet apple tree, producing the most delicious fruit, grows in concealment in the Caledonian wood. In vain will it be sought upon the bank of its stream, till Cadwaladyr comes to the conference of Rhyd Rheon, with Kynan, opposing the tumult of the Saxons. Then Cymru shall prevail. Her chief shall be splendid. All shall have their just reward. Britons shall rejoice. The horns of joy shall sound — the song of peace and serenity.'[100]

Such are the seemingly wild hints, which Merddin has thought proper to communicate upon the subject of his apple trees, and which, undoubtedly, were agreeable to the mystical lore of his order.

These trees, we find, were allegorical, and pointed to that mass of super-stition, which the bards of the sixth century had retained, and which they were desirous of concealing, preserving, and transmitting safely to posterity. The Christian princes and ministers, who diligently sought for the mystical orchard for the avowed purpose of destroying it root and branch, could have viewed it in no other light.

But though, under this type, the general system of Druidism may be represented, yet I am induced to conclude, from many circumstances which I need not recapitulate, that these trees more particularly refer to the practice of sortilege, and have a marked connection with the *coelbreni*, (omen sticks, lots or letters) of the bards.[101]

As Merddin was the most recent character, deemed by his fraternity to have possessed the gift of prophecy, his oracles were never superseded, during the long ages of superstition. But when new predictions were demanded for political purposes, the succeeding bards thought it most expedient either to interpolate the *Hoianau*,[102] or to make the prophet speak out of his grave.[103]

The vaticinations of our ancient priest are not much calculated to derive credit to his order, from the present age, but the absurdity of his pretentions was not peculiar to the Celtae. Odin, as well as Merddin, was deemed a prophet, and Partridge and Moore were renowned Gothic Seers, of more recent days. Both in their nature, and in the fate which attended them, the predictions of our Caledonian Druid, seem to have resembled the celebrated lots, or oracles of Musaeus, which are mentioned, and obliquely quoted by Herodotus. These were in such high credit amongst Greeks and barbarians, that men of rank and talents thought them worth interpolating, for political purposes. But the Athenians deemed the crime worthy of banishment, and with good reason: the sacred predictions had an authority which could embolden foreign princes to invade their country.[104]

When we have once closed the poems of Merddin the Caledonian, we hear no more of the Druidism of the North. Of the countenance which this ancient superstition experienced amongst the Welsh, for some centuries longer, and of the documents which their poetry and traditions furnish upon the subject, I have endeavoured to give a fair and impartial account, in the present essay, which it is now time to bring to a conclusion. It is hoped, that the general view here presented, will not be deemed superfluous in a British library, and that the cause of true religion cannot be injured by this delineation of the gloomy mazes of error.

I shall take a brief retrospect of what I have written, and add a few general reflections.

I have shown, that the bards pretend to the preservation of the mystical lore of the Druids; and that a comparison of their works with the documents of classical antiquity confirms the authenticity of their pretentions.

From the barren or desolated field of bardic philosophy, I hastened to the consideration of religious doctrines and rites; and here I have shown, that the superstition of the ancient Britons consisted of two principal branches, intimately blended together.

One of these was Mr Bryant's Arkite theology, which embraced some memorials of the history of the Deluge, together with an idolatrous commemoration of Noah, of his family, and of his sacred ship.

The other was *Sabian idolatry*, or the worship of the host of heaven, a superstition, which in many other countries has existed in conjunction with Arkite theology.

It has been remarked that the Britons constantly interweave the memorials of the Deluge with their remotest traditions of the origin of the country and the nation, whence arose an influence that this was the superstition of the earliest settlers in Britain, and the degenerate offspring of the patriarchal religion which our ancestors derived from the great stock of the Noachidae.

On the contrary, it was shown that British tradition clearly discriminates and steadily reports the worship of the sun and moon as an innovation, which found its way into Cornwall and from thence diffused itself into various parts of the British islands. And hence, I judged it a reasonable conjecture that this alloy was derived from the tin merchants of Phoenicia, in whose country a similar superstition confessedly prevailed.

From this analysis it appears that the religion of the Britons differed from that of most heathen nations only as a *variety* in the same *species*: that it presented no fundamental principle which can be accounted peculiar. Its two main branches, the *Arkite* and the *Sabian*, have been clearly traced, and in the same connection, over great part of the ancient world.

This intimate, and almost universal combination of two systems, which have no obvious relation to each other, I cannot contemplate without searching for some early cause of such connection. Why should Noah be the sun? Or why should the Arkite goddess be the moon? This is not the place for a new disquisition, but I may be allowed briefly to state a conjecture.

The righteous Noah and his family, who had been distinguished by a Supreme Providence, and miraculously preserved amidst a perishing world, must have been highly and justly reverenced by their pious and obedient children, whilst living, their prayers were besought, and their precepts received as the oracles of heaven.

After their death, their memory was revered, and a growing superstition may have begun to invoke these undoubted favourites of heaven as mediators with the supreme being (just so the saints of the Roman Church are invoked), and at last proceeded to worship them as gods.

The Ark, also, was the means of preservation to the righteous. Its figure may have been consecrated, as a religious memorial of that preservation, till superstition began to view it as a pledge of safety, and to put it under the charge of an ideal being who was worshipped as the universal mother.

Thus, the Arkite theology may have sprung from a corruption of the patriarchal religion, and in a manner which would not set the vain imaginations of man in immediate and open hostility with his fallible reason.

As to the incorporation of Sabian idolatry with this superstition, when I recollect that amongst the heathen Britons the sacred ship, or *ark*, the *zodiac* and the *circular temple* had equally the name of *Caer Sidi*, I cannot help surmising that the confusion arose from an abuse of the earliest post-diluvian astronomy.

Whether that science revived in Ararat or Chaldea, it was its evident design to commemorate the history and circumstances of the Deluge, in the disposition of signs and constellations. This device may have sprung from an innocent, or even laudable motive.

But from henceforth, the heavens represented those very scenes with which Noah and his sons had been conversant. These canonized patriarchs were acknowledged to be immortal, for the age which first paid religious homage to the deceased must of course have admitted the immortality of the soul, and the doctrine of future rewards.

The unbridled imagination of man no sooner contemplated the sun, moon, and planets, expatiating amongst the heavenly mansions of these immortals, than it also began to regard them as emblems of their persons, and of their sacred vessel, and therefore as mediators between the human race and the unknown and great Supreme. Thus, the Arkite and the Sabian idolatry became one and the same.

This union seems not to have been coeval with the earliest Arkite superstition of the Noachidae. Hence the traditions of the Greeks and other nations relative to the persecution of Latona and her children, of Hercules, Bacchus, and other characters which implied an adoration of the host of heaven. They were admitted, with reluctance, to the rank of gods. Mankind adopted the practice of Sabian idolatry, with an avowed consciousness that they were departing from the principles of their forefathers.

That the heathen Britons felt this consciousness, we have had abundant proof. It may also be urged, from their own traditions and acknowledgements, that their Arkite superstition was a manifest corruption of better principles.

They had become so gross in their ideas as to worship Hu the Mighty, or the patriarch, as a god. yet they had not absolutely forgotten his true history. The Triads view him as a righteous man, and ascribe to him the actions of a man. Taliesin says of him and his family — 'The just ones toiled; on the sea which had no land, long did they dwell; of their integrity it was that they did not endure the extremity of distress.'

If they were preserved *for their integrity*, it must have been by some super-intending power; and this power is acknowledged by the same bard, in his song upon Dylan, where we find that 'A sole supreme God, most wise unfolder of secrets, most beneficient', had destroyed a profligate world, and preserved the righteous patriarch. And again: the *sovereign, the supreme ruler of the land, extended his dominion over the shores of the world*, or destroyed it by the Deluge, but, at the same time *preserved the inclosure of the righteous patriarch in perfect security.*

So that the great Diluvian god, who was worshipped under the symbol of the bull and the dragon, and who was even identified with the luminary of the material heavens, is acknowledged to have been no other than a *saint of the most high.*

If such principles were admitted by heathens, when they came to the candid avowal of the truth, wherein did the great heinousness of heathenism, and its votaries, consist?

Not in an absolute ignorance of a great First Cause, and of his superintending Providence, but in giving *his* glory to another, and in acting against those better principles which their own minds could not but acknowledge.

'Because that which may be known of God is manifest to them, for God hath showed it unto them. For the invisible things of him, from the creation of the world, are clearly seen, being understood by the things that are made, even his eternal power and Godhead. So that they are without excuse, because that when they knew God they glorified him not as God, neither were thankful, but became vain in their imaginations, and their foolish heart was darkened.

'Professing themselves to be wise, they became fools, and changed the glory of the incorruptible God into an image, made like to corruptible man, and to birds, and four-footed beasts, and creeping things — who changed the truth of God into a lie, and worshipped and served the creature, more than the Creator, who is blessed for ever.'[105]

Such is the view of this subject, communicated by a true philosopher, a good antiquary, and no mean scholar.

The human mind is prone to such woeful lapses, when it gives way to vain imagination and self-conceit — to the opinions of fallible, or the views of designing men.

Thus, Druidism was removed but a few paces further from the religion of Noah, than popery, and some other modes of worship, denominated Chris-tian, are departed from the faith, the purity, and the simplicity of the gospel. Wherefore it behoves all men, who build their hopes upon the religion of Christ, not to place an implicit confidence in the practice of a corrupt age, or in the principles of an arrogant and presumptuous teacher, but to have a constant eye to the foundation once laid by the apostles and prophets.

Here another remark of some importance offers itself.

As Gentilism arose from a corruption of the patriarchal religion, it is reasonable to suppose that amongst a multiplicity of errors and absurdities it preserved some tincture of the venerable source from whence it sprung, in the same manner as popery is acknowledged still to possess some of the genuine forms and tenets of primitive Christianity, and a diligent comparison of heathen systems with the book of Job, and the first book of Moses, will evince that this was actually the case.

Whatever Gentilism had thus preserved without corruption must be regarded as derived from the revelations vouchsafed to the patriarchs, and therefore, *in its origin*, of Divine authority, like those uncorrupted forms and tenets in popery which are derived from the truth of the Gospel.

We are not, therefore, to conclude, *a priori*, that every form of sacrifice, every rite of purification, every sacred symbol, or even every fundamental doctrine, which may have prevailed amongst the ancient heathens, was of human device, and therefore could have nothing similar to it in the revealed will and ordinances of the Supreme Being. For this mode of argument would lead us to conclusions as unjust as the cavils of those scrupulous persons who assert that the Church of England must be superstitious because it retains some of the forms of the Church of Rome.

As this church has retained *some* of the institutes of true Christianity, so Gentilism had not lost every institute of the patriarchal religion, and these uncorrupted institutes are pure and sacred, notwithstanding the general corruption of the channels through which they have flowed.

Upon this ground, we may frame an answer to those adversaries of revelation who, having observed that some modes of sacrifice, some rites of purification, some sacred symbols, and many other particulars sanctioned in the writings of Moses and the prophets, have their parallel in the religion of Egypt, Syria, or Chaldea, boldly assert, that these things were adopted from the heathens, and, consequently, that the writings of the Old Testament and the religion of the Jews could not have been of divine communication.

The answer is ready. As God had revealed his will, and instituted a form of worship, by the prophets of the primitive world, Adam, Enoch, and Noah, so, when the primitive religion was corrupted by the vanity and wickedness of mankind, he renewed this revelation to the Israelites by Moses and the prophets of the Old Testament.

That Spirit, which has neither variableness nor shadow of turning, again inculcated to his chosen people the same expectation of the promised Redeemer, figured out by the same symbolical types which had been communicated to the patriarchs. And as the Gentiles also had retained some vestiges of the true primitive religion, an occasional analogy between their forms and symbols and those of the Israelites was a consequence that necessarily followed.

As certain rites and symbols were enjoined to the Israelites, not because they were heathenish but because they were patriarchal and of divine institution, so they were not omitted in consequence of the mere accident that the Gentiles had retained them.

The word of God, that word of which every jot and tittle must be fulfilled, never turns to the right hand, nor to the left — never gives way to the error or the petulence of man.

From the general and unequivocal vestiges of Arkite mythology, which were impressed upon the heathen world, some other important inferences may be drawn.

As the united voice of the early ages, they forcibly recall the candid sceptic, if such there be, to the acknowledgement of the true, that is, the scriptural account of the Deluge, and the consequent rejection of all those astronomical and geological fables which plunge the origin of mankind into the abyss of unfathomable antiquity and thus open the gap into the regions of darkness and infidel delusion. Let reason only be consistent with itself, in exploring even the history of heathenism, and it must acknowledge the truth of our sacred oracles.

The general voice of mythology, to which I may now add that of the sequestered Briton, admits that the personage who escaped in his bark from the great Deluge, was distinguished from the mass of perishing mortals by a divine providence, and miraculously preserved on account of his piety and righteousness.

This attestation to the character of the great patriarch, and from the mouth of heathenism itself, not only asserts the authenticity of his history but also the truth of his religion, as a man whose faith and conduct were eminently approved by heaven. And this religion regarded man as morally responsible to one supreme and over-ruling God, who mercifully accepted the offerings and the persons of those who sincerely obeyed him, and pardoned their offences, through the merits of a Redeemer, announced to our first parents.

1. Originally published by J. Booth, 1809 [Ed.]
2. Jacob Bryant, *A New System or an Analysis of Ancient Mythology*, six vols (London, 1807) [Ed.]
3. *Monde Primitif.* Tom. IV, p. 579.
4. *Archaiol.* V. II, pp. 6, 20, 72, 77.
5. Owen's *Cambrian Biog.* under the articles *Pryderi, Pwyll,* and *Meirig.*
6. *Analysis,* V. I, p. 40.
7. Ibid. V. II, p. 404.
8. Ibid. V. I, p. 124.
9. *Cambrian Register,* V. I, p. 177, and V. II, p. 382. From the *Red Book of Jesus College,* Oxford, a MS of the fourteenth century.
10. *Analysis,* V. II, p. 360.
11. Κυνεϛ οι Μαντειϛ, *Schol. in Lycoph.,* V. 469.
12. In the *Cambrian Register,* Arawn is oddly translated, 'of the silver tongue'. The word may imply eloquence; but considering his character, I rather think it comes from אֲדֹן, *Aron,* an *ark,* or *chest.*
13. In fact, to be found in the *Mabinogion,* 'The Tale of Pwyll' [Ed.].
14. *Myst. of the Cabiri,* V. I, p. 220.
15. Agath., apud Athens, *Deipnos,* Lib. IX, p. 575.
16. *W. Archaiol.* V. II, p. 67.
17. Ibid. pp. 7, 71, 77.
18. Owen's *Cambrian Biog.* V. *Coll.*
19. *Analysis,* V. II, p. 337.
20. Ibid. V. I, p. 78.
21. Ibid. p. 19.
22. *Pharaon* seems to be the British name of the Cabiri, their priests, called *Pheryll,* were skilled in metallurgy, and are said to have possessed certain books upon mysterious subjects.
23. Gibson's *Camden Col.* [Ed.]
24. Ibid. 804.
25. *W. Archaiol.* V. II, pp. 59, 65.
26. Beli is represented as the father of the brave *Cassivellaunus,* and the son of *Manhogan, radiated with splendour.* But *Beli* and *Prydain* are titles of the helio-arkite divinity.
27. *W. Archaiol.* V. II, pp. 9, 11, 66, 78.
28. Thus Mr Owen, in his *Dictionary,* explains the word *draig,* a '*generative principle,* or *procreator*; a fiery serpent; a *dragon*; the *supreme. Dreigian, silent lightnings.* In the mythology of the primitive world, the serpent is universally the symbol of the

*sun*, under various appellations, but of the same import as the *Draig, Adon, Addon; Bel* and *Bál* amongst the Cymry.'

29. *W. Archaiol.* p. 73.
30. Ibid. p. 44.
31. Cath *Fraith*, and Cath Ben *Vrith*.
32. *W. Archaiol.* V. II, pp. 6, 20, 72, 77.
33. Ibid. pp. 5, 63, 77.
34. Ibid. V. II, pp. 5, 12.
35. Ibid. pp. 19, 69.
36. Ibid. p. 80.
37. Ibid. pp. 13, 73.
38. Ibid. pp. 19s, 74, 80.
39. *Schol. in Lycopli.*, V, 766.
40. *Analysis*, V. II, p. 408.
41. *W. Archaiol.*, V. II, pp. 5, 13, 68. There was a prince called *Geraint ab Erbin*, in the beginning of the sixth century, but the name itself is borrowed from mythology, and the Geraint of the Welsh tales is a mystical character. See Ed. Llwyd's *Archaeol.*, p. 265.
42. See the second section of this Essay.
43. The character assigned to this prince in the Welsh tales is mythological. He seems to have occupied a distinguished place in the mystical drama — See the story told of him and the *lady of the fountain*.
    In the *Red Book of Jesus College*, Oxford, it is mentioned by Ed. Llwyd, *Archaeol.*, p. 265.
44. *W. Archaiol.* V. II, pp. 14, 73. Ida, the Northumbrian king, is supposed to be described under the name of Flamebearer. If such be the meaning of the term in this passage, I should conceive that *Bun* may allude to the mysteries of *Isis*, which Tacitus remarked amongst the ancient Germans, and which this pagan prince may have celebrated in Britain.
45. *Analysis*, V. II, p. 27, etc.
46. *W. Archaiol.*, V. II, pp. 3, 10, 13, 60. Caswallon, the son of Beli was attended by *Gwenwynwyn, thrice fair*, and *Gwanar, the ruler*, who were sons of Lliaws, *impeller of the wares*, sons of *Nwyvre, the firmament*, by *Arianrhod, goddess of the silver wheel* (the Isis daughter of Beli, the *sun*.
47. See the poem called the *Chair of Taliesin*. Every leaf of this plant is naturally impressed with a pale figure of a crescent, which was also a sacred symbol amongst the Druids, and other heathens.
48. Owen's *Cambrian Biog.* V., *Olwen*. From *Maill*, the name of this plant, we may derive *Cy-vaill*, an associate — one who mutually exhibits the *Maill*.
49. *W. Archaiol.* V. II, p. 74, Triad 118.
50. *Hanes Taliesin*.
51. This ambiguity arises from a general principle, which discovers itself in every page of the Irish vocabulary; namely, the appropriating of the same term to every object which presents the same general idea; and the primary and abstract meaning of *Triath* happens to be *bulkiness, eminence,* or *prominence*.
52. Gibson's *Camden Col.* 815.
53. Owen's *Dictionary*, V, *Glarn*.
54. *De Bell. Gall.* I., VI c. 13.
55. *W. Archaiol.* V. II, pp. 9, 13, 65.
56. Ibid. V. II, pp. 11, 65.
57. *Cambrian Register*, V. II, p. 313. In this contest, another mystical cannibal was destroyed, namely, *Gwrgi Garw lwyd — the hideous, grey, human dog.*
58. *W. Archaiol.* V. II, pp. 8, 12, 69.
59. Ibid. pp. 7, 16, 70. The poems of Merddin the *Caledonian* afford ground of conjecture, that these *days* were *years*, during which the votaries of Druidism

persisted in their superstitious practices after some severe laws had been promulgated against them.
60. Merddin's *Avallenau*, 1 and 6.
61. *W. Archaiol*. p. 166.
62. *Hoianau*, 3.
63. *Cyvoesi*, 1.
64. Ibid. 11.
65. Ibid. 11, 17.
66. Song 22.
67. *Cyvoesi*, 69.
68. Ibid. 195.
69. Ibid. 129.
70. So his age is fixed by our great antiquary, Ed. Llwyd. See his *Catalogue of British MSS*.
71. This fact will appear upon the examination of the very first line: *Oian a phorchellan, a pharchell dedwydd* — which would be thus expressed in Welsh:

> *Edrych o barchellyn, o barchell dedwydd.*
> 'Attend, thou little pig, thou initiated pig.'

It must here be remarked, that we have no such word as *Oian*: it certainly comes from the Irish and Caledonian verb *Oigham*, or *Oighanam*, *I behold*, *I attend*, whence the imperative *Oighan*, pronounced *Oi'an*, *Behold! Attend!*

Again, *a*, in Irish and Erse is a sign of the vocative case, but it is never so in Welsh; we write and pronounce *o*.

The initial *p* in *porchellan* is here changed into *ph*, after the sign of the vocative, as in Ireland and the Highlands, whereas in Welsh, it would necessarily become a *b*. Thus, instead of the exclamation of the Irish Ossian, *A Phadruig*, *O Patrick*, a Welshman would express himself, '*O Badrig!*' and in all parallel cases, the variations of the initials are the same.

*Porchell*, in this poem, takes the Irish and Erse diminutive termination *an*, which the Welsh express by *yn*. So that it is evident from these three first words that the *Hoianau* is not Welsh, and that we had our copy from the country of *Merddin*, for had it come from Ireland, it would have differed still more than it does from our native idiom.
72. *Hoianau*, 1, 2.
73. *W. Archaiol*. p. 132.
74. *Cambrian Register*, V. II, p. 513.
75. Bede, L. III, c. 4. Gibson's *Camden Col*. 1244, 1462.
76. I follow the order of a MS copy in my possession. The printed edition has transposed two stanzas.
77. *W. Archaiol*. V. II, p. 11.
78. *Tawy*, a principal river, that penetrates the centre of the Caledonian forest, must be the *Tay*.
79. These *whites* were Druids.
80. *W. Archaiol*. V. II, pp. 7, 20, 79.
81. Cadair Taliesin, in the third section of this Essay. See also Maurice's *Indian Antiquities*, V, VI, p. 190. Bryant's *Analysis*, V. II, p. 242.

In Montfaucon's *Antiquities*, V. II, fronting p. 276 is the figure of a bas relief, found at Autun, representing the Arch-Druid bearing his sceptre, and crowned with a garland of oak leaves, whilst another Druid approaches, and displays a crescent in his right hand.
82. Eliver is sometimes called *Eleuver*, the *luminary* (*W. Archaiol*., V. II, p. 64). *Gwgawn Gwron*, the *severely energetic*, herald of mysteries, is sometimes represented as his son, and other times as his grandson. Ibid., p. 15 and 63.

83. Ibid. pp. 8, 16, 70.
84. *Camb. Register* V. II, p. 313.
85. *W. Archaiol.* V, II, pp. 9, 13, 65.
86. Irish, *Earc a bee*: Welsh, *Haid, a swarm*.
87. *W. Archaiol.*, V. II, pp. 7, 20, 79.
88. Ibid. pp. 16, 17, 71.
89. Ibid. pp. 3, 68.
90. Ibid. pp. 14, 73.
91. Ibid. p. 68.
92. That is, the son of *Gwenddydd*, the *lady of the day*.
93. *W. Archaiol.* p. 150.
94. *Angar Cyryndawd.* Ibid. p. 34. This is the square of 7, multiplied by the mystical 3. The round number, 140 often occurs. This is the computed number of the stones, which completed the great temple upon Salisbury plain.
95. This identity will appear more clearly in the sequel. If it be said, that Tacitus describes a *German*, and not a *Celtic* rite, I would reply, that the *Barditus* or *Bardism*, which the Germans near the Rhine, possessed, in the days of that historian, was probably a shread of the Celtic institute, which had been expelled from Gaul. I do not find that any such term as *Barditus* was familiar to the Germans of Caesar, or to those of the *Edda*.
96. In another copy — 'On the *brow of a rock, without a stone in its circle.*'
97. Gwenddolen was the mystical daughter of an ancient king of Cornwall. She may represent, in general, the Cornish rites, but I think, more particularly, the lunar divinity. Thus she answers to *Gwenddoleu*, who represented the sun.
98. This surely alludes to the practice of divining by lots.
99. Merddin is foreboding the restoration of his lord Gwenddoleu's cannibal eagles.
100. This triumphant close very much resembles that of *Cadair Taliesin, Cadair Ceridwen*, and several other mystical poems. This seems to have been the style of the bards, at the completion of their Diluvian mysteries, in commemoration of the returning season of serenity.
101. That Merddin used them as means of divination may be further inferred from hence; in most of the stanzas, a prediction of some great event is immediately subjoined to the contemplation of these mystical trees.

   These predictions, of which I have inserted a specimen or two, are sometimes delivered by the bard himself; at other times, they are put into the mouth of the guardian goddess, who has the property of alternately appearing and disappearing.
102. *W. Archaiol.*, p. 135.
103. Ibid. p. 132.
104. See Herodotus, L. VII, c. 6—.
105. St Paul's Epistle to the Romans, 1.

# PART TWO: TROJAN OUTPOST — FROM TROIA NOVANT TO CELTIC BRITAIN

Just as there are Celtic myths, so there is a kind of proto-mythology which deals with the distant origins of the Celtic peoples themselves. Archaeology has taught us to believe in the Indo-European culture which spread from the Indus valley across most of present-day Europe, seeding various tribal groups which remained behind to found the La Tène and Hallstatt cultures which provided a foundation for the Celtic peoples as we know them today.

Just how the Celts saw themselves we cannot say. They almost certainly did not call themselves by the names we have attached to them. Probably they were just 'the People', with each tribe having its own unique identity, its carefully memorized genealogies. There are, however, traces within the mythology of the Celts which indicate that they saw themselves as deriving from, among others, the Greeks. References to heroes who married 'the Greek king's daughter' abound in folk-songs, and there are several bardic poems which eulogize Hercules.

Certainly there was a good deal of intercourse between the peoples of the Hellenic world and those of Gaul and Britain. References are found scattered throughout Classic literature which betray a considerable knowledge of the Celtic world; some of these are collected here in the chapter called 'Monumenta Historica Celtica', faithfully gathered together by W. Dinan.

Another, extremely pervasive, legend refers to the coming to Britain of the last remnant of fallen Troy. London was called Troia Novant. 'New Troy' and was for centuries believed to have been founded by Brutus, the grandson of Aeneas the Trojan.[1] A speculative examination of this whole sub-culture is made by R.W. Morgan in 'The Trojan Era'. This is followed by a further excursion into history and proto-history. 'The Pretanic Background', by Eoin MacNeill, looks into the significance of the name 'Britain', with its many variants in Classical and post-Classical writings, and attempts to discover the truth of Celtic origins within the larger context of archaeology and history.

Each of these writings deals in its own way with some neglected chapters in the history of the Celts. Whether or not we accept as even possible some of the claims made within this group of essays, we cannot ignore the fascination it holds for us still.

---

1. See my chapter 'London Before History' in *The Aquarian Guide to Legendary London*, eds. John Matthews and Chesca Potter (Aquarian Press, 1990).

# Chapter 4
# The Trojan Era
## by R.W. Morgan

The descent of the British people from Troy and the Trojans was never disputed
for fifteen hundred years. The 'Island of Brutus' was the common name of the
Island in old times. The word *tan* is the old British or Japhetic term for *land*
— Brutannia (pronounced Britannia, the British *u* being sounded as ë) is Brut's
or Brutus' Land. The term is also of very ancient use in Asia, as Laristan,
Feristan, Afghanistan. The only two national names acknowledged by the
Ancient Britons are *Kymry*, and *Y Lin Troia*, the race of Troy. The Trojan descent
solves all the peculiarities in the British laws and usages which would otherwise
be wholly inexplicable.

The Trojan War is the cardinal point in ancient history from which we can
trace events upwards for about four centuries, and downwards for about one
hundred and forty years — in Greece, to Codrus and Neleus; but in Britain,
for one thousand years, down to the era of Caswallon, and the Roman invasion
under Julius Caesar. The genealogies of all the British kings and princes trace
up through Beli the Great, to Aeneas, Dardanus, and Gomer.

The Trojan Colonization of Britain took place as follows —

After the Deluge 680 years, and 1637 BC, Iau and Dardan reigned over the
Umbrian Empire in Italy. Dardanus having in a rencontre slain his brother Iau
or Jasius, emigrated first to Crete, then to Samo — Thrace — lastly to Phrygia,
where at the foot of the mountain which, after the mountain in Crete, he called
Ida, he built Dardania. The king of Phrygia then reigning was Athus. He had
two sons, Lud and Tyrrhi (Lydus and Tyrrhenus). Dardanus having exchanged
his rights in Italy with Athus for a part of Phrygia, Tyrrhi sailed with a large
body of his father's subjects and took possession of that portion of Umbria in
Italy which belonged to Dardanus. From Tyrrhi, it was from that time called
Tyrrhenia. Dardanus married Batea, daughter of Teucer, king of Llydaw
(Lydia), and was succeeded by Eric, the wealthiest monarch of the East — Eric
by Tros, who removed the capital of the empire from Dardania to Troy. Tros had
three sons, Ili, Assarac, and Gwyn the Beautiful, (Ganymedi). Gwyn was
waylaid by Tantallon, king of Lydia, and sent for safeguard to Jove, king of
Crete. Tros made war on Tantallon and his son Pelops, expelled them from
Asia, and added Lydia to his empire. Pelops settled in that part of Greece called
after him Peloponnesus — from him descended the royal families at Argos and
Sparta, represented when the Trojan war broke out by Memnon and Maen
(Agamemnon and Menelaus). Tros was succeeded by Ili, Ili, by Laomedon.
Tros reigned sixty years. To commemorate the splendor of his career, the Kymri
of Italy, who had followed Dardanus, took the name of Trojans. His second
son, Assarac begat Anchises, who wedded Gwen (Venus) the daughter of Jove,
king of Crete. Their son was Aeneas or Aedd — the head of the royal tribe of
the Dardanidae, and patriarch of the Trojan lines of Rome and Britain. In the

reign of Laomedon the citadel and walls of Troy were rebuilt by Belin and Nêv, architects of Crete, after the model of the Cretan Labyrinth, which was also an exact representation of the stellar universe. Laomedon was succeeded by his eldest son, Tithon, who, marrying Ida, or Aurora, abdicated in favour of his youngest brother, Priam. The son of Tithon and Ida was Memnon, King of India. In the reign of Priam the Trojan war broke out. The cause of it was this —

Jason, nephew of Pelias, king of Thessaly, organized an expedition against Colchos in Asia, which was part of the mother country of the Kymri. The principal chiefs under him were Hercwlf (Hercules) and Telamon. These anchored, on their way to join Jason, off Troy, but were peremptorily forbidden to set foot on Trojan ground by Laomedon. On their return from the conquest of Colchos, Hercwlf, Telamon, and the other Greek chiefs surprised and slew Laomedon and five of his sons by a sudden attack on the city, carrying off also Hesione his daughter, who was afterwards wedded to Telamon, to whom she bore Ajax the Great. Priam on his accession to the throne immediately despatched an embassy to Greece, demanding the restoration of Hesione, and satisfaction for the outrage perpetrated by Hercwlf. The two most powerful monarchs of Greece at the time were Memnon and Maen, the descendants of the Pelops who was expelled from Asia by the Kymry under Tros. Instigated by them, the states of Greece unanimously refused redress; upon which Priam appointed his son Paris to the command of a fleet, ordering him at all hazards to effect the liberation of Hesione; instead of which, he bore down at once towards Sparta, the capital of the territories of Menelaus, and seizing his wife, Helen, the loveliest woman of the age, carried her off, first to Egypt and then home to Troy — Menelaus being at the time absent in Crete. All Greece, on hearing of this act of just retribution, flew to arms. A confederate Armada of 1301 ships, under forty-eight princes, was collected under Memnon, or Agamemnon, king of Argos, and Commander in Chief. The history of the war which ensued, the most celebrated of any in ancient or modern times, is given in its acetic form by Homer and Virgil, and in its historic by Dares of Phrygia, and Dietys of Crete, contemporary authors who served throughout it, and afterwards accompanied Brutus into Britain. It lasted for ten years, during which time eighteen pitched battles were fought, and the flower of the Trojan and Greek chivalry perished for the most part in single combats. The heroes who distinguished themselves most on the Greek side were Achilles, Ulior, (Ulysses), Ajax, Pedrocles, Meirion, Nestor, and Agamemnon — on the Trojan or Kymric, Hector, Troil, Paris, Memnon, Aeneas, and Sarph (Sarpedon). On the night of 21st June, 1184 BC, in the tenth year of the siege, the Faction of Autenor and Helenus, which had always been averse to the war, threw open the Scoean gate, surmounted by a statue of the white horse of the sun, to the Confederate Army. For forty-eight hours a battle of the most desperate description raged within the walls. The brave old king with most of his sons fell, fighting round the altar in his palace; the command then fell to Aeneas, who, giving orders to fire the city in every quarter to prevent its capture by the enemy, cut his way at the head of the Dardanidae, through sword and flame, to the forest of Mount Ida. There, being joined by other Trojans to the number of 88,000, he prepared to return to his ancestors, the Kymry of Italy. Accordingly, after various adventures, he landed at the mouth of the Albula or Tiber, was cordially received by the reigning sovereign, Latinus, and presented with Llawen (Joy), or Lavinia, his daughter, in marriage.

Antenor, sailing with six thousand Trojans up the Adriatic founded Padua and the kingdom of *Gwynedd*, or Venetia, in Italy.

Helenus, with a large body, settled in Albyn, or Albania in Greece, where he was afterwards joined by Brutus.

Aeneas, by his first wife Creusa, a daughter of Priam, had Julius Ascanius. From the second son of Ascanius Julius descended the family of Julius Caesar, and the emperors of Rome. The eldest son of Ascanius was Sylvius Ascanius. He married Edra, niece of Lavinia, who bore him Brutus, the founder of the Trojan dynasty of Britain.

The issue of the second marriage of Aeneas and Lavinia was Silvius Aeneas, from whom descended Romulus, the founder of Rome.

In his fifteenth year, Brutus accidentally slew his father in the chase. He was ordered by his grandfather, in consequence of this deplorable event, to quit Italy. Assembling three thousand of the bravest youths of Umbria, he put himself at their head, and sailed to his countrymen in Albania, afterwards called Epirus.

There in conjunction with Assaracus, another Trojan Prince, he raised the standard of independence against Pandrasus, who had succeeded Agamemnon in the sovereignty of Greece. A series of victories on the Trojan side resulted in a peace, Pandrasus giving his daughter, Imogene, in marriage to Brutus. The coasts of the Mediterranean were at this time studded by settlements founded by the Greek leaders at the siege of Troy, for Greece had been completely exhausted and disorganized by her enormous efforts during the ten years' war, and for more than two centuries a state of anarchy succeeded that of the old heroic civilization. Brutus, aware that a Trojan kingdom could not be established in Albania except at the cost of incessant hostilities, resolved on emigrating with all his people to the northern seat of the mainstock of his race — the White Island. The resolution was unanimously approved of. A navy of three hundred and thirty-two vessels was constructed — arms and provisions supplied — the pedestal of the Trojan Palladium consigned to the care of Geryou the augur, and the whole population embarked on board. The Crimean colonization took place by land, across the Continent of Europe — the Trojan was conducted by sea.

Coasting the southern shore of the Mediterranean, Brutus arrived the third day at Melita, then called Legetta. Finding on it a temple of Diana, or *Karidwen*, he consulted her oracle on the future destinies of his family and nation. The verses were afterwards engraved in Archaic Greek on the altar of Diana in New Troy, or London, and translated into Latin in the third century by Nennius, a British prince attached to the court of Claudius Gothicus, the emperor, uncle of Constantius. They have thus been rendered by Pope. With the exception of the predictions of Balaam, recorded by Moses in the Book of Numbers, the Prophecy is the oldest in the Gentile world, and is still in course of fulfilment.

BRUTUS

Goddess of Woods! tremendous in the chase
To mountain boars and all the savage race;
Wide o'er the ethereal walks extends thy sway
And o'er the infernal regions void of day —
Look upon us on earth! unfold our fate,
And say what region is our destined seat?

When shall we next thy lasting temples raise,
And choirs of Virgins celebrate thy praise?

DIANA
 Brutus! there lies beyond the Gallic bounds
An Island, which the Western Sea surrounds,
By Ancient Giants held — now few remain
To bar thy entrance or obstruct thy reign;
To reach that happy shore thy sails employ,
And found an Empire in thy royal line
Which time shall ne'er destroy nor bounds confine.

The bounds of the empire founded by Brutus are now measured only by the circumference of the world, and his lineal descendants still sway its sceptre and occupy its throne.

On the ninth day they passed the Philistoean Altars, and thence sailed on to Mount Azara. They gave the coast the name of Moritania (the land along the sea), which it yet retains. They then steered through the Straits of the Libyan Hercules, now those of Gibraltar, into the Atlantic, then called the Tyrrhenian Ocean. On the south coast of Spain they came upon four other Trojan colonies, under Troenius. These were readily persuaded to join them. The combined emigrations sailing northward were again joined by a body of Greeks, part of a Cretan colony, that under Teucer had settled in Calabria. They then anchored off the mouth of the Loire. The great plain between the Alps and the Atlantic had by this time been thickly peopled by the descendants of the Alpine and Auveruian Cymry; these called themselves Celts or Gael, and the country Gaul, or Gallia. The meaning of Gael is 'a Woodlander — a man of a forest land'. The lowlands being then everywhere covered with dense timber, the highlands alone were cleared and dry. The king of Gael was Goffar. His ambassador being killed in a rencontre with Troenius, Goffar made war on Brutus. In the first battle, Goffar was defeated and Subard his general slain. Brutus, advancing through Gascony, threw up his camp in the centre of Goffar's own domains. A second engagement was fought, in which Brutus lost a nephew, Tyrrhi. In honour of him, he built an immense tumulus, where now stands the city called after Tyrrhi, Tours. Goffar, being a third time routed, submitted to the terms imposed upon him by the conquerors. The fleet, repaired and revictualled, sailed next year round the Horn of Armorica, and finally anchored off Talnus, in Torbay. The disembarcation occupied three weeks, the first to place foot on the 'Isle of the Mighty Ones', being the Trojan hero himself, on the rock still pointed out at Totnes as 'the Stone of Brutus'. The three Pacific Tribes received their countrymen from the East as brethren. Brutus introduced the constitution and laws of Troy. Before his time the primitive tribes regulated their lives and intercourse by a few simple patriarchal usages, the law of natural kindness being their chief guide. Brutus, at a national convention of the whole Island, with its dependencies, was elected Sovereign Paramount. The throne and crown of Hu Gadarn thus devolved upon him, both by descent and suffrage. His three sons, born after his arrival in Britain, he named after the three Pacific Tribes, Locrinus, Camber, and Alban. Brutus is also celebrated in the Triads as one of the three king revolutionists of Britain, the Trojan system under him being incorporated with the patriarchal. The most memorable of his laws is that of the royal primogeniture, by which the succession to the throne of Britain was vested in the eldest son of the king. This was known as pre-eminently 'the Trojan law', and has in all ages regulated the succession to the British Crown among the British dynasties. It was eventually adopted by the Normans, and became the law of England. It is the only safe basis on which monarchy can rest. Elective monarchies have always fallen by internal disunion or foreign partition. Another fundamental ordinance established by Brutus was that the sovereigns of Cambria and Alban should be so far subordinate to the sovereign of Lloegria that they should pay him annually forty pounds weight of gold, for the military and naval defence of the Island. The whole Island was never to be regarded otherwise than one kingdom and one crown. This crown was called 'the crown of Britain', and the sovereignty over the whole Island rested in it — the Crownship of Britain, *Un Beanaeth Brydain*. The military leadership remained in the eldest tribe, the Kymry, and from it the *Pendragon* or military dictator, with absolute power for the time being, was in the case of foreign invasion or national danger to be elected. This leadership was the same as Sparta exercised in Greece and Rome in Italy. Every subject was as free as the king. There were no other laws in force than those which were known as *Cyreithian*, or 'common rights'. There were no slaves; the first slaves in aftertimes were the *Caethion*, or captives taken in war.

The Usages of Britain could not be altered by any act or edict of the crown or national convention. They were considered the inalienable rights to which every Briton was born and of which no human legislation could deprive him. Many of these usages are remarkable for their humane and lofty spirit, for instance, 'There are three things belonging to a man, from which no law can separate him — his wife, his children, and the instruments of his calling; for no law can unman a man, or uncall a calling.'

The most learned jurists refer the original institutes of our Island to the Trojan law brought by Brutus. Lord Chief Justice Coke (Preface to Vol. III of *Reports*) affirms, 'the original laws of this land were composed of such elements as Brutus first selected from the Ancient Greek and Trojan institutions.'

It is to these native laws and not, as has been absurdly alleged, to any foreign or continental source — German, Saxon, or Norman — Britons have in all ages been indebted for the superior liberties they have enjoyed as contrasted with other nations. Lord Chancellor Fortescue, in his work *On the Laws of England* justly observes — 'concerning the different powers which kings claim over their subjects, I am firmly of opinion that it arises solely from the different nature of the original institutions. So the Kingdom of Britain had its original from Brutus and the Trojans who attended him from Italy and Greece, and were a mixed government compounded of the regal and democratic.'

Another British or Trojan law remains in full force — that the sceptre of the Island might be swayed by a queen as well as a king. In the Pict kingdom the succession went wholly by the female side. Amongst the continental nations no woman was permitted to reign. The Saxon considered it a disgrace for a king to be seen seated on a throne with a queen.

The names of the leading Greek and Trojan families remained among their Cymric descendants till a very recent period. Some are still in use. All ought, as a matter of national honour, to be revived.

Homer is one of the mutative forms of the word Gomer — the *g* being under certain laws dropped. The epic poem of the *Iliad*, or *Fall of Troy*, assigned to

Homer, is a collection of the heroic ballads of the bards of the Gomeridæ or Kymry, on the great catastrophe of their race in the East. It was originally composed in the Kymric or bardic characters. These were afterwards changed by the Greeks into the Phoenician, and in so doing, they were compelled to drop the Cymric radical *Gw*. Hence the metrical mutilation in the present Greek form of the *Iliad*. The *gw* is the letter attempted to be restored by modern scholars under the name of the Aeolic Digamma.

The *Aenid* is similarly the epic of the British Kymry of Italy on the same subject, Virgil being a descendant of the Kymric conquerors of Italy under Breanus, and, as his writings everywhere evince, an initiated bard. Neither of these immortal poems have any connection, strictly speaking, with the historic races of Greece and Rome. They are the epics of the heroic race, or race of Gomer.

The chariot system of warfare, and the system of military castrametation, were introduced into Britain by Brutus. Caesar describes both as having attained in his time the highest perfection. The British castrametation was in some important respects superior to the Roman.

In the third year of his reign, Brutus founded Caer Troin, afterwards called Caer Lludd, now London (*Lud-din*, Lud's city), on a spot known as *Bryn Gwyn*, or the White Mount, on the north side of the estuary of the Thames. The White Mount is now occupied by the Tower. In the court of the temple of Diana he placed the sacred stone which had formed the pedestal of the Palladium of the mother city of Troy. On it the British kings were sworn to observe the usages of Britain. It is now known as 'London Stone', and is imbedded in another on the south side of St Saviour's church, Cannon street. The belief in old times was that as long as it remained, New Troy, or London, would continue to increase in wealth and power; with its disappearance, they would decrease and finally disappear. Faiths of this description were moral forces on the minds of our ancestors, impelling them sometimes to the wildest, sometimes to the sublimest achievements. The faith that the British Troy, or London, was destined to sway a wider empire than either the Asiatic or Italian Troy (Rome) had swayed is one of the most ancient traditions of the Kymry.

Brutus died after a memorable reign of twenty-four years, and was interred by the side of Imogene, at the White Mount. His career was one of gigantic events — that of the founder of a mighty empire in the West which, after various mutations of fortune and absorptions of races, still reposes on his name and institutions.

The portion of Britain assigned to Troenius was the Western Keryn or promontory, extending from Torbay to the Land's End, part of which is now known as Cornwall. From the Keryn, Troenius changed his name into Keryn or Corineus. The dukedom of Cornwall, thus founded, was a Dukedom Royal; that is, the duke within it exercised the same prerogatives as the kings of Lloegria, Cambria and Albyn did within their territories. Next to these crowns, it is the oldest title in Britain. Cornwall and Bretagne were in old times regarded as appanages of the same race and dynasty. Both have given lines of kings to each other and to Britain.

Brutus was succeeded in Lloegria by his eldest son, Locrinus; in Albyn, by his second son, Alban; in Cambria, by his youngest son, Camber, or Cumbyr. Before the demise of Brutus, Gwendolene, sole daughter and heiress of Corineus, had been betrothed to Locrinus. In the second year of the reign of

Locrinus occurred the first invasion of Britain on record by the northern nations. The vast countries extending from the lake districts of Upper Russia across Scandinavia and the lower Baltic to Germany may, from 1000 BC to AD 1000 be regarded as the piratic lands of the Pre-Roman, Roman, and Dark Ages. Periodically they produced a surplus population which, unable to procure the means of subsistence in these dreary and frost-bound regions, threw themselves, sometimes by land, sometimes by sea, on the cultivated countries of the West and South. The names they assumed or were known by varied in different eras — Scythians, Scots, Goths, Vandali, Sacae, Saxons, Llychlinians, Norsemen, etc. Their physical characteristics were — large but soft limbs, red or flaxen hair, blonde complexions, grey or blue eyes, broad and flat feet. Natives of Arctic climates, they carried everywhere with them strong animal appetites, and a passion for indulgence in intoxicating liquors. Their religion was for the most part either Materialism of the grossest kind, or consisted in the practice of the most cruel superstition; it must however be remembered, that our accounts on these points, being derived from their bitterest enemies, are to be received with extreme caution. The invasion which landed in the North of Britain consisted of a confederacy headed by Humber, king of the Scythians. Marching southward, Humber encountered Alban, at the present site of Nottingham castle. Alban, disdaining to wait for the arrival of his brothers, was defeated and slain in the battle which ensued. Humber then fell back before the advance of Locrinus and Camber, on the banks of the great eastern estuary. The British fleet, entering the mouth, prevented the escape of the Scythian armada. Humber, compelled to an engagement, was totally defeated, and plunging in his flight into the waters of the estuary was therein drowned; since which event, it has borne his name, the Humber. Locrinus after the victory divided the spoils amongst his army, reserving for himself such gold and silver as was contained in the king's own ship, together with three virgins of surpassing beauty, found on board, whom Humber had forcibly abducted from their own countries. One of these was a daughter of a king of Almaen (Germany) her name, Susa, or Estrildis. Struck with her extraordinary charms of mind and person, Locrinus declared his intention to marry her. Corineus on hearing of this intention was so incensed that it required the utmost efforts of their mutual friends to prevent the breaking out of a civil war. Eventually Locrinus found himself under the necessity of observing his engagement with Gwendolene. But retaining his passion for Estrildis, he secretly built a palace for her at Caerwys, near the banks of the river which divides Lloegria from Cambria. Here, with the connivance of his brother Camber, he indulged his affection for his beautiful captive without restraint. In this manner he concealed her for seven years. Estrildis gave birth to a daughter, Sabra, surpassing even the mother in loveliness, and rivalling in grace her ancestress, Venus, the mother of Aeneas, whom the Greeks and Romans had idolized into the goddess of beauty. Gwendolene also gave birth to a son, Madoc, or Mador, who was consigned to the guardianship of Corineus. But Corineus in process of time dying, and relieving Locrinus from his former apprehensions, the latter immediately divorced Gwendolene, and proclaiming Estrildis his wife advanced her to the throne. Infuriated at the discovery of the intrigue and the additional dishonour of her deposition, Gwendolene retired to Cornwall, and levying all the forces of her father's dukedom, declared war against her husband. The two armies met on the river

Stour, and in the battle Locrinus fell dead from the shot of an arrow. Gwendolene, hastening after the victory to the Cambriae frontier, seized Estrildis and Sabra. The former she ordered to immediate execution, but in despite of the recollection of her wrongs and the natural vindictiveness of her temper, was so moved by the supernatural loveliness of Sabra, that many days elapsed before she could be persuaded to condemn her to death. She was then taken by her guards to a meadow (*Dôl-forwyn*, the maiden's meadow), and cast into the river, which from that time has been called Sabra, or Sabrina (the Severn), after her name.

Gwendolene, during the minority of Madoc, conducted the government with great vigour and ability. On her decease at Tintagel castle, Madoc, whose favourite recreation was the chase, left the affairs of the kingdom entirely in the hands of his uncle, Camber. Madoc founded Caer Madoc, or Doncaster.

Membricius, son and heir of Madoc, transferred the college erected by Dares Phrygius from Cirencester to the present site of Oxford. The original name of Oxford is Caer Mymbyr. He inherited his father's attachment to the chase. His death was a singular one: pursuing a horde of wolves after nightfall, he was attacked by them and torn to pieces at Pontbleiddan, or Wolvaston, near Oxford. Evroc the Great, his son and successor, was the first British sovereign who turned his attention to continental acquisitions. His victorious arms overran France and Central Europe. The family alliances which had formerly existed between the Kymry of Italy and Britain were renewed by the inter-marriages of twenty-one of his daughters with the Umbrian houses of the Alban kingdom in Italy. His son, Assaracus, led the Kymry to the frontiers of Pwyl or Poland. Evroc founded Caer Evroc, or York; Caer Edin, or Edinburgh; Dunbarton, and Caer dolur, Bamborough castle. His reign, which lasted sixty years, is one of the most illustrious in our early annals.

He was succeeded by his son Brutus Darian Lâs (of the Blue Shield). Brutus was succeeded by Leil, the founder of Carlisle and Chester. Leil, by Rhun of the Strong Shaft (*paladr brâs*), who founded Shaftesbury, (*Caer paladr*), Winchester (*Caer wynt*), Canterbury (*Caer caint*). He built also many Druidic circles and temples.

In the reign of Rhun, 892 BC (the era when Zachariah prophesied in Judea), the first of the three Confederate Expeditions commemorated in the Triads went forth from Britain. Urb, grandson of Assaracus, the son of Evroc the Great, being driven from his territories in Scandinavia, or Lochlyn, landed at Caer Troia with but one attendant, Mathatta Vawr. Presenting himself before Rhun and the national council, he implored them to pledge their solemn oath that they would grant him his petition. Moved by this appeal of the royal exile, they inadvertently consented to his request. Urb asked that from every capital fortress in the kingdom he might take as many armed men as he entered it with. Rhun, bound by the oath of the council, was obliged to give the required permission, but immediately foreseeing the consequences, issued an edict that no Briton should on pain of death enter any fortress with Urb. Neither threats nor persuasion, however, could shake the fidelity of the prince's gigantic squire, and in defiance of all preventive measures, Urb entered the first fortress with Mathatta Vawr by his side. From this he took two, from the second, four, from the third, eight, and so on, till the fighting force of the Island was found insufficient to supply the demand exceeding 120,000 men made on the seventeenth city. Urb accordingly set sail with the 60,000 already levied, for

*Figure 2*: 'The Giant of Caer Drais' by *R. Machell*.

Scandinavia. By their assistance he soon recovered his throne. Part of this armament settled in the country called after them the Cimbric or Kymric Chersonese, now Denmark. From these descended, first, the terrible Cimbri, who, in alliance with the Teutones, overthrew and destroyed so many armies of Rome; and secondly, in after ages, the Norman race who conquered Normandy, Saxon England, and other lands. The facility with which the Normans fused and intermarried with the Kymry and Bretons, identifying themselves with their history and traditions, explains itself by this community of descent. The other moiety of the host of Urb followed up their career of conquest across Europe to the lands of Galas and Avena (Galatia and Ionia) in Asia Minor. These are the Kymry to whom the Greek and Latin authors assign the subjugation of the East prior to the foundation of the Persian Empire by Cyrus. No individual of the confederate host of Urb ever returned, state the Triads, to Britain. They settled in the conquered countries. The three confederate are also termed the three Silver Hosts of Britain. They were all picked men and their arms were of the three metals — gold, silver, and steel. This account is in harmony with the astonishment expressed by the Classic writers at the splendid character of the equipments of both infantry and cavalry in the Kymric armies. The three confederate are known too as the Three Inconsiderate Hosts, because they laid the Island open to the three Capital Invasions — those of the Coranidae, the Romans, and the Saxons.

The drain caused by this expedition on the military resources of the Island enabled the Coranidae, a marine tribe from the lowlands of the continent facing the eastern side of Britain, to establish themselves between the Humber and the Wash. This was the earliest Teutonic or German settlement: they are the Coritani of the Roman writers. They acknowledged allegiance and paid tribute to the British Crown at Caer Troia, but were invariably false in critical emergencies such as a foreign invasion to the national cause.

Rhun was succeeded by Bleddyn, or Bladud, who built Caer Badon, or Bath, and constructed therein a magnificent circular temple. He was succeeded by Lear (*Llyr*), the founder of Caer Llyr (Leicester), the closing scenes of whose long and peaceful reign in connection with the unnatural ingratitude of his two elder, and the affecting devotion of his youngest daughter, Cordelia, has been made familiar to the European world by the dramatic pen of Shakespeare. The succession then descended through Cordelia, Kynedda, Rivallo, Gorust, Cecil (Sitsyl), Iago, Cymac, to Gorvod. The two sons of Gorvod, Fer and Por, perished — one in civil war, the other by the machinations of a vindictive mother. In them ended the elder male line of the Britannidae, or dynasty of Brutus.

After an interregnum of some years, occupied by the contests of various claimants to the throne, Dyvnwal Moelmud, hereditary duke of Cornwall, and the representative by both paternal and maternal descent of the younger line of the Britannidae, was by general consent recognized Sovereign Paramount. His first act was to reduce to a code the civil and international usages which the late commotions had disturbed. The laws, thus systematized, are eminently distinguished for their clearness, brevity, justice, and humanity. They have come down to us in the Druidic form of Triads. We give a few examples.

'There are three tests of civil liberty — equality of rights, equality of taxation, freedom to come and go.

There are three causes which ruin a State — inordinate privileges, corruption of justice, national apathy.

There are three things which cannot be considered solid longer than their foundations are solid — peace, property, and law.

Three things are indispensable to a true union of Nations — sameness of laws, rights, and language.

There are three things free to all Britons — the forest, the unworked mine, the right of hunting wild creatures.

There are three things which are private and sacred property in every man, Briton or foreigner — his wife, his children, his domestic chattels.

There are three things belonging to a man which no law of men can touch, fine, or transfer — his wife, his children, and the instruments of his calling; for no law can unman a man, or uncall a calling.

There are three persons in a family exempted from all manual or menial work — the little child, the old man or woman, and the family instructor.

There are three orders against whom no weapon can be bared — the herald, the bard, the head of a clan.

There are three of private rank against whom no weapon can be bared — a woman, a child under fifteen, and an unarmed man.

There are three things that require the unanimous vote of the nation to effect — deposition of the sovereign, introduction of moralities in religion, suspension of law.

There are three civil birthrights of every Briton — the right to go wherever he pleases, the right, wherever he is, to protection from his land and sovereign, the right of equal privileges and equal restrictions.

There are three property birthrights of every Briton — five (British) acres of land for a home, the right of armorial bearings, the right of suffrage in the enacting of the laws, the male at twenty-one, the female on her marriage.

There are three guarantees of the society — security for life and limb, security for property, security of the rights of nature.

There are three sons of captives who free themselves — a bard, a scholar, a mechanic.

There are three things the safety of which depends on that of the others — the sovereignty, national courage, just administration of the laws.

There are three things which every Briton may legally be compelled to attend — the worship of God, military service, and the courts of law.

For three things a Briton is pronounced a traitor, and forfeits his rights — emigration, collusion with an enemy, surrendering himself and living under an enemy.

There are three things free to every man, Briton or foreigner, the refusal of which no law will justify — water from spring, river, or well, firing from a decayed tree, a block of stone not in use.

There are three orders who are exempt from bearing arms — the bard, the judge, the graduate in law or religion. These represent God and his peace, and no weapon must ever be found in their hand.

There are three kinds of sonship — a son by marriage with a native Briton, an illegitimate son acknowledged on oath by his father, a son adopted out of the clan.

There are three whose power is kingly in law — the sovereign paramount of Britain over all Britain and its isles, the princes palatine in their princedoms, the heads of the clans in their clans.

There are three thieves who shall not suffer punishment — a woman compelled by her husband, a child, a necessitous person who has gone through three towns and to nine houses in each town without being able to obtain charity though he asked for it.

There are three ends of law — prevention of wrong, punishment for wrong inflicted, insurance of just retribution.

There are three lawful castigations — of a son by a father, of a kinsman by the head of a clan, of a soldier by his officer. The chief of a clan when marshalling his men may strike his man three ways — with his baton, with the flat of his sword, with his open hand. Each of these is a correction, not an insult.

There are three sacred things by which the conscience binds itself to truth — the name of God, the rod of him who offers up prayers to God, the joined right hand.

There are three persons who have a right to public maintenance — the old, the babe, the foreigner who cannot speak the British tongue.'

These, and other primitive laws of Britain not only rise far superior in manly sense and high principle to the laws of Ancient Greece and Rome but put to shame the enactments of nations calling themselves Christians at the present day. They contain the essence of law, religion, and chivalry. A nation ruling itself by their spirit could not be otherwise than great, civilized, and free. One of their strongest recommendations is that they are so lucid as to be intelligible to all degrees of men and minds.

In addition to being one of the founders of British legislation, Dyvnwal designed and partly made the Royal British military roads through the Island. These were nine in number — 1. The *Sarn Gwyddelin* (corrupted into Watling Street), or Irish Road, in two branches, from Dover to Mona and Penvro. 2. The *Sarn Iken* (Iknield Street), the road from Caer Troia northward through the eastern districts. 3. *Sarn Uelia* (Iknield Street), from the mouth of the Tyne to the present St David's. 4. *Sarn Ermyn*, from Anderida (Pevensey) to Caer Edin (Edinburgh). 5. *Sarn Achmaen*, from Caer Troia to Meuevia (St David's). 6. *Sarn Halen*, from the salt mines of Cheshire to the mouth of the Humber. 7. *Sarn Halen*, from the salt mines to Llongborth (Portsmouth). 8. The second *Sarn Ermyn*, from Torbay to Dunbreton on the Clyde. 9. The *Sarn ar y Môr*, or military road following the coast around the Island. These roads were pitched and paved, and ran sometimes in a straight, sometimes a sinuous line, at a moderate elevation above the ground, forming a network of communication between the cities of Britain. Being completed by Belinus, they are known as the Belinian roads of Britain. The Romans followed these lines in their first and second invasions, and subsequently laid down in great measure their own military roads upon them. Hence the Belinian and Roman roads are found constantly running in and out of each other.

The reign of Dyvnwal was marked with signal prosperity. The trade in tin, copper, iron, lead, horses, carried on with Tyre and the East through the medium of the Phoenicians, attained dimensions hitherto unexampled. The manufactures of swords (hardened by some process now lost, to a temper superior to that of steel), statues, ornaments, doors, gates of bronze — into the composition of which tin largely enters — were carried on to such an extent that Asia appears to have been deluged with them. No tin mines but those of Britain existed then, nor are any to be found now but those of Malacca, of comparatively very recent discovery. Wherever, therefore, bronze is mentioned by the sacred or Classic authors, there is evidence of the trade and manufactures of Trojan Britain. From Phoenicia and the East in return poured a steady stream of the precious metals. British merchants frequented the mart at Tyre, and Ezekiel is literally correct in describing the city which rose 'very glorious and of great beauty, in the midst of the sea', as the merchant of the people of the Isles afar off. The wealth accruing from the commerce thus conducted affords an easy explanation of the profuse expenditure of gold and silver lavished by the Kymry on their arms and steeds.

After a memorable reign of forty years, Dyvnwal Moelmud died, and was interred at the White Tower in Caer Troia. He was succeeded by his eldest son, Belinus, the younger, Brennus, receiving Alban for his government.

Brennus (Bran), a young man of stern temperament and unbounded ambition, distinguished by a courage which no difficulties could daunt and a generosity towards his friends no funds, however princely, could supply, soon involved himself with his sovereign and brother. Instigated by the usual incentives which interested courtiers and diplomatists know so well to apply to the bosom of kings, he prepared to strike at the Crown Paramount. To strengthen himself for this unnatural enterprize, he sailed to Norway, and there won and married Anaor, daughter of Elsing, king of Llochlyn. Anaor had previously been betrothed to Guthlac, king of the Cimbric Chersonese, who, on hearing of the indignity thus practised upon him, fitted out a fleet to intercept Brennus on his return. Intelligence of the conspiracy being also in Britain conveyed to Belinus, he immediately marched northwards and possessed himself of all the fortified cities in his brother's dominions. Guthlac and Brennus meeting with their fleets, the engagement was broken off by a furious tempest, the ship in which Anaor was embarked happening in the confusion to be captured by Guthlac. The storm raged for five days, at the end of which Guthlac and Anaor were wrecked off Hamborough, where Belinus was encamped, prepared to repel the invasion of his brother. They were immediately conducted to him, and honourably received. A few days after Brennus, having weathered the storm, arrived with the remnant of his armada in Albania. News soon reached him of the capture of his wife, first by Guthlac, and then by Belinus, Maddened by the intelligence, he pressed forward towards Bamborough, giving out he would destroy the whole Island with fire and sword, if his bride and kingdom were not restored to him. Belinus absolutely refusing to comply with these demands, a battle took place at Culater. The Norsemen were defeated with the loss of fifteen thousand slain, and Brennus compelled to save himself by flight into Gaul. Guthlac, on signing a treaty by which the Cimbric Chersonese (Dacia, afterwards Denmark), became part of the British Empire, was dismissed with Anaor to his own kingdom. The next seven years were devoted by Belinus to the completion of the roads begun by his father. A law was made throwing them open to all, natives and foreigners, and placing them on the same footing of religious security as the river and the sanctuary. 'There are three things free to a country and its borders — the rivers, the road, and the place of worship. These are under the protection of God and his peace: whoever on or within them draws weapon against any one is a capital criminal.' In this law originated the expression 'the the King's highway', these highways, on which it was a capital offence to stop or commit an outrage on a traveller, being the nine Belinian roads thus placed under the protection of God and the nation.

Meanwhile Brennus, having in vain solicited aid from the kings of Celtica, betook himself to Seguin, prince of the Ligurians in Gaul. He was entertained as became his birth and the relationship which existed between the Ligurians of the Alps and Britain. His services in the field secured him the respect of the nation at large, whilst his personal qualities won him the affection of Rhonilla, the only child of the prince. They were married, Seguin promising his son-in-law his assistance to recover his government in Britain, and at the same time nominating him his successor to the throne of Liguria. At the end of the year Seguin died. Brennus on ascending the throne immediately divided the treasures which the old king had hoarded among the most influential chiefs in his new domains, thus securing their consent and co-operation to the intended invasion of Britain. A treaty was concluded with the Celts for a free passage through Gaul; forces collected from all quarters, and eventually embarked on board a fleet which had been constructed for the purpose by the Vencti (Gwynedd, Venedotia, La Vendée) of Armorica. A landing was effected at Anderida — the same spot where in after ages Vespasian, Ella the Saxon, and William the Norman, found ingress into Britain. Belinus, marching from Caer Troia, drew up his forces opposite to those of his brother, and the same ground which afterwards reeked with the best blood of Saxondom under Harold would have now streamed with that of Trojan Britain, but for the intervention of Corwenna, the aged mother of the two contending sovereigns. Reaching with trembling steps the tribunal from which Brennus was haranguing his army, she threw her arms around his neck, as he descended to receive her, and kissed him in transports of affection. She then adjured him by every appeal a mother could address to a son to save her from the horrible spectacle of seeing the children of her womb engaged in impious hostilities against God, the laws of nature, their country, and themselves. Pointing out the injustice of his cause, and the ease with which far nobler conquests than that over a brother might be achieved if two such armies, instead of destroying, would unite with each other, she entreated him to be reconciled to his rightful sovereign. Moved by these representations, Brennus deposited his helmet and arms on the tribunal, and bareheaded went with her, amidst the profound silence of both armies, to his brother. Seeing him approach, Belinus dismounted from his chariot, threw down his lance, and meeting him half way, folded him in his embraces. The cheers of the two armies on witnessing the scene rent the skies. In a few minutes all order was dissolved; Briton and Ligurian were no longer to be distinguished; the banners were bound together; the seamen of the fleet, informed of the event, poured on shore, and a day which threatened to be one of the most shameful and disastrous in British annals ended in a general jubilee of joy and festivities. Happy would it be for mankind if every mother of kings were a Corwenna — if every contending monarch listened to the remonstrances of nature and humanity with the like readiness of Belinus and Brennus.

After long consultation, Belinus decided on attempting, with the confederate forces, the conquest of Europe. The nation enjoyed tranquility at home — the sceptre was swayed by one powerful hand. A vast host with whose aspirations it was dangerous to tamper panted for employment — the means of transport were in the Thames. Gaul was torn with petty factions and the Umbrian population of Northern Italy, oppressed by the Etrurian domination, waited but the display of the great standard of their race — the Red Dragon —

on the crest of the Alps, to rise and vindicate their ancient liberties. The Armament accordingly landed to the number of 300,000 men at the mouth of the Seine. One battle on the plains of Tours decided the fate of Gaul. City after city, wearied of intestine struggles which led to no result, gladly accepted a conquest that promised to bring in its train a blessing to which they had long been strangers — security for life and property. The banditti which under the name of soldiers swarmed in Gaul were either exterminated or incorporated in the regular forces. Two years sufficed to reduce all Celtica to order under the British law and administration. The Cymro-Celtic army then moved under the brothers towards Italy. The Ligurians joined them, and the first military passage of the Alps was in the face of apparent impossibilities accomplished. The glory which has hitherto attached to the two names of Hannibal and Napoleon belongs in justice to those of the two British leaders Belinus and Brennus. They were the first that ventured — the first that succeeded in overcoming the snowy barriers which nature has built as if purposely to shield the sunny climes of Italy from the sword of the North. Of the nature of the forces which were about to re-establish the Kymric Empire in Italy, we have vivid accounts transmitted us by the classic authors. 'The greater and more warlike Cimbri,' states Plutarch, 'live in the Northern ocean, in the very ends of the earth. They are called Cimbri — not from their manners, it is the name of their race. As to their courage, spirit, force, and vivacity, we can compare them only to a devouring flame. All that came before them were trodden down, or driven onwards like herds of cattle.' Justin records an anecdote illustrative of the contempt with which they regarded the character and military science of the Greeks. After subduing the Triballi and Getae (Goths), the Cymro-Celts offered their alliance, in earnest of their pacific disposition towards him, to Antigonus, king of Macedonia. Antigonus treated the offer as if it proceeded from fear or policy. 'What are these Greeks?' asked the Kymry of their ambassadors, on their return. 'They are remarkable for two things,' replied the ambassadors, 'they call positions which have neither moats nor ramparts camps, and they think if they have plenty of gold they have no need of steel.' Over the plains of Northern Italy, the Kymric army swept in three divisions. The Etrurians made a gallant but ineffectual stand in defence of their empire. Defeated in five engagements, they withdrew their cognate population southwards, consigning each city, as they abandoned it, to the flames. The old Umbrian nationality was restored, the liberated and the liberators forming from this period one federation with equal rights and laws. The following cities are enumerated by Justin and Pliny as being founded by Brennus on the expulsion of the Tuscans — Milan, Como, Brescia, Verona, Burgamo, Mantua, Trent, and Vicentia. It is to be observed, that the conquests of the Kymry were those of civilization, not destruction. Wherever they settled, they proclaimed equality of laws, they erected temples, made roads, built cities, and cultivated literature, especially poetry. The conquests, on the other hand, of the German and the Northern nations in the Dark Ages were those of barbarism over civilization — of the principle of destruction over that of conservatism and consolidation. From the Cymro-Celts of Cisalpine Gaul sprang many of the first writers of the Roman Empire — Livy, Pliny, Catullus, Virgil, etc., etc.

Rome at this time is represented by her own writers as an independent metropolis, exercising considerable influence in the Italian peninsula. The British writers on the contrary state she was a dependent or tributary of

Etruria, and that the Porsena or King of Etruria was in right of such title, Consul also or Chief Magistrate of Rome. This account is confirmed by the Greek historians, and by the searching analysis which this particular part of the early traditions of Rome has recently undergone. The way in which the Kymry came into conflict with the city which had always been the sacred city of their race in Italy, and afterwards ruled the world, was as follows —

Belinus after the conquest of Cisalpine Keltica had with one half of his forces marched northwards and was engaged in subjugating the various tribes which in after ages became known in the aggregate as the German or Teutonic people. The Romans introduced greater confusion in history by giving nations not their generic name, or the name by which they called themselves, but some appellation fastened upon them from some peculiar habit or characteristic. German means in the Teutonic language the same as Belgae in the Kymric — war-men, warriors. The Belgae of the Continent were Kymry, not Celts. They were the descendants of the Kymry who conquered the country under Brennus, and in Caesar's time occupied one third of Gaul. Eastward of them lay the Teutons (Tudeschi, Deutch). These were now subdued by Belinus, and the most fertile part of their territory around the Hercynian forest divided among the Cymro-Celtic army. The Cymro-Celts in Caesar's time were known as the Volcae and retained their old superiority in arms and civilization over the surrounding Teutons. Brennus, taking up his headquarters at Mediolanum (Meifod, Milan), gradually extended his arms southwards. Among other cities, he besieged Clusium, a city of Lower Etruria. The inhabitants sent to Rome for aid. Three brothers of the Fabian Cenedl, or clan, accompanied the deputation back as ambassadors. An interview being requested and granted, Brennus was asked what injury he had received from the Clusians. He replied, 'These Etrurians have twice as much land as they can cultivate — we are powerful, numerous, and in want of land, yet they refuse to part with an acre of their useless territory.' 'But by what right do you advance such a claim?' again asked the ambassadors. 'By the oldest of all rights,' answered Brennus, with a stern smile, 'the law which pervades all nature, and to which all animals are subject — the right of the strong over the weak. It is by this law these Etrurians, and you Romans, originally obtained your possessions. Either restore these possessions to their former owners or abide by the law against yourselves.'

The next day, Quintus Ambustus Fabius headed a sortie of the Clusians against the besiegers. He slew a Celtic officer and, whilst stripping him of his arms, was recognized as one of the Roman ambassadors. Amongst the Kymry, an ambassador was always a sacred character and, as we have seen, prohibited from carrying any weapon himself; and it constituted a grave offence even to unsheath a weapon before him. Their indignation, therefore, at this double violation of the laws of nations, as recognized among themselves, was extreme. Striking his camp, Brennus despatched an embassy to Rome, demanding that Quintus Fabius should be given up to him. The Feciales, or college of heralds, at Rome, advised the Senate to comply, pointing out the grossness of an act which reflected dishonour on the whole nation. The people (plebs), however, not only overruled the motion, but creating the three brothers military tribunes, appointed them to the command of the army. Brennus at once gave the word 'for Rome'. 'His forces,' states Plutarch, 'injured no man's property; they neither pillaged the fields, nor insulted the towns.' On the 6th June, AU 363, 490 BC, the two armies met at the confluence of the little river Allia with the Tiber. The Romans were routed with great slaughter; and Rome itself, with the exception of the Capitol, fell three days afterwards into the hands of the conqueror. The anniversary of the battle of Allia was noted as 'the black day' in the Roman calendar. No business was transacted in it, and every citizen who appeared in public did so in mourning vestments. The Capitol stood a siege of six months. During it Fabius Dorso, proceeding in his pontifical robes to the Quirinal Hill, offered up there the sacrifice usual on the clan-day (dies gentilitia) of his family. The Roman writers express surprise that he was permitted to do this and return in safety. But the Kymry would as soon have throught of striking their sovereign as of unsheathing a weapon against both a priest and the head of a clan. In making way for him and escorting him back to the Capitol, they only observed the usages of Britain. An attempt made by the Porsena of Etruria to raise the siege being defeated by a second victory on the part of Brennus, the Romans agreed to ransom the citadel for one thousand pounds weight in gold. When the gold was being weighed in the presence of the different commanders, Brennus, taking off his belt and sword, threw them into the opposite scale: 'What means that act?' asked the Roman consul. 'It means,' replied Brennus, 'gwae gwaethedigion (vae victis) — woe to the vanquished.' The Romans endured the taunt in silence. The gold was transferred to Narbonne in Gaul. Brennus withdrew his troops, and shortly afterwards concluded an offensive and defensive alliance with Dionysius of Sicily.

The once accepted account of the recovery of the gold and the defeat of Brennus by Camillus is now abandoned by all scholars as a fiction of Roman vanity. Rome indeed only comes into the province of history after her capture by the Kymry.

Virgil, whose archaeological accuracy cannot be too highly spoken of, describes the uniform and arms of the conquerors of Rome: their vest was a mass of gold lace (aurea vestis), they wore the gold torque round their necks, a sword by their side, two javelins with heavy steel heads were their principal missiles; oblong shields, borne on their shoulders during a march, covered their whole bodies in action. In Kymric, ysgwydd means the shoulder — hence 'scutum', the shoulder-piece shield. It is one of the most striking proofs of the subserviency and littleness of modern scholarship that it should have permitted itself to be Romanized into the idea that an army thus described was not far in advance of the Romans themselves in every element of civilization.

Brennus reigned thirty years in Northern Italy. The Cymro-Celtic kingdom thus established was henceforth known as Cisalpine Gaul. Its subsequent history is connected with the Roman. Its people were the first nation admitted to the full rights of Roman citizenship.

Belinus, after the conquest of Germany, founded Aquileia, where he was afterwards worshipped as a god. Returning through Gaul, he divided its territories amongst his five younger sons, retaining the government of Britain alone in his own hands. He employed the latter years of his long and glorious reign in peaceful legislation and the construction of public works. Belin's castle (Billingsgate) and the stupendous embankment of the Thames were begun and completed under this monarch. He built also Caer leon (originally Caer usc), and repaired the Druidic temples of Côr gawr (Stonehenge), and Ambri. He died in the 80th year of his age. His body was burnt, and the ashes deposited in a golden urn on the top of the highest tower of his palace on the Thames.

He was succeeded by Gwrgant the Peaceful, the chief incident in whose reign was the reduction of Dacia (Denmark), which had attempted to separate itself, to its former state of annexation. Returning to Britain, he met an Iberian or Hispanian fleet, seeking a country to colonize. Their leader was Partholyn. Gwrgant assigned them the South of Erin, or Ierne, (Ireland). From them descended the Milesian kings and clans of the sister island.

Gwrgant was buried at Caerlleon.

From this date to about fifty years preceding the Julian invasion, Britain enjoyed a long era of peace and prosperity.

The sceptre was swayed by the following kings: Gorvonian the Just, Artegal, Elidyr the Pious, Vigen, Peredur, March, Morgan, Einion, Rhûn, Geraint, Cadell, Coel, Por, Corineus, Fulgen, Eldad, Androgeus, Urien, Eliud, Cledor, Cleton, Geraint, Meriou, Bleddyn, Cap, Owen, Cecil, Blegàbred, Arthmail, Eldol, Redion, Rhydderch, Sawl, Pir, Cap II, Manogan, to whom succeeded his son, Beli Mawr. The Kymric genealogies are generally headed with his initials — B.M. The succession upward from him to Brutus, the founder of the Trojan dynasty, is readily found by reference to any of the ancient royal pedigrees. Beli reigned forty years. He had three sons, Lud, Caswallon (Cassibellanus), and Nennius. Lud succeeded him. He rebuilt the walls of Caer Troia, with seven principal towers and gates. One of these, Ludgate, retains his name. He issued an edict, commanding the city to be henceforth called Llud-din (Londinium, *Caer Lludd*), instead of Caer Troia. The people, headed by Nennius, threatened to rise and depose Lud, if the edict were not rescinded. He was compelled to give way. After the death of Nennius, a second attempt, supported by Androgeus, was more successful. The name of Londinium gradually superseded the old heroic one of Troy. Lud was buried in the vault under his tower at Ludgate. He left two sons of tender age. Androgeus and Tenuantius. The Irish having invaded Mona, and the Roman arms under Caesar threatening at this time the total subjugation of Gaul and Bretagne, Caswallon was during their minority appointed Regent of the kingdom. He immediately marched upon Mona and defeated the Irish at Manuba, with such slaughter that a pestilence arose from the number of the dead bodies exposed to the heat of the summer. The bones were afterwards collected into pyramids on the nearest point to Irland, *Caer gybi*, Holyhead. On his return to London, embassies from Gaul requesting aid against Caesar, waited upon him.

1.   Originally published as part of *The British Kymry*, by R.W. Morgan, (H. Humphries, Carnavon, 1857) [Ed.].

# Chapter 5
# Monumenta Historica Celtica
## by W. Dinan[1]

## HECATAEUS OF MILETUS

In the *Iliad*[2] we find mention of Miletus, a Greek city situated near the mouth of the river Meander. Its favourable position enabled it to secure a monopoly of the trade of the Black Sea, while the energy and enterprise of its citizens made it in the sixth century BC the most important of the Greek cities. By 700 BC it had founded more than sixty cities, chiefly on the Hellespont, including Abydos, Cyzicus, Sinope, Dioscurias, Panticapaeum and Olbia. It entered into commercial relations with the Phoenicians and became distinguished as a seat of literature, history, philosophy, and geographical enterprise. Towards the end of the seventh century BC Anaximander of Miletus designed the first map of the world. Hecataeus, born at Miletus *c*540 BC, continued the researches of Anaximander and travelled extensively in Egypt, Asia and Europe. He wrote an account of his observations, largely used by Herodotus in his history, and of which 331 fragments have come down to us. It is to these fragments we owe the first mention of the Celts. The fragments are collected in the scholarly work of C. and T. Miller: *Fragmenta Historicorum Graecorum*, 5 vols., published by Didot, Paris.

  I Narbon,[3] a market and city of the Celts.
 II Nyrax,[4] a Celtic city.
III Massalia,[5] a city of the Ligurians, near the Celts, a colony of the Phocaeans.

## HIMILCO

Himilco, a Carthaginian explorer, made a voyage round the west coast of Europe and explored as far as Britain and Ireland about 500 BC. An account of his expedition, giving details of the coast and the tribes who dwelt on it, written probably by himself, was known to the ancients but is now lost. Eratosthenes (*c*.275–195 BC), librarian to Ptolemy III, king of Egypt, translated this account into Greek, but this work too is lost. Rufus Festus Avienus, who was proconsul for Africa AD 366, and an elegant writer of Latin, had a copy of the Greek version of Himilco's work and amused himself by rendering it into Latin verse. Of this Latin translation, written 850 years after the events it narrates, we have a fragment of some 4015 lines. These have been carefully published by Alfred Holder, under the title of *Rufi Festi Arieni Carmina*.

It should be noted that at the time of Himilco's expedition the Celts had not conquered Spain. Polybius and, following him, Strabo blame Eratosthenes for stating that the Celts held all Spain except Cadiz, which belonged to the

*Figure 3*: Himilco's voyage to the west coast of Europe *c.* 500 BC.

Carthaginians, and then omitting the Celts from his list of peoples occupying the west coast of Spain. There is, however, no contradiction here. Eratosthenes, writing *c*240 BC, correctly states that the Celts held dominion over the greater portion of the Iberian peninsula, but when copying the account of the voyage of Himilco, which relates to 500 BC, he does not find the Celts among the tribes occupying Iberia. We must conclude they had not yet conquered the peninsula. We know, however, from Herodotus that about fifty years after the expedition of Himilco the Celts had conquered the Iberian peninsula. The conquest therefore took place in the fifth century BC. We shall see they were subsequently conquered by the Carthaginians.

*Literature.* — An exhaustive list of the literature dealing with this voyage will be found in the edition of A. Holder, pp. xxxi-lxy, to which should be added Mr Elton's *Origins of English History,* pp. 20 *et seq.*

> By the Pillars of Hercules the land of Europe
>     nourishes
> On its level sward the generous Iberian race.
> These people touch the northern ocean's frozen
>     waters
> And scattered far and wide occupy the cultivated
> Land, near — too near — to the hardy folk of
>     Britain.
> Germania with her race of flaxen hair stretches
>     out her borders
> Along the woody limits of the Hercynian Forest.
>     From these same Pillars the snow-clad
>         Pyrenees rear
> Their swelling backs, and here the fiery Gaul
>     toils through life
> On a barren soil. Next the Po vomits forth
>     its sky-blue wave from its cavern.
> And with its mighty volume weighs down the
>     spreading plains.
> Here in olden times, along the wooded waters
>     of Heridanus,
> The tearful sisters wept the fallen Phaethon,
> And with their hands, now changed to branches,
>     beat their breasts.
> Here lies the land of Spain, and, beyond, the
>     rich Iberian soil:
> Yonder Tartessus towers aloft: and then the
>     Cempses toil, dispersing their people to the
>     foot of the rocky Pyrenees.
> And further on the eastern part holds the Tartesii
> And Cilbiceni. The isle of Cartare lies beyond,
> And this in former days . . . as is well known
> The Cempses held.
> The Cempses and the Saefes dwelt on the
>     towering heights
> That deck Ophiussa's land: and next to them
>     the fleet Ligurians,
> And the offspring of the Draganes, towards the
>     snowy north,
> Have placed their seats.

By the side of the Saefes lies the isle of Poetanion
With its broad harbour: then bordering on the
    Cempses
Come the tribes of the Cynetes: and then,
    where the starlit night
Marks the lofty limits of fertile Europe,
The Cynetic mountain range extends towards
The shores of the monster-tenanted ocean.
There flows the river Guadiana through the
    Cynetes
Furrowing their land . . .

Here ends the country of the Cynetes. The
    Tartesian
Land adjoins, whose sward is watered by the
River Tartesus.
Behind the Atlantic main an Ethiopian race,
    to wit,
The Hesperides, dwell; and here swells forth
    the broad back of Erythia,
And here again, that of the Sacred Mountain,
    for so the people name its slopes:
The broad land draws out its mountain chain,
    which rears its lofty head o'er
Wide-extending Europe: the coast produces
    metal
Giving forth veins of white-blue tin. The fleet
    Iberian
Of these parts oft speeds o'er the shallows in
    his swift bark.
And other coasts some distance off braving the
    north-wind's frosty blast
Tower o'er the waters with their mighty cliffs.
Twin cliffs are they, with their rich soil clothed
    in spreading sward, stretching to
Where in the turbid western sea the Rhine is
    hid, and where
Upon their bosoms dread bands of Britons live.
From there the ocean's foaming wave spreads out
    its tide,
And fills a gulf close by the main. Here a
    large chorus
Of female bands practise the orgies of seductive
    Bacchus:
Their sacred rites lengthen the night, and
    make the air vibrate
With their cries, while far and wide they stamp
    the earth in rapid dance.
Here stands the city, Gadir, once named
    Tartessus:
Here too are the Pillars of much enduring
    Hercules,
Abila and Calpe (that to the left of the land
    we speak of,
And nearest Libya is Abila). Swept by the

cold north blast
Unmoved they stand.
Here towers aloft the peak of the higher chain
(Known as Oestrymnin by an earlier race)
Whose pile with its rocky top
Bends straight towards the warm south wind.
Beneath its threatening brow
Yawns the Oestrymnic Bay before the inhabi-
    tants;
In which the isles, Oestrymnides, raise their
    heads.
Scattered they lie, and rich in the metals,
Tin and lead. A vigorous race inhabits them,
Noble-minded and skilful at their trades;
All along the mountain range business is carried
    on:
And in their well-known skiffs they widely
    plough the turbid sea
And the storm-pit of the monster-tenanted
    Ocean.
These folk indeed do not build their keels of pine,
Nor do they know how to fashion them, neither
    do they round their
Barks from fir, as is the common practice, but
    with wondrous
Skill they make each skiff with skins bound
    together,
And often in their hide-bound crafts, skim o'er
    the mighty deep.
      From here a two days' voyage the
        Sacred Island[6] lies
(For by this name the Ancients knew it),
Rich in green sward amid the waves it lies,
Peopled thickly by the folk of the Hierni.
Near them lies the broad isle of the Albiones.
The Tartesii were accustomed to trade even to
The boundaries of the Oestrymnides. Even
    the Carthaginians
And the people dwelling round the Pillars of
    Hercules
Were accustomed to make visits to these seas.
Four months would scarce suffice to make the
    voyage
There and back, as Himilco the Carthaginian
    had
Proved by sailing thither himself:
So sluggish are the breezes to propel the
    bark,
And so dead are the waters of the heavy sea.
Himilco tells us too, that there is much seaweed
In the whirls of that sea, which, like the osier
    withes,
Retards the bark: and yet, he adds, the
    ocean-bed
Is here of no great depth, and

Covered with but a scanty flow of water.
The wild denizens of the deep meet one on
  every side,
And monstrous fish swim among the slowly
  sailing
Barks: he who shall dare
To urge his bark beyond the Oestrymnic isles into
The waves, where 'neath the Great and Little
  Bear
The air grows rigid, shall reach the Ligurians'
  land,
Tenantless now, and wasted long by bands of
  Celts
And by many a bloody foray:
The Ligurians, put to flight, as fate so oft
  decrees,
Came to these parts, and 'mid the bristling
  thickets
Hold their own: on all sides here is barren
  rock,
Stern crags, and threatening mountains
Towering to the sky; and here these fugitives
Long passed their days in the rocky crevices,
Safe from the waves, for mindful of their former
  lot,
They feared the sea. But in after-days repose
  and leisure
— When security had bred courage —
Induced them from their mountain homes,
And led them to the sea-shore once again.
  Beyond the places we have just described,
A mighty gulf of wide-expanding sea runs down
Even to Ophiussa. The distance from this shore
  to the
Land-bound sea, where the waters, as I have set
  out
In another verse, embrace land known as Sardum,
Is a journey, to one on foot, of seven days.
The Ophiussian shore winds on a distance
As far as that we consider the isle of Pelops
In the Grecian land to lie from us: this once
  was called Oestrymnis,
For here the Oestrymnii tilled the soil;
But after many years a serpent made the
  cultivators flee
And gave its name to the desert tract.

1. Originally published by David Nutt, (London, 1911) [Ed.].
2. *Iliad*, ii, 484–7, and *Iliad*, ii, 867–8.
3. Narbon is now Narbonne.
4. Nyrax is probably modern Noriqire, but this is not certain.
5. Massalia is now Marseilles.
6. The old name for Ireland was *Eriu*. The copy of Himilco's work by Eratosthenes
   would represent the word by ιερ, which would suggest *Sacer*. The title Holy Island
   so frequently applied to Ireland thus originated in bad etymology?

## Chapter 6

# The Pretanic Background in Britain and Ireland[1]

## by Eoin MacNeill

The name Brittania for the island of Britain and the name Brittani for a people of Britain are not found before the invasion of the island by Julius Caesar, and are first found in the writings of Caesar himself and of his contemporaries, Catullus and Cicero. Catullus belonged to the circle of Caesar's intimacy. A brother of Cicero, Quintus, held a command under Caesar and accompanied Caesar in Britain, and from Britain the orator received letters written to him by his brother and by Caesar. The landing of a Roman army in that island was a grand event, certain and doubtless intended to make fame throughout the Roman world. In this way the newly adopted names Brittania and Brittani at once came into use and became established in the Latin language.[2]

The byform *Brittones* makes appearance later in Juvenal and Martial. It is probably a Gallic substitute for *Brittani*, perhaps favoured by the need of a distinct name.

The older name of the island, known to Greek writers, was Albion. This was also the name known to the Celts. In Irish it became Albu, with genitive Alban, and was the name of the whole island of Britain down to the tenth century. It became then restricted in application to the northern part of Britain, the realm of the Irish dynasty of Dál Riada, perhaps because this dynasty and its kindred in northern Britain were called Fir Alban in Irish, 'the Men of Albion', meaning the Irishmen of Albion. In like manner Gwyr y gogledd, 'the Men of the North', meant in Welsh usage 'the Cymry of the North'.[3]

The Greeks are certain to have learned the name Albion from the Celts of Gaul, with whom their colonies on the Gulf of Genoa had been in active intercourse long before the Romans obtained power in that region. Through the same medium the Greeks learned to call Britain and Ireland, with the smaller adjoining islands, 'the Pretanic Islands'. This name, which, after Caesar's invasion, took the form Insulae Brittanicae in Latin, means the islands of the Pretani. It has long been recognized that Pretani is the Gallo-Brittonic equivalent of the name which in Old Irish is Cruithin, representing an older 'Goidelic' name Qreteni. In later Irish usage, Cruithin is replaced by the adjectival derivative Cruithnigh, just as Lagin by Laighnigh, Saxain by Sasanaigh, Uluith by Ultaigh. The Irish equivalent enables us to identify the Pretani with the people who are now commonly called the Picts. Thus we learn that the Celts of pre-Roman Gaul regarded Britain and Ireland as 'Pictish islands'. A caution is necessary in regard of the use and precise signification of the name Picts. It comes to us from the Latin Picti. The Welsh form Picht also comes from Latin, and at a relatively late time through literature. Had it come by Cymric tradition from a Celtic origin, or by an early borrowing from Latin, it should have taken the form Peith. Picti, as the name of a people of Britain, is found for the first time in a Latin document of AD 297, the panegyric of the

Emperor Constantius. Thenceforward the name appears frequently in Latin writings, but, while the Roman occupation of Britain lasted, it appears to be applied indiscriminately to *all* the inhabitants of that part of Britain which lay to the north of the Roman military frontier. During the Roman occupation the Britons of the North were the dominant population of the region north of the Roman Wall from Tynemouth to the Solway Firth, and held power as far north as Stirlingshire and Perthshire. Yet, among the northern enemies who troubled the Romans and their British subjects by raids and attacks, no mention of the Britons by name is found. It is not credible that the northern Britons had not an active share in these hostilities and that the incursions which 'wearied' the Roman provincials were wholly or even mainly made by a people who dwelt still farther north and by whom a wide belt of territory which the Britons held must be traversed to reach the Roman frontier and to carry back the plunder of the Roman lands. The name Picti, therefore, in its earliest use may be taken to mean all the inhabitants of Britain north of the Roman frontier and not a particular ethnic division of these.[4]

It has been sought to derive the name Picti from a Celtic root *pik*, *qik*, meaning to carve or engrave. Such an explanation might hold good, if we had any evidence that Picti was a name given by the Celts of Britain or Ireland to the people who are named Picti in Latin. The known evidence indicates that neither Britons nor Irish knew that people to be so named except in Latin. The name is sufficiently explained as a byname given in Latin. It could well have originated among the Roman soldiers and as a term of depreciation. We may note that in Stapleton's translation, printed in 1565, of Bede's *Historia Ecclesiastica*,[5] Picti is invariably translated by 'Redshanks', which was an English byname for the Scottish Highlanders, showing how names given in this way can come to be used as proper appellatives. I think that Scotti and Góidil also became proper names in this way.

We have now to consider Caesar's division of the inhabitants of Britain into two distinct populations, native and colonist. His account of their geographical distribution is not based on his own or on Roman observation, for he and his forces did not penetrate to any part of the island outside of the zone of Belgic colonization. Hence his statement that the interior is inhabited by natives, the maritime part by colonists, is drawn from hearsay. It was probably heard by him in Gaul, and it appears to represent not so much the state of things at that time as a longstanding tradition. Modern archaeology represents a division of Britain, before the Roman occupation, into two zones, the 'Highland Zone' and the 'Lowland Zone', lying mainly to the north-west and to the south-east, respectively, of a line drawn between Devonshire and the middle of Yorkshire, or thereabouts, the Highland Zone being notably less permeated by late development than the Lowland Zone, therefore retaining in the mass a population less changed by invading elements. Nevertheless, in the process of colonization from over sea, there is likely to have been an early stage in which the colonists were distributed mainly along the seaboard, leaving the older population relatively undisturbed in the interior regions.

It must be evident that Caesar, when he ascribes certain distinctive customs to the Brittani, has in mind the population which he classes as native, and not the colonists. The colonists he considered to be in a large measure offshoots from states of Gaul whose names they continued to bear. If he had included these among the Brittani whose customs are described by him, his terms of description would have been different, for he had not observed these customs in any part of Gaul, and he would not have failed to remark and specify any large departure, on the part of the colonists, from the manner of life of their continental kinsfolk. Neither he nor any other writer of antiquity professed to have found painted skins or the polyandrous family among the continental Celts of any region: nor do these customs appear to have belonged to the insular Celts in their tenacious traditions. The Irish law of marriage, set forth in *Cāin Lānamna*, preserves in fulness a tradition derived from heathen antecedents, unmodified by the Christian and ecclesiastical law of monogamy, but its divergences from monogamy are not at all in the direction of polyandry. In short, painting the skin and polyandry were not Celtic customs.

These customs, too, were known to Caesar by report, not by actual observation, for he did not visit the Brittani of the 'interior'. In the case of both customs, we may judge that the reports which came to his ears were exaggerations, we may say caricatures of fact. The extracts cited above show how later writers, as Britain became better known to the Roman world, qualify Caesar's statement as regards the dyeing of the skin. Tacitus, who had more to tell and better sources of information regarding the Britons than any other known writer before Gildas, says not a word about dyeing the skin to produce a formidable show in battle or for any other purpose. So far as Caesar's statement had any basis in fact, it is likely to be in what Pliny tells, that married women, when they took part in certain religious rites, had their bodies artificially coloured.

On the matter of polyandry, likewise, the opportunities of fuller and more direct information did not induce later writers to confirm the statement of Caesar. The tradition indeed persisted for centuries, but the homeland of the alleged polyandry shows a remarkable aptitude to shift from more accessible to less accessible regions. Dio Cassius places it among the Maiatai, just beyond the northern bounds of Roman Britain. Solinus makes it a feature in the systematic communism of the distant Hebrides. St Jerome, writing at a time when the Britons were all accounted Christians, ascribes the custom, in a vaguely promiscuous form, to the still heathen Irish. This persistent tradition was not indeed without a foundation in fact. It was no singular case, that of two neighbouring but ethnically distinct populations, one of which esteems itself to be on a higher plane of civilization than the other: to seize upon divergent features in the other's way of life, to exaggerate these and to caricature them, is found entertaining, self-flattering, and therefore quite acceptable. When Caesar speaks of the distinctive customs of the people whom he calls Brittani, he tells what he has found to be commonly reported among the Celts of Gaul.

It will be recognized as an implication that the Celts of Gaul regarded Caesar's Brittani as an alien people, characterized by an inferior civilization. Let us recall to mind that the Celts of Gaul knew Britain and Ireland as 'Pretanic islands', that is, islands of the Pretani. For the name Pretani, Caesar substituted Brittani. The Brittani were a folk of no great prominence, inhabiting a part of Belgic Gaul between the Morini and the Ambiani, as Pliny shows, his testimony being corroborated by the persistence of their name, preserved by the village of Bretagne, near the mouth of the river Somme.[6] Near by in the territory of the Morini, was the port of Ition, where Caesar embarked his legions for Britain, and the Brittani were doubtless among the maritime peoples from whom he levied ships and supplies for the expedition. Like other Gallic states of which he speaks, they may have been represented by a colony of the same name beyond the Channel. It is possible that Caesar imagined their name to be a variant and more authentic form of the name Pretani.

The main point to be noted is that the known evidence enables us to date from Caesar's expedition, and not earlier, the use of the name Brittania for the island of Albion, and of Brittani for its inhabitants.

From the Celts of Gaul the Greeks learned that Ireland also was a Pretanic island, an island of the Pretani. Diodorus writes expressly of 'those of the Pretani who inhabit the country called Iris'. He says that these are reported to be man-eaters. Here we observe another trait of the caricature of an alien people on a lower plane of civilization. This part of the hostile Gallic tradition of the Pretani was still vigorous in the time of St Jerome, who could persuade himself that in his boyhood he had been an eye-witness of a party of Scotti enjoying a cannibal feast.

The chief conclusion to be drawn from these premisses is that, as late as the time of Julius Caesar, the Celts of Gaul regarded Britain and Ireland as countries having for their native and main population a people named Pretani, and that they held this people to be alien to them in race, differing from them in social structure, and living on an inferior plane of civilization. The evidence has been obscured by the substitution, in Latin writings following Caesar's lead, of the name Brittani for Pretani, the restriction of the substituted name to the people of Britain only, and its extension to comprise the latest Celtic colonies in Britain.

Modern writers have created a certain amount of illusion for themselves and others by adopting a precise use of the terms Brythonic and Goidelic, as though the adoption of these terms enabled us to recognize and distinguish ancient populations properly so named. 'Brythonic' is a gross anachronism in its very form, as much out of place as 'Yankeic' would be in a serious treatment of North American history. 'Goidelic' stands on a little better footing. I hold that 'Góidil' originated in a Cymric distortion of the name Venii, which in Old Irish takes the form Féni and denotes the land-owning freeman element of the people of Ireland.[7] The persistence of the second syllable of Góidel when a third syllable is added (as in Góidelu, Góidelaib, Góidelach) shows that the name, if it had existed in an earlier Irish form, must already have lost a syllable, and that 'Goidelic' simulates a spurious antiquity.

We have seen that, in the light of the statements by later writers, when Caesar says that 'all the Brittani' dye themselves in order to appear more formidable in battle, his statement is incredible. The later writers, too, vary so much from each other as to suggest that they are distant echoes of the fact, probably best represented by Pliny when he says that the women colour their skins for the purpose of taking some part in religious rites. More consistently preserved is the story of the Brittanic community of husbands and children. This means that, in the structure and nexus of the family, there was a population in Britain which differed fundamentally from the Celts and the other Indo-Europeans. Caesar's account contains in one part an obscurity which is in contrast to Caesar's habitual and careful clarity of expression and which may not be indeliberate: *qui sunt ex iis nati*, eorum *habentur liberi*, quo *primum virgo quaeque deducta est*. This should mean: 'those who are born of them (the various husbands) are held to be children of *those*, *where* the virgin was first married.' Instead of *eorum* one might expect *eius*, and instead of *quo*, *a quo*: 'children of him by whom the virgin was first married'. Caesar, however, may have recognized good reason for avoiding a statement in this form. He gives no information regarding the structure of the family among the Celts of Gaul, but it is likely that for them, as for the Celts of Ireland and Wales, the unity of the family extended to all the descendants of the same great grandfather, in popular phrase, to second cousins. This, in Ireland, was the *derbfhine*, the 'true kin', and for every child of the free class it was a matter of prime importance to himself, to his kinsfolk, and to all who might have relations with him involving legal rights or dues, that the *fine* or joint family to which he belonged should be known. Caesar's choice of pronouns may be held to signify that the children of a woman, irrespective of paternity, belonged to the kin to which she belonged at the time of her first marriage. This really means that legal kinship among Caesar's Brittani was decided by maternity and not, as in Indo-European custom generally, by paternity. It also implies that when a marriage was made the husband joined the kin of the wife, whereas in Indo-European custom the wife joined the kin of the husband.

Thus what is said of the structure of the family among the Brittani by Caesar, among the Maiatai by Dio Cassius, among the Ebudaci by Solinus, among the Scotti by St Jerome, has for a basis in fact the well-attested law or custom of succession, that is to say, of kinship, in the maternal line, which was a distinctive institution of the people whom we are accustomed to call the Picts; and in this we have corroborative evidence that the substitution of the name Brittani for the older name of the Picts, Pretani, is to be ascribed to Caesar himself.

The problem of the relations of the Picts, more properly called the Pretani, to the other ancient peoples of Britain and Ireland, has been the subject of much writing and has given rise to a variety of conclusions or rather of opinions. For the most part, the consideration of the problem has been vitiated by the notion that the Picts were specifically the people of unlimited geographical area, the northern half of Scotland, with a small outlying extension in the south-western part of Scotland, the region of Galloway.

The Picts of Galloway retain their identity as a distinct people just long enough to come into documentary history. We learn of their conversion to Christianity by St Ninian about the beginning of the fifth century. Irish tradition points to their monastery of Candida Casa as a centre of the monastic discipline during the fifth century. It was probably in this region of Picts that Palladius died within the first year of his mission to Ireland. St Patrick, in his letter against Coroticus, makes reference twice to 'the apostate Picts' who were associates in barbarity of that British prince. After this time they disappear from history. Bede records that in their country a bishopric was created for the Angles in his own time, sufficient evidence that a colony of the Angles had been established there. The region came successively under the power of the Scots from Ireland and of the Norsemen, and its population became known to both as a mixture of Irish and Norse, Gall-Ghaedhil. [8]

The Picts of northern Scotland are veiled in obscurity until St Columba comes among them in the third quarter of the sixth century. From first to last they are an unlettered people, their known use of letters being confined to a few inscriptions in imitation of the Britons and the Scots; and so they have left no written records of themselves. In the middle of the ninth century they came under the power of the Scots, and thenceforward their ethnic and national existence becomes merged. Yet they had achieved a real advance in power and relative prominence during the century that followed their decisive victory over the invading Angles in 685. The next turning point is appropriately recorded by the *Annals of Ulster* in 756: 'The ebb[9] of the reigning power of Oingus.' Before this time the same annals show the Picts pressing hard on the Scots of Argyle, whose power appeared to Adamnan to be declining in his own time.[10]

To the Greek writers, Ireland, as well as Britain, was a Pretanic island, as has been mentioned above, and this is sufficiently proved by strictly historical records and by the evidence of the oldest traditions preserved in writing.

In early Irish writings the people called by the Gallo-Brittanic name Pretani are named by the equivalent Irish word Cruithin. Two grades of the Cruithin are recognized, autonomous communities under dynasties of their own race, and subject folks under other dynasties.

The autonomous Cruithin are found for the most part in eastern Ulster, over a large range of territory extending from Loch Foyle to Dundalk Bay. There is evidence of the existence of seven, and possibly of nine, petty kingdoms of the Cruithin in this region as late as AD 563. An entry for that year, dated 562, in the *Annals of Ulster* records an event of great significance, the battle of Móin Dairi Lothair. The opposing parties were led, on one side, by 'seven kings of the Cruithin, with Aed Brecc at their head', and, on the other side, by a certain Baetán with two [kings of the] Cruithin in alliance with the Northern Uí Neill, who were 'hired with the reward of the Léi and Arda Eolairg'. The victory went to these allies, and the Uí Neill in consequence obtained a stretch of territory, held till then by the Cruithin, which extended on the western side of the river Bann from the Moyola river northward to Magilligan Point at the mouth of Loch Foyle.

After this reduction of territory the Cruithin, under two branches of the dynasty of Dál Araidhe, continued to hold territory in the present counties of Antrim and Down. In Antrim their territory in the seventh century extended from Loch Neagh northward to the sea between the mouths of the rivers Bann and Bush, and included Coleraine and 'the Liberties of Coleraine' which now form part of the county of Londonderry; also from the Bann eastward to the sea at Larne; but it did not comprise the north-eastern part of the county, forming the territory of Dál Riada, between the Giants' Causeway and Glenarm Bay. In Down the territory of the Cruithin comprised the baronies of Upper and Lower Iveagh and Kinelarty; the maritime part of this county belonged in the main to the territory of the Ulaidh, whose relations to the Cruithin demand special investigation. The Ulaidh also, until the eighth century, held the greater part of Louth county, but not the barony of Ferrard in the south. In the eighth century the dynasty of Conaille seems to have displaced the rule of the Ulaidh in this region, apparently by favour of the kings of Ailech and as a part of their policy to keep the Ulaidh in check.[11]

Dubhaltach Mac Fir Bhisigh quotes some ancient document: 'Of the Cruithin of Ireland are Dál Araidhi, the seven [subdivisions of the] Lóigsi of Leinster, the seven Soghain of Ireland, and every [branch of the] Conaille that is in Ireland.' In the altered tradition of his time and class, this statement appeared questionable, and Dubhaltach offers an explanation of it: 'How strangely the Gaedhil of the race of 'Ir took the name of Cruithin, by reason

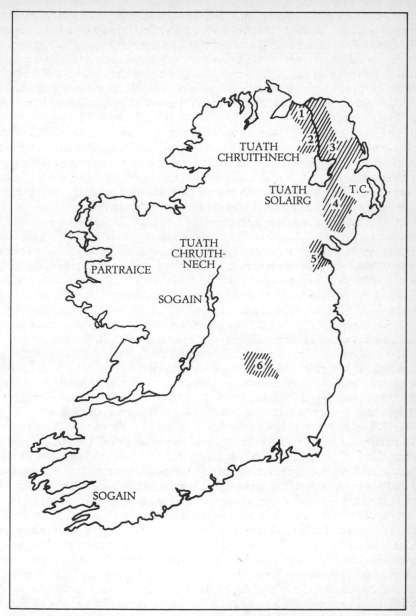

*Figure 4*: Explanation of the map — the shaded portions mark autonomous territories of the Cruithia (Picts), distinguished by numbers: 1 Arda Eolairg; 2 Lēi or Li — these came under the Northern Ui Néill from AD 563; 3 Northern Dál Araidi — the territory came under Ui Tuirtri, a sept of Airgialla, about AD 1000; 4 Southern Dál Araidi, remaining autonomous during the eighth, ninth and tenth centuries; 6 Lóigse (Leix), autonomous until the sixteenth century. The names printed in capital letters denote subject populations indicated in ancient writings to have been of Pictish origin. 'T.C.' is an abbreviation for Tuath Chruithnech, a section.

of the firm headship which they acquired over the Cruithin of Scotland!' It was the dynasty of Dál Riada, however, who acquired that headship, and they were not of 'the race of 'Ir' and did not take the name of Cruithin. The territorial scope of Dál Araidhe and Conaille has been explained above. The quotation implies that there were branches of the Conaille folk in various parts of Ireland, and *Onomasticon Goedelicum* shows one branch in Fernmag, that is, in Monaghan county, and another branch on the river Suilide, the Swilly, in Tír Conaill. The principal group of the Lóigsi held the territory named from them, in English form 'Leix', a portion of the county now so named, formerly Queen's County. Another branch, Lóigis Ua nEcnechglais, was seated near Arklow. The main group was ruled by a native dynasty from the earliest period until modern times.

The Soghain folk were seated on both sides of the river Suck in the present counties of Galway and Roscommon. They were also called Senchenél, 'the ancient kindred', implying that they were the ruling kindred of that region before it came under the rule of the Sept Ui Maini. Their displacement from territorial autonomy dates at earliest in the fifth century, since at that time the Sept Ui Maini branches from the royal kindred of Connacht and Tara. An account of their displacement is cited by Dubhaltach[12] and also by O'Donovan in a note to the *Book of Rights* (p.106), indicating a date towards the end of the fifth century. O'Donovan here calls their king, Cian, 'the Firbolg king of the district', but in this instance we must understand 'Firbolg' in its widest sense, meaning not Gaelic. In a poem on the Aithechthuatha (subject folks) of Ireland, preserved by Dubhaltach,[13] there is mention of 'the Ancient Kin of the old plain of the Soghain', who 'stretched eastward across the Suck'. Other branches of the Soghain are shown by *Onom*, *Goed*, in Mide (Westmeath, etc.) and Fernmag (Monaghan) and in the district of Benntraige (Bantry, Co. Cork), and their name is found (MUCOI SOGINI 'of the gens of Sogenos') in an ogham of East Muskerry (Co. Cork, Macalister, *Irish Epigraphy*, III, 153).

Beginning with the account, already cited, of the battle of Móin Dairi Lothair in 563, the *Annals of Ulster* contain various notices of the Cruithin by that name or the Latin equivalent Picti. Its seems not unlikely that the oldest Irish chroniclers were the first to make a specific identification of the Picti with the Cruithin or Pretani. The notices in the *Annals* for the most part have reference to the autonomous Cruithin under the dynasty of Dál Araidhe.

AD 607.[14] Death of Finchra Caech, son of Baetán among [or at the hands of] the Cruithin.

AD 628. *Bellum Feda Euin, in quo Mael Caich mae Seannail, rex Cruithne, victor fuit, Dal Riati ceciderunt.*

AD 644. *Locheni mac Fingin, ri Cruithne obiit.*

AD 645. *Guin Scannail mc. Bēcce mc. Fiachrach, regis Cruitne.*

AD 665. *Mael Caich mac Scannail di Cruithnib* ('of the Cruithin') etc. *obierunt.*

AD 680. *Combustio regum i nDun Ceithirnn .i. Dungal mac Scannail. rex Cruithne,* etc.

AD 681. *Bellum Ratha More Maighi Line contra Britones, ubi ceciderunt Cathusach mac Maele Duin, ri Cruithne,* etc.

AD 690. *Dal Raiti* (Dál Riada) *populati sunt Cruthniu et Ultu* (the Cruithin and the Ulaidh).

AD 707. *Canis Cuarani* (= Cú Chúaráin). *rex Cruithne, iugulatus est.*

AD 709. *Fiacra mac Dungaile apud Cruithne iugulatus est.*

AD 726. *Dub Da Inber mac Congalaigh, rex Cruithne, iugulatus est.*

AD 730. *Bellum inter Cruithne et Dal Riati in Murbuilgg, ubi Cruithni devicti fuerunt.*

AD 773. *Flathruae mac fiachrach, rex Cruithne, moritur.*

It is a matter of special significance that from AD 774 onward the name Cruithin and its Latin equivalent Picti cease in the *Annals of Ulster* to be written of the Irish population hitherto so named and are henceforth written only of the Picts of northern Britain. The dropping of the name does not correspond to any change in the population or in its rulers. People and dynasty remain undisturbed in the northern part of their territory until the tenth century, when the rulers are displaced by the Airgialla sept of Uí Tuirtri coming from the western side of Loch Neagh, and in the southern part until the English expropriations in the seventeenth century. It is only the fashion of naming that is changed. The title 'King of the Cruithin' is replaced by 'King of Dál Araidhe', that is to say, the name of the dynastic sept is substituted for the name of the ancient population. The title 'King of Dál Araidhe' is used twice before AD 774. In the annal of 616 (written 615) it is used of Mongán, who died in 625. This is the king of whom a saga [15] tells that he was a reincarnation of Find Mace Cumaill. In the annal of 698 (written 697) the death in battle is recorded of 'Aed Airdd, rex Duil Araide'. It is possible that neither Mongán nor Aed held the superior kingship of the Cruithin. We have seen that in the sixth century these formed a number of subordinate kingships under a principal king. In the fifth century one of their subordinate kings was Míliuce, to whom St Patrick had been a slave. Muirchu, in his life of St Patrick, through a prophecy attributed to the saint, shows that the kingship in the kindred of Míliuce, Dál Buain, had become extinct, and that the sept Dál Buain had been reduced to subject status before Muirchu wrote in the latter part of the seventh century: '*nemo de filiis eius sedebit rex super sedem regni eius a generatione in generationem; insuper et semen eius serviet in sempiternum.*' Muirchu knew the people of the regions bordering on the Ulaidh, and as far north as Sliabh Mis, where Míliuce ruled, by the name of Cruithin: '*relicta ibi navi apud Dichoin, coepit per terras dirigere viain in regiones Cruidnenorum,* [16] *donec pervenit ad Montem Miss . . . convertit cito iter suum ad regionem Ulutorum per eadem vestigia quibus venerat, et rursum pervenit in Campum* Inis ad Dichoin.'

From the evidences of autonomous communities of the Cruithin existing in the documentary period we are led to infer that indications of a subject population of the same origin should be forthcoming. In the chief document treating expressly of the subject communities, the Aithechthuatha, [17] the following are named —

Tuath Senchene(oi)l, 'the *tuath* (populus) of the Ancient Kin', in northern Uí Maini. They have been identified above with the Sogain of that region.

Tuath Chruithnech (this is the adjective corresponding to Cruithin) in Magh Aoi and in Magh Luirg, from Loch Cé to Bruigheol and to the Shannon. The extent indicated covers the north-eastern part of the Co. Roscommon, bordering on the Shannon and Co. Sligo.

Tuath Chruithen ('of the Cruithin') in the territory of the Ulaidh and in Magh Cobha. Here Magh Cobha represents the territory of Uí Echach Cobha or southern Dál Araidhe, and the two territories together form the present county of Down.

Tuath Buain in Dál Araidhe. A synonym of Dál Buain, the sept of Míliuce moccu Buain above-mentioned. Its inclusion among the Aithechthuatha explains 'serviet' in Muirchu's story of the prophecy by St Patrick. [18]

Tuath Nemluirg (Nebliarg, Nebluirg) in Airgialla from Glenn Rigi to Loch Erne and from Banna (Buaid) to Loch Febail. Instead of ocus 'and', the Book of Lecan has . i. 'id est', in correction of the preceding clause. I would read Tuath Eoluirg. The extent indicated is across Airgialla from east to west and also the district between Loch Foyle and the most northern part of the river Bann. This comprised Arda Eolairg, 'the forelands of Eolorg', part of the territory annexed from the Cruithin by the Northern Uí Néill as a result of the battle of AD 563. Tuath Eoluirg would thus denote the older population remaining in subjection to the Northern Uí Néill.

Tuath Chruithnech of the North, from the Sídán of Sliabh in Chairn to Loch Febail and from Bernus Tíre Aeda to Banna. The extent indicated appears to be that of the territory of Cenél Eoghain at a particular stage of its expansion, and to overlap in part the extent of Airgialla inhabited by Tuath Neblairg. Such overlapping is not likely to have been a feature of the tract as originally drawn up. Sliabh in Chairn may be the mountain now named Mullaghearn, near Omagh, in Tyrone. Loch Febail is Loch Foyle. Bernus Tíre Aeda is the Gap of Barnesmore on the boundary of the baronies of Tirhugh and Raphoe in Tír Conaill. Banna is the river Bann. A poem in the same volume (GT 77) on the topography of the Aithechthuatha names Tuath Eolairg for Eoghan oirdherc 'T. E. on [the territory of] famous Eoghan'. At the beginning of its list, this poem has 'Clan Chathraighe in the territories of the Cruithin, from which sprang Cairbre Cinn Cuit'. In the story of the revolt of the Aithechthuatha (GT 108), Cairbre is their leader. The barony of Cary in the north of Co. Antrim takes its name from the Cathraighe sept, and this barony formed part of the ancient territory of Dál Riada, ruled by a dynasty which is not accounted to be of the Cruithin. There can be no doubt, however, that the subject population there was of the same stock as the Cruithin of Dál Araidhe, whose territory adjoined that of Dál Riada on every side except the seaward.

The same poem names 'the tuatha of the Cruithnigh around Cruachain': 'the Cruithnigh were the pillars of Cruachain.' These are the same as the Tuath Chruithnech of Magh Ai in the prose tract aforesaid. Dubhaltach Mac Fir Bhisigh (GT 108) quotes from an older source a list of tribes of the Fir Bolg 'descendants of Genann': including among them the Craithentuath of Cruachain. This is important, as affording explicit evidence that the Fir Bolg of Lebor Gabála [19] comprising the descendants of Genann, are an artificial category in an artificial scheme, and are designed to provide a place for all the elements of the ancient population of Ireland other than the Góidil. We shall revert later to the curious account of the Cruithin in the scheme of Lebor Gabala.

Dubhaltach quotes on the same page another source (sliocht cle) in which the Cruithentuath of Cruachain is prominently mentioned. It will be shown that there is a general tendency in Irish genealogical lore to disavow or disguise an ancestry from the Cruithin stock. It is quite exceptional to find such an ancestry expressly claimed for an extant family. We find it in the Book of Ballymote 103b, col. 3, in a genealogical account of the families of the old territory of Corcu Ochlann, there called 'Na Tuatue', inhabiting a district between Cruachain and the Shannon eastward: 'Ua Guairican, do Chruithnechaibh doibb', 'those of the surname Ua Guairicán are of the

Cruithin stock'. It is thus evident from various testimonies that Cruachain, the ancient seat of the kings of Connacht, was surrounded by a subject population of the Cruithin, recognized as such during centuries of the documentary period.

It is therefore reasonable to think that a large element of the same ancient population persisted in other and remoter areas of Connacht. In view of the tendency above-mentioned, the silence of genealogical writings should not be taken as proof to the contrary. The Partraige folk inhabited an area around Loch Mask and westward to the coast. Their name consists of a Celtic element *rigion* added to the specific element *Part* — which is not Irish Celtic. [20] I have proposed to identify *Part* — as an eponym which is found in the form *Partha* in the genealogical account of the Cruithin. Indeed I think it likely that the name Partraige has supplied the genealogists with the name of this ancestor of the Cruithin, Parta or Partha. This would imply that the Partraige folk were known to the genealogists as a prominent and typical branch of the Cruithin stock. In corroboration of this view, Kuno Meyer drew my attention to genealogical statements that the Partraige and the Cruithin likewise were descendants of Genann. [21]

In Munster, and still more in Leinster, these being the regions of Ireland most open to the influx of migration from the Continent, we should not expect to find the Cruithin so permanent and persistent as in Connacht and Ulster. The instance of the Lóigse above-mentioned shows, however, that even in Leinster a community of the Cruithin could persist and could preserve its autonomy down to the modern period of English expropriations. The instance of the Soghain in Munster has been already cited. The story of the Déssi migration, dating from the middle of the eighth century, names among the migrant folks Celrige, descendants of 'Celer of the Cruithin'. [22] Their geographical position is not known. I hope to produce evidence in a sequel to this paper, showing a probability of a tradition of Cruithin origin, presented under a typical disguise, for a number of Munster septs.

Let us now consider the part assigned to the Cruithin in relation to Ireland by LG. The Cruithin, we read, were a branch of the Agathyrsi from Thrace, and were descendants of Gelonus, son of Hercules. This, with the story of their migration, appears already in a poem of Mael Muru, who died in 887. [23] It exemplifies the metamorphic effect of intrusive Latin learning in the treatment of Irish traditional origins, having its source in Virgil's epithet *picti Agathyrsi*, *picti Geloni*. The Cruithin, thus identified with the Picti, arrive in Ireland during the reign of Eremón, son of Mil, that is to say, a short time after the Gaelic conquest. Eremón did not allow them to settle in Ireland, but caused them to pass on to Britain. They had brought no women with them, and Eremón provided them with wives, but on this condition, that succession to kingship among them should come thenceforward by maternal not paternal descent. The fiction was adopted to explain the fact of matrilinear succession in the custom of the Picts.

No straining of critical judgement is needed to distinguish between a legend of this kind and authentic popular tradition. A recent French writer [24] imagines this legend to voice authentic tradition, particularly as regards the order in time of the Gaelic and Pictish migrations:

'*Mais pourquoi supposer que les Pictes ont précédé les Goidels? Pour une fois que* la tradition mythique irlandaise, *qui fait venir avant eux en Irlande la plupart des étrangers qu'ils ont reduits ou assimilés, les fait suivre, eux [c'est à dire, les Goidels], par* un autre peuple celtique [*les Pictes*], *quel besoin a-t-on de la corriger?'* (p. 255.)

The main feature demanding attention in this legend is the underlying postulate that the Cruithin are a people of Britain only and are not and have never been a people of Ireland. In view of the data collected above, which are probably a small part of similar data known to the authors and redactors of LG, the question arises, why is it that LG, designed to give an account of the peopling of Ireland from the beginning, nowhere expressly recognizes the existence of a Pretanic element in the population of Ireland. The true character of LG must be kept in view. It is an essay to construct a history of Irish origins in conformity with a scheme of world-history derived from Biblical and Latin sources. It is the work of many hands, moulded and recast during successive centuries, but always subject to that rule of conformity. Beyond doubt it embodies much of ancient native traditions. These traditions, however, in their native form, knew nothing of Genesis and Exodus, nothing of Eusebius and Orosius. A Procrustean process of lopping and stretching was necessary to fit them into their new frame. In many parts we can recover from other sources material of earlier date, and so, if it comes from tradition, closer to tradition than the form in which it is presented by LG. It is therefore a grave error to depend, as Hubert has done in the case in question, on LG for evidence of authentic tradition.

The incongruous story of the Picts in LG was known to Mael Muru, and may well have been invented by him. It was not known to the author or authors and redactors of the *Historia Brittonum*, reputed to be the work of Nennius. In this work the first inhabitants of Britain are of Trojan origin. Their story is purely of learned invention, a duplication and extension of Virgil's story of the origin of Rome. Next after these, 'after an interval of many years, not less than 900, the Picti came and occupied the islands which are called the Oreades. And afterwards from the islands they wasted many regions and occupied them in the northern part of Britain. And they remain there, holding a third part of Britain until the present day. *Last, however, came the Scotti from part of Spain to Ireland.*' Hence we may infer that the story of the Cruithin in LG was not in the older version of that work which is cited under the name of *Liber Occupationis* in the *Historia Brittonum*.

It is interesting to note that the rule of the Picts in Britain came to an end in the time of Mael Muru. Cinaed, king of the Scots in Britain, became king of the Picts also, probably about the year 850. He died 'king of the Picts' in 858. His daughter Mael Muire became wife of Aed Findliath, who was king of Ireland from 862 to 879. She died in 913. Mael Muru's poem refers expressly to the end of the Pictish *régime* in Britain, and to its lasting until the reign of Cinaed. His poem is the work of an author who had witnessed the disappearance of the Cruithin into a half historical and half legendary obscurity.[25]

It must then be evident that the story of the Cruithin, as it is told by Mael Muru and in an expanded form in LG and in the Irish version of HB does not represent Irish tradition. We may contrast it with the origin-story of Dál Cuinn, preserved in the manuscript Laud 610, and published without translation by Kuno Meyer in ZCP, vol. viii, p. 313. The language of this story and of the other 'tribal histories' as Meyer calls them, which accompany it, except the last of these, entitled *Senchas Airgiall*, which is of somewhat later date, belongs to the oldest period of Irish prose, AD 650 to 750. I have shown evidence that the accompanying synchronic lists were drawn up in 743, and Zimmer has dated a portion of the prose material about 750. This brings us back to a time when the Cruithin of Ireland are still known by that name in the *Annals*, and it brings us closer to authentic tradition than does any extant version of LG.

The story is based on what is likely to be the oldest version, as it is the simplest, of the legend of Míl of Spain. Míl is here ancestor, not of the Gaelic race in general, but only of the kin of the high-kings, Dál Cuinn, and of their congeners, the dynastic kin of the Dési, Dál Fiachach.[26] When Míl and his followers came to Ireland they find the Cruithin in possession of the country. A contest for sovereignty results in a compromise, the descendants of Míl and the kings of the Cruithin holding the sovereignty in alternation. This arrangement lasts until the time of Conn, who earns his byname Céichathach from the hundred battles fought by him against the Cruithin. The contest is maintained against these in many battles by Art, son of Conn, and by Cormac, son of Art. The headship of the Cruithin in opposition to Cormac belongs to Fiachu Aride, eponymous ancestor of Dál Araidhe. Cormac is driven out of Tara and seeks the aid of the king of Munster. With this help he returns and wins the decisive victory over the Cruithin at Fochairt. It is implied that the sovereignty of Ireland was held thenceforward by Dál Cuinn. 'By force,' the story says, 'they gained the sovereignty, and by force they hold it always.' The story also implies that the power of the Cruithin was centred at Emain. Fiachu Aride is king of Emain in the oldest Irish chronicle. This aspect of the case, in which Emain is the centre of a Pictish power, requires fuller consideration. For the present it is enough to observe that here, in a story older than any extant version of LG, the Gaelic invaders, when they came to Ireland, find it a Pretanic island, and it remains half Pretanic after the Roman conquest of Britain.

There are echoes of this tradition in the early part of the Annals of Inisfallen. 'Seven kings of the Pictish peoples (Cruithentuathaib) ruled over Ireland until Conn of the Hundred Battles came . . .'[27] The battle at Fochairt of Muirthemne was gained over the Cruithin and over Fiachu Araide by Fiachu Mullachlethan, son of Eogan, from Munster, and by Cormac Longbeard.'[28]

LG virtually denies the existence of a permanent Pretanic element in the population of Ireland at any time. We may connect this negative position with the disappearance of the names Cruithin and Picti from the *Annals of Ulster* after AD 774. Mael Muru's poem on the Cruithin ignores the Cruithin of Ireland. We have seen evidence that the Cruithin within strictly historical time inhabited the greater part of Ulster and were especially prominent in the eastern parts, yet the sagas of the Ulster Cycle are silent about them. All this brings us to think that before the end of the eighth century traditions of Pictish origin had come to be held in low esteem in Ireland, especially among the nobility and the literate. Let us recall the entry in the *Annals of Ulster*, 'the ebb of the power of Oingus' in 750, which marks a turning-point in the history of the Pictish realm in Britain. The fall of this realm was hastened by the arrival of the Norsemen, who quickly took possession of the northern and western islands of Scotland, and whose inroads on every side must have crippled the military power of the northern Pictland, of all regions the most exposed to this new and formidable enemy. A sense of racial hostility may have spread to Ireland from the long struggle between Scots and Picts in northern Britain, with such incidents as the expulsion of the Columban monks from Pictland in 717. If it were not for the transcription and citation of Irish documents written before the ninth century we might be led by LG and other late writings to imagine that Ireland was not rightly called a Pretanic island and did not continue in later times to be largely inhabited by people of Pretanic origin. In writings produced anew from about AD 800 onward there is a kind of conspiracy of silence in regard of the Irish Picts. In the synthetic scheme of the genealogies no place is accorded to them.

I propose to show that LG is not content with excluding the Picts from Ireland. It actually introduces an older legend or origin-story of the Irish Picts, but handles it in such a manner as to blot them out of existence before the favoured Gaelic race comes to Ireland.

In the artificial framework of LG, Ireland is inhabited by five successive populations, the people of Partholón, the people of Nemeth, the Fir Bolg, the Tuatha Dé Danann, and the Góidil. The scheme is drawn up in relation to accepted notions of Biblical chronology, and also, as I have shown elsewhere, in relation to accepted notions of world history derived from Latin histories. The beginning and the duration of the five colonies are timed so as to account for the estimated number of years between Noah's Flood and the missions of Palladius and Patrick. The writings of Bede on chronology and history obtained great authority in Ireland. Bede reduced the reckoning between the Deluge and the Christian era by more than a thousand years. Successive redactions of LG adopted different dates for the Gaelic invasion, the later redactions as a rule favouring earlier dates. Consequently, the chronology of the colonies in LG shows large variations. As far back, however, as the version cited and used by HB, the scheme is already fixed in one respect, and remains afterwards unchanged: the colonies of Partholón and Nemeth are each wholly exterminated and are followed by intervals during which Ireland is without inhabitants. These blank intervals belong to the artificial chronology of the scheme. When we examine in detail the story of Partholón's colony the artificial factor becomes fairly obvious. In the time of this colony the various arts and institutions of ancient civilization have their commencement in Ireland. All to no purpose, if Partholón's people are to perish utterly in a plague, the dead burying their dead in a single cemetery.

The people of Nemeth do not perish. They are driven out of every part of Ireland by enemies, the Fomori, who, strange to say, do not take possession of the country and have never inhabited it at any time, earlier or later. A remnant of Nemeth's people, the Fir Bolg, migrate to Greece, where they acquire their name, 'Men of Bags', from their employment in servile labour. Their descendants return to Ireland and form the colony of the Fir Bolg.

Our knowledge of the ancient civilizations of stone and bronze, derived from their finished products, is greatly augmented and, so to speak, vitalized when we come upon sites of their industry abounding in rejected fragments of their craft. For the study of LG and the associated scheme of the genealogical synthesis, certain manuscripts, and especially the *Book of Lecan*, contain material that is somewhat analogous to the leavings found on such ancient sites of industry. A collection of material of this kind is found in GT, and among its contents is a particular excerpt, printed and translated at p. 197. A second version is given on p. 198. The beginning is omitted from the second, the end from the first version. The second version is used by a redactor of LG in the *Book of Lecan* to supplement his exemplar; hence the omission of the beginning, which could not be reconciled with the scheme of LG. The language of this tract points to an original probably of the eighth century. The collocation and order of its contents, dealing with Partholón, Nemeth, the Fir Bolg, and the Tuatha Dé Danann, show that it was written as a commentary on an early version of LG, correcting this by citing alternative accounts. Especially interesting is its account of the Tuatha Dé Danann, whom it declares to be demons and to be still in existence, inhabiting the *sida* and holding communication with mortals.

According to this tract, Partholón and Nemeth (Nemed) were brothers, sons of Agnoman,[29] dwelling in Ireland at the same time, not separated, as in LG, by centuries. In this form of the legend, a plague coming upon Partholón's people could not leave Ireland uninhabited. The people of Nemeth are not driven out of Ireland. They engage in trade with the Greeks, exporting Irish earth in bags to be spread around cities for protection against venomous reptiles. 'They used to travel to the east and back with that commerce', and so they got the name of Fir Bolg. There was thus no separate invasion of Ireland by the Fir Bolg.

It will be seen that Partholón, brother of Nemeth, is ancestor of the Cruithin. Nemeth is ancestor of the Fir Bolg. Setting aside the Tuatha Dé Danann, shown in the same tract to be gods who were formerly adored, we see that the tract has in view an original population of Ireland consisting of Cruithin and others, not Cruithin, who are comprehensively called Fir Bolg.

The pedigree of Partholón in this tract is as follows: 'Mac Agnomain mc. Stairte mc. Thaet mc. Beim mc. Mair mc. Aireacht mc. Fortheacht mc. Iathacht mc. Iathfeth [= Japhet] mc. Nói [= Noah].' In HB, the pedigree of Alanus, ancestor of many European nations, is as follows: '*Alanus autem, ut aiunt, filius fuit Fetebir* [= Irish Fetheuir], *filii Ougomun, filii Thoi, filii Boib, filii Simeon, filii Muir, filii Ethagh, filii Aurthach, filli Eethet*[here follow seven names not found in the pedigree of Partholón above] . . . *filii Iovan, filii Iafeth, filii Noe.*'

Lebor Bretnach, p. 5, embodies an Irish excerpt entitled 'Do Bunad Cruithuech' ('Of the Origin of the Cruithnigh'). In this, the eponymous ancestor is Cruithne, and his pedigree is given as follows: 'Cruithne mac Cinge mc. Luchtai mc. Parthalón mc. Agnon mc. Buain mc. Muis mc. Fathecht mc. Iafeth mc. Noe.' Another version of the pedigree is also given, p. 23: 'Cruithne mac Ingu [Ingi, Inge, Cinge] mc. Luithe mc. Pairte [Partai, Parthaloin] mc. Istoreth mc. Agammain [Agnon] mc. Buain mc. Mair [Mais] mc. Faithect mc. Ianad [= Iavan] mc. Infeth.' The same pedigree, with merely scribal variations, is found in other manuscripts.

I take Partholón here to be an artificial extension of Parte, Parta, Partha, which should be the eponym of Part-rige. We find a somewhat similar extension of the eponym Cruithne in an interesting variant of the story of the Cruithin, showing perhaps the main basis of their story as it is given in LG. It is used by a redactor to supplement the story in L Bret (p. 9). Here the eponymous ancestor is Cruithnechan mac Lochit meic Ingi. It is he who founds the colony of Cruithentuath in Britain, and in consideration of obtaining wives for his men from the sons of Míl, he takes an oath by heaven, earth, etc., that rulership over the Cruithin shall ever shall come through mothers — *bad ó máithriv flaith ferro co bráth.*[30]

In the well attested fact that the maternal and not the paternal relation was the basis of the Pictish family and kindred, we may recognize the source of the accounts of polyandry and community of offspring among the older native populations of Britain and Ireland. In the case of those who were powerful and wealthy, kinship and succession based on the mother, in the absence of an ethical rule of monogamy, must have favoured a plurality of connections with men, as the ancient Celtic law, preserved, apparently unmodified by the Christian ethical rule, in the Irish law tract *Cáin Lánamna*,[31] favoured a plurality of connections with women. The children were common to a number of fathers in the sense that, being members of their mother's kin and not of their father's, they belonged no more to one of their mother's mates than to another.

This was not Celtic law and custom. It is the converse of what we find in *Cáin Lánamna*. Nevertheless there is evidence that it prevailed more or less in pre-Christian Ireland. The Ulster Saga-cycle is recognized to be a repository of pre-historic traditions. The sagas of this cycle contemplate a division of Ireland into five principal kingdoms. Each of these kingdoms should have had its own dynastic kindred, but the sagas show three of the five kingdoms ruled by three kings who were brothers, sons of one father. This should imply that two at least of the three came into kingship by 'marrying into' the dynastic kindreds of their kingdoms. The case is clear in one instance. Ailill is one of the three brothers, son of Russ Ruad, a Leinster king, and becomes king of Connacht by marrying Medb, daughter of a king of Connacht. Táin Bó Cuailngi, in the *Book of Leinster*, begins with a dramatic scene, in which Ailill and Medb hold a dialogue of significance. Ailill opens the dialogue with a sententious pronouncement, as if he had come to the conclusion of a piece of silent thinking: 'A woman of worth is one who is the wife of a man of worth.' He expresses the Celtic and the Indo-European idea. Medb at once repudiates it. In a woman's way she comes from the general to the particular, from the abstract to the concrete, and applies the king's remarks to herself. She was as worthy a woman before ever they were married as she was that day. Moreover, it was she who accepted him for a mate, not he who accepted her. It was she who laid down the conditions of their union. The chief condition was one that turns the light upon what was said of old by the Celts of Gaul about the marital life of the Pretanic Islands. Medb accepted Ailill for a husband, she says, because she understood that he was free from jealousy. She gave him ample opportunity for proving his virtue in this respect. 'I have never been,' she proclaims, 'without a paramour.' The narrative tells these things, as the Gallic Celts told similar things to Caesar, in the language of another civilization. In the times to which the story has reference it was not a matter of jealousy and paramours, but simply of maternity as the bond of kinship and consequent succession to rulership and ownership through the maternal line. Medb was queen in Cruachain — Medb of Cruachain she is often called, and the tracts on the Aithechthuatha show that, as late as the eighth century, Cruachain was still the centre of an old Pretanic population: *Tuath Chruithnech imm Chruachain*.

Traces of reckoning kinship through the mother have been recognized in names belonging to the saga tradition, such as Conchobur mace Nessa (son of a mother Ness), Conaire mace Messe Buachalla, etc. A late instance in the documentary period is Dallún mace Móire, towards the end of the sixth century. An ogham of the ancient territory of Ciarraige Luachra (Macalister, *Irish Epigraphy*, II, 55, no. 71) is read: DUMELI MAQI GLASICONAS NIOTTA COBRANORa.[32] If NIOTTA (from něōtos = Latin *něpōtis*) is the genitive of the word which is *nia* in Old Irish and is explained to mean 'sister's son', this inscription shows a blending of the two traditions. Dameliios is his father's son, but the kin to which he belongs is that of his father's mother.

The unified framework of the Irish genealogies is closely associated with the artificial synthesis of LG, both forming parts of the same synthetic scheme of history. Like LG, the genealogical synthesis shows abundant evidence of redaction in successive periods and not always consistently, for the modifications point often to a number of remodellers working independently of each other. Like LG, the genealogical synthesis ignores and virtually denies the existence of a permanent Pretanic population in Ireland. The pedigrees of Cruithne, eponymous ancestor of the Cruithin, which are quoted above, are expressly and exclusively made relative to the Cruithin of northern Britain.

In the genealogical synthesis, pedigrees are traced to four sons of Míl, namely, Eremón, Eber, Ir, and Aireach (or Erech[33]) Februad. There are strong indications that an earlier form of the scheme existed in which pedigrees were traced only to Eremón and Eber, and that Ir and Aireach Februad are relatively late additions to the legend.

LG (BB 39a 41) gives a list of the wives of the sons of Míl, without mention of Ir or Erech. The story of the landing of the sons of Míl in Ireland is duplicated, partly in identical words. In the first telling (BB 39a 19), Ir is not mentioned. In the second telling (39b 5), he dies before the landing is effected. A third version (40b 13) has Arannán instead of Ir in the same incident. In the poem *Génair Pátriac* ('Fiacc's Hymn'), the Irish nation is called *tuatha Hérenn*, *Scotaib, tuath Herenn tuatha Fénc*, and *maicc Emir maicc Erimon* 'sons of Eber and Erem (Eremón)'.

Two versions of LG 'record nine sons of Míl, only two of whom left children, Erimon and Eber' (Van Hamel, *On Lebor Gabala*, ZCP X 167).

It is to be inferred that Ir and Aire Februad are relatively late genealogical inventions. All the dynastic families of the Irish Cruithin are among the descendants of these two in the genealogies, and in some cases the same pedigree has alternative versions leading up to Ir and Aire Februad. That is to say, at some stage in the growth of the genealogical synthesis a place was found for the Cruithin of Ireland among the descendants of Míl, but two accounts of their descent from Míl were independently invented.

Thus we see that in the annals, before the end of the eighth century, the Cruithin of Ireland ceased to be called by that name or by its Latin equivalent, Picti; in the ninth century (before 887), in a poem on the Cruithin, Mael Muru recognizes only the Cruithin of northern Britain; in LG likewise, the Cruithin of Ireland are ignored and those only of Britain are recognized; the sagas of the Ulster Cycle are seemingly unaware of the existence of a large population of Cruithin inhabiting the greater part of Ulster. In face of the evidence of the earlier annals and of various other early documents cited above, we cannot well avoid the conclusion that a common accord was reached among the literati, probably in the second half of the eighth century, to ignore the separate identity of the Irish Cruithin.

Such an accord is likely to have been preceded and evoked by a change of sentiment among the patrician element of that stock. Between this element and the Gaelic nobility in Ireland there was no boundary and no distinction except that of traditional origin. Moreover, the older Pictish law of succession in the maternal line must have reduced the factor of traditional origin to something merely nominal. It facilitated intermarriage of Pictish women of rank with men of the dominant Gaelic race, and this inevitably led in time to the prevalence of the whole Gaelic tradition among the Picts themselves. Before the laws of Ireland began to be written in the seventh century, and probably long before, succession in the paternal line was law for all Ireland. There can be little doubt that the Picts of Ireland had once a language of their own, distinct from Gaelic, but it had been displaced by Gaelic at so early a time that no memory of its existence can be traced in writing. No sentiment of racial opposition between Picts and Gaels survived in the documentary period. It was otherwise in Britain. There the Gaels were newcomers, encroaching and aggressive, there was a distinction in language, and the Pictish law of succession was still operative. The victory of the Picts over the Angles in 685, as Bede, a contemporary and keenly interested witness, has fully recognized, was a turning point in the history of northern Britain. It broke the prestige of the Angles, stopped their career of conquest which had lasted over a century and a half, and forced them to abandon large stretches of territory. It enabled the Picts to regain much territory and to become an aggressive power. Already in the lifetime of Adamnan, as he himself testifies — he died in 704 — the Irish kingdom in Argyle had 'come under the power of its enemies', and the great abbot of Iona bewails its downcast state. The hostile relations between Picts and Scots in Britain at this period must have had a sensible influence in Ireland, especially in north-eastern Ireland where dynasties and a nobility preserved their continuity from Pictish antecedents and where the cultural influence of Iona radiated strongly. In short, at the very time when a reconstruction of Irish prehistoric antiquity was the main theme of writers in the vigorous springtime of a new literature, we can trace a complex of causes and conditions operating to merge the Irish Cruithin in a common Gaelic origin, in harmony with a visible tendency to reduce the diverse racial elements of tradition to an artificial unity comprising all who were of free status in the population of Ireland.

The conclusions to be drawn from the evidences brought together above may be stated in summary.

1  As late as the time of Julius Caesar, and probably much later, the main native population of Britain and Ireland was known to the Celts of Gaul by the name Pretani. From the Gallic Celts, Greek writers learned to call Britain and Ireland the Pretanic Islands. The name Pretani is represented in the earliest Irish documents by Cruithin, which is translated by the Latin Picti, and is the specific designation of the ethnic group now called the Picts.

2  For Pretani, Julius Caesar substituted Brittani or Britanni, which was probably the name of a subdivision of the Belgae in Gaul, perhaps also in Britain. For Albio or Albion, the older name of Britain, Caesar substituted Brittania (Britannia), and thenceforward in Latin writings Brittani became the name of the people of the island in general. From Brittani the by-form Brittones also came into use.

3  Where Caesar ascribes to the Brittani the distinctive customs of dyeing the skin and of forming polyandrous unions, he relates what came to him by report and with exaggeration from the Gallic Celts regarding the Pretani, whom they looked upon as an alien race of inferior civilization.

**4** The name Picti is of Latin origin, based on the reported custom of dyeing the skin. In Latin writings of the time of Roman Britain, Picti has no specific ethnic application, but is said indiscriminately of all the inhabitants of Britain to the north of the Roman frontier.

**5** The earliest Irish traditions and historical records justify the ancient description of Ireland as a Pretanic island. The negative position of later writings is deceptive.

## ABBREVIATED REFERENCES USED THROUGHOUT

Holder = *Altceltische Sprachschatz*, by Alfred Holder. The quotations in Greek and Latin are taken mainly from this work, where they are found under proper names (Brittania, etc.) in alphabetical order, and under each article in chronological order.

GT = *Genealogical Tracts*, *I*, ed. by T. Ua Raithbheartaigh for the Irish Manuscripts Commission.

ZCP = *Zeitschrift für Celtische Philologie*.

LG = *Lebor Gabála*, 'The Book of Invasions'. The older versions remain unpublished. For a comprehensive study of their growth and contents, see Van Hamel 'On *Lebor Gabála*', ACP, vol. X.

LBret = *Lebor Bretnach*, ed Van Hamel for the Irish Manuscripts Commission. It contains the *Historia Brittonum* ascribed to Nennius, the Irish version of the same work, and a critical study based on both.

HB = *Historia Brittonum*, text in LBret.

GPM = A collection of Irish genealogical poems edited by Kuno Meyer, *Uber die alteste irische Dichtung, I*.

1. Originally published in vol. 63 of the *Journal of the Royal Society of Antiquaries of Ireland*, 1933 [Ed.].
2. The form in which the name first became current in Roman usage was either *Britanni* or *Británi*, shown by the metrical use of the name in the poetry of Catullus, Propertius, Virgil and Horace. In general Latin usage however, perhaps from the outset, *Brittáni* is well attested. See Holder.
3. It seems to have become quite a fixed fashion for English writers to miscall these 'the Britons of Strathclyde'. Strathclyde, represented approximately by the modern Lanarkshire, was a small fraction of the territory held by the northern Britons during centuries of the post-Roman period. An amusing outcome of the misnomer is the name Strathclyde extending from the Clyde into northern Lancashire on maps designed to give special historical information.
4. In corroboration, see Wade-Evans, *Welsh Medieval Law*, pp. xxviii, xxix, and especially the quotation, p. xxix, from the Peniarth MS, 118, *nid oedhynt y Picteit onyd yr hef Gymry* 'the Picts were none other than the old Cymry'.
5. See the recent edition in Loeb Classical Library.
6. Holder.

7. Whitley Stokes has explained *Gwynedd*, old Welsh *Guined*, as the equivalent of Irish *Féni*. The name, denoting a large part of Wales, should have arisen from the Irish migrations to Wales during the later years of the Roman occupation of Britain. *Guined* in popular usage, as applied to the *Féni*, would have been changed to *Guidel*, modern Welsh *Gwyddel*, whence Irish *Góidel*. At all events, the evidence goes to show that *Góidel* does not replace *Féni* in Irish usage until the latter part of the seventh century at earliest. The early lawtracts have always *Féni*, never *Góidil*, and the poem *Génair Pátric* uses *tuatha Féne* as a name for the people of Ireland.

8. The name Galloway seems to be a mere transformation of the Latin Galvia, which in turn represents Gallaibh, still the name of that region in Scottish Gaelic. The index of the *Annals of Ulster* translates Gall-Goidhil by 'Galloway', but the Gall-Goidhil of the ninth century in those *Annals* have no such geographical limitation.

9. In Irish, *aithbe*, mistranslated 'end of the reign of Oengus'.

10. *Vita Columbae*, III, 5, end of chapter.

11. See my note in the *Journal of the Royal Society of Antiquaries of Ireland*, vol. LVII, 1927, p. 155.

12. GT 73.

13. GT 75.

14. The dates in this list of excerpts are to be corrected by the addition of one year to each.

15. Edited by Kuno Meyer in *The Voyage of Bran*.

16. *Crunneorum* in the Brussels MS. Read *Cruithneorum*.

17. Four versions in GT 69, 107, 114, 119.

18. The same sense is implied in the text by the scribal addition (*Tuath Buain*) *dimbuain* 'not lasting', a play of words.

19. Van Hamel's view (ZCP, X, 188) that the Fir Bolg of LG represent 'the lower mythology' seems to me quite untenable. If mythological elements are present in the story of the Fir Bolg, the same is true of the story of the Góidil.

20. *Rigon* from OI *rige*, meaning 'kingship' not 'a kingdom'. Names containing the component *-rige*, *-raige*, must have primarily denoted ruling septs, but the usage was extended before the documentary period, e.g. in *Bolgraige* 'Bag-folk'.

21. GT 88, 178. At p. 88 is a list of other septs and tribes in various parts of Connacht, which are said to be descendants of Genann.

22. *Eriu*, III, 139.

23. LBret, 10.

24. Hubert, *Les Celtes et l'Expansion Celtique*, 1932. The author died before the publication of his book.

25. In this poem the adjective form *Cruithnig* begins to replace the older name *Cruithin*.

26. The descent of Dál Fiachach from a brother of Conn is likely to be a genealogical fiction, and the inclusion of Dál Fiachach among the descendants of Míl would in that case belong to a redaction of the older legend. Cormac being a grandson of Conn, his kinsmen, the chiefs of the Dési, grandsons of Fiachu Suigde, brother of Conn, could not be at the head of a distinct people in Cormac's time and in hostility to Cormac, as they are in the story of the Dési migration (*Eriu*, III, 135, and *Anecdota from Irish Manuscripts*, I, 15).

27. Folio 7v col. 2.

28. 8r, col. 1. The MS has *Criunu* for *Cruithniu*, an attempted correction by a scribe who had the alternative story of the battle of Crinna in mind.

29. A scribal form of Ogomun 'the unifying', common ancestor of Cruithin, Fir Bolg, and Goidil, and also, in HB, of the Britons and various continental nations. This piece of cosmic genealogy is of Irish origin: '*hanc peritiam inveni ex traditione vetcrum*' (LBret, p. 7). The Irish genealogists use *peritia* in this limited and concrete sense.

30. The redactor did not understand that this was a way of explaining the Pictish law of succession. He adds ineptly: 'And so rule over the Cruithin belongs ever since to the men of Ireland' — a *régime* established first by Cinaed mac Ailpin in the ninth century.
31. *Ancient Laws of Ireland*, Vol.II.
32. A fracture, of extent not stated, leaves the letter or letters at the end doubtful. If the space permits, I suggest as a possible reading COBRANORigas, the first component being a variant of the word which is written *comrann*.
33. *Erech* is found both as nominative and genitive. The original nominative is likely to have been *Aire*. *Aire Februad* should mean 'worthy-strong nobleman'.

# PART THREE:
# THE FIRST STORIES —
# MABINOGI AND SAGA

The Art of Story was as important to the Celts as their religion — with which it may be said to interact. The position of the bard and story-teller was recognized as equally important by his position in the court — seated close to the side of the lord, served a tender portion of meat before even the hero.

Thus, in the long dark nights of winter, with the wind howling around the wooden halls or turf bothies of the warriors, stories of love, adventure and magic were woven. Many, alas, are now lost to us forever, or exist only in a fragmentary or corrupt state. But many others we have, in particlar the great collection of stories from the Welsh collected under the title of The *Mabinogion*. These were first edited by Lady Charlotte Guest in the nineteenth century, and still read as well as any modern translation — though several now exist which supersede Lady Guest's in details and accuracy. None are printed here because of their general availability, but all who are concerned with the Celtic myths are urged to seek them out. [1]

An account of the mythic background to the *Mabinogion* itself, by the great Celtic scholar Edward Anwyl, whose work has still to be bettered in many cases, opens this section, and is followed by a story from the equally fascinating Irish sagas, 'The Second Battle of Moytura', in the shortened translation of T.P. Cross and C.H. Slover. A vast number of Irish texts remain untranslated, and until they are all before us it is hard to judge the intricate mythology they contain. Theirs is a wildness and otherworldliness which exceeds even that of the Welsh. Further examples will be found in Parts Five and Six.

1.  See also: *Mabon and the Mysteries of Britain* and *Arthur and the Sovereignty of Britain* by Caitlín Matthews (Arkana, 1987 and 1989) for a full discussion of the *Mabinogion*.

# Chapter 7
# Myth in the Mabinogion [1]
## by Edward Anwyl

In dealing with the *Mabinogion* for the present purpose, it is clear at the outset that the romances of Owein and Luned, Peredur, and Geraint and Enid, which are substantially identical in narrative with Chrétien de Troyes' *Yvain*, *Perceval*, and *Erec et Enide*, whatever Celtic elements they may ultimately be found to contain, are in a different category from tales such as The Four Branches of the Mabinogi, Macsen Wledig, Lludd and Llevelys, and Kulhwch and Olwen. In these latter stories there are such numerous and obvious allusions to Welsh topography that it is not unreasonable to suppose that some of their material, at any rate, is derived from local legend and folklore, and that when they were written they were composed by men who were in touch with living medieval narrative. In spite of the fact that, as literary works of imagination, they contain elements derived from the fancy of their writers, yet, the more they are examined, the more clearly they seem to contain traces of strata of narrative; these traces, though often very faint, are yet linked to the pre-Christian ideas of Wales, and so cast some rays of light on the early religious conceptions of the principality.

The main stories which form the *Mabinogion* are linked together in the bonds of a common tradition, probably as the professional stock-in-trade of the bards and storytellers of Wales. The agglomeration of narrative in question as a more or less united whole reveals itself in other portions of literature connected with medieval Wales, in Geoffrey of Monmouth, in the Welsh Triads, in the older body of Welsh poetry, and in the various legendary allusions that are scattered through the works of the Welsh medieval poets. The stories connected with the various characters are not everywhere identical, nor are they combined together everywhere in the same proportions; but the body of narrative as a whole is substantially the same, and the connections in which it is found lead forcibly to the view that its basis is a professional tradition, handed down and developed by the bards, who were officially connected, in Wales as in Ireland, with the courts of the Welsh princes. The very term *mabinogi*, as Sir John Rhys has pointed out, appears to mean 'the stock-in-trade of a "mabinog" or apprentice-bard'. That the bards of Wales combined with their purely poetic functions those of storytellers is clear from statements in the Four Branches themselves, as, for example, the reference in Math ab Mathonwy to Gwydion and Gilvaethwy's skill in storytelling, when they went as bards to the court of Dyfed.

From the purely bardic circles the stories in question appear to have passed into the Welsh monasteries and abbeys, and it is in MSS copied in these institutions that they have come down to us. Before arriving at their present form, they appear to have undergone several recensions, both oral and literary, and many of their earlier features have doubtless been obscured in the process.

In their present form, as the writer has endeavoured to show in articles in the *Zeitschrift für Celtische Philologie*, they reflect, in their references to gradations of rank and to homage, the ideas of feudal times, and, as he has suggested later in the *Celtic Review*, the collection as a whole in its final form shows signs of being arranged on a chronological basis (parallel to that of Geoffrey of Monmouth's *Historia Regum Britanniae*, where we seem to have stories of the pre-Roman, the Roman, and the post-Roman periods. It is even possible that the compilation of the collection as a whole was suggested by the desire to supplement and to rival the work of Geoffrey of Monmouth. The stories of Lludd and Llevelys and of Macsen Wledig have all of them the appearance of being supplementary to Geoffrey's narrative, and with Lludd and Llevelys and Macsen certain of the narratives of the Four Branches are linked both topographically and otherwise. The three chief literary recensions which the Four Branches of the *Mabinogi* appear to have undergone before reaching their present form appear to be those of Gwynedd (Western North Wales), Dyfed (Western South Wales), and Gwent (Eastern South Wales). The first recension may have been made at Clynnog or Beddgelert in Carnarvonshire, the second at Whitland or Talyllychau (Talley) in Carmarthenshire, and the third in one of the large abbeys of Glamorgan or Monmouth, possibly in the Benedictine Priory of Monmouth itself. There are several linguistic points of contact between the Gwentian recension of the Four Branches and the Welsh versions of the Chrêtien romances, and, consequently, it may well be surmised that they are products of the same literary school. According to Mr Egerton Phillimore, the story of Kulhwch and Olwen probably reached its present form at Talyllychau in Carmarthenshire; but, before reaching that form, it has clearly undergone a process of development similar to that of the Four Branches, though probably not in the same districts. With some of its oldest strata the present writer has dealt in his article in the *Celtic Review* on 'Wales and the Ancient Britons of the North'. In the case of the Four Branches it is probably to the Gwentian recension that the story belongs of Gwri Wallt Euryn and Teyrnon Twryf Vliant. As for Gwri, however, it is not impossible that a story originally associated with Caerlleon (Chester) and the Wirral promontory of Cheshire, called in Welsh Cil Gwri (the retreat of Gwri), has, owing to the identity of the two names, been transplanted into Gwent into association with Caerleon-on-Usk. The local connection of Teyrnon with Gwent shows itself clearly in the name Llantarnam, anciently known as Nant Teyrnon (the brook or valley of Teyrnon). The transplanting of stories from one district to another is one of the chief difficulties in the way of a thorough analysis of all ancient documents, and the *Mabinogion* in this matter is no exception.

In the earliest or Gwynedd recension the majority of the stories are topographically connected with Carnarvonshire and Anglesey and with the adjoining parts of Merionethshire. This recension shows traces of stories from the Dee Valley, especially from the neighbourhood of Llangollen and the Hirae-thog district, relating to Bran and his family. From some of the allusions in the Gogynfeirdd poetry, we know that Gwynedd (Western North Wales) bore the name of Bro Beli (the land of Beli), while Eastern North Wales was called Bro Bran (or 'y Vran vro'). It is not improbable that the conception of the rivalry of the families of Beli and Llyr (the father of Bran), which is implied in the framework of the Four Branches, reflects the rivalry that existed at one period between the two districts in question, and something of this tradition has passed into Geoffrey of Monmouth's account of the feud between Belinus and Brennus. It is from the eastern portion of North Wales that the name Matholwch (also known as Mallolwch) comes; the name being found, according to Mr Egerton Phillimore, in that of Caer Vallwch (= Vallolwch) in Flintshire. Closely linked to the Gwynedd recensions of the Four Branches are the stories of Macsen Wledig and Lludd and Llevelys. In some genealogies Macsen is represented as the father of Peblig and Raglan, the saints of Llanbeblig and Llanfaglan, the two parishes of Carnarvon. Perhaps it might not be inopportune here to mention that both Beli and Llyr were associated with the sea. Llyr (the Irish *Ler*, gen. *Lir*) is in Welsh a common noun meaning the sea, while the name Beli, in its association with the sea, survived in the expressions Biw Beli (the cattle of Beli) for the waves, and Gwirawt Veli (the liquor of Beli) for brine. In the story of Macsen Wledig, Macsen is said to have conquered the Isle of Britain from the sons of Beli, and to have driven them 'upon the sea', an evident allusion to their connection in popular legend with that element. In the story of Math ab Mathonwy, the fortress of Aranrot, daughter of Beli and Don, is accessible over the sea; and it is therefore not unlikely that Beli and his family were associated in the popular mind with the sea and its islands.

In the Four Branches of the *Mabinogi* as we now have them, there is no reference to Arthur, but this is probably due to an attempt in their latest recensions at a chronological treatment. In the Book of Taliessin, as well as in Kulhwch and Olwen, which give the bardic body of legend in a less clarified form, Arthur is made to associate freely with the 'men of Caer Dathyl', Pwyll, Pryderi, Taliessin, and others. In Kulhwch and Olwen, Arthur is even said to have been related to the men of Caer Dathyl (i.e. the Don family) on his mother's side, a statement which is probably an echo of ancient Arthurian legends in Arfon.

The question now arises, in view of these various recensions, whether there are any portions of the *Mabinogion* in which traces are visible of pre-Christian religious ideas; and the writer suggests that such traces may be safely looked for in connection with the following features.

1  The existence in these stories of aetiological myths.

(a) Myths explanatory of certain place names. The value of these is that they seem to spring, in some cases at any rate, from living medieval folklore, and so may, through their association with definite place names, go back in some of their features to a remote antiquity. There is here the possibility, as in local folklore generally, that stories and explanations may be handed on from generation to generation, containing strata of ideas that were psychologically and sociologically natural under the earlier conditions, but which could hardly have been spontaneously invented at a later stage, owing to their incongruity with the later psychological and sociological situations. The place name stories of the Four Branches have been discussed by Sir John Rhys in various articles, and by the present writer in the *Zeitschrift für Celtische Philologie*. In the Four Branches, they relate mostly to Gwynedd, Ardudwy, Dyfed, and Gwent; in Macsen Wledig they relate to Gwynedd. In Lludd and Llevelys to Gwynedd, in Kulhwch and Olwen to Dyfed, Baullt, Ewyas, Erging, and Gwent. It is impossible to enter here into an exhaustive account of these place name explanations, but it is worthy of mention that there is a marked interest shown in some of them in the sea, the element which probably played a prominent part in the religious conceptions of the Welsh coast population.

(b) Aetiological myths explanatory of games, proverbial expressions, Triads, etc. In the *Mabinogion* we have, for example, the explanation of the game 'Broch ygkot' (a badger in a bag); 'A vo penn bit pont' (let him who is a head be a bridge); numerous explanations of Triads and the like. In the case of traditional practices and expressions, there is always a possibility that, like the practices and expressions themselves, certain stories connected with them may survive. The analysis of stories of this type is often delicate and tentative enough; but occasionally a passing reference, for example, to such a significant date for the old Celtic year as the First of May (Calan mai) may give a clue to the earlier *milieu* in which the story was evolved. In the account of Teyrnon Twryf Vliant's mare, and of the feud between Gwythur and Gwyn fab Nudd for Creurdilad, the reference to the first of May is perhaps an ancient feature.

2  Certain of the ideas embodied in the *Mabinogion* and closely connected with religious and kindred conceptions. The chief of these conceptions is that of Annwfn, the Welsh other-world. This is first mentioned in connection with Arawn, one of its kings, whose home is said to have been there situated. It is clear from the picture of Annwfn here given that it was regarded as a kind of counterpart of this world, containing, like this world, countries and kingdoms. For example it contains, besides Arawn, another king, Havgan, with whom Arawn is at war. It is clear, too, that the inhabitants of the lower world were thought to have access to this world, and to be engaged in similar pursuits, such as fighting and hunting. In the story of Pwyll the dogs that are mentioned as belonging to Arawn are probably those still known in Welsh folklore as Cwn Annwfn. In this story Annwfn is regarded as more advanced in civilization than the upper world, inasmuch as it is from Annwfn that certain of the boons of civilization, such as swine, are said to have come. It is interesting to note the prominence given in this narrative to swine, a trait which suggests that at an older stage Welsh folklore was greatly preoccupied with them. We know that among the Celts there was a god Moccus (Welsh Moch), and we know too that the men of Pessinus did not eat swine. It cannot be said, however, that in the inscriptional allusions to Celtic religion the pig holds a prominent place. Yet it is not impossible that, in these references to swine in the *Mabinogi* and to Arthur's hunting of the Boar Trwyth in Kulhwch and Olwen, we touch a very ancient stratum of folklore. Again, we find closely associated with Annwfn the ideas of change of form and magic. Probably Celtic religion regarded the denizens of its other-world as possessing powers much greater than those of the men of the world above, though these powers may not have been regarded as greater physically. Thus the conception of Annwfn appears to be related to the conception, so prevalent in Celtic countries and elsewhere, of local δαιμόνια, whether viewed singly or in groups, who had the power of influencing the life of the world above. That Annwfn played an important part in Welsh medieval folklore we clearly see from the allusions to it in the poetry of Dafydd ab Gwilym (fourteenth century), who even alludes to the summer as 'going to Annwfn to rest for the winter'. The allusions to Annwfn in Welsh medieval poetry and in Dafydd ab Gwilym are of importance, as showing how living the idea of it was in the folklore of the time.

Another point that comes to view in the folklore of the *Mabinogion* is that the older conception of Annwfn appears to have been, not that of one homogeneous other-world, but rather that of a number of local other-lands, not necessarily all related to the upper world in the same way. Caer Aranrot, for example, appears to have been regarded as an island, and certainly in the *Book of Taliessin* some expeditions to Annwfn are regarded as having been made in ships, as for example, in Prydwen, the ship of Arthur. In the *Book of Taliessin* Annwfn is expressly stated to have been 'beneath the world' (is eluyd); but other allusions suggest a view of it as being on the same plane as the countries of the upper world, and accessible not simply by sea, but by land. In the story of Kulhwch and Olwen, Arthur is represented as going thither by an expedition to the North. All these considerations lead to the belief that the primitive conceptions of the Celts implied a number of other-lands varying in character and situation and not simply an other-world. This earlier conception is in some respects not unlike that of the fairy lands of Welsh folklore of modern times. In the story of Math ab Mathonwy it is not improbable that Math himself and Gwydion were originally on the same plane as Arawn rather than on that of Pwyll and Pryderi, and were, in the original story, represented as dwellers in a local Annwfn rather than as inhabitants of the upper world. Their close association with magic and with such a spot as Caer Aranrot suggests that their narrative was originally of this kind. The story of Ysbaddaden Bencawr also suggests that it had a similar origin, and it may well be considered whether some of the magical sections of the Arthurian legend itself may not have had similar sources.

Another type of story which seems to have affinities with early folklore in the matter of Annwfn is that of Rhiannon. There are certain features connected with this story, which suggest that it contains matter of a very ancient kind. For example, the association of Rhiannon as a rider with a horse, and the further association of her son Gwri Wallt Euryn with horses, raise the question whether Rhiannon herself may not once have been a kind of deity like Epŏna, a goddess in the form of a mare. The allusion also to the mare of Teyrnon, which foaled every year on the First of May (the beginning of the second half of the Celtic year), suggests forcibly the idea that there may at one time have been an attempt to explain the growth of summer by the rebirth, from a divine mare, of the spirit of vegetation in the form of a foal. The great Earth-Mother may well have been herself represented as a mare, since it does not in the least follow that she, while regarded as a mother, would be represented in human form. The year's period of gestation of a mare would also help this conception. In the older conception Gwri Wallt Euryn may not have been regarded as human at all, but simply as a foal. That similar stories were found in Wales is suggested by the local story of Castellmarch in Lleyn, where the original owner March is said to have had horse's ears. In view of the fact that Rhiannon's father's name was Heveyd, it is not impossible that one form of her story came from the Radnorshire (Builth) zone, the name of Radnorshire in Welsh being Maesyfed, that is 'Maes Hyfeidd', the plain of Hyfeidd. In one of the poems of the *Myvyrian Archaeology*, Elfael in Radnorshire is called 'Bro Hyfeidd', 'the land of Hyfeidd'. The search for local other-lands in the *Mabinogion* may thus be very fruitful for the student of Celtic religion, and the same method may with advantage be pursued in the study of Irish legend, and even in that of Arthur himself.

3 The existence among the heroes and heroines of names which are undoubtedly survivals of divine names from the pre-Christian period. The

*Figure* 5: 'Two sorceresses capture and bind two warriors' by *Beatrice Elvery*.

most obvious of these names are those ending in -on. This ending in the older form was -ŏnos for gods, -ŏna for goddesses. Among the most authentic names of Celtic deities there are several instances of this type, as, for example, Măpŏnos, Epŏna, Sīrŏna, Dămŏna. In the *Mabinogion* we find several examples of names of this formation, such as Mabon (Măpŏnos), Modron (Mātrŏna), Rhiannon (Rīgantŏna), Teyrnon (Tigernŏnos), Amaethon (Ambactŏnos), Gofannon (Gobannŏnos), Gwydion (Vītiŏnos). To this type possibly belong also the curious forms Blathaon, Afaon, Amathaon, Ffaraon, where it is probable that a 'g' has vanished between the 'a' and the 'o'. A name like Geirion (unless it be Gāriānus) might also be referred to this type. To this type may also possibly be referred such a name as Dreon Lew (Ox. Mab. 302, 19), Eidon Vaur Vrydic (107, 29), Gamon (109, 3), Gwryon the father of Hunabwy (110, 8), Banon, given also as Panon, (108, 3, 138, 22). The river name Gwrangon, found in the Welsh name of Caer Wrangon, Worcester, is also probably of this type. The root here is probably 'Gwrang' (youth). The name Cynon is undoubtedly of this type, too, and also Godybrion or Gotyvron in the name Gwynn godybrion (Gwynn beneath the water). The place of dogs in the ancient Celtic religion is well worthy of separate investigation.

It is probably to this type, too, that we are to refer the name Saranhon (107, 25), and with this name we may compare the river name Taranhon (the Thunderer), a river in Montgomeryshire. Another type of name that is of a religious significance is that which corresponds clearly to a name prominent in Irish legend, for example, Llyr to Irish Lor, Bran to Irish Bran, Manawyddan to Irish Manannan, Nudd to Irish Nuada, Lleu to Irish Lug (with a difference of vowel gradation), Ellyll to Irish Ailill. In the case of Nudd we know the proto-Celtic form Nodens, or Nodons, from an inscription at Lydney, while the corresponding form Lludd probably goes back to Lodens or Lodons. Nudd may have meant 'mist', since the derivative 'nudden' is still used for 'mist' in some of the dialects of South Wales. The name Llyr is undoubtedly that of a sea-god, like Neition (the swimmer), a name, however, which does not occur in the *Mabinogion*. A name like Bran (raven) suggests the survival of animal deities in the form of birds, as well as of other animals. There may be also a hint of such a survival in the terms Adar Rhiannon (the birds of Rhiannon), while the fabulous creatures whose names had become proverbial, such as Carw Rhedynre, Cuan Cwm Dawlwyt, y Twrch Trwyth (or Trwyd in pure Brythonic), Mwyaleh Cilgwri, Eog Llyn Lliw, Eryr Gwernabwy, and Gast Rymi, may have been originally worshipped. Proverbial names such as these may well be very ancient. With the fabulous birds of Rhiannon may be compared the fabulous birds of Gwendoleu, mentioned in the Triads (Ox. Mab. 303, 24). Possibly Gwalchmei (the Hawk of May) and Gwalchhaued (the Hawk of Summer) are names of this type. There may be also some suggestion of a similar kind in the name Gwrgi (Man-dog), such as Gwrgi Garwlwyt, Gwrgi Gwastra, and Gwrgi Seueri. The fabulous monster, Cath Paluc, and the others that Arthur is represented as hunting, may well have been at one time revered deities in certain localities. The same is also possible in the case of the fabulous stag mentioned in Peredur (245–6), though here the romance narrative is too remote from any definite local folklore to make it possible to attach to it any clear mythological significance. In the *Mabinogion* there are no names of the same type as Arthen (Artogĕnos), which might be due to this order of ideas, but in Welsh place names several names of this type are to be found. The proper names of the *Mabinogion* fall into various types, but an analysis of them in respect to formation and structure falls beyond the scope of the present work. At the same time, attention may be called to the type of name like Pryderi, Blodeuwedd, which had a distinct significance at the time when they were given.

**4** The survival of reflections of the grouping of deities on the basis of a matriarchal rather than of a patriarchal family. In the Four Branches of the *Mabinogi* the most conspicuous instance of this is the Don family, which contains certain names that have an undoubtedly religious significance, such as Amaethon (Ambactŏnos) and Gofannon (Gobannŏnos). Another instance of the same type is Modron, the mother of Mabon (Măpŏnos). We find the same phenomenon in Irish legend as, for instance, in the case of Conchobar mac Nessa. The name Modron (i.e. Mătrŏna) is clearly of a religious significance, and has a link of connection with Gaul, since it is the origin of the river name Marne. This vein seems to be distinctly fruitful for the study of the earlier groupings of Celtic religion.

**5** The conception of man's relation, whether active or passive, in relation to the future. As passive he receives omens (coelion), some of which come to him accidentally, while others come by deliberate search. In the latter category were those obtained through fire, and the Welsh name for a 'bonfire' is still 'coel certh' (a sure omen). The idea of omens appears but to a slight degree in the *Mabinogion*, though we know from the *Black Book of Carmarthen* that it was prevalent in medieval Wales, and that omens were derived, for example, from sneezing. In the *Mabinogion*, however, there comes to view a conception which is more important from a religious point of view than this, namely, the idea that one person could influence the destiny of another by the process called 'tyngu tynghed' (the swearing of a destiny). Evidently we have here a kind of verbal sympathetic magic, which probably belongs to an ancient cycle of ideas, of which the *Mabinogion* preserve in their present form only a few passing traces.

**6** In close conjunction with the latter conception — that of 'góidonot' (witches). The precise significance of this name is uncertain; but it seems to suggest from the narrative that they were belligerent women, whose weapons were not merely magical. The stories concerning them are more interesting sociologically than religiously in the *Mabinogion*; but they are indirectly valuable for the latter purpose, since they suggest the possibility of survival in legend of reflections of older sociological conditions. Of the same type are the allusions found in fairy-tales to the fairy dislike of iron. It is a very delicate task to trace out with certainty these sociological survivals; but all folklore contains them, and it is because they consist so largely of local folklore that this aspect of the *Mabinogion* is one that has to be continually kept in view. It is remarkable that the allusions to struggles with witches should appear above all in the Arthurian legend, both in the *Black Book of Carmarthen* and in the *Mabinogion*, while in the Four Branches they are not to be found.

**7** The conception of magic. In dealing with this aspect of the *Mabinogion* it is necessary to distinguish between magic as the favourite machinery of popular medieval narrative, and magic as a real belief that had a religious bearing. In the former sense it is much more characteristic of the purely Welsh tales than of the Chrétien romances. In Dyfed the great magician is Llwyd fab Cilcoed (the Irish Liath mac Celtchair), while in Gwynedd it is Math ab Mathonwy and Gwydion who are the chief characters of this type. From the fact that in Irish, as well as in Welsh, Liath mac Celtchair was famous as a magician, it is impossible not to believe that here we have a survival from an early Celtic period of a belief in beings with superhuman magical powers. Moreover, there appears to have been a similar belief as to the existence of races of superhuman acuteness, for example, the Coranyeit (possibly = the Pigmies) who are mentioned in Lludd and Llevelys. The characteristics of these and that of Math ab Mathonwy are so much alike, and the topographical allusions in the stories are so clearly akin, that it is not unnatural to regard them as belonging to the same zone of ideas, and we know from the proper names of the Don-series that they are in several cases religious in their connections. From these and similar data we may gather that Celtic religion held the belief not only in individual beings of superior powers, but also in tribes and other social groups of this kind. It was probably with tribes of this kind that the Celtic other-lands were peopled, and there is no suggestion in the *Mabinogion* that the inhabitants of these other-lands had anything necessarily to do with the spirits of the dead. In the case of Llew Llaw Gyffes the spirit of Llew takes the form of an eagle, and it is not at all improbable that the conception of a spirit as obtaining a winged form, whether during life or death, was fairly common.

Such are some of the considerations which appear to the present writer in regard to the *Mabinogion*, when critically studied as a valuable document for the study of Celtic religion; though, as already stated, the number of modifications and recensions which the stories have undergone make it necessary to use them for this purpose with the utmost care.

1. Originally published as 'The Value of the Mabinogion for the Study of Celtic Religion' in *Transactions of the 3rd International Congress for History of Religion* (Oxford University Press, 1908) [Ed.].

# Chapter 8
# The Second Battle of
# Mag Tured (Moytura)[1]

The central heroic tale of the group dealing with the Tuatha De Danann and the so-called Mythological Cycle is 'The Second Battle of Mag Tured'. The text, though not so early in date as most of the stories of the Ulster Cycle, still preserves much of the rugged strength and directness for which the older tales are admired. It also exhibits something of the rough exaggerated humour of the earlier texts. The diversity of material, the repetitions, and the contradictions all go to show that the story as we now have it is a compilation made up of a number of independent narratives.

The Tuatha De Danann lived in the northern isles of the world, learning lore and magic and Druidism and wizardry and cunning, until they surpassed the sages of the arts of heathendom. There were four cities in which they learned lore and science and diabolic arts, to wit Falias and Gorias, Murias and Findias. Out of Falias was brought the Stone of Fal, which was in Tara. It used to roar under every king that would take the realm of Ireland. Out of Gorias was brought the Spear that Lug had. No battle was ever won against it or him who held it in his hand. Out of Findias was brought the Sword of Nuada. When it was drawn from its deadly sheath, no one ever escaped from it, and it was irresistible. Out of Murias was brought the Dagda's Cauldron. No company ever went from it unthankful. Four wizards (there were) in those four cities. Morfesa was in Falias: Esras was in Gorias: Uscias was in Findias: Semias was in Murias. Those are the four poets of whom the Tuatha De learnt lore and science.
    Now the Tuatha De Danann made an alliance with the Fomorians, and Balor grandson of Net gave his daughter Ethne to Cian son of Diancecht, and she brought forth the gifted child, Lug.
    The Tuatha De came with a great fleet to Ireland to take it from the Fir Bolg. They burnt their ships at once on reaching the district of Crocu Belgatan (that is, Connemara today), so that they should not think of retreating to them; and the smoke and the mist that came from the vessels filled the neighbouring land and air. Therefore it was conceived that they had arrived in clouds of mist.
    The first battle of Moytura was fought between them and the Fir Bolg; and the Fir Bolg were routed, and a hundred thousand of them were slain, including their king Eochaid son of Erc.
    In that battle, moreover, Nuada's hand was stricken off — it was Sreng son of Sengann that struck it off him — so Diancecht the leech put on him a hand of silver with the motion of every hand; and Credne the brazier helped the leech.
    Now the Tuatha De Danann lost many men in the battle, including Edleo son of Alla, and Ernmas and Fiachra and Turill Bicreo.
    But such of the Fir Bolg as escaped from the battle went in flight to the Fomorians, and settled in Arran and in Islay and in Mann and Rathlin.

*Figure 6*: 'Partholon, the first king of Ireland' by *Vera Bock*.

A contention as to the sovereignty of the men of Ireland arose between the Tuatha De and their women; because Nuada, after his hand had been stricken off, was disqualified to be king. They said that it would be fitter for them to bestow the kingdom on Bres son of Elotha, on their own adopted son; and that giving the kingdom to him would bind the alliance of the Fomorians to them. For his father, Elotha son of Delbaeth, was king of the Fomorians.

Now the conception of Bres came to pass in this way:

Eri, Delbaeth's daughter, a woman of the Tuatha De, was one day looking at the sea and the land from the house of Maeth Sceni, and she beheld the sea in perfect calm as if it were a level board. And as she was there she saw a vessel of silver on the sea. Its size she deemed great, but its shape was not clear to her. And the stream of the wave bore it to land. Then she saw that in it was a man of fairest form. Golden-yellow hair was on him as far as his two shoulders. A mantle with bands of golden thread was around him. His shirt had trimmings of golden thread. On his breast was a brooch of gold, with the sheen of a precious stone therein. He carried two white silver spears, and in them two smooth riveted shafts of bronze. Five circlets of gold adorned his neck, and he was girded with a golden-hilted sword with inlayings of silver and studs of gold.

The man said to her: 'Is this the time that our lying with thee will be easy?'

'I have not made a tryst with thee, verily,' said the woman. But they stretched themselves down together. The woman wept when the man would rise.

'Why weepest thou?' said he.

'I have two things for which I should lament,' said the woman. 'Parting from thee now that we have met. And the fair youths of the Tuatha De Danann have been entreating me in vain, and my desire is for thee since thou hast possessed me.'

'Thy anxiety from these two things shall be taken away,' said he. He drew his golden ring from his middle-finger, and put it into her hand, and told her that she should not part with it, by sale or by gift, save to one whose finger it should fit.

'I have another sorrow,' said the woman. 'I know not who hath come to me.'

'Thou shalt not be ignorant of that,' said he. 'Elotha son of Delbaeth, king of the Fomorians, hath come to thee. And of our meeting thou shalt bear a son, and no name shall be given him save Eochaid Bres, that is Eochaid the beautiful; for every beautiful thing that is seen in Ireland, whether plain or fortress or ale or torch or woman or man or steed, will be judged in comparison with that boy, so that men say of it then ''it was a *bres*'''

After that the man went back again by the way he had come, and the woman went to her house, and to her was given the famous conception.

She brought forth the boy, and he was named, as Elotha had said, Eochaid Bres. When a week after the woman's lying-in was complete the boy had a fortnight's growth; and he maintained that increase till the end of his first seven years, when he reached a growth of fourteen years. Because of the contest which took place among the Tuatha De the sovereignty of Ireland was given to the boy, and he gave seven hostages to Ireland's champions, that is, to her chiefs, to guarantee the restoring of the sovereignty if his own misdeeds should give cause. His mother afterwards bestowed land upon him, and on the land he had a stronghold built, called Dun Brese. and it was the Dagda that built that fortress.

Now when Bres had assumed the kingship, the Fomorians — Indech son of Dea Domnann, and Elotha son of Delbaeth, and Tethra, three Fomorian kings, laid tribute upon Ireland, so that there was not a smoke from a roof in Ireland that was not under tribute to them. The champions were also reduced to their service; to wit, Ogma had to carry a bundle of firewood, and the Dagda became a rath-builder, and had to dig the trenches about Rath Brese.

The Dagda became weary of the work, and he used to meet in the house of an idle blind man named Cridenbel, whose mouth was out of his breast. Cridenbel thought his own ration small and the Dagda's large. Whereupon he said: 'O Dagda! of thy honour let the three best bits of thy ration be given to me!' So the Dagda used to give them to him every night. Large, however, were the lampooner's bits, the size of a good pig. But those three bits were a third of the Dagda's ration. The Dagda's health was the worse for that.

One day, then, as the Dagda was in the trench digging a rath, he saw the Mac Oc coming to him. 'That is good, O Dagda,' says the Mac Oc.

'Even so,' says the Dagda.

'What makes thee look so ill?' said the Mac Oc.

'I have cause for it,' said the Dagda; 'every evening Cridenbel the lampooner demands the three best bits of my portion.'

'I have a counsel for thee,' said the Mac Oc. He put his hand into his purse, took out three crowns of gold, and gave them to him.

'Put these three gold pieces into the three bits which thou givest at close of day to Cridenbel,' said the Mac Oc. 'These bits will then be the goodliest on thy dish; and the gold will turn in his belly so that he will die thereof, and the judgment of Bres thereon will be wrong. Men will say to the king. "The Dagda has killed Cridenbel by means of a deadly herb which he gave him." Then the king will order thee to be slain. But thou shalt say to him: "What thou utterest, O king of the warriors of the Fene, is not a prince's truth. For I was watched by Cridenbel when I was at my work, and he used to say to me 'Give me, O Dagda, the three best bits of thy portion. Bad is my housekeeping tonight.' So I should have perished thereby had not the three gold coins which I found today helped me. I put them in my ration. I then gave it to Cridenbel, for the gold was the best thing that was before me. Hence, then, the gold is inside Cridenbel, and he died of it."' The Dagda followed this advice, and was called before the king.

'It is clear,' said the king. 'Let the lampooner's belly be cut open to know if the gold be found therein. If it be not found, thou shalt die. If, however, it be found, thou shalt have life.'

After that they cut open the lampooner's belly, and the three coins of gold were found in his stomach, so the Dagda was saved. Then the Dagda went to his work on the following morning, and to him came the Mac Oc and said: 'Thou wilt soon finish thy work, but thou shalt not seek reward till the cattle of Ireland are brought to thee, and of them choose a heifer black-maned.'

Thereafter the Dagda brought his work to an end, and Bres asked him what he would take as a reward for his labour. The Dagda answered: 'I charge thee,' said he, 'to gather the cattle of Ireland into one place.' The king did this as the Dagda asked, and the Dagda chose of them the heifer which the Mac Oc had told him to choose. That seemed weakness to Bres: he thought that the Dagda would have chosen somewhat more.

Now Nuada was in his sickness, and Diancecht put on him a hand of silver

with the motion of every hand therein. That seemed evil to his son Miach.
Miach went to the hand which had been replaced by Diancecht, and he said
'joint to joint of it and sinew to sinew,' and he healed Nuada in thrice three
days and nights. The first seventy-two hours he put it against his side, and it
became covered with skin. The second seventy-two hours he put it on his breast
. . . That cure seemed evil to Diancecht. He flung a sword on the crown of his
son's head and cut the skin down to the flesh. The lad healed the wound by
means of his skill. Diancecht smote him again and cut the flesh till he reached
the bone. The lad healed this by the same means. He struck him a third blow
and came to the membrane of his brain. The lad healed this also by the same
means. Then he struck the fourth blow and cut out the brain, so that Miach
died, and Diancecht said that the leech himself could not heal him of that
blow.

Thereafter Miach was buried by Diancecht, and herbs three hundred and
sixty-five, according to the number of his joints and sinews, grew through the
grave. Then Airmed opened her mantle and separated those herbs according
to their properties. But Diancecht came to her, and he confused the herbs, so
that no one knows their proper cures unless the Holy Spirit should teach them
afterwards. And Diancecht said 'If Miach be not, Airmed shall remain.'

So Bres held the sovereignty as it had been conferred upon him. But the
chiefs of the Tuatha De murmured greatly against him, for their knives were
not greased by him, and however often they visited him their breaths did not
smell of ale. Moreover, they saw not their poets nor their bards nor their
lampooners nor their harpers nor their pipers nor their jugglers nor their fools
amusing them in the household. They did not go to the contests of their
athletes. They saw not their champions proving their prowess at the king's
court, save only one man, Ogma son of Ethliu. This was the duty which he had,
to bring fuel to the fortress. He used to carry a bundle every day from the Clew
Bay islands. And because he was weak from want of food, the sea would sweep
away from him two thirds of his bundle. So he could only carry one third, and
yet he had to supply the host from day to day. Neither service nor taxes were
paid by the tribes, and the treasures of the tribe were not delivered by the act
of the whole tribe.

Once upon a time there came a-guesting to Bres's house, Cairbre son of
Etain, poet of the Tuatha De. He entered a cabin narrow, black, dark, wherein
there was neither fire nor furniture nor bed. Three small cakes, and they dry,
were brought to him on a little dish. On the morrow he arose and he was not
thankful. As he went across the enclosure, he said:

> Without food quickly on a dish:
> Without a cow's milk whereon a calf grows:
> Without a man's abode in the gloom of night:
> Without paying company of story-tellers, let that be Bres's
>     condition.
> Let there be no increase in Bres.

Now that was true. Nought save decay was on Bres from that hour. That is the
first satire that was ever made in Ireland.

Now after that the Tuatha De went together to have speech with their
fosterson, Bres son of Elotha, and demanded of him their sureties. He gave
them the restitution of the realm, and he was not well-pleased with them for
that. He begged to be allowed to remain till the end of seven years. 'That shall

be granted,' said the same assembly; 'but thou shalt remain on the same security. Every fruit that comes to thy hand, both house and land and gold and silver, cows and food, and freedom from rent and taxes until then.'

'Ye shall have as ye say,' said Bres.

This is why they were asked for the delay: that he might gather the champions of the fairy-mound, the Fomorians, to seize the tribes by force. Grievous to him seemed his expulsion from his kingdom.

Then he went to his mother and asked her whence was his race. 'I am certain of that,' said she; and she went on to the hill whence she had seen the vessel of silver in the sea. She then went down to the strand, and gave him the ring which had been left with her for him, and he put it round his middle-finger, and it fitted him. For the sake of no one had she formerly given it up, either by sale or gift. Until that day there was none whom it suited.

Then they went forward till they reached the land of the Fomorians. They came to a great plain with many assemblies. Tidings were demanded of them there. They replied that they were of the men of Ireland. They were then asked whether they had hounds; for at that time it was the custom, when a body of men went to an assembly, to challenge them to a friendly contest. 'We have hounds,' said Bres. Then the hounds had a coursing-match, and the hounds of the Tuatha De were swifter than the hounds of the Fomorians. Then they were asked whether they had steeds for a horse-race. They answered, 'We have'; and their steeds were swifter than the steeds of the Fomorians. They were then asked whether they had anyone who was good at sword-play. None was found save Bres alone. So when he set his hand to the sword, his father recognized the ring on his finger and enquired who was the hero. His mother answered on his behalf and told the king that Bres was a son of his. Then she related to him the whole story even as we have recounted it.

His father was sorrowful over him. Said the father: 'What need has brought thee out of the land wherein thou didst rule?'

Bres replied: 'Nothing has brought me save my own injustice and arrogance. I stript them of their jewels and treasures and their own food. Neither tribute nor taxes had been taken from them up to that time.'

'That is bad,' said the father. 'Better were their prosperity than their kingship. Better their prayers than their curses. Why hast thou come hither?'

'I have come to ask you for champions,' said he. 'I would take that land by force.'

'Thou shouldst not gain it by injustice if thou didst not gain it by justice,' said the father.

'Then what counsel hast thou for me?' said Bres.

Thereafter he sent Bres to the champion, to Balor grandson of Net, the king of the Isles, and to Indech son of Dea Domnann the king of the Fomorians; and these assembled all the troops from Lochlann westwards unto Ireland, to impose their tribute and their rule by force on the Tuatha De, so that they made one bridge of vessels from the Foreigners' Isles to Erin. Never came to ireland an army more horrible or fearful than that host of the Fomorians. Men from Scythia of Lochlann and men out of the Western Isles were rivals in that expedition.

Now as to the Tuatha De, this is what they were doing. After Bres, Nuada was again in sovereignty over the Tuatha De. At that time he held a mighty feast at Tara for them. Now there was a certain warrior on his way to Tara, whose name was Lug Samildanach. And there were then two doorkeepers at Tara, namely Gamal son of Figal and Camall son of Riagall. When one of these was on duty he saw a strange company coming towards him. A young warrior fair and shapely, with a king's trappings, was in the forefront of that band. They told the doorkeeper to announce their arrival at Tara. The doorkeeper asked: 'Who is there?'

'Here there is Lug Lamfada (i.e., Lug Long-Arm) son of Cian son of Diancecht and of Ethne daughter of Balor. Fosterson, he, of Tailltiu daughter of Magmor king of Spain and of Eochaid the Rough son of Duach.'

The doorkeeper asked of Lug Samildanach: 'What art dost thou practise? For no one without an art enters Tara.'

'Question me,' said he: 'I am a wright.'

The doorkeeper answered: 'We need thee not. We have a wright already, even Luchta son of Luachaid.'

He said: 'Question me, O doorkeeper! I am a smith.'

The doorkeeper answered him: 'We have a smith already, Colum Cualleinech of the three new processes.'

He said: 'Question me: I am a champion.'

The doorkeeper answered: 'We need thee not. We have a champion already, Ogma son of Ethliu.'

He said again: 'Question me: I am a harper.'

'We need thee not. We have a harper already. Abcan son of Bicelmos whom the Tuatha De Danann chose in the fairy-mounds.'

Said he: 'Question me: I am a hero.'

The doorkeeper answered: 'We need thee not. We have a hero already, even Bresal Etarlam son of Eochaid Baethlam.'

Then he said: 'Question me, O doorkeeper! I am a poet and I am a historian.'

'We need thee not. We have already a poet and historian, even En son of Ethaman.'

He said, 'Question me: I am a sorcerer.'

'We need thee not. We have sorcerers already. Many are our wizards and our folk of might.'

He said: 'Question me: I am a leech.'

'We need thee not. We have for a leech Diancecht.'

'Question me,' said he; 'I am a cupbearer.'

'We need thee not. We have cupbearers already, even Delt and Drucht and Daithe, Tae and Talom and Trog, Glei an Glan and Glesi.'

He said: 'Question me: I am a good brazier.'

'We need thee not. We have a brazier already, Credne Cerd.'

He said again, 'Ask the king,' said he, 'whether he has a single man who possesses all these arts, and if he has I will not enter Tara.'

Then the doorkeeper went into the palace and declared all to the king. 'A warrior has come before the enclosure,' said he. 'His name is Samildanach (many-gifted), and all the arts which thy household practise he himself possesses, so that he is the man of each and every art.'

The king said that the chess-boards of Tara should be taken to Samildanach, and he won all the stakes, so that then he made the *Cro* of Lug. (But if chess was invented at the epoch of the Trojan war, it had not reached Ireland then, for the battle of Moytura and the destruction of Troy occurred at the same time.)[2]

Then that was related to Nuada. 'Let him into the enclosure,' says he; 'for never before has man like him entered this fortress.'

Then the doorkeeper let Lug pass him, and he entered the fortress and sat down in the sage's seat, for he was a sage in every art.

Then the great flagstone, to move which required the effort of four-score yoke of oxen, Ogma hurled through the house, so that it lay on the outside of Tara. This was a challenge to Lug. But Lug cast it back, so that it lay in the centre of the palace; and he put the piece which it had carried away into the side of the palace and made it whole.

'Let a harp be played for us,' said the company. So the warrior played a sleep-strain for the hosts and for the king the first night. He cast them into sleep from that hour to the same time on the following day. He played a wail-strain, so that they were crying and lamenting. He played a laugh-strain, so that they were in merriment and joyance.

Now Nuada, when he beheld the warrior's many powers, considered whether Samildanach could put away from them the bondage which they suffered from the Fomorians. So they held a council concerning the warrior. The decision to which Nuada came was to change seats with the warrior. So Samildanach went to the king's seat, and the king rose up before him till thirteen days had ended. Then on the morrow he met with the two brothers, Dagda and Ogma, on Grellach Dollaid. And his brothers Goibniu and Diancecht were summoned to them. A full year were they in that secret converse, wherefore Grellach Dollaid is called Amrun of the Tuatha De Danann.

Thereafter the wizards of Ireland were summoned to them, and their medical men and charioteers and smiths and farmers and lawyers. They held speech with them in secret. Then Nuada inquired of the sorcerer whose name was Mathgen, what power he could wield? He answered that through his contrivance he would cast the mountains of Ireland on the Fomorians, and roll their summits against the ground. And he declared to them that the twelve chief mountains of the land of Erin would support the Tuatha De Danann, in battling for them, to wit, Sliab League, and Denna Ulad and the Mourne Mountains, and Bri Ruri and Sliab Bladma and Sliab Snechtai, Sliab Mis and Blai-sliab and Nevin and Sliab Maccu Belgadan and Segais and Cruachan Aigle.

Then he asked the cupbearer what power he could wield. He answered that he would bring the twelve chief lochs of Ireland before the Fomorians, and that they would not find water therein, whatever thirst might seize them. These are those lochs: Dergloch, Loch Luimnigh, Loch Corrib, Loch Ree, Loch Mask, Strangford Loch, Belfast Loch, Loch Neagh, Loch Foyle, Loch Gara, Loch Reag, Marloch. They would betake themselves to the twelve chief rivers of Ireland — Bush, Boyne, Baa, Nem, Lee, Shannon, Moy, Sligo, Erne, Finn, Liffey, Suir — and they will all be hidden from the Fomorians, so that they will not find a drop therein. Drink shall be provided for the men of Ireland, though they bide in the battle to the end of seven years.

Then said Figol son of Mamos, their Druid: 'I will cause three showers of fire to pour on the faces of the Fomorian host, and I will take out of them two thirds of their valour and their bravery and their strength, and I will bind their urine in their own bodies and in the bodies of their horses. Every breath that the men of Ireland shall exhale will be an increase of valour and bravery and strength to them. Though they bide in the battle till the end of seven years, they will not be weary in any wise.'

Said the Dagda: 'The power which ye boast I shall wield it all by myself.' 'It is thou art the Dagda (good hand), with everyone': wherefore thenceforward the name 'Dagda' adhered to him. Then they separated from the council, agreeing to meet again that day three years.

Now when the provision of the battle had then been settled, Lug and Dagda and Ogma went to the three Gods of Danu, and these gave Lug the plan of the battle; and for seven years they were preparing for it and making their weapons.

The Dagda had a house in Glenn Etin in the north, and he had to meet a woman in Glenn Etin a year from that day, about Samain (Hallowe'en) before the battle. The river Unius of Connacht roars to the south of it. He beheld the woman in Unius in Corann, washing herself, with one of her two feet at Allod Echae (i.e. Echumech), to the south of the water, and the other at Loscuinn, to the north of the water. Nine loosened tresses were on her head. The Dagda conversed with her, and they made a union. 'The Bed of the Couple' is the name of the place thenceforward. The woman that is here mentioned is the Morrigu. Then she told the Dagda that the Fomorians would land at Mag Scetne, and that he should summon Erin's men of art to meet her at the Ford of Unius, and that she would go into Scetne to destroy Indech son of Dea Domnann, the king of the Fomorians, and would deprive him of the blood of his heart and the kidneys of his valour. Afterwards she gave two handfuls of that blood to the hosts that were waiting at the Ford of Unius. 'Ford of Destruction' became its name, because of that destruction of the king. Then that was done by the wizards, and they chanted spells on the hosts of the Fomorians.

This was a week before Samain, and each of them separated from the other until all the men of Ireland came together on Samain. Six times thirty hundred was their number, that is, twice thirty hundred in every third.

Then Lug sent the Dagda to spy out the Fomorians and to delay them until the men of Ireland should come to the battle. So the Dagda went to the camp of the Fomorians and asked them for a truce of battle. This was granted to him as he asked. Porridge was then made for him by the Fomorians, and this was done to mock him, for great was his love for porridge. They filled for him the king's cauldron, five fists deep, into which went four-score gallons of new milk and the like quantity of meal and fat. Goats and sheep and swine were put into it, and they were all boiled together with the porridge. They were spilt for him into a hole in the ground, and Indech told him that he would be put to death unless he consumed it all; he should eat his fill so that he might not reproach the Fomorians with inhospitality.

Then the Dagda took his ladle, and it was big enough for a man and woman to lie on the middle of it. These then were the bits that were in it, halves of salted swine and a quarter of lard. 'Good food this,' said the Dagda . . .

At the end of the meal he put his curved finger over the bottom of the hole on mould and gravel. Sleep came upon him then after eating his porridge. Bigger than a house-cauldron was his belly, and the Fomorians laughed at it. Then he went away from them to the strand of Eba. Not easy was it for the hero to move along owing to the bigness of his belly. Unseemly was his apparel. A cape to the hollow of his two elbows. A dun tunic around him, as far as the swelling of his rump. It was, moreover, long-breasted, with a hole in the peak. Two brogues on him of horse-hide, with the hair outside. Behind him a wheeled fork to carry which required the effort of eight men, so that its track after him was enough for the boundary-ditch of a province. Wherefore it is called 'The Track of the Dagda's Club'.

Then the Fomorians marched till they reached Scetne. The men of Ireland were in Mag Aurfolaig. These two hosts were threatening battle. 'The men of Ireland venture to offer battle to us,' said Bres son of Elotha to Indech son of Dea Domnann. 'I will fight anon,' said Indech, 'so that their bones will be small unless they pay their tributes.'

Because of Lug's knowledge the men of Ireland had made a resolution not to let him go into the battle. So his nine fosterers were left to protect him, Tollusdam and Ech-dam and Eru, Rechtaid the white and Fosad and Fedlimid, Ibor and Scibar and Minn. They feared an early death for the hero owing to the multitude of his arts. Therefore they did not let him forth to the fight.

The chiefs of the Tuatha De Danann were gathered round Lug. And he asked his smith, Goibniu, what power he wielded for them. 'Not hard to tell,' said he. 'Though the men of Erin bide in the battle to the end of seven years, for every spear that parts from its shaft, or sword that shall break therein, I will provide a new weapon in its place. No spear-point which my hand shall forge,' said he, 'shall make a missing cast. No skin which it pierces shall taste life afterwards. That has not been done by Dolb the smith of the Fomorians.'

'And thou, O Diancecht,' said Lug, 'what power canst thou wield?'

'Not hard to tell,' said he. 'Every man who shall be wounded there, unless his head be cut off, or the membrane of his brain or his spinal marrow be severed, I will make quite whole in the battle on the morrow.'

'And thou, O Credne,' said Lug to his brazier, 'what is thy power in the battle?'

'Not hard to tell,' said Credne. 'Rivets for their spears, and hilts for their swords, and bosses and rims for their shields, I will supply them all.'

'And thou, O Luchta,' said Lug to his wright, 'what service wilt thou render in the battle?'

'Not hard to tell,' said Luchta. 'All the shields and javelin-shafts they require, I will supply them all.'

'And thou, O Ogma,' said Lug to his champion, 'what is thy power in the battle?'

'Not hard to tell,' said he. 'I will repel the king and three enneads of his friends, and capture up to a third of his men.'

'And ye, O sorcerers,' said Lug, 'what power will you wield?'

'Not hard to tell,' said the sorcerers. 'We shall fill them with fear when they have been overthrown by our craft, till their heroes are slain, and deprive them of two thirds of their might, with constraint on their urine.'

'And ye, O cupbearers,' said Lug, 'what power?'

'Not hard to tell,' said the cupbearers. 'We will bring a strong thirst upon them, and they shall not find drink to quench it.'

'And ye, O Druids,' said Lug, 'what power?'

'Not hard to tell,' said the Druids. 'We will bring showers of fire on the faces of the Fomorians, so that they cannot look upwards, and so that the warriors who are contending with them may slay them by their might.'

'And thou, O Cairbre son of Etain,' said Lug to his poet, 'what power canst thou wield in the battle?'

'Not hard to tell,' said Cairbre. 'I will make a satire on them. And I will satirize them and shame them, so that through the spell of my art they will not resist warriors.'

'And ye, O Be-culle and O Dianann,' said Lug to his two witches, 'what power can ye wield in the battle?'

'Not hard to tell,' said they. 'We will enchant the trees and the stones and the sods of the earth, so that they shall become a host under arms against them, and shall rout them in flight with horror and trembling.'

'And thou, O Dagda,' said Lug, 'what power canst thou wield on the Fomorian host in the battle?'

'Not hard to tell,' said the Dagda. 'I will take the side of the men of Erin both in mutual smiting and destruction and wizardry. Under my club the bones of the Fomorians will be as many as hailstones under the feet of herds of horses where you meet on the battlefield of Moytura.'

So thus Lug spoke with every one of them in turn; and he strengthened and addressed his army, so that each man of them had the spirit of a king or a mighty lord. Now every day a battle was fought between the tribe of the Fomorians and the Tuatha De, save only that kings or princes were not delivering it, but only keen and haughty folk.

Now the Fomorians marvelled at a certain thing which was revealed to them in the battle. Their spears and their swords were blunted and broken and such of their men as were slain did not return on the morrow. But it was not so with the Tuatha De. For though their weapons were blunted and broken today, they were renewed on the morrow, because Goibniu the smith was in the forge making swords and spears and javelins. For he would make those weapons by three turns. Then Luchta the wright would make the spearshafts by three chippings, and the third chipping was a finish and would set them in the ring of the spear. When the spearheads were stuck in the side of the forge he would throw the rings with the shafts, and it was needless to set them again. Then Credne the brazier would make the rivets by three turns, and would cast the rings of the spears to them; and thus they used to cleave together.

This then is what used to put fire into the warriors who were slain, so that they were swifter on the morrow. Because Diancecht and his two sons, Octriuil and Miach, and his daughter Airmed sang spells over the well named Slane. Now their mortally wounded men were cast into it as soon as they were slain. They were alive when they came out. Their mortally wounded became whole through the might of the incantation of the four leeches who were about the well. Now that was harmful to the Fomorians, so they sent a man of them to spy out the battle and the actions of the Tuatha De, namely Ruadan son of Bres and of Brig the Dagda's daughter. For he was a son and a grandson of the Tuatha De. Then he related to the Fomorians the work of the smith and the wright and the brazier and the four leeches who were around the well. He was sent again to kill one of the artisans, that is Goibniu. From him he begged a spear, its rivets from the brazier and its shaft from the wright. So all was given to him as he asked. There was a woman there grinding the weapons, Cron mother of Fianlug; she it is that ground Ruadan's spear. Now the spear was given to Ruadan by a chief, wherefore the name 'a chief's spear' is still given to weavers' beams in Erin.

Now after the spear had been given to him, Ruadan turned and wounded Goibniu. But Goibniu plucked out the spear and cast it at Ruadan, so that it went through him, and he died in the presence of his father in the assembly of the Fomorians. Then Brig came and bewailed her son. She shrieked at first, she cried at last. So that then for the first time crying and shrieking were heard in Erin. Now it was that Brig who invented a whistle for signalling at night.

Then Goibniu went into the well, and he became whole. There was a warrior with the Fomorians, Octriallach son of Indech son of Dea Domnann, son of the Fomorian king. He told the Fomorians that each man of them should bring a stone of the stones of Drowes to cast into the well of Slane in Achad Abla to the west of Moytura, to the east of Loch Arboch. So they went, and a stone for each man was cast into the well. Wherefore the cairn thus made is called Octriallach's Cairn. But another name for that well is Loch Luibe, for Diancecht put into it one of every herb (*lub*) that grew in Erin.

Now when the great battle came, the Fomorians marched out of their camp, and formed themselves into strong battalions. Not a chief nor man of prowess of them was without a hauberk against his skin, a helmet on his head, a broad spear in his right hand, a heavy sharp sword on his belt, a firm shield on his shoulder. To attack the Fomorian host on that day was 'striking a head against a cliff', was 'a hand in a serpent's nest', was 'a face up to fire'. These were the kings and chiefs that were heartening the host of the Fomorians, namely, Balor son of Dot son of Net, Bres son of Elotha, Tuiri Tortbuillech son of Lobos, Goll and Irgoll Loscennlomm son of Lommglunech, Indech son of Dea Domnann the king of the Fomorians, Octriallach son of Indech, Omna and Bagna, Elotha son of Delbaeth.

On the other side the Tuatha De Danann arose and left their nine comrades keeping Lug, and they marched to the battle. When the battle began, Lug escaped from his guardians with his charioteer, so that it was he who was in front of the hosts of the Tuatha De. Then a keen and cruel battle was fought between the tribe of the Fomorians and the men of Ireland. Lug was heartening the men of Ireland that they should fight the battle fervently, so that they should not be any longer in bondage. For it was better for them to find death in protecting their fatherland than to bide under bondage and tribute as they had been . . .

The hosts uttered a great shout as they entered the battle. Then they came together and each of them began to smite the other. Many fine men fell there. Great the slaughter and the grave-lying that was there. Pride and shame were there side by side. There was anger and indignation. Abundant was the stream of blood there over the white skin of young warriors mangled by hands of eager men. Harsh was the noise of the heroes and the champions mutually fending their spears and their shields and their bodies when the others were smiting them with spears and swords. Harsh, moreover, was the thunder that was there throughout the battle, the shouting of the warriors and the clashing of the shields, the flashing and whistling of the glaives and the ivory-hilted swords, the rattling and jingling of the quivers, the sound and winging of the darts and the javelins, and the crashing of the weapons. The ends of their fingers and of their feet almost met in the mutual blows, and owing to the slipperiness of the blood under the feet of the soldiers, they would fall from their upright posture and beat their heads together as they sat. The battle was a gory, ghastly mêlée, and the river Unsenn rushed with corpses.

Then Nuada Silver-Hand and Macha, daughter of Ernmass, fell by Balor grandson of Net. And Cassmael fell by Octriallach son of Indech. Lug and Balor of the Piercing Eye met in the battle. An evil eye had Balor the Fomorian. That eye was never opened save only on a battlefield. Four men used to lift up the lid of the eye with a polished handle which passed through its lid. If an army looked at that eye, though they were many thousands in number, they could not resist a few warriors. It had a poisonous power. Once when his father's Druids were concocting charms, he came and looked out of the window, and the fume of the concoction came under it, so that the poison of the concoction afterwards penetrated the eye that looked. He and Lug met. 'Lift up mine eyelid, my lad,' said Balor, 'that I may see the babbler who is conversing with me.'

The lid was raised from Balor's eye. Then Lug cast a sling-stone at him, which carried the eye through his head while his own army looked on. And the sling-stone fell on the host of the Fomorians, and thrice nine of them died beside it, so that the crowns of their heads came against the breast of Indech son of Dea Domnann, and a gush of blood sprang over his lips. Said Indech: 'Let Loch Half-green my poet be summoned to me!' Half-green was he from the ground to the crown of his head.

Loch went to the king. 'Make known to me,' said Indech, 'who has flung this cast on me.'

Then the Morrigu, daughter of Ernmass, came, and heartened the Tuatha De to fight the battle fiercely and fervently. Thereafter the battle became a rout, and the Fomorians were beaten back to the sea. The champion Ogma son of Ethliu, and Indech son of Dea Domnann the king of the Fomorians, fell in single combat. Loch Half-green besought Lug for quarter. 'Give me my three wishes,' said Lug.

'Thou shalt have them,' said Loch. 'Till Doom I will ward off from Ireland all plundering by the Fomorians, and, at the end of the world, every ailment.' So Loch was spared. Then he sang to the Gael the 'decree of fastening'.

Loch said that he would bestow names on Lug's nine chariots because of the quarter that had been given him. So Lug told him to name them. [3]

'What is the number of the slain?' said Lug to Loch.

'I know not the number of peasants and rabble. As to the number of Fomorian lords and nobles and champions and kings' sons and overkings, I know, even five thousand three score and three men: two thousand and three fifties: four score thousand and nine times five: eight score and eight: four score and seven: four score and six: eight score and five: two and forty including Net's grandson. That is the number of the slain of the Fomorian overkings and high nobles who fell in the battle. Howbeit, as to the number of peasants and common people and rabble, and folk of every art besides who came in company with the great army — for every champion and every high chieftain and every overking of the Fomorians came with his host to the battle, so that all fell there, both his freemen and his slaves — we reckon only a few of the servants of the overkings. This then is the number that I have reckoned of these as I beheld: seven hundred, seven score and seven men . . . together with Sab Uanchennach son of Cairbre Colc, son was he of a servant of Indech son of Dea Domnann, that is, a son of a servant of the Fomorian king. As to what fell besides of 'half-men' and of those who reached not the heart of the battle, these are in no wise numbered till we number stars of heaven, sand of sea, flakes of snow, dew on lawn, hailstones, grass under feet of herds, and Manannan mac Lir's horses (waves) in a sea-storm.'

Thereafter Lug and his comrades found Bres son of Elotha unguarded. He said: 'It is better to give me quarter than to slay me.'

'What then will follow from that?' said Lug.

'If I be spared,' says Bres, 'the cows of Erin will always be in milk.'

'I will set this forth to our wise men,' said Lug.

So Lug went to Maeltne Mor-brethach, and said to him: 'Shall Bres have quarter for giving constant milk to the cows of Erin?'

'He shall not have quarter,' said Maeltne; 'he has no power over their age or their offspring, though he can milk them so long as they are alive.'

Lug said to Bres: 'That does not save thee: thou hast no power over their age and their offspring, though thou canst milk them. Is there aught else that will save thee, O Bres?' said Lug.

'There is in truth. Tell thy lawyer that for sparing me the men of Ireland shall reap a harvest in every quarter of the year.'

Said Lug to Maeltne: 'Shall Bres be spared for giving the men of Ireland a harvest of corn every quarter?'

'This has suited us, saith Maeltne: 'the spring for ploughing and sowing, and the beginning of summer for the end of the strength of corn, and the beginning of autumn for the end of the ripeness of corn and for reaping it. Winter for consuming it.'

'That does not rescue thee,' said Lug to Bres; 'but less than that rescues thee.'

'What?' said Bres.

'How shall the men of Ireland plough? How shall they sow? How shall they reap? After making known these three things thou wilt be spared.'

'Tell them,' said Bres, 'that their ploughing be on a Tuesday, their casting seed into the field be on a Tuesday, their reaping on a Tuesday.' So through that stratagem Bres was let go free.

In that fight, then, Ogma the champion found Orna the sword of Tethra, a king of the Fomorians. Ogma unsheathed the sword and cleansed it. Then the sword related whatsoever had been done by it; for it was the custom of swords at that time, when unsheathed, to set forth the deeds that had been done by them. And therefore swords are entitled to the tribute of cleansing them after they have been unsheathed. Hence, also, charms are preserved in swords thenceforward. Now the reason why demons used to speak from weapons at that time was because weapons were worshipped by human beings at that epoch, and the weapons were among the safeguards of that time . . .

Now Lug and the Dagda and Ogma pursued the Fomorians, for they had carried off the Dagda's harper, whose name was Uaitne. Then they reached the banqueting-house in which were Bres son of Elotha and Elotha son of Delbaeth. There hung the harp on the wall. That is the harp in which the

Dagda had bound the melodies so that they sounded not until by his call he summoned them forth; when he said this below:

> Come Daurdabla!
> Come Coir-cethar-chuir!
> Come summer, come winter!
> Mouths of harps and bags and pipes!

Now that harp had two names, Daur-da-bla 'Oak of two greens' and Coir-cethar-chuir 'Four-angled music'.

Then the harp went forth from the wall, and killed nine men, and came to the Dagda. And he played for them the three things whereby harpers are distinguished, to wit, sleep-strain and smile-strain and wail-strain. He played wail-strain to them, so that their tearful women wept. He played smile-strain to them, so their women and children laughed. He played sleep-strain to them, and the company fell asleep. Through that sleep the three of them escaped unhurt from the Fomorians though these desired to slay them.

Then the Dagda brought with him the heifer which had been given to him for his labour. For when she called her calf, all the cattle of Ireland which the Fomorians had taken as their tribute grazed.

Now after the battle was won and the corpses cleared away, the Morrigu, daughter of Ernmas, proceeded to proclaim that battle and the mighty victory which had taken place, to the royal heights of Ireland and to its fairy hosts and its chief waters and its rivermouths. And hence it is that Badb (i.e., the Morrigu) also describes high deeds. 'Hast thou any tale?' said everyone to her then. And she replied:

> Peace up to heaven,
> Heaven down to earth,
> Earth under heaven,
> Strength in every one, etc.

Then, moreover, she was prophesying the end of the world, and foretelling every evil that would be therein, and every disease and every vengeance. Wherefore then she sang this lay below:

> I shall not see a world that will be dear to me.
> Summer without flowers,
> Kine will be without milk,
> Women without modesty,
> Men without valour,
> Captures without a king . . .
> Woods without mast
> Sea without produce . . .
> Wrong judgments of old men,
> False precedents of lawyers,
> Every man a betrayer,
> Every boy a reaver.
> Son will enter his father's bed,
> Father will enter his son's bed,
> Everyone will be his brother's brother-in-law . . .
> An evil time!

Son will deceive his father,
Daughter will deceive her mother.


1.  Originally published in *Ancient Irish Tales*, eds. Tome Pette Cross and Clark H.
    Slover (Dublin, Figgis, 1936) [Ed.]
2.  This is the author's own comment.
3.  At this point the original gives a list of the names of the chariots, charioteers, and
    their equipment.

# PART FOUR:
# THE HIDDEN WORLD — TALIESIN
# AND THE ART OF INSPIRATION

The figure of the bard was among the most important at the courts of the Celtic princes. Their task was to remember the songs and stories which told of every man's ancestors. Thus the Celts buried their dead in unmarked graves since they knew that while the bards survived so would the memory of the mighty dead.

Undoubtedly the most famous of these men was Taliesin, an actual historic personage who lived towards the middle of the sixth century and left a substantial body of material behind, though in a form much muddled and misunderstood. His fame as a semi-mythical character in the *Hanes Taliesin* (Story of Taliesin) wrought a curious circumstance whereby a vast amount of mythical and mystical teaching constellated around the figure of the historical bard.

An entire system of Celtic magical teaching lies buried within the poems and stories about Taliesin and many attempts have been made to decipher it. Among the first to attempt a serious and reasonably accurate translation was the nineteenth-century scholar W.F. Skene, who published the text and translation of *The Four Ancient Books of Wales* (including 'The Book of Taliesin') in 1868. His work was shortly followed by a lengthy commentary with further translations by D.W. Nash, whose vituperative attack on his predecessors is often, in retrospect, amusing. The extract given here gives the best of his commentary, which is exhaustive and lively. His book remains the most reliable until now on the subject.[1]

A brief excursion into the Irish bardic heritage follows, in which the great Celtic scholar Henri d'Arbois de Jubainville examines the similarites between the writings of Taliesin and those of his Irish equivalent Amairgen.

Finally in this section we have one of the most curious and difficult documents of this collection, a chapter from *Barddas* edited by J. Williams ab Ithel from the writings of Edward Williams, better known as Iolo Morgannwg. The work of this brilliant eighteenth-century antiquarian has probably given rise to more argument and discussion on the question of the authenticity of the bardic tradition than any other writer of any age. Iolo's brilliance is beyond question. The problem is that we no longer know how much he translated and how much he made up on the spur of the moment, having reached a point where he could no longer fill out the gaps in his knowledge by any other means. Most of the material reprinted here is clearly a forgery; yet for all that it is fascinating as an example of the way a tradition can be extended in such a way that it complements rather than contradicts the original material. Thus it is with Iolo, whose 'Bardic Triads' and discussions between master and pupil are as much in the spirit of the originals as they might be. I include them here without apology to the purists, as a fascinating document which is a valid part of Celtic Tradition.

1. But see my forthcoming *Taliesin: Shamanic Mysteries of Britain and Ireland* (Unwin Hyman, 1990).

# Chapter 9
# Taliesin in Story and Song[1]
## by D.W. Nash

Before proceeding to an examination of the various compositions attributed to the celebrated chief of bards, Taliesin, we may offer a few observations on his history and the legends connected with his name.

If Taliesin really flourished in the sixth century, his genuine poems may be expected to contain references to historical events and personages, which will readily identify the age and locality of their author. It may also reasonably be anticipated, that, even should they fail to supply important authentic materials of history, they will at least, as Mr Rees has observed, be interesting as records of a valiant and high-spirited people, nobly struggling against overwhelming odds, to preserve their liberties and the independence of their country.

Although it is now admitted by the better informed Welsh scholars that the poems which constitute the *Hanes Taliesin*, or romantic history of the bard, as well as the majority of the other poems attributed to him, were composed in their present form as late as the thirteenth century, it is nevertheless contended that the ideas and traditions embodied in the romance composed by Thomas ap Einion Offeiriad had previously existed in the form of tales and poems which had already acquired an extensive popularity and circulation, and that from these earlier fragments the Druidism, philosophy and superstition of the bards of the sixth century are still capable of being eliminated.

Before entering upon that investigation of the poems which is necessary for deciding on the truth or falsehood of this opinion, we may endeavour to ascertain something of the personal history of Taliesin from other sources than the romance with which he is connected.

The generally received statement on this point is that Taliesin lived in the sixth century, and that his principal patron was Urien Rheged, a British chieftain to whose history we shall presently advert. The poems of Taliesin in honour of, or addressed to, this prince and his family, have generally been received as genuine historical documents, contemporary monuments of an age which abounded in bards and heroes of the ancient British race. Yet, upon a review of the historical poems of Taliesin, we are at a loss to discover the grounds of the great reputation which has attached to his name, as chief bard of the West, and the most celebrated among the poets of Wales, a reputation which had reached its height in popular estimation as early, certainly, as the middle of the twelfth century.

Taliesin is mentioned in terms of respect and as an example of bardic excellence by the poets of that epoch, by Cynddelw, Llywarch ab Llywelyn and Elidir Sais, and in the following century by Philip Brydydd, Davyd Benvras, and Gwilym Ddu. A fragment of a poem attributed to Taliesin, employed as evidence in support of the privileges claimed by the men of Arvon, is found in a MS copy of the laws of Howel Dda, in a handwriting, it is said, of the twelfth century. The contents of the historical poems of Taliesin do not however disclose the reason for the great estimation in which this bard has been held by his countrymen. Supposing him to have flourished in the sixth century, we must adjudge him, as a poet, inferior to his contemporaries, Llywarch Hen and Aneurin, and to the Caledonian Merlin, if the compositions of the latter are also regarded as of the same epoch. The subjects of these poems, admitting them to be genuine and written at the date of the events to which they allude, are limited in their scope, confined to the description of combats comparatively unimportant (altogether so, in a national view) and record the deeds of only one family of British chieftains, leaving unsung events and personages of far greater importance and more widely spread reputation.

It is impossible that the great celebrity of Taliesin in the twelfth century can have been founded solely on the historical poems which have been preserved, and it would seem therefore that Taliesin must have been the author of poetical works which have not come down to our time but which were known to, and highly appreciated by, the bards of the twelfth century, or that his reputation rests less upon his own compositions than on the fame which attached to his name as a character or romance, a prophet and magician.

To the first of these suppositions it must be objected that had other historical poems of Taliesin been in existence in the twelfth century, had his name been employed in rendering famous the names of other chieftains than Urien and his son Owain, some notice of such compositions could not fail to have been preserved. To the latter view two circumstances appear to give great probability. The name Tal-iesin, 'shining forehead' is connected with the romance history of the bard, and was given to him on his miraculous appearance at the fishing weir of Gwyddno Garanhir. It is more probable that this significant name was invented by the writer of the romance than that the adventure was composed to account for the origin of the name.

Llywarch ab Llewelyn in the twelfth century mentions Taliesin in connection with the romance history of the liberation of Elphin:[2]

> Cyvarchaf ym ren cyvarchuawr awen
> Cyvren kyrridwen rwyf bartoni
> Yu dull Talyesin yn dillwng Elfin
> Yn dyllest bartrin, beirt uannyeri —

> I address my Lord, in eulogistic song,
> With the treasures of Ceridwen, ruler of poets,
> In the manner of Taliesin, at the liberation of Elphin,
> In the fashion of the bardic lore of the leaders of the bards.

Davyd Benvras, in the thirteenth century, refers to Taliesin as a diviner, gifted with supernatural genius, and Gwilym Ddu somewhat later mentions him by his name of Gwion, by which he evidently refers to the romantic history of the bard.[3]

> Da fn ffawd y wawd i Wiawn ddewin
> Da Fyrddin ai lin o lwyth Meirchiawn —

> Good was the fortunate song of Gwiawn the diviner,
> Good was Merddin of the line of the tribe of Meirchiawn.

It would seem from these references that in the twelfth century the fame of Taliesin as chief of bards was chiefly connected with the romance attached to his name. It is true that Cynddelw at the same epoch appears to refer to the Song on the Battle of Argoed Lwyfain, but without connecting the name of Taliesin with that poem. It is very probable, as Mr Turner has shown, that the last-named poem was in existence in the twelfth century, but there is nothing more than opinion to connect its authorship with Taliesin.

We are necessarily led to the conclusion, that the romance or *Mabinogi* of Taliesin was in vogue in the twelfth century, and that the present form of that story was compiled from an older romance, in which the name of Taliesin had already become an object of popular adulation. But we have great difficulty in connecting the Taliesin of the romance with the Bard of Urien Rheged. The scene of the romance is laid in North Wales and in the sixth century, the era of the most celebrated personages of Welsh history and romance. We must not forget that the writers of the Welsh romances were so discordant in their views of the era of Taliesin that while one *Mabinogi* makes him a chief bard at the court of Arthur, and another places his adventures in the reign of Maelgwn Gwynedd, a third makes him a companion of Bran the Blessed, father of the celebrated Caractacus, who flourished in the first century of the Christian era.

But none of these romances connect the name of Taliesin with Urien Rheged, or the events in which that chieftain played a conspicuous part. This diversity of legendary statements respecting a personage so celebrated leads to some doubts on his genuine historical character. If the position of Taliesin as the bard of Urien Rheged was a fact well known to the Welsh, and if his genuine poems in honour of that chieftain had obtained in the eleventh or twelfth century a general acceptation, it is highly improbable that the romancers should have connected him with adventures six centuries earlier in date. But if known as Taliesin the Diviner, who claimed to have been contemporary with Alexander the Great, and to have been with Noah in the Ark, he might well find a place in companionship with the blessed Bran. These considerations lead us to hesitate in admitting the claims of Taliesin as an undoubted historical bard of the sixth century.

It must however be admitted that the writers of the twelfth and succeeding centuries, though evidently acquainted with the romance history of Taliesin, deal with him as a historical person and not as the mere creation of a popular fiction. We have moreover, in addition to the evidence to be derived from this general and great reputation which his name had acquired among his countrymen in the twelfth and thirteenth centuries, an independent testimony, which, though also given by a Briton, and most probably by a Briton of Wales, is of the greatest historical value, as having all the character of a legitimate and serious historical statement; though made at least four centuries after the era of Taliesin.

The compiler or transcriber of the genealogies of the Saxon kings, annexed to one copy of the *History* of Nennius, when relating the pedigree of the Deiri and the wars of the Angles against the British chieftains of Cumbria, mentions Taliesin among the notable bards who flourished in the time of Ida, about the middle of the sixth century.

'Ida, the son of Eoppa, possessed countries on the left-hand side of Britain, i.e., of the Humbrian Sea, and reigned twelve years, and united Dinguayth Guarth-Berneich. Then Dutigirn, at that time, fought bravely against the nation of the Angles. At that time Talhaiarn Cataguen was famed for poetry, and Neirin, and Taliesin, and Bluchbard, and Cian, who is also called Guenith Guant, were all famous at the same time in British poetry.'

On the other hand, we must remark that the personage whom Geoffrey of Monmouth presents to his readers as the chief bard and diviner of the Cymry is not Taliesin, but Merlin.

Whether Geoffrey were the original author of the *History of the Britons*, or, according to the opinion of the Revd Rice Rees, the translator of an original Welsh version of the Armorican history, it seems certain that the fame of Taliesin had not, in the early part of the twelfth century, reached the ears of the Archdeacon of Monmouth, though a curious passage in the commencement of the seventh book shows that the prophecies of Merlin had at that period attracted public attention: 'I had not got thus far in my history, when the subject of public discourse, happening to be concerning Merlin, I was obliged to publish his prophecies at the request of my acquaintance.' It may be, however, that the reputation of Taliesin among his countrymen, was that of a bard or poet merely, not that of a prophet; and the public attention was directed to Merlin in the twelfth century, on account of his supposed prophecies respecting the Norman kings.

Still, if the genealogies are true which represent him as a native of South Wales, the absence of all notice by Geoffrey of so famous a character as Taliesin is represented to have been, is, at least, somewhat extraordinary.

According to the genealogies of Taliesin, which have been published from manuscripts of which the dates are not known,[4] he was the son of Henwg the Bard, otherwise Saint Henwg, of Caerlleon-upon-Usk, and of the College of Saint Cadocus, whose pedigree, as a matter of course, ascends to Bran the Blessed, the father of Caractacus.

It is even said in one manuscript that Taliesin, chief of the bards, erected the church of Llanhenwg, at Caerlleon-upon-Usk, which he dedicated to the memory of his father, called St Henwg, who went to Rome on a mission to Constantine the Blessed, requesting that he would send SS Germanus and Lupus to Britain, to strengthen the faith, and renew baptism there.[5]

In the Triads,[6] Taliesin is named as one of the three baptismal bards of the Isle of Britain, Merddin Emrys and Merddin son of Madoc Morvryn being the other two, and in the Iolo MSS, chair president of the nine impulsive stocks of the baptismal bards of Britain. In the notes to the *History of Taliesin*,[7] it is considered probable that he was educated, or completed his education, at the school of the celebrated Cattwg, at Llanveithin, in Glamorgan. He is reported to have died in Cardiganshire, probably at Bangor Teivy, and tradition has handed down a cairn near Aberystwith as the grave of Taliesin.

Jones, in his *Historical Account of the Welsh Bards*,[8] states that 'Taliesin was the master or preceptor of Myrddin ap Morvryn; he enriched the British prosody with five new metres; and has transmitted in his poems such vestiges as throw new light on the history, knowledge, and manners, of the Ancient Britons and their Druids, much of whose mystical learning he imbibed.'

As the romance or *Mabinogi* of Taliesin is supposed to exhibit in great fullness the Druidical philosophy and doctrine of the metempsychosis, or transmigration of the soul, it is curious to find that a tradition exists which affects to place his early history, and some of the circumstances which have formed the groundwork of the romance, on a reasonable and historical footing.[9]

*Figure* 7: 'A Celtic bard harps before his lord' by *R. Machell*.

'Taliesin, chief of the bards, the son of St Henwg of Caerlleon-upon-Usk, was invited to the court of Urien Rheged, at Aberllychwr. He, with Elphin the son of Urien, being once fishing at sea in a skin coracle, an Irish pirate ship seized him and his coracle, and bore him away towards Ireland; but while the pirates were at the height of their drunken mirth, Taliesin pushed his coracle to the sea, and got into it himself, with a shield in his hand which he found in the ship, and with which he rowed the coracle until it verged the land; but the waves breaking then in wild foam, he lost his hold on the shield, so that he had no alternative but to be driven at the mercy of the sea, in which state he continued for a short time, when the coracle stuck on the point of a pole in the weir of Gwyddno, Lord of Ceredigion, in Aberdyvi; and in that position he was found, at the ebb, by Gwyddno's fishermen, by whom he was interrogated; and when it was ascertained that he was a bard, and the tutor of Elphin the son of Urien Rheged, the son of Cynvarch, "I too have a son named Elphin," said Gwyddno; "be thou a bard and teacher to him also, and I will give thee lands in free tenure." The terms were accepted; and for several successive years he spent his time between the courts of Urien Rheged and Gwyddno, called Gwyddno Garanhir, Lord of the Lowland Cantred. But after the territory of Gwyddno had become overwhelmed by the sea, Taliesin was invited by the Emperor Arthur to his court at Caerlleon-upon-Usk, where he became highly celebrated for poetic genius, and useful, meritorious sciences.

'After Arthur's death, he retired to the estate given him by Gwyddno, taking Elphin, the son of that prince, under his protection.

'It was from this account that Thomas, the son of Einion Offeiriad,[10] descended from Gruffyd Gwyr, formed his romance of Taliesin the son of Caridwen, Elphin the son of Gwyddno, Rhun the son of Maelgwn Gwynedd, and the operations of the cauldron of Caridwen.'

According to another legend, Taliesin, having escaped from the ship of the Irish pirates as before described, was extricated from the weir by Elphin, the supposed son of Gwyddno. Elphin was, however, in fact 'the son of Elivri, daughter of Gwyddno, but by whom was then quite unknown; it was, however, afterwards discovered that Urien, king of Gower and Aberllychwr, was his father, who introduced him to the court of Arthur at Caerlleon-upon-Usk, where his feats, learning, and endowments were found to be so superior that he was created a Golden-tongued Knight of the Round Table. After the death of Arthur, Taliesin became Chief Bard to Urien Rheged, at Aberllychwr in Rheged.'

Another legend in the Iolo MSS states that Talhaiarn, the father of Tangwn, presided in the chair of Urien Rheged, at Caer Gwyroswydd, after the expulsion of the Irish from Gower, Carnwyllion, Cantref Bychan, and the Cantref of Iscennen. The said chair was established at Caer Gwyroswydd, or Ystum Llwynarth, where Urien Rheged was accustomed to hold his national and royal court.

'After the death of Tallhaiarn, Taliesin, chief of the bards, presided in three chairs namely, the chair of Caerlleon-upon-Usk; the chair of Rheged at Bangor Teivy, under the patronage of Cedig ab Ceredig ab Dunedda Wledig; but he afterwards was invited to the territory of Gwyddnyw, the son of Gwydion in Arllechwedd, Arvon, where he had lands conferred on him, and where he resided until the time of Maelgwn Gwynedd, when he was dispossessed of that property, for which he pronounced his curses on Maelgwn, and all his possessions; whereupon the Vad Velen[11] came to Rhos, and whoever witnessed it became doomed to certain death. Maelgwn saw the Vad Velon through the keyhole in Rhos church, and died in consequence. Taliesin, in his old age, returned to Caer Gwyroswydd, to Rhiwallon, the son of Urien; after which he visited Cedig, the son of Ceredig, the son of Cunedda Wledig, where he died, and was buried with high honours, such as should always be shown to a man who ranked among the principal wise men of the Cimbric nation; and Taliesin, chief of the bards, was the highest of the most exalted class, either in literature, wisdom, the science of vocal song, or any other attainment, whether sacred or profane. Thus terminates the information respecting the chief bards of the chair of Caerlleon-upon-Usk, called now, the chair of Glamorgan.'

Unfortunately, it is impossible to ascertain whether these legends contain the foundation of the romance, or were written after the composition of the *Mabinogi* of Taliesin, by persons of a neologizing tendency. The only authority given in the Iolo MSS is that the first of the two legends was copied from Anthony Powel of Llwydarth's MS; the second from a MS at Havod Uchtryd; the last is from the MSS of Llwelyn sion of Llangwydd, who lived at the close of the sixteenth century.

There is another piece of evidence of the existence of Taliesin as a bard in the sixth century, which has been strongly insisted on by Mr Sharon Turner and others. This is the passage in the *Gododin* of Anenrin,[12]

Mi na vi Aneurin
Ys gwyr talyessin
Oveg Kywrenhin
Neu cheing c ododin
Kynn gwawr dyd dilin.

In the translation of Mr Williams —

I Aneurin will sing
What is known to Taliesin,
Who communicates to me his thoughts
Or a strain of Gododin
Before the dawn of the bright day.

Whether this translation be considered correct or no,[13] the occurrence of the name of Taliesin in this, the only poem of early date not attributed to Taliesin himself in which it occurs, is a testimony of considerable weight. Still, the passage in question is not altogether above suspicion.

According to the view taken by Mr Williams, the 'bedin Ododin', or 'troops of Gododin', were, at the battle of Catraeth, allied with the men of Deira and Bernicia, and opposed to the British chieftains eulogized or lamented by the poet.

Aneurin therefore, in the lines above quoted, gives to his poem made in honour of his countrymen a title taken from the appellation of one, and that certainly the least important of the three hostile tribes engaged in the conflict. How what Aneurin sung or would sing of the battle of Cattraeth should be known to Taliesin, or why the former should state that Taliesin communicated to him his thoughts, or thought with him, no other passage in this poem, or elsewhere, explains.

If the stanza be genuine, and the generally received translation the true one, it must bring down the date of the poem to a time when Taliesin had become sufficiently famous to be introduced with effect into a popular poem.

The difficulty lies in the true correspondence of the first line of the passage with the rest. If it belongs to and concludes the former part,

> And I am manacled
> In the earthen house,
> An iron chain
> Over my two knees;
> Yet of the mead and the horn,
> And of the men of Cattraeth,
> I Aneurin will sing.

this is the reasonable termination of the passage. The remainder will be an independent passage —

> It is known to Taliesin
> the skilful-minded —
> Shall there not be a song of the Gododin
> Before the dawn of the fair day?

which may well be a fragment of one of the numerous songs which we know to have been framed on the subject of the battle of Cattraeth, probably at very various dates.[14]

A somewhat similar passage occurs at the end of one of the so-called historical poems of Taliesin, the 'Anrhec Urien', in which Aneurin is mentioned among the thirteen princes of the North —

> And one of them was named Aneurin, the panegyrical poet,
> And I myself Taliesin from the banks of Llyn Ceirionydd.

The poem in which these lines occur is, however, a composition of the twelfth century, or later, and no weight therefore can be attached to the union of the names Aneurin and Taliesin in this quotation.

If we adopt the conclusion that a Taliesin, a bard of repute, really flourished in the middle of the sixth century, and that the halo of poetic glory which surrounded his memory, pointed him out to the romancers as a fit subject for the exercise of their art, we have still some difficulty in ascertaining the locality of the bard, or the part of the country under the dominion of the British chieftains, in which he resided and laid the foundation of his fame.

It will be observed that all the genealogies and prose legends relating to Taliesin describe him as a native of South Wales, and of the celebrated seat of the Arthurian Round Table, Caerlleon-upon-Usk.

Taliesin Williams, in a note on one of the above legends, observes on this, and remarks that 'Taliesin's intercourse with Gower (Rheged) and its Reguli is sufficiently decided by the several poems, addressed by him to those personages. He also wrote in the Gwentian dialect, of which district he was doubtless a native.' In proof of this latter opinion, the editor of the Iolo MSS actually quotes two lines from the *Cad Goddeu* —

Chwarycis yn Llychwr
Cysgais yn mhorphor —

I have played in Longhor;
I have slept in purple;

showing that he, at least, believed the *Cad Goddeu* to have been written by
Taliesin in the sixth century. As there are but two persons to whom any poems,
referred to Taliesin, are addressed — namely, Urien or Urien Rheged, and
Gwallawg or Gwallawg ap Lleenawg — Taliesin Williams must, of course, refer
to these.

The period at which Taliesin flourished must, if the poems addressed to
Urien Rheged are genuine, be that at which this prince can be ascertained to
have lived.

If it were clear that the Urien Rheged of the poems is the Urien mentioned
by the genealogist in Nennius, then the era of Taliesin must be that in which
Ida the Angle was carrying on that obstinate and eventful struggle with the
British chieftains of the northern and north-western portions of the island,
which resulted in the establishment of the great Anglian kingdom of
Northumbria.

Conspicuous among the British leaders, as well by his personal valour as by
his military skill, was a chieftain named Urien, who is mentioned in the
genealogy of the kins of the Deiri appended to one MS of the *British History*
of Nennius. Contemporary with this Urien were three other princes named in
the same genealogy, Ryderthen, Gwallauc, and Morcant. 'Theodoric, son of
Ida, fought bravely, together with his sons, against that Urien.'

Ida died in 560. His son Adda, according to Nennius, reigned eight years;
Ethelric, son of Adda, four years; Theodoric, son of Ida, seven years. It was
while besieging this Theodoric, as it is said, in the island of Lindisfarne, that
Urien was treacherously slain by Morcant. This brings the death of Urien
down, at the latest, to the year 579; and, as the poems which appear to have
been composed by Taliesin speak of that prince as living, it is probable that the
bard himself had not survived his patron.

The territories of this Urien would seem to have been situated in some
portion of the Cumbrian region, or the country occupied by the Cumbrian
Britons. This region, at the era of Ida's wars, extended from the vale of the
Clyde on the north, to the Ribble in Lancashire on the south, having the sea
for its western boundary. On the east the territories of the British chieftain had
a variable boundary depending on the fortune of war, where it was con-
terminous with the great Saxon or Anglian kingdoms of Deira and Bernicia,
of which the former extended northwards from the Humber to the Tyne, the
latter from the Tyne to the Firth of Forth.

That district of the Cumbrian region called Rheged, which in the middle of
the sixth century was under the sway of Urien, Sir Francis Palgrave places in
the forests of the south of Scotland, 'where the floating traditions of Arthur
and Merlin have survived the storms of many centuries.' As, however, portions
of Cumberland retained their independence to a much later period, and as the
friends and clansmen of Urien appear, very shortly after his death, to have
taken refuge in North Wales, it seems probable that Rheged had a more
southerly position. The battle of Cattraeth, the subject of the celebrated poem

of Aneurin, the *Gododin*, appears to have been particularly fatal to the clans of Rheged.

In whatever part of the Cumbrian territory Rheged may have been situated, its neighbourhood would appear to have been the seat of war between those Britons with whom Taliesin was connected and the Anglian chieftains of Deira and Bernicia. The only historical poems properly attributed to Taliesin relate to battles in which Urien of Rheged was engaged, or refer to that prince, to his son Owain, or to his confederate chieftains.

The only Saxon chief mentioned in these poems is one who, under the name of 'Flamddwyn' — the flame-bearer or incendiary — is supposed, but apparently on no sufficient grounds, to be Ida, the Anglian king of Northumbria.

There is no mention of the personages celebrated in history or tradition as having taken part in the long-continued and obstinate struggle between the Southern, Eastern, and Midland Britons, and the tribes of Jutes and Saxons who incessantly enlarged the Saxon and contracted the British boundary in those regions. Neither Aurelius Ambrosius, nor Uther Pendragon,[15] nor the world-renowned Arthur, nor the battles of Badon, of Salisbury, or of Camlan, find any place in the bardic eulogies of Taliesin. Yet all these personages, and all these important events, if historical, belong to the period when Taliesin is supposed to have flourished. It is evident that the sympathies of the bard, and of the tribes with whom he was associated, were engrossed by persons and events different from those connected with the wars of the Britons against the Saxons in the central and southern portions of the island. It is indeed very probable that the Northern Britons knew little of the events occurring in the other parts of Britain.

The want of anything like unity of government, or a central authority, must have tended very greatly to isolate the several British states and prevent anything like common action against the foe. For the story of a succession of Pendragons, or kings paramount of Britain, from Owain ap Maxen Wledig, down to Cadwallader, is a fiction invented by the compilers of the Triads, and the authors of those histories of which that of Geoffrey of Monmouth is an example. The Unbennaeth Prydain is (though there certainly was a song so called in the tenth century) as visionary as the imperatorship of Arthur. All the historical facts, from the time of Caesar downwards, demonstrate the falsity of the assumption.

Such are the views generally entertained of the locality of this celebrated British chieftain, and it seems to be supported by the evidence of the Saxon genealogies in Nennius. But a most unhappy confusion is introduced into this matter by a series of traditions,[16] which represent this same Urien as the chief of the district of Rheged, in South Wales, being the country between the Tawy and Towy, comprising the territories of Gower, Kidwely, Carnwyllion, Iscennen, and Cantref Bychan; his royal residence being Aberllychwr,[17] in Gower, where he constructed a strong castle called the Castle of Aberllyw.[18]

According to this tradition, Urien Rheged was king of Rheged in Glamorgan, and of Moray in Scotland. 'In the time of the Emperor Arthur, Glaian Ecdwr[19] and his fellow Irishmen came to Gower in Glamorgan where they resided for nine months. But Arthur sent his nephew, Urien, and 300 men, against them, and they drove them from there, whereupon the Irish, their king, Glaian Ecdwr, being slain, went to Anglesea, where they remained with their countrymen who had settled there previously. Arthur bestowed Rheged (so called from the name of a Roman who was lord of that country before it was subdued by the said Glaian and his Irishmen) on Urien, as a royal conquest for his heroic achievements in war.

'Urien Rheged had a daughter named Eliwri, who became the wife of Morgan Morganwg; and a son called Pasgen, who was a very cruel king, and a great traitor to his country, for which he was dethroned; and the country of Rheged, because of its original position, was reunited to Glamorgan, in which state it continued to the time of Owen, the son of Howell the Good, the son of Cadell, the son of Rhodri the Great, king of all Wales.'

It is difficult to suppose that a chief of North Britain, whose energies were devoted incessant warfare with the Angles, and who lost his life while engaged in the prosecution of those wars, should at the same time have acquired a territory in the very extremity of South Wales. It is, however, evident that all the legends which relate to Taliesin describe Urien Rheged as of the latter portion of the principality, and also represent his son Rhiwallon as reigning in the same district after him; but they make no mention of the assassination of Urien by Morcant in North Britain, or of the wars of the former against Ida; while the romance history of Taliesin connects him with Maelgwn Gwynedd, prince of Gwynedd, Venedotia, or North Wales, who fell a victim to the pestilence called 'Y mad felen', or the yellow plague, which devastated the principality of Wales, according to the chronology of the *Red Book of Hergest*, in the year 586.

The French romances of Arthur introduce Urien under the name of Sir Urience of Gore, that is, of Gower in Glamorganshire, agreeing in this with the legends above cited. We have, therefore, a double uncertainty introduced by these legends, both as to the person of Urien himself and as to the situation of his territory. It is evident that the Welsh genealogists and legend-writers placed Rheged in South Wales, and were ignorant of the existence of a kingdom of the same name in Cumbria, or Northern Britain. The derivations which they offer of the word Rheged — in one instance from 'rheged', a gift, because the territory was bestowed as a free gift upon Urien, in the other, from the name of a Roman so called — demonstrate the want of any genuine information on the subject in the eleventh and twelfth centuries.

Whatever doubts may rest on the individuality of the Taliesin of these legends, there seems to be none that the name had acquired a reputation as early as the eleventh century, and that in the twelfth and succeeding centuries it became significant of all that was great and glorious in literature and song.

We have before mentioned that no less than seventy-seven out of the 124 compositions of the Cynveirdd contained in the Myvyrian Collection[20] are attributed to Taliesin and that even down to the present day, many, if not all, of these compositions are cited under this celebrated name as evidence of the learning, the civilization, and the mythology of the Welsh of the sixth century.

There have not, however, been wanting eminent Welsh scholars who have exhibited a sounder judgement on the subject of these poems. Edward Jones, as long ago as 1792,[21] asserted that many of the poems attributed to Taliesin were the productions of the thirteenth and fourteenth centuries. He says that after the dissolution of the princely government in Wales, that is, after the death of Llywelyn ap Gruffyd in 1282, 'such was the tyranny exercised by the English over the conquered nation that the bards who were born ''since Cambria's fatal day'', might be said to rise under the influence of a baleful and

*Figure 8*: 'Meeting with a mysterious harper' by *R. Machell*.

malignant star. They were reduced to possess their sacred art in obscurity and sorrow, and constrained to suppress the indignation that would burst forth in the most animated strains against their ungenerous and cruel oppressors. Yet they were not silent or inactive. That their poetry might breathe with impunity the spirit of their patriotism, they became dark, prophetic, and oracular. As the monks of the Welsh Church, in the controversy with Rome, had written to countenance their doctrines several religious poems which they feigned to be the work of Taliesin, the bards now ascribed many of the political writings to the same venerable author, and produced many others as the prophecies of the elder Merlin. Hence much uncertainty prevails concerning the genuine remains of the sixth century, a great part of which has descended to us mutilated and depraved; and hence that mysterious air which pervades all the poetry of the later periods I am now describing. The forgery of those poems, which are entirely spurious, though they may have passed unquestioned even by such critics as Dr Davies and Dr J.D. Rhys, may, I think, be presently detected. They were written to serve a popular and a temporary purpose, and were not contrived with such sagacity and care as to hide from the eye of a judicious and enlightened scholar their historical mistakes, their novelty of language, and their other marks of imposture.'

The critical sagacity of Sharon Turner led him, while maintaining the genuineness of the British poems in general, to speak very cautiously on the subject of the poems attributed to Taliesin. 'The most important,' he says, 'are those which concern the battles between the Britons and the Saxons; and these are the poems for whose genuineness I argue.'

The poems of Taliesin which Turner asserted to be genuine, are —

The Poems to Urien, and on his Battles.
His Dialogues with Merddin.
The Poems on Elphin.
His Historical Elegies.

A list which, however, embraces many pieces of a much later date than the sixth century.

Dr John Jones, a Welshman, who, in 1824, published a *History of Wales*, spoke very plainly on this subject. 'The writings of the Welsh bards,' he says, 'are numerous. The largest collection is in the first volume of the *Myvyrian Archaeology*; they consist of ingenious trifles, very often on humble topics, and vested in coarse language; and do not include one epic poem. Aneurin, Llywarch Hen, and Taliesin, are said to have flourished in the sixth century; if that was the case, the Muse of Cambria fell dormant for five hundred years, and awoke again in the eleventh century. The times in which these bards flourished have been matter of great anxiety to antiquarians, who have informed the world, that Llywarch was buried in the church of Llanfor, drawing the inconsistent conclusion that Taliesin was buried in that church seven hundred years before the building could have been erected. The oldest Welsh MSS do not recur further than the twelfth century. Merddin treats of the orchard, which had no existence in Wales before the Conquest; Aneurin, Llywarch Hen, Merddin, and Taliesin, make use of the English words, *frank*, *venture*, *banner*, *sorrow*, etc., and introduce the names of places not built, and the names of saints who had not been canonized, in the sixth century.'

The Revd Thomas Price, author of the *Hanes Cymru*, had pointed out some of these poems as spurious. The Revd Rice Rees also intimates that the bardic records contain but few authentic materials of history, and that all the poems ascribed to the sixth century are not genuine. 'The number of these poems in the *Myvyrian Archaeology* is upwards of a hundred; and those which are spurious may be distinguished from the rest by the modern style in which they are written.' But no one has undertaken to point out and distinguish the genuine poems of Taliesin from those of a later era, falsely ascribed to that bard, except Mr Stephens.

'It has long been suspected,' says Mr Stephens,[22] 'that many of the poems attributed to Taliesin could not have been produced in the sixth century. These conjectures were undoubtedly correct; but as many of the poems may, upon most substantial grounds, be shown to be genuine, it becomes of importance to distinguish between those which are and those which may not be of his production. I have carefully read them; but, as a minute examination of seventy-seven poems would require a volume for itself, we shall here present the result. The classification, in the absence of the data on which it is based, can have no strong claims to attention, apart from the weight attached to the opinion of the critic. I have, as the result of my examination, classed these poems, thus —

## Historical, and as old as the sixth century

| | |
|---|---|
| Gwaith Gwenystrad | The Battle of Gwenystrad |
| Gwaith Argoed Llwyvain | The Battle of Argoed Llwyvain |
| Gwaith Dyffryn Gwarant | The Battle of Dyffryn Gwarant (part of the Dyhuddiant Elphin) |
| I Urien | To Urien |
| I Urien | To Urien |
| Canu I Urien | A Song to Urien |
| Yspail Taliesin | The Spoils of Taliesin |
| Canu I Urien Rheged | A Song to Urien Rheged |
| Dadolwch Urien Rheged | Reconciliation to Urien Rheged |
| I Gwallawg | To Gwallawg (the Galgaens of Tacitus) |
| Dadolwch i Urien | Reconciliation to Urien |
| Marwnad Owain ap Urien | The Elegy of Owain ap Urien |

## Doubtful

| | |
|---|---|
| Cerdd i Wallawg ab Lleenawg | A Song to Gwallawg ab Lleenawg |
| Marwnad Cunedda | The Elegy of Cunedda |
| Gwarchan Tutvwlch | The Incantation of Tulvwlch |
| Gwarchan Adebon | The Incantation of Adebon |
| Gwarchan Kynvelyn | The Incantation of Kynvelyn |
| Gwarchan Maelderw | The Incantation of Maelderw |
| Kerdd Daronwy | The Song to Daronwy |
| Trawsganu Cynan Garwyn | The Satire on Cynan Garwyn |

## Romances belonging to the twelfth and thirteenth centuries

| | |
|---|---|
| Canu Kyntaf Taliesin | Taliesin's First Song |
| Dyhuddiant Elphin | The Consolation of Elphin |
| Hanes Taliesin | The History of Taliesin |
| Canu y Medd | The Mead Song |
| Canu y Gwynt | The Song to the Wind |
| Canu y Byd Mawr | The Song of the Great World |
| Canu y Byd Bychan | The Song of the Little World |
| Bustl y Beirdd | The Gall of the Bards |
| Buarth Beirdd | The Circle of the Bards |
| Cad Goddeu | The Battle of the Trees |
| Cadeir Taliesin | The Chair of Taliesin |
| Cadeir Teyrnon | The Chair of the Princes |
| Canu y Cwrwf | The Song of the Ale |
| Canu y Meirch | The Song of the Horses |
| Addfwynen Taliesin | The Beautiful Things of Taliesin |
| Angar Kyvyndawd | The Inimical Confederacy |
| Priv Gyvarch | The Primary Gratulation |
| Dyhuddiant Elphin (2nd) | The Consolation of Elphin |
| Arymes Dydd Brawd | The Prophecy of the Day of Judgment |
| Awdl Vraith | The Ode of Varieties |
| Glaswawd Taliesin | The Encomiums of Taliesin |
| Divregwawd Taliesin | Poesy of Taliesin |
| Mabgyvreu Taliesin | Taliesin's Juvenile Accomplishments |
| Awdl etto Taliesin | Another Ode by Taliesin |
| Kyffes Taliesin | The Confession of Taliesin |

## Poems forming part of the Mabinogion, or Romance of Taliesin, composed by Thomas ap Einion Offeiriad in the thirteenth century

| | |
|---|---|
| Cadair Keridwen | The Chair of Keridwen |
| Marwnad Uthyr Bendragon | The Elegy of Uther Pendragon |
| Preidden Annwn | The Spoils of Annwn |
| Marwnad Ercwlf | The Elegy of Ercwlf |
| Marwnad Mad Drud ac Erov Greulawn | The Elegy of Madoc the Bold, and Erov the Fierce |
| Marwnad Aeddon o Von | The Elegy of Aeddon of Mon |
| Anrhyveddodan Alexander | The Not-wonders of Alexander |
| Y Gofcisws Byd | A Sketch of the World |
| Lluryg Alexander | The Lorica of Alexander |

## Predictive Poems of the twelfth and succeeding centuries

| | |
|---|---|
| Ymarwar Lludd Mawr | The Appeasing Lludd the Great |
| Ymarwar Lludd Bychan | The Appeasing of Lludd the Little |
| Gwawd Lludd Mawr | The Praise of Lludd the Great |
| Kerdd am Veib Llyr | Song to the Sons of Llyr ab Brochwel |
| Marwnad Corroi ab Dairy | The Elegy of Corroi the Son of Dairy |

| | |
|---|---|
| Mic Dinbych (or Myg Dinbych) | The Glory of Dinbych |
| Arymes Brydain | The Prophecy of Britain |
| Arymes | Prophecy |
| Arymes | Prophecy |
| Kywrysedd Gwynedd a Dehcubarth | The Contention of North and South Wales |
| Awdl | An Ode |
| Marwnad y Milveib | Elegy of the Thousand Saints |
| Y Macu Gwyrth | The Miraculous Stone |
| Can y Gwynt | The Song of the Wind |
| Anrhce Urien | The Gift of Urien |

## Theological — same date

| | |
|---|---|
| Plaen yr Aipht | The Plagues of Egypt |
| Llath Moesen | The Rod of Moses |
| Llath Voesen | The Rod of Moses |
| Gwawd Gwyr Israel | Eulogy of the Men of Israel' |

The result of the investigation by Mr Stephens is to assign with certainty, to the sixth century twelve only out of the seventy-seven poems bearing the name of Taliesin, and to place eight others doubtfully as belonging to the same era. It will be seen that even this expurgated list must be still farther curtailed.

In the Notes to the Iolo MSS,[23] the *Hanes Taliesin* is declared to be 'an evidently fictitious poem, attributed until recently to Taliesin, and still passing current as his production with general readers'.

'But,' says the editor of the MSS, Taliesin Williams, the son of Edward Williams or Iolo Morganwg, who collected them, 'to rescue the genuine fame of the chief bard of the West from the annihilation of such as have lately denied the originality of his works and would fain even pronounce his very existence a romance, it is high time to divest his compositions of the spurious productions commixed with them, productions that are characterized by comparatively modern expressions and idioms, and (like other similar deceptions) by their anachronisms, and other denouncing incongruities. Nor would this expurgation materially affect the literary remains of this remote votary of the Cimbric Muse; *for his numerous and genuine poems*, being intrinsically sustained by consistency of allusions, primitive features of versification, and originality of sentiment, would still extensively vindicate the palm so long conceded to his hoary merit. Iolo Morganwg, in his manuscript compositions, frequently laments the injurious effects of the counterfeit pieces;[24] and the Revd Thomas Price, whose *Hanes Cymru* (History of Wales) ably supplies the desideratum heretofore so long the object of hope, impugns, occasionally, their originality.'

It would have been satisfactory if Iolo Morganwg or his editor had pointed out these numerous and genuine poems of Taliesin, and the evidences of their originality. All the evidence at present before us shows that there is not extant a single poem or metrical composition in the Welsh language, with the exception of the lines from the copy of Juvencus before mentioned, the manuscript of which is older than the twelfth century. For the proof of an earlier date of the compositions themselves, we have only such internal evidence as they may afford.

And in this statement the works of Aneurin and Llywarch Hen must be included with those of Taliesin. The materials of these compositions in all probability did exist, perhaps for some centuries before, in the mouths of the professional minstrels and storytellers; but there is no evidence that they were reduced into writing at an earlier period than the twelfth century. Zeuss[25] is of opinion that all the extant poems have been transcribed in a modern orthography, in many instances by persons unacquainted with the meaning of the older forms, and that in consequence they have, in undergoing this change of form, suffered considerable alteration and interpolation, and we have sufficient proof in the Myvyrian Collection that poems which were written in the Llyvr Ddu in the twelfth century were transcribed at a later period in a more modern orthography, but we can go no farther back than the former manuscript.

That the form in which these compositions now appear in the oldest MSS is not that in which they originally existed, if written in the sixth or seventh century, is too clear for discussion.

It is, however, supposed that these poems, though worked up and brought into their present form by writers or bards of the twelfth and thirteenth centuries, contain materials of far more ancient date, and were, in fact, originally composed in the sixth century.

So little importance has indeed been attached to the critical views of Mr Stephens by his countrymen, and so little effect has his work published in 1849 produced upon this question of the antiquity and nature of the Welsh poems, that the old opinion, that they contain philosophical dogmas and notices of Druid or pagan superstitions of a remote origin, has been as distinctly promulgated in 1853 by the chairman of the society which adjudged the prize to Mr Stephens's Essay in 1848, as they were by the Revd Edward Davies in 1809. In truth, as Mr Stephens has himself observed, any opinion on the date or character of these poems, unaccompanied by translations has no very strong claims to attention, apart from the weight attached to the opinion of the critic.

It is somewhat remarkable that these remains of the earliest Welsh literature, and especially the poems attributed to Taliesin, so constantly appealed to and cited in evidence not only for the history and condition of the Welsh at the period during which he flourished but also for the verification of traditions of a much earlier period, have never been translated *in extenso* by the learned Welshmen who rely on his authority. Isolated pieces and fragments in abundance have appeared, but a complete edition of these works in a language which would make them common property has never been ventured.

In 1792, Dr Owen advertised the *Works of Taliesin*, with a literal English version and notes, but the work never appeared.

The reason assigned for this apparent neglect has been that the language in which they are written is obsolete, and that they are filled with mystical and mythological allusions which are no longer intelligible.

But the best authorities on this subject are agreed that no insuperable difficulty of this kind exists. This was asserted nearly sixty years ago by the editors of the *Myvyrian Archaeology*. 'These ancient poems,' they state, in a *Review of the Present State of Welsh Manuscripts*,[26] 'have for ages been secluded from the eyes of the public; and some of the collections are very difficult of access. Very mistaken ideas of them have for a long time circulated through every part of Wales; there are consequently preconceptions from which many will too rashly criticize; but a long course of study is absolutely necessary to understand them properly. Facts of which no other records remain are often alluded to; opinions that are forgotten, manners that no longer exist, idioms and figurative modes of expression that are obsolete and obscured by various schemes of orthography, arising from the inadequacy of the Roman alphabet to represent the ancient British one, render many passages almost unintelligible to novices. It is not from a supposed loss or corruption of our language that they are difficultly understood: they contain very few, if any words, either radicals or derivations that are not at this day in common use in one part or other of Wales, nor have any of those words materially changed their acceptation. Our language, as some have imagined, is not altered; it is therefore to be regretted that the Revd Evan Evans did not, in his *Dissertatio de Bardis*, investigate and point out the various things which embarrassed him, instead of assigning all the difficulties to the language. In many of the allusions, indeed, they are dark; mutilations are occasionally met with out of the question, which equally confuse in every age, the present as well as the past, and are matters not of language, but of accident.'

Archdeacon Williams, though he maintains that a great orthographical change had taken place in the interval between the eighth and twelfth century (as would necessarily be the case), admits that 'restoration and interpretation of all the more valuable portion of the ancient poems is possible, without any further discovery, as instruments sufficient for that purpose are within our reach.'[27]

Mr Stephens, also, has recorded his opinion[28] that as to the majority of the poems attributed to Taliesin, 'though many of them contain allusions which are now unintelligible, yet a large portion of them and the intentions of the whole may be understood. They were written when the language was in an advanced state of development, as most of the words are in use at the present day, and, as will be seen, cannot be supposed to have been prior to the twelfth and succeeding centuries.'[29]

In fact, the result has been, as far as Taliesin is concerned, whenever any of these poems have been fairly translated, to cut down their claims to antiquity, and gradually to strip their reputed author, leaf after leaf, of the laurels assigned to him by the partial voice of his countrymen; and this may, in some degree, account for the want of any general translation of these works.

This has been eminently the case with another celebrated bard, said to be of the sixth century — Merlin or Merddin. Translations of the most important pieces attributed to this bard, the *Avellanau*, and the *Hoianau*, have been published by Mr Stephens in his *Literature of the Kymry*. From these translations we are enabled to decide, not only that there is a total absence of all these mysterious allegories which have been supposed to enshroud fearful superstitions and Druidic oracles but also that they contain allusions to personages and events belonging to the eleventh and twelfth centuries. The fourth stanza of the *Hoianau* is decisive as to the date of the composition being, at least, as late as the end of the twelfth century —

> Hear, O little pig! it was necessary to pray
> For fear of five chiefs from Normandy;
> And the fifth going across the salt sea,
> To conquer Ireland of gentle towns,
> There to create war and confusion,

> And a fighting of son against father — the country knows it;
> Also will be going the Loegrians of falling cities,
> And they will never go back to Normandy.

This stanza, Mr Stephens observes, clearly refers to the conquest of Leinster by Richard Strongbow, who went to Ireland AD 1170. He was the *fifth* Norman, having been preceded by *four* others — Robert Fitzstephens, Maurice Fitzgerald, Hervé de Montmarais, and David Barry. Even if this were not apparent, the two last lines could not have been written before AD 1066, unless we really believe the Cambrian bard to have been actually gifted with the spirit of prophecy.

The other bard of the sixth century is Aneurin. The famous poem which passes under his name, *Y Gododin*, has recently been carefully translated by the Revd John Williams ab Ithel. [30]

An excellent translation of the *Gododin*, of some of the compositions of Llywarch Hen, and of the historical pieces ascribed to Taliesin, was published by M. de la Villemarqué, [31] who has paid great attention to the traditional remains of the ancient Armorican nation still preserved among the peasantry of Bretagne.

This celebrated poem, the *Gododin*, so unintelligible in the tradition of Davies, and by him and Mr Herbert supposed to relate to the massacre of the British chiefs by Hengist at Stonehenge, is now known to describe a combat between the Strathclyde Britons and the Saxons of Deira and Bernicia, north of the Humber, the date of which Mr Williams places at about AD 567. It contains no Druidism, and its author was a Christian.

> The heroes marched to Cattraeth, loquacious was the host,
> Blue mead was their liquor, and it proved their poison.
> In marshalled army they cut through the engines of war;
> And after the joyful cry, silence ensued.
> They should have gone to churches to have performed penance;
> The inevitable strife of death was about to pierce them. [32]

Again —

> They put to death Gelorwydd with blades.
> The Gem of Baptism was thus widely taunted;
> Better that you should ere you join your kindred
> Have a gory unction, and death far from your native home. [33]

We certainly could not, prima facie, expect to find any other than Christian allusions in poems of this age. For, whatever may be thought of the story of the introduction of Christianity into Britain by Bran the Blessed, the father of Caractacus, by Joseph of Arimathea, or by Aristobulus, in the first century of the Christian era, there is no doubt that in the sixth century, the period when the authors of these poems are supposed to have flourished, the Christian religion was firmly established in Wales. St David, apart from the monkish legends and absurd fables connected with his name, has every claim to be considered a historical character, and his era is precisely that of Taliesin. There is hardly a piece in the collection of the *Mywyrian Archaeology* which does not bear direct testimony to the fact of the writer having been a Christian, and that the persons to whom these poems were addressed were Christians also. Such arguments, however, are of little weight in the opinions of those who maintain that the Druidical doctrines to be found in these poems were cherished in secret, as esoteric, and carefully hidden from the eye of the people at large, though known to and acknowledged by the select initiated among the higher classes. A little reflection will teach us that it was impossible any such doctrines could have been kept secret through a course of ages, and remain unnoticed by the Christian authorities, or by such writers as Giraldus Cambrensis, who was evidently ignorant of any such heresy existing in the bosom of the community over which he presided, unless we are to consider him, in common with every other writer, equally bound to secrecy as a member of the institution.

While on the subject of the *Gododin*, we ought not to omit to mention, that there is a still later translation of this poem, which shows it to be 'an Aramitic composition which purports to have been delivered orally at a school meeting in Wilts, at some period before the Christian era', principally composed of a treatise on the game of chess. At the 322nd line we have —

> The game of chess. It rains
> Out of doors; let chess spread relaxation.

Afterwards, line 332 —

> Here's the game of chess, the game
> Of ivory troops in four squads.
> The Indian game with care consider,
> Chief game celebrated afar among the Anakim.

It is satisfactory to be informed from the *Gododin*, line 251 —

> There was a Chinese hero Sk-m-sk Kon Caph,
> First of bard chiefs, after the genius of the Britons.

and that

> The fat Chinese heroes have skill to find out little marks.

We have here also veritable Druids who have informed us what the *Gododin* really is; line 474 —

> 'Lech' is joined. Here's 'la'. La is weary.
> What is 'Gododin',
> What? A trifle to Cherubim.

It may be so; but, as we are afterwards told, line 515 —

> Cast at it quickly. Give it up! Turn it over.
> Consider! Risk! Hurry on! Stand still! Go back!
> A pleasant game of games.

We must say, we prefer giving it up. [34]

As a preliminary to the examination of these poems, we may present an example of one of these compositions, which was, no doubt, recited to delight audiences by vagrant minstrels many years before it was reduced to writing in the fourteenth century. It is certainly one of the most corrupt examples of its class, but is not singular in the mixture of topics contained in it, and enables us to appreciate the condition in which many of these pieces have come down to us.

## PRIF GYFARCH TALIESIN

Prif gyfarch gelvyd par rylent
Puy Kyntac tyuyll ac goleuat
Neu adaf pan vu pa dyd y
  great
Neu y dan tylwet py ry
  Scilyat
A vo Lleion nys myn
  pwyllyat
Est qui peccator am nivereit
Collant gulad nef vy pluyf
  Offeiryeit.
  Boreu neb ni del
  Or ganon teir pel
  Eingngyl gallwydel
  Gunnont en ryvel
  Pan dau nos n dyd
  Pan vyd lluyd Eryr
  Pan yw tyuyll nos
  Pan iu guyrd llinos
  Mor pan dyverwyd
  Cud anys guelyd
  Yssit teir ffynnaun
  Y mynyd Fuaun
  Yssit Gaer Gwarthawn
  A dan don eigiawn
  Gorith gyvarchawr
  Puy enw y Porthawr
  Pwy y periglawr
  Y vab Meir mwynvawr
  Pa vessur muynaf
  A orug Adaf
  Puy vessur Uffern
  Puy tuet y llen
  Puy llet y gencu
  Puy meint cu mein heu
  Neu vlaen gwydd ffalsum
  Py estung mor grum
  Neu pet anat llon
  Yssyd yn eu bon
  Neu leu a gwydion
  A vuant gelvydon
  Nen a rodant lyvyryon
  Pan wnant

Pan dau nos a lliant
Pan vyd y diviant
Cud anos rac dyd
Pater Noster ambulo
Gentis tonans in
    adjuvando
Sibilem signum
Ro gentes fortium
Am gwiw gwiwam gwmya
Am geissyant deu Gelvydd
Am Kaer Kerindan
    Kerindydd
Rys tyneirch *pector* Dauyd
Y mwyngant ys cwant
Ym Kaffwynt yn dirdau
Kymry yggridvan
Provater eneit
Rac Lluyth eissyffleit
Kymry prif diryeit
Rann ry goll buyeit
Gwnedd hir neheneit
As guyar honneit
Dydoent guarthvor
Gwydveirch dyarvor
Eingyl yghygvor
Guelattor aruyddion
Guynyeith ar Saesson
Claudus in Sion
O ruyvannussion
Bydaut penn Sciron
Rac ffichit lewon
Marini Brython
Ryd a roganon
A medi heon
Am Hafren Avon
Lladyr ffadyr Ken a
    Massuy
Ffis amala ffur flir Sel
Dyrnedi trinct tramoed
Creaudyr oro hai — huai
Gentil divlannai gyspell
Codigni ceta gosgord mur
Gan nath ben gau
    Govannon
Corvu . . . dur
Neu bum gan vyr Kelydon
Gau Vatheu gan Govannon
Gan Eunyd gan Elestron
Ry ganhymdeith achuysson
Bluydyn yg Kaer Govannon
Wyf hen wyf neuyd wyf
    guion
Wyf lluyr wyf synwyr
    Keinyon
Dy gy vi dyheu vrython

Guydyl Kyl diaerogyon
Meddut medduon
Wyf bardd wyf ny rivaf
   yeillyon
Wyf llyu wyf syu amrysson
Sihei a rahei nys medry
Si ffradyr yn y ffradri
Pos Verdein bronrhein a
   dyvi
A ddeuont uch medlestri
A ganont gam vardoni
A geissent gyvarnys nys
   deubi
Ileb gyvreith heb reith heb
   rodi
A guedy hynny dyvysgi
Brithvyt a byt dyoysci
Nac cruyn dy hedduch
   nyth vi
Reen nef rymnvyr dy wedi
Rac y gres rym guares dy
   voli
Ri Rex gle am gogyvarch
   yn gelvyd
A ueleisty Dominus ffortis
Darogan dwfn Domini
Budyant Uffern
Hic nemor i por progenii
Ef a dyllyngys ci thuryf
Dominus virtictum
Kaeth naut Kynhulluys
   estis iste — est
(Est) a chyn buassun a
   simsei
Ruyf deruin y duu diheu
A chyn mynnuyf dervyn
   ereu
A chyn del ewyn friw ar
   uyggeneu
A chyn vyg Kyvalle ar y
   llatheu pren
Poet ym heneit yd a
   Kyvadeu
Abreid om dyweit llythyr
   llyvreu
Kystud dygyn guedy guely
   aghen
Ar saul a gigleu vy
   mardly-freu
Ry bryn huynt wlat Nef
   adef goren
Ry prynwynt, etc.

*Diwedd y Prif Gyv.*

# THE 'FRIF GYFARCH', OR FIRST ADDRESS OF TALIESIN

First tell the secret you who are in the superior place,
What was before darkness and light?
Or of Adam, where was he the day he was created?
Or what could he see in the darkness?
Or was he, like a stone, without intellect?
Est qui peccator, innumerable,
The ministers of my people lose the kingdom of heaven,
In the morning let nobody come
Within three cannon balls
Of the Irish of Eingyngl
Who are making a disturbance.
Whence are night and day distinct?
Whence is the eagle grey?
Whence is the night dark?
Whence is the linnet green?
Whence is the boiling up of the sea?
Hidden and not exposed.
Is it the three fountains
In the mountain of Fuawn?
Is it Caer Gwarthawn
Under the wave of the ocean?
The illusive questioner.
What is the name of the porter?
Who is the priest?
The very kind son of Mary.
What is the greatest measure
That Adam made?
What is the measure of Hell?
How thick its covering?
How wide its jaws?
How many its stones?
Was not the measuring rod false?
What is the extent of the raging sea,
Or what kind of creatures
Are at the bottom of it?
Neither Lleu nor Gwydion,
And they were wise,
Nor do books inform
How they are made.
Whence come night and dawn,
Whither the earth is moving on slowly,
The hiding-place of night before day.
    Pater noster ambulo
    Gentis touans in adjuvando
    Sibilem signum
    Ro genics fortium.
To the worthy, the worthy is a companion.
They ask me two secrets
Concerning Caer Kerindydd.
Very gentle was the breast of Davyd,
In gentle song his pleasure,
They seek after thy song,
The Cymry in their grief,

It is profitable to the soul.
On account of the poverty of the land,
The chief misfortune of the Cymry,
On account of the loss of food,
Long is the cry of sorrow.
There is blood upon the spears.
The waves are bearing
Ships upon the sea.
Angles, the sea-rovers
Displaying their banners,
The false tongue of the Saxon.
Claudus in Sion
From the rulers.
They shall be the chief workmen
Before twenty chiefs.
Marini Brython
Are prophesying
A reaping of the ripe crop
By the river Severn.
Slain is the father of Ken and Massny,
Ffiis amala ffur fir sel,
It is impossible to comprehend the Trinity.
I pray to the Creator, hai — huai,
The Gentiles may be illuminated by the Gospel,
Equally worthy of the great assembly.
Have I not been with the wise Kelydon,
With Math and with Elestron,
Accompanying them with great labour
A year in Caer Govannon,
I am old, I am young, I am Gwion;
I am a soldier, I am knowing in feasts;
I am equal to the Southern Britons.
The Irish distil from a furnace
Intoxicating liquor.
I am a bard, I have an abundance of melodies;
I am a scholar, I am constant in (musical) contests;
In . . . there is none more accomplished.
Si frater in fratri.
Broad-chested rhyming bards there are,
And they prophesy over bowls of mead,
And sing evil songs,
And seek gifts which they will not get
Without law, without justice, without gifts;
And after this there will be a tumult,
There will be quarrelling and confusion.
I am not opposed to thy peace,
Lord of Heaven, I seek thee in prayer,
Through grace it is pleasant to me to praise thee.
Ri rex . . . I am worshipping thee in secret.
Who has seen Dominus fortis?
(Who can) relate the deep things of the Lord?
They have been victorious over Hell.
Hie nemor i por progenii.
He hath set free its multitudes.
Dominus virtictum,

He is the protector of the assembled captives.
And before I had been . . .
I was actively travelling in the southern parts;
And before I cease from active motion,
And before my face becomes pale,
And before I am joined to the wooden boards,
May there be to me a good festival in my lifetime.
I have scarcely finished the letters of my book.
There will be sore affliction after the sleep of death.
And whosoever has heard my bardic books
Shall surely obtain the most blessed mansions of the land of
    Heaven.

*End of the Prif Gyvarch*

This remarkable farrago has apparently been the property of some of the vagrant monks with whom, previous to the Reformation, Wales swarmed almost equally with the vagrant minstrels or bards, of whom they were at once the rivals and bitter enemies. The bardic poets abundantly repay the scorn and hatred exhibited for them by the ecclesiastics.

The poem, in its present condition, is evidently made up of several unconnected fragments, as is indeed the case with most others in the Myvyrian Collection. Though this condition of the oldest Welsh compositions may be in some measure ascribed to their having been subjects of oral recitation long before they were committed to writing, it is probable that in many instances it represents, though imperfectly, the original condition of the ballad, arising out of the customs of the Welsh minstrels.

In the great musical contests of the earlier and better age of Welsh minstrelsy, the competitors were obliged each to produce a composition of his own, and the prize was award to the successful candidate. According to the laws of Gruffyd ap Cynan,[35] 'When the congress hath assembled, they shall choose twelve persons skilled in the Welsh language, poetry, music, and heraldry, who shall give to the bards a subject to sing upon in any of the twenty-four metres, but not in amoechean carols, or any such frivolous compositions. The umpires shall see that the candidates do not descend to satire or personal invective, and shall allow to each a sufficient time for composing his Englyn or Cywydd, or other task that they shall assign.'

In less dignified stations, the practice of contesting by the recitation of known compositions, or the production of extempore verses, appears to have been a favourite and universal pastime.

'Two clerwyr' (or wandering minstrels), says Dr Rhys,[36] 'were wont to stand before the company, the one to give in rime at the other extempore, to stirre mirth and laughter with wittie quibbes,' etc.

Something of the same kind also took place even on more important occasions, and in the presence of dignified personages, when a kind of Saturnalia was permitted. At such times, and especially at the marriage of a prince, or any person of princely extraction, the higher and lower orders of bards intermingled in the appointment of a *Cyff Cler*, a 'butt' or object on whom the rest exercised their talent of ridicule. A year and a day before the celebration of the nuptials, notice was given to a Pencerdd to prepare himself to support that character. When the time came he appeared in the hall, and, a facetious subject being proposed, the inferior bards surrounded him and attacked him with their ridicule. In these extempore satirical effusions, they were restrained from any personal allusion or real affront. The Cyff Cler sat in a chair in the midst of them, and silently suffered them to say whatever they chose that could tend to the diversion of the assembly. For this unpleasing service he received a considerable fee. The next day he appeared again in the hall and answered his revilers, and provoked the laughter and gained the applause of all who were present, by exposing them in their turn, retorting all their ridicule upon themselves.

Of this custom we have a curious notice in a piece called the *Buarth Beirdd*, the 'Fold (or Enclosure) of the Bards', in which the minstrel, among other self-commendations, says —

> Wyf bardd Nenodd wyf Kyv Kadeir,
> Digonaf i feirdd llafar llestair —

> I am the Bard of the Hall, I am the Cyff of the Chair;
> I am able to stop the tongues of the bards.

In Pennant's time this species of musical contest, though the subjects of song had somewhat degenerated, was in full activity in Wales. 'Even at this day,' he observes, 'some vein of the ancient minstrelsy survives amongst our mountains. Numbers of persons of both sexes assemble and sit around the harp, singing alternately pennillon or stanzas of ancient or modern composition. Often, like the modern *improvisatori* of Italy, they sing extempore verses, and a person conversant in this art readily produces a pennill opposite to the last that was sung.'

'Many have their memories stored with several hundreds, perhaps thousands, of pennillion, some of which they have always ready for answers to every subject that can be proposed; or, if their recollection should ever fail them, they have invention to compose something pertinent and proper for the occasion.'

This is, no doubt, the key to the condition of many of those pieces which contain apparently unconnected fragments, and to the kind of question and answer which they frequently exhibit.

An example of the somewhat hasty manner in which a remote antiquity has been ascribed to some of the compositions in the Welsh language, which have been preserved in the *Red Book of Hergest* or other MSS of that age, will not be out of place here.

There is in the *Myvyrian Archaeology* a piece containing the following stanzas composed in the metre called 'Triban Milwr'. Three of these were given by the Revd Evan Evans, in a paper published in the *Cambro-Briton* in 1820, as the genuine production of the Druids. In 1853 the Ven. Archdeacon Williams, speaking of this same metre, says, 'There is every reason to believe that this was the medium through which the instruction of the Druids was generally conveyed to the initiated. Hence we have monitory stanzas, and hints conveyed in symbols respecting the observation of secrecy, with respect to "guid", whether knowledge of wood or trees. It is impossible to fix the relative antiquity of such stanzas as these' —

**1**

Marchwiail bedw briglas
A dyn fy nlíroed o wanas
Nae addef dy rin i was

**2**

Marchwiail derw mewn llwyn
A dyn fy nhroed o gadwyn
Nae addef dy rin i forwyn,

**3**

Marchwiail derw deiliar
A dyn fy nhroed o garchar
Nae addef dy rin i lafar.

**4**

Eurtirn ai cirn ni clwir
Oer lluric lluchedic awir
Bir diwedit blaen guit gwir.

Translation —

**1**

Saplings of the green-topped
    birch,
Which will draw my foot from
    the fetter.
Repeat not thy secret to a
    youth.

**2**

Saplings of the oak in the
    grove,
Which will draw my foot from
    the chain,
Repeat not thy secret to a
    maiden.

**3**

Saplings of the leafy oak,
Which will draw my foot from
    prison,
Repeat not thy secret to a
    babbler.

**4**

Golden princes with their
    horns are heard,
Cold is the breastplate, full of
    lightning the air,
Briefly it is said; true are the
    tree-sprigs.

It at once occurs, on reading these stanzas, that we have here a specimen of that triadic form of composition, so frequently met with in the productions of the Welsh, wherein of a stanza of three lines, the last is a proverbial phrase or moral maxim, having no necessary connection with the two preceding lines.

Mr E. Davies, however, regarded them as 'the oldest remains of the Welsh language, and as genuine relics of the Druidical ages.' Mr Williams, we have seen, follows in the same track.

But, on turning to the original piece in the *Myvyrian Archaeology*,[37] we find that there are no less than fifty-two of these stanzas and are at a loss to know why the Ven. Archdeacon, who refers to the *Myvyrian Archaeology*, has selected the 8th, 9th, 10th and 26th stanzas, omitting the 11th, which clearly is in the same category with the three former. It is this —

Marchwiail drysi a mwyar arni
A mwyalch ar ci nyth
A chelwyddawg ni theu byth —

Saplings of the thorn with berries on it,
The blackbird is on her nest;
The liar will not be silent.

Or the next —

Gwlaw allan gwlychyd rhedyn
Gwyn gro mor goron cwyn
Tecav canwyll pwyll i dyn —

There is rain without, wetting the fern;
White is the sand of the sea with its crown of foam;
Reason is the fairest light of man.

Or the seventh, the one which precedes those selected —

Hir nos gorddyar morva
Guawd tervysg yn nghymmynva
Ni chyvyd diriaid a da —

Long is the night, roaring the seashore;
Usual is a disturbance in an assembly;
The evil with good do not agree.

Or, indeed, any other of the series.

It may be difficult to fix the age of these and similar stanzas, though not in the sense meant by the Revd J. Williams. We find, in fact, that the editors of the *Myvyrian Archaeology* ascribe these 'Tribanau' to Llywarch Hen, the famous warrior bard of the sixth century; and Dr Owen has given a translation of twelve of them in his *Heroic Elegies* of that bard. They are precisely similar in form and character to the *Gorwynion*, attributed to the same poet, and may be of any age down to the time when they were written in the *Red Book of Hergest*. In fact, the stanzas commencing 'Marchwiail', etc., are said to have been composed in the fourteenth century, or in the reign of King Edward III.

In the Iolo MSS published by the Welsh MSS Society in 1848, five years before the publication of *Gomer*, the following notices occur respecting these very stanzas —

### The Lineage of Marchwiail in Maelor[38]

Llywelyn the son of Gruffyd, called Llewelyn Llogell Rhison, who composed *Englynion Marchwiail*, in the ancient style of poetry, when the great Eisteddvod was held there, in the time of King Edward III, under the patronage of Lord Mortimer.

Also —

### 'The Eisteddvod of Gwern-y-Cleppa, and the Brothers of Marchwiail. Memoirs of Bards and Poets

In the time of King Edward III, the celebrated Eisteddvod of Gwern-y-Cleppa took place, under the patronage and gifts of Ivor Hael, and to it came the three brothers of Marchwiail in Maelor, in Powys, and Llywelyn ab Gwilym of Dôl Goch in Ceredigion. The three brothers of Marchwiail, and with them Davydd ab Gwilym, had been scholars in bardism to Llywelyn the son of Gwilym at Gwern-y-Cleppa — that is, the seat of Ivor Hael.

After that, an Eisteddvod was held at Dôl Goch, in Emlyn, under the patronage of Llywelyn, the son of Gwilym, which was attended by John of Kent and Rhys Goch of Snowdon in Gwynedd. Upon this occasion, Llywelyn the son of Gruffyd, one of the three brothers of Marchwiail, sang the Englynion of *Marchwiail bedw briglas* in the ancient style of poetry.

Whether this story is true or false — and it is to be supposed that the Ven. Archdeacon does not give any credit to it, as he does not notice it — it is evident that the authors of this relation did not imagine that there was any Druidic mystery concealed under these triplets — a discovery which was reserved for the nineteenth century.

The most ancient piece of British poetry extant is composed in this style of stanzas of triplets. Lhuyd was in doubt whether it was in the language of the Strathclyde Britons, or of the Pictish or old Caledonians, and Archdeacon Williams pronounces it 'an unique surviving specimen of the Pictish composition in the language mentioned by Beda, as a living speech in his day, and as the representative of the language of Galgaeus and his Caledonians, partially, perhaps, affected by the intercourse established between the Picts and Scots during their long-continued struggles against imperial Rome.'

The composition in question, which was discovered by Lhnyd inscribed in an old copy of Juvencus, might, in his opinion, have been written in the seventh century, and may fairly be supposed to be as old as the ninth, the verbal forms being similar to those of the glosses in the Bodleian MSS, which Zeuss refers to about the latter date. The Juvencus lines are the only independent composition preserved in which those forms appear, the MSS of the twelfth and thirteenth centuries, as seen in the *Black Book of Caermarthen* differing only in unimportant particulars from those of the fourteenth.

In the original MS the lines are written continuously without division, but are evidently metrical in form, and constitute three stanzas of three lines each. Archdeacon Williams has printed them in a modernized form, and gives the following translation —

### 1
I will not sleep even an hour's sleep tonight
My family is not formidable,
I and my Frank servant and our kettle.

### 2
No bard will sing, I will not smile nor kiss tonight,
Together — to the Christmas mead.
Myself and my Frank client and our kettle.

### 3
Let no one partake of joy tonight,
Until my fellow-soldier arrives.
It is told to me that our lord the king will come.

'This,' says the Archdeacon, 'is the trifling effusion of a young officer given to literary pursuits, who otherwise would not have carried his Juvencus with him. The writer of the stanzas seems to have been on a midnight watch, at a military outpost, whence he was not to move until a superior officer should arrive, whom he styles a fellow-soldier. His *callaur*, or *padell*, was his camp-kettle. The last line alludes to the rumoured arrival of their common prince. The Frank servant is evidently a Frank by birth serving with the Pictish army — the name often occurring among the Cymric poets of this age.'

The idea of an officer of the Pictish army, in the seventh century, carrying about with him, a Frank servant, a copy of Juvencus, and a camp-kettle, appears a little far-fetched. We can see, however, that the words admit of a somewhat different division from that adopted by the Archdeacon, and that the lines contain what we should expect from them — the effusion of a bard desirous of obtaining a share of the feast in return for the display of his musical or poetic skill.

**1**
Ni guorcosam nemheunaur henoid
Mi telun it gurmaur
Mi am franc dam an calaur.

**2**
Ni can ili ni guardam ni cusam henoid
Cet iben med nouel
Mi am franc dam an patel.

**3**
Na mereit nep legucnid henoid
Is discinn mi coweidid
Dou nam Riccur imguctid.

The substitution of 'telun', 'telyn', a harp, for 'teuln', a family, or household, renders the first stanza intelligible, and gives the key to the meaning of the whole. Instead of reading the word 'franc' as a proper name, a Frank, we give it the meaning ascribed to it by Dr Owen, 'a play, frolic, prank', or, as an adjective, 'active, sprightly'. The following translation, though not free from objections, presents a more reasonable rendering of the meaning of these antique lines, and more in accordance with the tenor and contents of those fragments of British minstrelsy with which we are, in other instances, familiar

**1**
I shall not sleep a single hour tonight,
My harp is a very large one.
Give me for my play a taste of the kettle.

**2**
I shall not sing a song nor laugh or kiss tonight,
Before drinking the Christmas mead.
Give me for my play a taste of the bowl.

**3**
Let there be no sloth or sluggishness tonight,
I am very skilful in recitation.
God, King of Heaven, let my request be obtained.

We know so little of the Picts, or the dialect of the British language spoken by that people, that we cannot affirm or deny that these lines present a specimen of the Pictish dialect; the close affinity with the Cambric glosses of the Bodleian MSS which they present is, perhaps, no reason for denying their Pictish origin.

1. Originally published as Chapter 2 *Taliesin: or the Bards and Druids of Britain* (John Russell Smith, 1858) [Ed.].
2. *Myvyrian Archaeology* [eds. O. Jones, E. Williams and W.O. Pughe (London, 1801), Ed.], vol. i, p. 303
3. Ibid. p. 411.

4. Iolo MSS, and notes to the *Mabinogi* of Taliesin, by Lady Charlotte Guest.
5. The name of St Henwg is not to be found in the lists of Welsh saints in Rees's *Essay*; and the dedication of the church of Llanhenwg is there attributed to St John the Baptist.
6. Triad, 125.
7. *Mabinogion*, vol. iii.
8. Published in 1784.
9. Iolo MSS, p. 458.
10. The priest.
11. A pestilence, called the yellow plague, represented as a serpent.
12. Stanza 45 in edition of the Revd J. Williams ab Ithel.
13. Without offering any opinion adverse to the general correctness of this translation by a writer who evinces a very intimate acquaintance with his subject and the circle of ancient Welsh literature, we may observe that the difficulty of executing such a translation is evidenced in the stanza above quoted, in which the line

> A dan droet ronin

is translated by Mr Williams,

> This particle shall go under foot;

that is, says the author in a note, 'this treatment I despise; it is beneath my notice; I will regard it as a particle of dust under my feet.' The poet is describing his lamentable condition in the earthen house or prison in which he is confined, and says,

> Under my feet is gravel,
> And my knees tied tight.

In the same way the adage, cited by Mr Williams,

> Nid a gwaew yn ronyn,

which he translates

> Pain will not become a particle,

must be

> A spear will not go into (or pierce) a grain of corn;

importing that the means should be proportioned to the object.
   The word *gronyn* is the singular of *grawn*, grains; and there are abundant instances where a singular is put with a plural meaning, and vice versa, on account of the rhyme; or very probably the word may have originally been *graian*, gravel, coarse sand. Villemarqué translates 'a ring' from *cron*, round, circular, which agrees very fairly with the context.
14. The 93rd stanza was certainly composed after the death of Aneurin. The expression,

> Er pan aeth daear ar Aneirin —
> Since the time when the earth went upon Aneirin —

has reference to his death, as may be seen in the corresponding passages in the same poem.

15. The elegy of Uthyr Pendragon, falsely attributed to Taliesin, is of late date, and not historical.

16. Iolo MSS, p. 457.

17. Lloughor, near Swansea.

18. The river Llyw falls into the Llychwr near the remains of this old castle. Iolo MSS.

19. This tradition, published in the Iolo MSS, is of some interest, as it is an instance of a legend which is found in Nennius, adapted to the history of Arthur. Nennius, after describing the colonization of Ireland by Partholanus and Nimech many centuries before the Christian era, says, 'Afterwards others came from Spain (i.e. the Milesians of Irish history) and possessed themselves of various parts of Britain. Last of all came one Hoctor (called in other MSS Damhoctor, Clamhoctor and Elamhoctor), who continued there, and whose descendants remain there to this day. The sons of Liethali obtained the country of the Dimetae, where is a city called Menevia, and the province Guoher and Cetgueli (Gower and Kidwelly), which they held till they were expelled from every part of Britain by Cunedda and his sons.'

20. *Myvyrian Archaeology*, eds. O. Jones, E. Williams and W.O. Pughe (London, 1801) [Ed.].

21. *Historical Account of the Welsh Bards*, p. 21.

22. *Literature of the Kymry*, p. 281.

23. English Translation p. 335, *note*.

24. When Taliesin Williams wrote this paragraph, he had forgotten that his father, Iolo Morganwg, had stated in his essay on the Barddas, printed in the 2nd vol. of his *Poems, Lyric and Pastoral*, 'that the poems of Taliesin in the sixth century exhibit a complete system of Druidism', not hinting for a moment that he considered any of the poems attributed to that bard to be counterfeit or spurious.

25. *Grammatica Cellica*, vol. ii, p. 950.

26. *Myvyrian Archaeology*, vol. i. p. xviii (London, 1801).

27. *Gomer*, part ii, p. 17.

28. *Literature of the Kymry.*

29. A proposal to publish by subscription, an English Translation of the *Myvyrian Archaeology*, including those bardic remains of the older British poets which present most interesting materials calculated to throw light upon the history, the manners, the literature, the philosophy, and the mythology of our British ancestors, was advertised by the Revd J. Williams, Archdeacon of Cardigan, as long ago as 1840; but up to the present time it has not appeared. What such a translation would have been may be inferred from the late publication of the Archdeacon — *Gomer; a Brief Analysis of the Language and Knowledge of the Ancient Cymry* (London, 1854).

30. *Y Gododin*: a poem of the Battle of Cattraeth, by Aneurin, a Welsh bard of the sixth century, with an English translation, and numerous historical and critical notes, by the Revd John Williams ab Ithel, MA (Llandovery, 1852).

31. *Poëmes des Bardes Bretons du 6e Siècle*, by M. Hersart de la Villemarqué (Paris, 1850).

32. Stanza 8.

33. Stanza 12.

34. *Ancient Oral Records of the Cimri or Britons in Asia and Europe, recovered through a literal Aramitic Translation of the Old Welsh Bardic Relics*, by G.D. Barber, AM, author of *Suggestions on the Ancient Britons* (London, 1855).

The same writer has translated the *Hoianau* of Merlin, and finds it to contain an account of the Institution of the Order of the Garter by the Ken or Britons, at their original site near Lake Van and the sources of the Zah, in Asia Minor, long before the Christian era.

35. Jones's *History of the Welsh Bards*, p. 16.

36. *Cambrobrytannicae Cymraecaeve Linguae Institutiones Accuratae* (London, 1592).

37. Vol. i. p. 129.

38. Near Wrexham.

# Chapter 10
# Poems From the Four Ancient Books of Wales[1]

## by W. F. Skene

### Book of Taliessin, XLI

Madawg, the joy of the wall,
Madawg, before he was in the grave,
Was a fortress of abundance
Of games, and society.
The son of Uthyr before he was slain,
From his hand he pledged thee.
Erof the cruel came,
Of impotent joy;
Of impotent sorrow.
Erof the cruel caused
Treacheries to Jesus.
Though he believed.
The earth quaking
And the elements darkening,
And a shadow on the world,
And baptism trembling.
An impotent step
Was taken by fierce Erof,
Going in the course of things
Among the hideous fiends
Even to the bottom of Uffern.

### Book of Taliessin, XLVI

I am Taliesin the ardent;
I will enrich the praise of baptism.
At the baptism of the ruler, the worshipper wondered,
The conflict of the rocks and rocks and plain.
There is trembling from fear of Cunedda the burner,
In Caer Weir and Caer Lliwelydd.
There is trembling from the mutual encounter.
A complete billow of fire over the seas,
A wave in which the brave fell among his companions.
A hundred received his attack on the earth,
Like the roaring of the wind against the ashen spears.
His dogs raised their backs at his presence,
They protected, and believed in his kindness.
The bards are arranged according to accurate canons.
The death of Cunedda, which I deplore, is deplored.
Deplored be the strong protector, the fearless defender,
He will assimilate, he will agree with the deep and shallow,
A deep cutting he will agree to.

(His) discourse raised up the bard stricken in poverty.
Harder against an enemy than a bone.
Pre-eminent is Cunedda before the furrow (*i.e.* the grave)
And the sod. His face was kept
A hundred times before there was dissolution. A door-hurdle
The men of Bryniich carried in the battle.
They became pale from fear of him and his terror chill-moving.
Before the earth was the portion of his end.
Like a swarm of swift dogs about a thicket.
Sheathing (swords is) a worse cowardice than adversity.
The destiny of an annihilating sleep I deplore,
For the palace, for the shirt of Cunedda;
For the salt streams, or the freely-dropping sea.
For the prey, and the quantity I lose.
The sarcasm of bards that disparage I will harrow,
And others that thicken I will count.
He was to be admired in the tumult with nine hundred horse.
Before the communion of Cunedda,
There would be to me milch cows in summer,
There would be to me a steed in winter,
There would be to me bright wine and oil.
There would be to me a troop of slaves against any advance.
He was diligent of heat from an equally brave visitor.
A chief of lion aspect, ashes become his fellow-countrymen,
Against the son of Edern, before the supremacy of terrors,
He was fierce, dauntless, irresistible,
For the streams of death he is distressed.
He carried the shield in the pre-eminent place,
Truly valiant were his princes.
Sleepiness, and condolence, and pale front,
A good step, will destroy sleep from a believer.

## THE CHAIR OF THE SOVEREIGN

### Book of Taliessin, XV

The declaration of a clear song,
Of unbounded Awen,
About a warrior of two authors,
Of the race of the steel Ala.
With his staff and his wisdom,
And his swift irruptions,
And his sovereign prince,
And his scriptural number,
And his red purple,
And his assault over the wall,
And his appropriate chair,
Amongst the retinue of the wall.
Did not (he) lead from Cawrnur
Horses pale supporting burdens?
The sovereign elder.
The generous feeder.
The third deep wise one,
To bless Arthur,
Arthur the blessed,

In a compact song.
On the face in battle,
Upon him a restless activity.
Who are the three chief ministers
That guarded the country?
Who are the three skilful (ones)
That kept the token?
That will come with eagerness
To meet their lord?
High (is) the virtue of the course,
High will be the gaiety of the old,
High (is) the horn of travelling,
High the kine in the evening.
High (is) truth when it shines,
Higher when it speaks.
High when came from the cauldron
The three awens of Gogyrwen.
I have been Mynawg, wearing a collar,
With a horn in my hand.
He deserves not the chair
That keeps not my word.
With me is the splendid chair,
The inspiration of fluent (and) urgent song.
What the name of the three Caers,
Between the flood and the ebb?
No one knows who is not pressing
The offspring of their president.
Four Caers there are,
In Prydain, stationary,
Chiefs tumultuous.
As for what may not be, it will not be.
It will not be, because it may not be.
Let him be a conductor of fleets.
Let the billow cover over the shingle,
That the land becomes ocean,
So that it leaves not the cliffs,
Nor hill nor dale,
Nor the least of shelter,
Against the wind when it shall rage.
The chair of the sovereign
He that keeps it is skilful.
Let them be sought there!
Let the munificent be sought.
Warriors lost,
I think in a wrathful manner.
From the destruction of chiefs,
In a butchering manner,
From the loricated Legion,
Arose the Guledig,
Around the old renowned boundary.
The sprouting sprigs are broken,
Fragile in like manner.
Fickle and dissolving.
Around the violent borders.
Are the flowing languages.

The briskly-moving stream
Of roving sea-adventurers,
Of the children of Saraphin.
A task deep (and) pure
To liberate Elphin.

## Black Book of Caermarthen, XXXI

What man is the porter?
Glewlwyd Gavaelvawr.
Who is the man that asks it?
Arthur and the fair Cai.
How goes it with thee?
Truly in the best way in the world.
Into my house thou shalt not come,
Unless thou prevailest.
I forbid it.
Thou shalt see it.
If Wythnaint were to go,
The three would be unlucky —
Mabon, the son of Mydron,
The servant of Uthir Pendragon;
Cysgaint, the sea of Banon;
And Gwyn Godybron.
Terrible were my servants
Defending their rights.
Manawydan, the son of Llyr,
Deep was his counsel.
Did not Manawyd bring
Perforated shields from Trywruid?
And Mabon, the son of Mellt,
Spotted the grass with blood?
And Anwas Adeiniog,
And Llwch Llawynnog —
Guardians were they
On Eiddyn Cymminog,
A chieftain that patronized them.
He would have his will and make redress.
Cai entreated him,
While he killed every third person.
When Celli was lost,
Cuelli was found; and rejoiced
Cai, as long as he hewed down.
Arthur distributed gifts,
The blood trickled down.
In the hall of Awarnach,
Fighting with a hag,
He cleft the head of Palach.
In the fastnesses of Dissethach,
In Mynyd Eiddyn,
He contended with Cynvyn;
By the hundred there they fell,
There they fell by the hundred,
Before the accomplished Bedwyr.
On the strands of Trywruid,

Contending with Garwlwyd,
Brave was his disposition,
With sword and shield;
Vanity were the foremost men
Compared with Cai in the battle.
The sword in the battle
Was unerring in his hand.
They were stanch commanders
Of a legion for the benefit of the country —
Bedwyr and Bridlaw;
Nine hundred would to them listen;
Six hundred gasping for breath
Would be the cost of attacking them.
Servants I have had,
Better it was when they were.
Before the chiefs of Emrais
I saw Cai in haste.
Booty for chieftains
Was Gwrhir among foes;
Heavy was his vengeance,
Severe his advance.
When he drank from the horn,
He would drink with four.
To battle when he would come
By the hundred would he slaughter;
There was no day that would satisfy him.
Unmerited was the death of Cai.
Cai the fair, and Llachan,
Battles did they sustain,
Before the pang of blue shafts.
In the heights of Ystavingon
Cai pierced nine witches.
Cai the fair went to Mona,
To devastate Llewon.
His shield was ready
Against Cath Palug
When the people welcomed him.
Who pierced the Cath Palug?
Nine score before dawn
Would fall for its food.
Nine score chieftains.

## Book of Taliessin, XXX

I    I will praise the sovereign, supreme king of the land,
Who hath extended his dominion over the shore of the world.
Complete was the prison of Gweir in Caer Sidi,
Through the spite of Pwyll and Pryderi.
No one before him went into it.
The heavy blue chain held the faithful youth,
And before the spoils of Annwvn woefully he sings,
And till doom shall continue a bard of prayer.
Thrice enough to fill Prydwen, we went into it;
Except seven, none retured from Caer Sidi.

**II**     Am I not a candidate for fame, if a song is heard?
In Caer Pedryvan, four its revolutions;
In the first word from the cauldron when spoken,
From the breath of nine maidens it was gently warmed.
Is it not the cauldron of the chief of Annwvn? What is its intention?
A ridge about its edge and pearls.
It will not boil the food of a coward, that has not been sworn,
A sword bright gleaming to him was raised,
And in the hand of Lleminawg it was left.
And before the door of the gate of Uffern the lamp was burning.
And when we went with Arthur, a splendid labour,
Except seven, none returned from Caer Vedwyd.

**III**    Am I not a candidate for fame with the listened song
In Caer Pedryvan, in the isle of the strong door?
The twilight and pitchy darkness were mixed together.
Bright wine their liquor before their retinue.
Thrice enough to fill Prydwen we went on the sea,
Except seven, none returned from Caer Rigor.

**IV**    I shall not deserve much from the ruler of literature,
Beyond Caer Wydyr they saw not the prowess of Arthur.
Three score Canhwr stood on the wall,
Difficult was a conversation with its sentinel.
Thrice enough to fill Prydwen there went with Arthur,
Except seven, none returned from Gaer Golud.

**V**     I shall not deserve much from those with long shields.
They know not what day, who the causer,
What hour in the serene day Cwy was born.
Who caused that he should not go to the dales of Devwy.
They know not the brindled ox, thick his head-band.
Seven score knobs in his collar.
And when we went with Arthur of anxious memory,
Except seven, none returned from Caer Vandwy.

**VI**    I shall not deserve much from those of loose bias,
They know not what day the chief was caused.
What hour in the serene day the owner was born.
What animal they keep, silver its head.
When we went with Arthur of anxious contention,
Except seven, none returned from Caer Ochren.

**VII**   Monks congregate like dogs in a kennel,
From contact with their superiors they acquire knowledge,
Is one the course of the wind, is one the water of the sea?
Is one the spark of the fire, of unrestrainable tumult?
Monks congregate like wolves,
From contact with their superiors they acquire knowledge.
They know not when the deep night and dawn divide.
Nor what is the course of the wind, or who agitates it,
In what place it dies away, on what land it roars.
The grave of the saint is vanishing from the altar-tomb.
I will pray to the Lord, the great supreme,
That I be not wretched. Christ be my portion.

# GERAINT, SON OF ERBIN

## Black Book of Caermarthen, XXII.

## Red Book of Hergest, XIV

Before Geraint, the enemy of oppression
I saw white horses jaded and gory,
And after the shout, a terrible resistance.

Before Geraint, the unflinching foe,
I saw horses jaded and gory from the battle,
And after the shout, a terrible impulsion.

Before Geraint, the enemy of tyranny,
I saw horses white with foam,
And after the shout, a terrible torrent.

In Llongborth I saw the rage of slaughter,
And biers beyond all number,
And red stained men from the assault of Geraint.

In Llongborth I saw the edges of blades in contact,
Men in terror, and blood on the pate,
Before Geraint, the great son of his father.

In Llongborth I saw the spurs
Of men who would not flinch from the dread of the spears,
And the drinking of wine out of the bright glass.

In Llongborth I saw the weapons
Of men, and blood fast dropping,
And after the shout, a fearful return.

In Llongborth I saw Arthur,
And brave men who hewed down with steel,
Emperor, and conductor of the toil.

In Llongborth Geraint was slain,
A brave man from the region of Dyvnaint,
And before they were overpowered, they committed slaughter.


# THE BATTLE OF GODEU

## Book of Taliessin, VIII

I have been in a multitude of shapes,
Before I assumed a consistent form.
I have been a sword, narrow, variegated,
I will believe when it is apparent.
I have been a tear in the air,
I have been the dullest of stars.
I have been a word among letters,
I have been a book in the origin.
I have been the light of lanterns,
A year and a half.
I have been a continuing bridge,
Over three score Abers.

I have been a course, I have been an eagle.
I have been a coracle in the seas:
I have been compliant in the banquet.
I have been a drop in a shower;
I have been a sword in the grasp of the hand:
I have been a shield in battle.
I have been a string in a harp,
Disguised for nine years.
In water, in foam.
I have been sponge in the fire,
I have been wood in the covert.
I am not he who will not sing of
A combat though small,
The conflict in the battle of Goden of sprigs.
Against the Guledig of Prydain,
There passed central horses,
Fleets full of riches.
There passed an animal with wide jaws,
On it there were a hundred heads.
And a battle was contested
Under the root of his tongue;
And another battle there is
In his *occiput*.
A black sprawling toad,
With a hundred claws on it.
A snake speckled, crested.
A hundred souls through sin
Shall be tormented in its flesh.
I have been in Caer Vevenir,
Thither hastened grass and trees,
Minstrels were singing,
Warrior-bands were wondering,
At the exaltation of the Brython,
That Gwydyon effected.
There was a calling on the Creator,
Upon Christ for causes,
Until when the Eternal
Should deliver those whom he had made.
The Lord answered them,
Through language and elements:
Take the forms of the principal trees,
Arranging yourselves in battle array,
And restraining the public.
Inexperienced in battle hand to hand.
When the trees were enchanted,
In the expectation of not being trees,
The trees uttered their voices
From strings of harmony,
The disputes ceased.
Let us cut short heavy days,
A female restrained the din.
She came forth altogether lovely.
The head of the line, the head was a female.
The advantage of a sleepless cow
Would not make us give way.

The blood of men up to our thighs,
The greatest of importunate mental exertion
Sported in the world.
And one has ended
From considering the deluge,
And Christ crucified,
And the day of judgment near at hand.
The alder-trees, the head of the line,
Formed the van.
The willows and quicken-trees
Came late to the army.
Plum-trees, that are scarce,
Unlonged for of men.
The elaborate medlar-trees,
The objects of contention.
The prickly rose-bushes,
Against a host of giants,
The raspberry brake did
What is better failed
For the security of life.
Privet and woodbine
And ivy on its front,
Like furze to the combat
The cherry-tree was provoked.
The birch, notwithstanding his high mind,
Was late before he was arrayed.
Not because of his cowardice,
But on account of his greatness.
The laburnum held in mind,
That your wild nature was foreign.
Pine-trees in the porch,
The chair of disputation,
By me greatly exalted,
In the presence of kings.
The elm with his retinue,
Did not go aside a foot;
He would fight with the centre,
And the flanks, and the rear.
Hazel-trees, it was judged
That ample was thy mental exertion.
The privet, happy his lot,
The bull of battle, the lord of the world.
Morawg and Morydd
Were made prosperous in pines.
Holly, it was tinted with green,
He was the hero.
The hawthorn, surrounded by prickles,
With pain at his hand.
The aspen-wood has been topped,
It was topped in battle.
The fern that was plundered.
The broom, in the van of the army,
In the trenches he was hurt.
The gorse did not do well,
Notwithstanding let it overspread.

The heath was victorious, keeping off on all sides.
The common people were charmed,
During the proceeding of the men.
The oak, quickly moving,
Before him, tremble heaven and earth.
A valiant door-keeper against an enemy,
His name is considered.
The bluebells combined,
And caused a consternation.
In rejecting, were rejected,
Others, that were perforated.
Pear-trees, the best intruders
In the conflict of the plain.
A very wrathful wood,
The chestnut is bashful,
The opponent of happiness,
The jet has become black,
The mountain has become crooked,
The woods have become a kiln,
Existing formerly in the great seas,
Since was heard the shout —
The tops of the birch covered us with leaves,
And transformed us, and changed our faded state.
The branches of the oak have ensnared us
From the Gwarchan of Maelderw.
Laughing on the side of the rock,
The lord is not of an ardent nature.
Not of mother and father,
When I was made,
Did my Creator create me.
Of nine-formed faculties,
Of the fruit of fruits,
Of the fruit of the primordial God,
Of primroses and blossoms of the hill,
Of the flowers of trees and shrubs.
Of earth, of an earthly course,
When I was formed.
Of the flower of nettles,
Of the water of the ninth wave.
I was enchanted by Math,
Before I became immortal,
I was enchanted by Gwydyon
The great purifer of the Brython,
Of Eurwys, of Euron,
Of Euron, of Modron.
Of five battalions of scientific ones,
Teachers, children of Math.
When the removal occurred,
I was enchanted by the Guledig.
When he was half-burnt,
I was enchanted by the sage
Of sages, in the primitive world.
When I had a being;
When the host of the world was in dignity,
The bard was accustomed to benefits.

To the song of praise I am inclined, which the tongue recites.
I played in the twilight,
I slept in purple;
I was truly in the enchantment
With Dylan, the son of the wave.
In the circumference, in the middle,
Between the knees of kings,
Scattering spears not keen,
From heaven when came,
To the great deep floods,
In the battle there will be
Four score hundreds,
That will divide according to their will.
They are neither older nor younger,
Than myself in their divisions.
A wonder, Canhwr are born, every one of nine hundred.
He was with me also,
With my sword spotted with blood.
Honour was allotted to me
By the Lord, and protection (was) where he was.
If I come to where the boar was killed,
He will compose, he will decompose,
He will form languages.
The strong-handed gleamer, his name,
With a gleam he rules his numbers.
They would spread out in a flame,
When I shall go on high.
I have been a speckled snake on the hill,
I have been a viper in the Llyn.
I have been a bill-hook crooked that cuts,
I have been a ferocious spear
With my chasuble and bowl
I will prophesy not badly,
Four score smokes
On every one what will bring.
Five battalions of arms
Will be caught by my knife.
Six steeds of yellow hue
A hundred times better is
My cream-coloured steed,
Swift as the sea-mew
Which will not pass
Between the sea and the shore.
Am I not pre-eminent in the field of blood?
Over it are a hundred chieftains.
Crimson (is) the gem of my belt,
Gold my shield border.
There has not been born, in the gap,
That has been visiting me,
Except Goronwy,
From the dales of Edrywy.
Long white my fingers,
It is long since I have been a herdsman.
I travelled in the earth,
Before I was a proficient in learning.

I travelled, I made a circuit,
I slept in a hundred islands.
A hundred Caers I have dwelt in.
Ye intelligent druids,
Declare to Arthur,
What is there more early
Than I that they sing of.
And one is come
From considering the deluge,
And Christ crucified,
And the day of future doom.
A golden gem in a golden jewel.
I am splendid
And shall be wanton
From the oppression of the metal-workers.

## Book of Taliessin, I

## Red Book of Hergest, XXIII

A primitive and ingenious address, when thoroughly elucidated.
Which was first, is it darkness, is it light?
Or Adam, when he existed, on what day was he created?
Or under the earth's surface, what the foundation?
He who is a legionary will receive no instruction.
Est qui peccator in many things,
Will lose the heavenly country, the community of priests.
In the morning no one comes
If they sing of three spheres.
Angles and Gallwydel,
Let them make their war.
Whence come night and day?
Whence will the eagle become gray?
Whence is it that night is dark?
Whence is it that the linnet is green?
The ebullition of the sea,
How is it not seen?
There are three fountains
In the mountain of roses,
There is a Caer of defence
Under the ocean's wave.
Illusive greeter,
What is the porter's name?
Who was confessor
To the gracious Son of Mary?
What was the most beneficial measure
Which Adam accomplished?
Who will measure Uffern?
How thick its veil?
How wide its mouth?
What the size of its stones?
Or the tops of its whirling trees?
Who bends them so crooked?
Or what fumes may be
About their stems?

Is it Lleu and Gwydyon
That perform their arts?
Or do they know books
When they do?
Whence come night and flood?
How they disappear?
Whither flies night from day;
And how is it not seen?
Pater noster ambulo
Gentis tonans in adjuvando
Sibilem signum
Rogantes fortium.
Excellent in every way around the glens
The two skilful ones make inquiries
About Caer Cerindan Cerindydd
For the draught-horses of pector David.
They have enjoyment — they move about —
May they find me greatly expanding.
The Cymry will be lamenting
While their souls will be tried
Before a horde of ravagers.
The Cymry, chief wicked ones,
On account of the loss of holy wafers.
There will long be crying and wailing,
And gore will be conspicuous.
There came by sea
The wood-steeds of the strand.
The Angles in council
Shall see signs of
Exultation over Saxons.
The praises of the rulers
Will be celebrated in Sion.
Let the chief builders be
Against the fierce Ffichti,
The Morini Brython.
Their fate has been predicted;
And the reaping of heroes
About the river Severn.
The stealing is disguised of Ken and Masswy
Ffis amala, ffur, ffir, sel,
Thou wilt discern the Trinity beyond my age
I implore the Creator, hai
Huai, that the Gentile may vanish
From the Gospel. Equally worthy
With the retinue of the wall
Cornu ameni dur.
I have been with skilful men,
With Matheu and Govannon,
With Eunydd and Elestron,
In company with Achwyson,
For a year in Caer Gofannon.
I am old. I am young. I am Gwion,
I am universal, I am possessed of penetrating wit.
Thou wilt remember thy old Brython

(And) the Gwyddyl, kiln distillers,
Intoxicating the drunkards.
I am a bard; I will not disclose secrets to slaves;
I am a guide: I am expert in contests.
If he would sow, he would plough; he would plough, he would not
     reap.
If a brother among brothers,
Didactic Bards with swelling breasts will arise
Who will meet around mead-vessels,
And sing wrong poetry
And seek rewards that will not be,
Without law, without regulation, without gifts.
And afterwards will become angry.
There will be commotions and turbulent times,
Seek no peace — it will not accrue to thee.
The Ruler of Heaven knows thy prayer.
From his ardent wrath thy praise has propitiated him
The Sovereign King of Glory addresses me with wisdom —
Has thou seen the dominus fortis?
Knowest thou the profound prediction domini?
To the advantage of Uffern
Hic nemo in por progenie
He has liberated its tumultuous multitude.
Dominus virtutum
Has gathered together those that were in slavery,
And before I existed He had perceived me.
May I be ardently devoted to God!
And before I desire the end of existence,
And before the broken foam shall come upon my lips,
And before I become connected with wooden boards,
May there be festivals to my soul!
Book-learning scarcely tells me
Of severe afflictions after death-bed;
And such as have heard my bardic books
They shall obtain the region of heaven, the best of all abodes.

# POEMS REFERRING TO EARLY TRADITIONS WHICH BELONG TO A LATER SCHOOL

## THE CHAIR OF CERIDWEN

### Book of Taliessin, XVI

Sovereign of the power of the air, thou also
The satisfaction of my transgressions.
At midnight and at matins
There shone my lights.
Courteous the life of Minawg ap Lleu,
Whom I saw here a short while ago.
The end, in the slope of Lleu.
Ardent was his push in combats;
Avagddu my son also.

Happy the Lord made him,
In the competition of songs,
His wisdom was better than mine,
The most skilful man ever heard of.
Gwydyon ap Don, of toiling spirits,
Enchanted a woman from blossoms,
And brought pigs from the south.
Since he had no sheltering cots,
Rapid curves, and plaited chains.
He made the forms of horses
From the springing
Plants, and illustrious saddles.
When are judged the chairs,
Excelling them (will be) mine,
My chair, my cauldron, and my laws,
And my pervading eloquence, meet for the chair.
I am called skilful in the court of Don.
I, and Euronwy, and Euron.
I saw a fierce conflict in Nant Frangeon
On a Sunday, at the time of dawn,
Between the bird of wrath and Gwydyon.
Thursday, certainly, they went to Mona
To obtain whirlings and sorcerers.
Arianrod, of laudable aspect, dawn of serenity,
The greatest disgrace evidently on the side of the Brython,
Hastily sends about his court the stream of a rainbow,
A stream that scares away violence from the earth.
The poison of its former state, about the world, it will leave.
They speak not falsely, the books of Beda.
The chair of the Preserver is here.
And till doom, shall continue in Europa.
May the Trinity grant us
Mercy in the day of judgment.
A fair alms from good men.

## THE DEATH-SONG OF UTHYR PENDRAGON
### Book of Taliessin, XLVIII

Am I not with hosts making a din?
I would not cease, between two hosts, without gore.
Am I not he that is called Gorlassar?
My belt was a rainbow to my foe.
Am I not a prince, in darkness,
(To him) that takes my appearance with my two chief baskets?
Am I not, like Cawyl, ploughing?
I would not cease without gore between two hosts.
Is it not I that will defend my sanctuary?
In separating with the friends of wrath.
Have I not been accustomed to blood about the wrathful,
A sword-stroke daring against the sons of Cawrnur?
Have I not shared my cause.
A ninth portion in the prowess of Arthur?
Is it not I that have destroyed a hundred Caers?
Is it not I that slew a hundred governors?
Is it not I that have given a hundred veils?

Is it not I that cut off a hundred heads?
Is it not I that gave to Heupen
The tremendous sword of the enchanter?
Is it not I that performed the rights of purification,
When Hayarndor went to the top of the mountain?
I was bereaved to my sorrow. My confidence was commensurate.
There was not a world were it not for my progeny.
I am a bard to be praised. The unskilful
May he be possessed by the ravens and eagle and bird of wrath.
Avagddu came to him with his equal,
When the bands of four men feed between two plains,
Abiding in heaven was he, my desire,
Against the eagle, against the fear of the unskilful.
I am a bard, and I am a harper,
I am a piper, and I am a crowder.
Of seven score musicians the very great
Enchanter. There was of the enamelled honour the privilege,
Hu of the expanded wings.
Thy son, thy barded proclamation,
Thy steward, of a gifted father.
My tongue to recite my death-song.
If of stone-work the opposing wall of the world.
May the countenance of Prydain be bright for my guidance,
Sovereign of heaven, let my messages not be rejected.


# Book of Taliessin, XLV

Disturbed is the isle of the praise of Hu, the isle of the severe
    recompenser
Mona of the good bowls, of active manliness. The Menei its door.
I have drunk liquor of wine and bragget, from a brother departed.
The universal sovereign, the end of every king, the ruinator.
Sorrowful (is) the Dean, since the Archdeacon is interred.
There has not been, there will not be in tribulation his equal.
When Aeddon came from the country of Gwydyen, the thickly
    covered Seon.
A pure poison came four nightly fine-night seasons.
The contemporaries fell, the woods were no shelter against the wind
    on the coast.
Math and Eunyd, skilful with the magic wand, freed the elements.
In the life of Gwydyon and Amaethon, there was counsel.
Pierced (is) the front of the shield of the strong, fortunate, strong
    irresistibly.
The powerful combination of his front rank, it was not of great
    account.
Strong (in) feasting; in every assembly his will was done.
Beloved he went first; while I am alive, he shall be commemorated.
May I be with Christ, so that I may not be sorrowful, when an
    apostle,
The generous Archdeacon amongst angels may he be contained.
Disturbed (is) the isle of the praise of Hu, the isle of the severe
    ruler.
Before the victorious youth, the fortress of the Cymry remained
    tranquil.

The dragon chief, a rightful proprietor in Britonia.
A sovereign is gone, alas! the chief that is gone to the earth.
Four damsels, after their lamentation, performed their office.
Very grievous truly on sea, without land, long their dwelling.
On account of his integrity (it was) that they were not satiated with distress.
I am blameable if I mention not his good actions.
In the place of Llywy, who shall prohibit, who shall order?
In the place of Aeddon, who shall support Mona's gentle authorities?
May I be with Christ, that I may not be sorrowful, for evil or good.
Share of mercy in the country of the governor of perfect life.

1. Originally published in *The Four Ancient Books of Wales* by William F. Skene (Edmonston & Douglas, 1868) [Ed.].

# Chapter 11
# Taliesin and Amairgen[1]
## by H. D'Arbois de Jubainville

I

*Arrival of the Sons of Mile in Ireland*

The companions of Ith returned to the Land of the Dead, or, as the Christian redaction puts it, to Spain, bringing the body of their chief with them. The race of Mile regarded the murder of Ith as a declaration of war. To avenge him they resolved to set out in a body for Ireland and take possession of the island. Thirty-six chiefs, whose names are recorded, commanded the race of Mile.

Each of them had his ship, with his family and all his men on board. But they did not all arrive at their journey's end. One of the sons of Mile having climbed to the masthead to get a distant view of Ireland, fell into the sea and perished. Amairgen, surnamed *Glungel*, 'the white kneed', son of Mile, was the scholar, the *file*, of the fleet; and his wife died on the way. They reached the coast of Ireland, and came to shore at the south-western point, where Ith had landed before them. And they called the name of the place, *Inber Scene*,[2] after Amairgen's wife, whom they buried there.

It was on a Thursday, the First of May, and the seventeenth day of the moon,[3] that the sons of Mile arrived in Ireland. Partholon also landed in Ireland on the First of May, but on a different day of the week and of the moon — on a Tuesday, the fourteenth day of the moon; and it was on the First of May, too, that the pestilence came, which in the space of one week destroyed utterly his race. The First of May was sacred to Beltene one of the names of the god of death, the god who gives life to men, and takes it away from them again. Thus, it was on the feast day of this god that the sons of Mile began their conquest of Ireland.

II

*The First Poem of Amairgen. its pantheistic doctrine. Comparison of same with a Welsh poem ascribed to Taliesin and with the philosophical system of Joannes Scotus, surnamed Erigena*

As he set his right foot upon the soil of Ireland, the *file* Amairgen chanted a poem in honour of the science which rendered him superior to the gods in power, though it came originally from them; he sang the praise of that marvellous science which was to give the sons of Mile victory over the Tuatha De Danann. This divine science, indeed, penetrating the secrets of nature, discovering her laws, and mastering her hidden forces, was, according to the tenets of Celtic philosophy, a being identical with these forces themselves, with the visible and the material world; and to possess this science was to possess nature in her entirety.

'I am,' said Amairgen, 'the wind which blows over the sea;

I am the wave of the ocean;
I am the murmur of the billows;
I am the ox of the seven combats;
I am the vulture upon the rock;
I am a tear of the sun;
I am the fairest of plants;
I am a wild boar in valour;
I am a salmon in the water;
I am a lake in the plain.

I am a word of science;
I am the spear-point that gives battle;
I am the god who creates or forms in the head [of man] the fire [of
   thought];
Who is it that enlightens the assembly upon the mountain?
[And here a gloss adds: Who will enlighten each question, if not I?]
Who telleth the ages of the moon? [And a gloss adds: Who telleth
   you the ages of the moon, if not I?]
Who showeth the place where the sun goes to rest? [If not the *file*,
   adds another gloss]

There is a lack of order in this composition; the ideas, fundamental and
subordinate, are jumbled together without method. But there is no doubt as
to the meaning: the *file* is the word of science, he is the god who gives to man
the fire of thought; and as science is not distinct from its object, as God and
nature are but one, the being of the *file* is mingled with the winds and the
waves, with wild animals, and the warrior's arms.

In a Welsh MS of the fourteenth century we find an analogous composition.
It is ascribed to the bard Taliesin. Amairgen, the Irish *file*, has said: 'I am a tear
of the sun.' And the Welsh poem puts a similar utterance in the mouth of
Taliesin, who says: 'I have been a tear in the air.'[4] The following are further
utterances:

Amairgen: 'I am the vulture upon the rock.'
Taliesin: 'I have been an eagle.'[5]
Amairgen: 'I am the fairest of plants.'
Taliesin: 'I have been wood in the covert.'[6]
Amairgen: 'I am the spear-point that gives battle.'
Taliesin: 'I have been a sword in the grasp of the hand; I have been a shield
in battle.'[7]
Amairgen: 'I am a word of science.'
Taliesin: 'I have been a word among letters.'[8]

The Welsh poem alters the primitive meaning of the formula in putting the verb
in the past tense. It substitutes the idea of successive metamorphoses for the
vigorous pantheism which is the glory, as it is the error, of Irish philosophy. The
*file* is the personification of science, and science is identical with its object.
Science is Being itself, of whom the forces of nature and all sensible beings are
but manifestations. Thus it is that the *file*, who is the visible embodiment of
science in human form, is not only man but also eagle or vulture, tree or plant,
word, sword or spear; thus it is that he is the wind that blows over the sea, the
wave of the ocean, the murmuring of the billows, the lake in the plain. He is
all of these because he is the universal being, or, as Amairgen puts it, 'the god

who creates in the head' of man 'the fire' of thought. He is all of these because it is he who has the custody of the treasure of science. 'I am,' he says, 'the word of science,' and there are many proofs of his possessing this treasure. Amairgen is careful to recall them. For instance, when the people who are gathered together on the mountain are perplexed by some difficult question, it is the *file* who gives the answer. Nor is this all: he knows how to calculate the moons, upon which the calendar is based, and, consequently, it is he who fixes the periods of the great popular assemblies, which are the common foundation of the social and religious life of the people. Astronomy has no secrets for him; he even knows the place, hidden from the rest of men, where the sun sinks to rest at evening, wearied with his journey over the heavens. Science, therefore, belongs to him; he is himself science; now science is the one only being of whom the whole world, and all the subordinate beings it contains, is but the changing and manifold expression.

This is the doctrine that the Irish philosopher, Joannes Scotus, taught in the ninth century in France, at the court of Charles the Bald, clothing it in the forms of Greek philosophy. M. Haurēau has summarized the fundamental doctrine of the Irish philosopher in the following extracts from his great work, *de Divisione Naturae*:

'We are informed by all the means of knowledge that, beneath the apparent diversity of beings, subsists the one being who is their common foundation.' [9]

'When we are told that God makes all things,' says Joannes Scotus, 'we are to understand that God is in all things, that He is the substantial essence of all things. For He alone possesses in Himself the veritable conditions of being; and He alone is in Himself all that which is among the things that are truly said to exist. For nothing which is, is really of itself, but God alone, who alone truly is in Himself, spreading Himself over all things, and communicating to them all that which in them responds to the true notion of being.' [10]

And again: 'Do not you see how the Creator of the universality of things holds the first rank in the divisions of nature? Not without reason, indeed, since He is the principle of all things, and is inseparable from all the diversity He has created; without which He could not exist as Creator. In him, indeed, immutably and essentially, are all things; He is Himself division and collection, the genus and the species, the whole and the part of the created universe.' [11]

Finally, 'What is a pure idea?' According to Joannes Scotus, 'it is, in proper terms, a theophany, that is to say, a manifestation of God in the human soul.' Such is the doctrine taught by Scotus Erigena in France, in the ninth century. [12] It is the doctrine the Irish mythological *épopee* puts into the mouth of Amairgen, when it makes him say: 'I am the god who puts in the head of man the fire of thought, I am the billow of the ocean, I am the murmur of the waves,' etc. The *file*, the being in whom science, that is to say, the divine idea, is manifested, and who thus becomes the personification of that idea, can, without boasting, proclaim himself identical with the one universal being of whom all other beings are but appearances or manifestations. His own existence is confounded with that of these beings.

This is the explanation of the old poem which the Irish legend puts in the mouth of the *file* Amairgen, at the moment this primitive representative of Celtic science, coming from the mysterious regions of death, set his right foot for the first time on the soil of Ireland.

III

*The two other Poems of Amairgen. Their Naturalistic Doctrine*

The *Book of Invasions* accredits Amairgen with two other poems, the philosophy of which is, however, of a less elevated character than the foregoing, being almost identical with that by which Hesiod explains the origin of the world, in his *Theogony*. Matter preceded the gods. That which existed at the beginning was Chaos, the father of Darkness and Night; then came the Earth, who produced the mountains and the sea and the sky; and after being united to the sky, gave birth, first of all to the Ocean, and then to the Titans, the fathers of gods and men. Matter, therefore, existed from the beginning of things, and has the same supremacy over the gods as a father has over his son. Material nature is above the gods. Thus Amairgen, who is at war with the gods, invokes the forces of nature, by whose aid he hopes to overcome them. Hence the last two poems of Amairgen are invocations to the forces of nature. The second runs as follows; as in the *Theogony*, the earth takes the first place:

> I invoke the land of Ireland!
> Shining, shining sea(?)!
> Fertile, fertile mountain!
> Gladed, gladed wood!
> Abundant river, abundant in water!
> Fish-abounding lake! [13]

It is thus the land of Ireland, the sea that surrounds it, its mountains and rivers and lakes, that Amairgen calls to his aid against the gods that dwell there. Here we have a form of prayer taken from the Celtic ritual. It must have been consecrated by long usage, and was not written for the literary work in which we find it. It is a pagan invocation to Ireland deified, and one that could be employed in any circumstance that might call for the intervention of the tutelar divinity.

This text calls others to mind in which we see material nature regarded as the greatest of the gods. We have referred in another place to the oath which Loegaire, High King of Ireland, was constrained to take before being set at liberty by the people of Leinster, by whom he had been defeated and taken prisoner. He called to witness the sun and moon, water and air, day and night, sea and land; and these were the only gods he spoke of; and when he had broken his oath, these powers of nature whom he had given as his sureties punished him by taking away his life. [14]

The *Book of Invasions* ascribes a second poem to Amairgen, the meaning of which is clear when read after the third. It is an invocation to the sea; the earth is also named, but here holds the second place only, whereas in the preceding it occupied the first:

> Fish-abounding sea!
> Fruitful Earth!
> Irruption of fish!
> Fishing there!
> Bird under wave!
> Great fish!

Crab hole!
Irruption of fish!
Fish-abounding sea![15]

Thus Amairgen, about to do battle with the gods, calls both matter and the forces of nature to his aid, offering up two prayers to them. His prayers are answered, and the gods overthrown.


IV

*First invasion of Ireland by the sons of Mile*

We shall now return to the account of the conquest of Ireland by the sons of Mile. The *file* Amairgen, when he came to land with his brethren and his men, says the old text, chanted the two invocations given above, namely, the first and the third. The second we shall return to later. Then after the three days and three nights had elapsed, the sons of Mile fought their first battle. Their adversaries, according to the *Book of Invasions*, were 'demons, that is to say, the Tuatha De Danann.' The battle took place a short distance from the shore, in the place called Sliab Mis, now written Slieve Mish, in the County Cork.

The *Book of Invasions* makes this the scene of one of those curious legends which the mania for etymology has given rise to in Ireland. Near Slieve Mish was a lake which was called Loch Lugaid, after Lugaid, the son of Ith, who bathed there. His wife, who was called Fial, or 'modesty', bathed in a river which flowed out of the lake. One day Lugaid, following the stream, came to the place where his wife was in the act of bathing, and the latter was so overcome with shame at being thus discovered by her husband that she expired forthwith, and her name was given to the stream in memory of the event.

The sons of Mile now marched in the direction of the northeast. They were still in the vicinity of Slieve Mish when they were met by Queen Banba, who said to them: 'If it is to make the conquest of Ireland that you are come, the aim of your expedition is not just.' And the *file* Amairgen replied: 'It is for that, indeed, we are come.' Then said Banba: 'Grant me at least one favour — that the island be called by my name.' 'It shall be so,' said Amairgen.

A little further on the sons of Mile met the second queen, who was called Fotla. She also begged that the island be named after her. And Amairgen answered: 'So be it; the island shall be called Fotla.'

At Usnech, the central point of Ireland, the sons of Mile were met by the third queen, whose name was Eriu. 'Welcome, O warriors,' said she. 'You come from afar. This island will belong to you for all time, and from here to the furthest east there is none better. No race will be so perfect as yours.' 'These are good words,' said Amairgen, 'and a good prophecy.' 'It is not to you that we owe any thanks,' cried Eber Dond, the eldest of the sons of Mile, 'but to our gods and our own prowess.' 'What I announce has no concern for you,' replied Eriu; 'you shall not enjoy this island; it will not belong to any descendants of yours.' So, indeed, it befell, for Eber Dond was fated to perish before the race of Mile had completed the conquest of Ireland. Then the queen Eriu, like the other two queens, begged that the island should be called by her name. 'That will be its chief name,' said Amairgen.

V

*The Judgment of Amairgen*

The sons of Mile came at length to Tara, the capital of Ireland, then known as *Druim Cain*, Fair Hill. There they found the three kings, MacCuill, MacCecht, and McGrene, who were then reigning over Ireland and the Tuatha De Danann, upon whom they were come to make war. The sons of Mile called upon them to surrender the island.

The three kings demanded an armistice, in order to have time to consider whether they should give battle or deliver up hostages and make terms. They thought to take advantage of the delay by making themselves invincible, for at that moment their Druids were preparing enchantments which would drive the invaders out of the country. And MacCuill, the first of the three Tuatha De Danann kings, said: 'We will accept the judgment of your *file* Amairgen; but if he render a false judgment we shall put him to death.' 'Pronounce thy judgment, Amairgen,' cried Eber Dond, the eldest of the sons of Mile. 'This is my judgment,' replied Amairgen. 'You will temporarily abandon the island to the Tuatha De Danann.' 'To what distance shall we go?' asked Eber. 'You will put between you and them the distance of nine waves,' answered Amairgen. This was the first judgment given in Ireland.

Such is the account of the *Book of Invasions*. It may be asked what is the meaning of the expression 'nine waves', what exact distance it indicated. All we can say is that it was a magical formula to which a certain superstitious potency was still attributed in Ireland in the early days of Christianity. In the seventh century there was an ecclesiastical school at Cork, presided over for some time by Colman, son of Hua Cluasaig, the *fer Leigind*, or professor of written literature, that is to say, of Latin and theology. At the time Colman was giving instruction in this school, Ireland was stricken by a famine, accompanied by great loss of life. Two-thirds of the people perished, among them being the two kings of Ireland, Diarmait and Blathmac, both sons of Aed Slane. This was in 665.[16] To escape the scourge himself, and to safeguard the lives of his scholars, Colman had recourse to two means: first he wrote a hymn in Irish verse, which has come down to us in two MSS of the late eleventh century;[17] then he withdrew along with his scholars to an isle lying off the coast of Ireland, at a distance of nine waves. 'For,' remarks the Irish text recording the incident, 'this is a distance at which the men of learning say maladies cannot attain one.'[18] Thus, in the seventh century of our era, the Irish Christians attributed to the distance of nine waves a certain magic power, in whose protecting influence they had not ceased to believe, and we find this pagan doctrine in the legendary history of the conquest of Ireland by the sons of Mile.

VI

*Retreat of the Sons of Mile*

The sons of Mile submitted to the judgment of Amairgen. They returned by the way they had come, and going on board their ships withdrew from the shore to the mysterious distance of nine waves, in accordance with the judgment of Amairgen. As soon as the Tuatha De Danann found them

*Figure 9*: 'In the land of Tir-na-og' by *Vera Bock*.

launched upon the sea, their Druids and *file* began to chant magic poems, which caused a furious tempest to arise, so that the fleet of the sons of Mile was driven far out to sea and dispersed. Thereupon a great sorrow fell upon the sons of Mile. 'This must be a magic wind,' said Eber Dond, who, as the eldest of them, appears to have been in command of the expedition. 'See if the wind is blowing above the masthead,' said he. They sent a man up to the topmast, who reported that there was no wind blowing there. 'Let us wait until Amairgen comes,' cried the pilot of Eber Dond, who was a pupil of the celebrated *file*. When all the ships were gathered together again, Eber Dond called out to Amairgen that this tempest put their men of learning to shame. 'It is not true,' replied Amairgen. And it was then that he chanted his invocation to the land of Ireland, calling upon the benevolence of that natural power to aid him against the enmity of the gods:

> I invoke the land of Ireland!
> Shining, shining sea!
> Fertile, fertile mountain! etc. [19]

When he had ended, the wind changed and became favourable to them. Eber Dond thought immediate success was secured. Said he: 'I am going to put all the inhabitants of Ireland to the sword.' But he had hardly uttered the words when the wind turned against them again. A violent tempest arose and the ships were scattered; several of them foundered and all on board perished, Eber Dond being among the number. Those who escaped landed at a great distance from the place where they had re-embarked, after the judgment of Amairgen.

## VII

*Second Invasion of Ireland by the sons of Mile. Their conquest of the island*

It was at the mouth of the Boyne, on the eastern coast of Ireland, facing Great Britain, that the sons of Mile landed for the second time in Ireland; and, as Eriu had foretold, Eber Dond, the eldest, was no longer among them. He was dead, and it was his brothers and not he, as the goddess Eriu had prophesied, who made the conquest of Ireland. [20]

The fate of the island was decided by a battle fought at Tailtiu, celebrated for its great annual fair, said to have been instituted by Lug. The three kings and three queens of the Tuatha De Danann were slain. [21] Thenceforth the Tuatha De Danann took refuge in the caves and depths of the mountains, where they dwell in marvellous palaces. They go to and fro over the land, invisible, rendering in secret good or ill services to men, as the occasion arises. Sometimes they assume visible form, and no mystery enshrouds the operations of their divine power. The end of their history belongs to the heroic period of Ireland. Their life is mingled with the lives of heroes, like that of the Greek gods in the *Iliad* and the *Odyssey*. [22] We shall return to them in the succeeding chapters.

The sons of Mile took possession of Ireland. The eldest, Eber Dond, being dead, his two brothers disputed with each other for the royalty. Eremon, the second son of Mile, had become the eldest on his brother's death; but the third

son, Eber Find, refused to recognize his claim. The matter being put before
Amairgen, he decided that Eremon should possess the sovereignty during his
life, and that on his death it should pass to Eber Find. This was the second
judgment of Amairgen. But it was less favourably received than the first. On
the word of Amairgen the sons of Mile had consented to beat a retreat and
temporarily abandon Ireland, which they had almost taken possession of. But
this time Eber Find declined to submit to the judgment of Amairgen. He
demanded an immediate division of Ireland, and he obtained it. [23] This
arrangement, however, was not permanent. At the end of a year the two
brothers were at war with each other. Eber Find was slain, and Eremon became
sole king of Ireland. [24]

## VIII

### Comparision of Irish and Gaulish traditions

The leading characteristics of this tale are evidently derived from traditions
which are not exclusively Irish, but the common property of the Celtic race.
The Gauls, like the Irish, believed themselves to be descended from the god
of the dead; and they also believed that the dominion of this god was a
territorial one, a real country lying beyond the ocean. It was the mysterious
region whither the Gaulish mariners, with one strike of the oar, or in one hour's
voyage, conducted the invisible dead at night, in ships of unknown origin. The
pre-Celtic population of Gaul did not come from thence.

The Druids of the first century BC affirmed that there was once a native
population in Gaul; it was the population anterior to the Celtic conquest, that
which was known in Ireland as the Fir-Bolg, Fir-Domnann, and Galioin. A
second group, added the Druids, came thither from the most distant isles, in
other words, from the land of the dead, the Isles of the Blest, or the all-
powerful, of Greek mythology. This was the population that first crossed the
Rhine and settled down on its western borders in pre-historic times, anterior
to the fifth century BC, and to the time of Hecateus of Miletus. [26] When
Timagenus obtained this information from the Druids, about the first century
before Christ, the Celts of this first immigration had lost all recollection of their
arrival in Gaul, and had no other belief than the Druidical doctrine of the
mythic origin of the Celt. However, a third group had been formed by the Celts
of the second immigration, originally settled on the right bank of the Rhine,
and whom the Germanic invasions, from the third to the first century BC, had
gradually driven thence, forcing them over to the left bank, or more to the west
rather, into various parts of Gaul. [26] On this side of the Rhine they remembered
the circumstances of their early immigration.

Of the three articles containing the teaching of the Druids on Gaulish
ethnology, the second is mythological, that, namely, which makes the oldest
established Celtic population in Gaul come from the most distant islands
beyond the ocean. The third article, which assigns a trans-Rhenish origin to
the later arrivals, is historical. As for the first article in which the earliest
inhabitants of Gaul, that is, the pre-Celtic populations, are described as native,
this is the belief generally admitted in ancient times, when races were considered as native all memory of whose migration was forgotten, and it has been
proved by experience that the recollection of early migrations gradually fades

away from the minds of peoples who possess no written annals.

## IX

### *The Fir-Domnann, the Britons, and the Picts in Ireland*

But to return to Ireland and the legendary tales upon which the traditional theories of her origin have been founded. Eremon, having become sole master of Ireland, divided the north, the west, and the south-west portions of the island among the conquerors, that is, he assigned to them the provinces of Ulster, Connacht and Munster. He left Leinster to the primitive inhabitants of the country, and gave the sovereignty of it to Crimthan Sciathbel, who was a Fir-Domnann. Before long, Crimthan was at war with a British tribe known as the Fir-Fidga or Tuath-Fidga, the 'men of Fidga'. They had invaded the kingdom of Crimthan, and were superior to his soldiers, their envenomed arrows causing mortal wounds.

It was at this moment that the Picts, in Irish, *Cruithnich*, arrived in Ireland. They landed on the southern coast of Leinster, at the mouth of the river Slaney, which flows into the sea near Wexford. Crimthan joined forces with them, and learned from a Druid of the Picts how to heal the wounds inflicted upon his soldiers by the poisoned arrows of the Fir-Fidga. The recipe was to take a bath near the field of battle, in a hole filled with the milk of a hundred and twenty white hornless cows. The treatment proved efficacious, and Crimthan's soldiers obtained a victory over the Fir-Fidga at Ard-Lemnacht. The Picts, who brought about the victory, held for a time considerable power in Ireland. Then Eremon drove them out, and they settled down in Great Britain.

But he consented to give them for wives the widows of the Milesian warriors who had perished at sea before the conquest of Ireland. He attached one condition to this gift, namely, that among the Picts all inheritances should go down in the female line, and not in the male. The chiefs of the Picts agreed to this, and they swore by the sun and the moon for ever to observe the same. [27] Thenceforth the Goidels or Scots, otherwise called the sons of Mile, were the sole possessors of Ireland. It would be hard to say at what exact point in this tale fable ends and history begins.

1.  Originally published in *The Irish Mythological Cycle* (Dublin, O'Donoghue & Co., 1903) [Ed.].
2.  This appears to be the ancient name of the river Kenmare in the County Kerry (Hennessy, *Chronicum Scotorum*, p. 389). It was there also that Nemed was said to come to land.
3.  *Flathiusa hErend*, in *Book of Leinster*, p. 14, col. 2, lines 50-51; *Chron. Scot.* ed. Hennessy, p. 14. According to the document known as the *Flathiusa hErend*, the sons of Mile arrived in Ireland in the time of King David, that is, in the eleventh century before the present era. The Four Masters assign the same event to the year 1700 BC.
4.  *Kat Godeu*, verse 5, in Skene's *Four Ancient Books of Wales*, ii, 137 seq. Cf. i, 276 seq.
5.  *Kat Godeu*, verse 13.
6.  Ibid. verse 23.
7.  Ibid. verses 17 and 18.
8.  Ibid. verse 7.

9. *Histoire de la Philosophie Scholastique*, pt. I, p. 171.
10. Hauréan, Ibid. p. 159. Cf. Joannes Scotus, *De Divisione Naturae*, i, chap. 72; Migne, *Patrologia Latina*, cxxii, col. 518, A.
11. *De Div. Naturae*, iii, chap. I; Hauréau, ibid. p. 160; Migne, *Patrologia Latina*, cxxi, col. 621, BC.
12. Hauréau, ibid. pt. 1, pp. 156–7. Cf. Scotus, *De Div. Nat*, i, chap 7; Migne, *Pat Latin*, cxxii, col. 446, D.
13.         Aliu iath n-hErend.
        Hermach [hermach] muir,
        Mothach mothach sliab,
        Srathach srathach caill,
        Cithach cithach aub,
        Essach essach loch.

    *Aliu* is glossed by *alim*, and *aub* by *aband* (*Book of Leinster*, p. 13, col. 2, lines 6 seq.; cf, *Book of Ballymote*, fol. 21, v/, col. 2, lines 20 seq. *Book of Lecan*, fol. 285 recto, col 1; Tr. Ossianic Society, v, 232.

14. Introd. *Litt. Celtique*, pp. 181–2.
15.         Iascach muir,
        Mothach tir,
        Tomaidm n-eisc,
        Iasca and,
        Fo thuind en,
        Lethach mil,
        Partach lag,
        Tomaidm n-eisc,
        Iascach muir.

    (*Book of Leinster*, p. 12, col. 2, lines 49 seq.; cf. *Book of Ballymote*, fol. 21, r, col. 3, line 21; *Book of Lecan*, fol. 284, v, col. 1; Tr. Ossianic Society, v, 237.
16. Annals of Tigernach, in O'Conor's *Rerum Hibernicarum Scriptores*, ii, p. 205. According to the *Chronicum Scotorum*, ed. Hennessy, pp. 98-9, this plague took place in the year 661, and in 664, according to the Four Masters, ed. O'Donovan, i, pp. 274–6. The year 664 is also given by Bede, *Historia Ecclesiastica*, iii, 27; and in Migne's *Pat. Latina*, xcv, col. 165.
17. MS E 4, 2, fol. 5, Trin. Coll., Dublin; MS classed by Golbert, 1, p. 28, in Franciscan Monastery, Dublin; Whitley Stokes, *Goidelica*, 1st ed., p. 76; 2nd ed., p. 121; Windisch, *Irische Texte*, p. 6.
18. *Goidelica*, 2nd ed., p. 121, line 34.
19. *Supra*, sec. 3.
20. *Leabhar Gabhala*, in *Book of Leinster*, p. 13, col. 4, lines 34–40.
21. *Flathiusa hErend*, in *Book of Leinster*, p. 14, col. 2, line 51; p. 15, col. 1, lines 1–4.
22. See *Odyssey*, xvii, 485–8. The gods, in the guise of strangers, says the poet, are everywhere to be seen, going about the cities, observing men and their evil doings.
23. *Leabhar Gabhala*, in *Book of Lienster*, p. 14, col. 1, lines 47–51.
24. *Flathiusa hErend*, *Book of Leinster*, p. 15, col. 1, lines 8–14.
25. *Fragmenta Historicorum Graecorum*, i, p. 2.
26. Timagenus, cited by Ammianus Marcellinus, xv, chap. 9, in Didot-Muller, *Fragmenta Historicorum Graecorum*, iii, p. 323. Timagenus flourished in the time of the Emperor Augustus.
27. *Flathiusa hErend*, *Book of Leinster*, p. 15, col. 1, line 15, seq.; cf. *Book of Ballymote*, fol. 23 r; and *Book of Lecan*, fol. 287 r. Two different redactions, one in verse, the other in prose, are contained in the 'Irish version of the *Historia Britonum* of Nennius', pp. 122-7; 134-49. See also the article in the *Dinnsenchus* commencing with the words 'Senchass Ardda-Lemnacht' (*Book of Leinster*, p. 196, col. 2, line 12).

The war between Crimthan Sciathbel and the Fir-Fidga was the subject of the piece entitled *Forbais Fer Fidga*. It is contained in the oldest catalogue of Irish epic literature.

# Chapter 12
# Barddas[1]
## edited by J. Williams ab Ithel

### THE BOOK OF BARDISM

Here is the Book of Bardism, that is to say, the Druidism of the bards of the Isle of Britain, which I, Llywelyn Sion of Llangewydd, extracted from old books, namely, the books of Einion the Priest, Taliesin, the Chief of Bards, Davydd Ddu of Hiraddag, Cwtta Cyvarwydd, Jonas of Menevia, Edeyrn the Golden-tongued, Sion Cent, Rhys Goch, and others, in the Library of Rhaglan, by permission of the Lord William Herbert, Earl of Pembroke, to whom God grant that I may prove thankful as long as I live. The first is a treatise in the form of Question and Answer, by a bard and his disciple — the work of Sion Cent, which contains many of the principal subjects of the primitive wisdom, as it existed among the bards of the Isle of Britain from the age of ages. In this dialogue, the disciple first puts the question, and the bard, his teacher, answers, and imparts to him information and knowledge. In the second place the bard examines, and the disciple answers.

### The Second Examination

**Question**   Prithee, who art thou? And tell me thy history.
   **Answer**   I am a man in virtue of God's will, and the necessary consequence that follows, for 'what God wills must be.'
   **Q**   Whence didst thou proceed, and what is thy beginning?
   **A**   I came from the Great World, having my beginning in Annwn.[2]
   **Q**   Where art thou now, and how camest thou to where thou art?
   **A**   I am in the Little World, whither I came, having traversed the circle of Abred,[3] and now I am a man at its termination and extreme limits.
   **Q**   What wert thou before thou didst become a man in the circle of Abred?
   **A**   I was in Annwn the least possible that was capable of life, and the nearest possible to absolute death, and I came in every form, and through every form capable of a body and life, to the state of man along the circle of Abred, where my condition was severe and grievous during the age of ages, ever since I was parted in Annwn from the dead, by the gift of God, and His great generosity, and His unlimited and endless love.
   **Q**   Through how many forms didst thou come, and what happened unto thee?
   **A**   Through every form capable of life, in water, in earth, and in air. And there happened unto me every severity, every hardship, every evil, and every suffering, and but little was the goodness and Gwynvyd[4] before I became a man.
   **Q**   Thou hast said that it was in virtue of God's love thou camest through all these, and didst see and experience all these; tell me how can this take place

through the love of God. And how many were the signs of the want of love during thy migration in Abred?

A   Gwynvyd cannot be obtained without seeing and knowing everything, but it is not possible to see and to know everything without suffering everything. And there can be no full and perfect love that does not produce those things which are necessary to lead to the knowledge that causes Gwynvyd, for there can be no Gwynvyd without the complete knowledge of every form of existence, and of every evil and good, and of every operation and power and condition of evil and good. And this knowledge cannot be obtained without experience in every form of life, in every incident, in every suffering, in every evil and in every good, so that they may be respectively known one from the other. All this is necessary before there can be Gwynvyd, and there is need of them all before there can be perfect love of God, and there must be perfect love of God before there can be Gwynvyd.

Q   Why are the things, which thou has mentioned, necessary, before there can be Gwynvyd?

A   Because there can be no Gwynvyd without prevailing over evil and death, and every opposition and Cythraul,[5] and they cannot be prevailed over without knowing their species, nature, power, operations, place and time, and every form and kind of existence which they have, so that all about them may be known, and that they may be avoided, and that wherever they are they may be opposed, counteracted and overcome, and that we may be cured of them, and be restored from under their effect. And where there is this perfect knowledge there is perfect liberty, and evil and death cannot be renounced and overcome but where there is perfect liberty; and there can be no Gwynvyd but with God in perfect liberty, and it is in perfect liberty that the circle of Gwynvyd exists.

Q   Why may not perfect knowledge be obtained, without passing through every form of life in Abred?

A   On this account, because there are no two forms alike, and every form has a use, a suffering, a knowledge, an intelligence, a Gwynvyd, a quality, an operation, and an impulse, the like and complete uniformity of which cannot be had in any other form of existence. And as there is a special knowledge in each form of existence, which cannot be had in another, it is necessary that we should go through every form of existence before we can acquire every form and species of knowledge and understanding, and consequently renounce all evil, and attach ourselves to every Gwynvyd.

Q   How many forms of existence are there, and what is the use of them?

A   As many as God saw necessary towards the investigation and knowledge of every species and quality in good and evil, that there might be nothing capable of being known and conceived by God without being experienced, and consequently known. And in whatsoever thing there may be a knowledge of good and evil, and of the nature of life and death, there is a form of existence which corresponds with the attainment of the knowledge required. Therefore, the number of the kinds and modes of forms of existence is the sum that could conceive and understand with a view to perfect goodness, knowledge, and Gwynvyd. And God caused that every living and animate being should pass through every form and species of existence endued with life, so that in the end every living and animate being might have perfect knowledge, life and Gwynvyd, and all this from the perfect love of God which in virtue of His

Divine nature He could not but exhibit towards man and every living being.

Q Art thou of opinion that every living being shall attain to the circle of Gwynvyd at last?

A That is my opinion, for less could not have happened from the infinite love of God, God being able to cause, knowing the manner how to cause, and continually willing everything to exist that can be conceived and sought in His own love, and in the desire of every animation while opposed to evil and death.

Q When will this condition happen to every living being, and in what manner will occur the end of the life of Abred?

A Every living and animate being shall traverse the circle of Abred from the depth of Annwn, that is, the extreme limits of what is low in every existence endued with life; and they shall ascend higher and higher in the order and gradation of life until they become man, and then there can be an end to the life of Abred by union with goodness. And in death they shall pass to the circle of Gwynvyd, and the Abred of necessity will end for ever. And there will be no migrating through every form of existence after that, except in right of liberty and choice united with Gwynvyd, with a view to re-experience, and re-seek knowledge. And this will remain for ever, as a variation and novation of Gwynvyd, so that no one can fall into Ceugant, [6] and thence into Abred; for God alone can endure and traverse the circle of Ceugant. By this it is seen that there is no Gwynvyd without mutual communication, and the renewal of proof, experience, and knowledge, for it is in knowledge that life and Gwynvyd consists.

Q Shall every man, when he dies, go to the circle of Gwynvyd?

A No one shall at death go to Gwynvyd, except he who shall attach himself in life, whilst a man, to goodness and godliness, and to every act of wisdom, justice and love. And when these qualities preponderate over their opposites, namely, folly, injustice, and uncharitableness, and all evil and ungodliness, the man, when he dies, shall go to Gwynvyd, that is heaven, from whence he will no more fall, because good is stronger than evil of every kind, and life subdues death, prevailing over it for ever. And he shall ascend nearer and nearer to perfect Gwynvyd, until he is at its extreme limits, where he will abide for ever and eternally. But the man who does not thus attach himself to godliness, shall fall in Abred to a corresponding form and species of existence of the same nature as himself, whence he shall return to the state of man as before. And then, according as his attachment may be to either godliness or ungodliness, shall he ascend to Gwynfyd, or fall in Abred, when he dies. And thus shall he fall for ever, until he seeks godliness, and attaches himself to it, when there will be an end to the Abred of necessity, and to every necessary suffering of evil and death.

## ABRED — GWYNVYD — AWEN

Q How often may one fall in Abred?

A No one will fall once of necessity, after it has been once traversed, but through negligence, from cleaving to ungodliness, until it preponderates over godliness, a man will fall in Abred. He will then return to the state of man, through every form of existence that will be necessary for the removal of the evil, which was the cause of his fall in Abred. And he will fall only once in Abred on account of the same ungodliness, since it will be overcome by that fall; nevertheless, because of many other impieties he may fall in Abred, even numberless times, until every opposition and Cythraul, that is all ungodliness, shall have been vanquished, when there will be an end to the Abred of necessity.

Q  How many have fallen in Abred, and for what cause have they fallen?

A  All living beings below the circle of Gwynvyd have fallen in Abred, and are now on their return to Gwynvyd. The migration of most of them will be long, owing to the frequent times they have fallen, from having attached themselves to evil and ungodliness; and the reason why they fell was that they desired to traverse the circle of Ceugant, which God alone could endure and traverse. Hence, they fell even unto Annwn, and it was from pride, which would ally itself with God, that they fell, and there is no necessary fall as far as Annwn, except from pride.

Q  Did all who reached the circle of Gwynvyd after the primary progression of necessity from Annwn fall in Abred from pride?

A  No; some sought after wisdom, and hence saw what pride would do, and they resolved to conduct themselves according to what was taught them by God, and thereby became divinities, or holy angels, and they acquired learning from what they beheld in others, and it was thus that they saw the nature of Ceugant and eternity, and that God alone could endure and traverse it.

Q  Does not the danger of falling in Abred, from the circle of Gwynvyd, exist still as it did formerly?

A  No; because all pride and every other sin will be overcome before one can a second time reach the circle of Gwynvyd, and then by recollecting and knowing the former evil, every one will necessarily abhor what caused him to fall before, and the necessity of hatred and love will last and continue for ever in the circle of Gwynvyd, where the three stabilities, namely, hatred, love and knowledge, will never end.

Q  Will those who shall return to the circle of Gwynvyd after the fall in Abred be of the same kind as those who fell not?

A  Yes; and of the same privilege, because the love of God cannot be less towards one than towards another, nor towards one form of existence than another, since He is God and Father to them all, and exercises the same amount of love and patronage towards them all, and they will all be equal and co-privileged in the circle of Gwynvyd, that is, they will be divinities and holy angels for ever.

Q  Will every form and species of living existence continue for ever as they are now? If so, tell me why.

A  Yes, in virtue of liberty and choice, and the blessed will go from one to another as they please, in order to repose from the fatigue and tediousness of Ceugant, which God only can endure, and in order to experience every knowledge and every Gwynvyd that are capable of species and form; and each one of them will hate evil of necessary obligation, and know it thoroughly, and consequently of necessity renounce it, since he will perfectly know its nature and mischievousness — God being a help, and God being chief, supporting and preserving them for ever.

Q  How are these things to be known?

A  The Gwyddoniaid, from the age of ages, from the time of Seth, son of Adam, son of God, obtained Awen[7] from God, and thence knew the mystery of godliness; and the Gwyddoniaid were of the nation of the Cymry from the age of ages. After that, the Gwyddoniaid were regulated according to privilege and usage, in order that unfailing memory might be kept of this knowledge. After that, the Gwyddoniaid were called bards according to the privilege and usage of the bards of the Isle of Britain, because it was after the arrival of the Cymry in the island of Britain that this regulation was made; and it is through the memorials of bardism and Awen from God that this knowledge has been acquired, and no falsehood can accrue from Awen from God. In the nation of Israel were found the holy prophets, who through Awen from God knew all these things as described in the Holy Scriptures. And after Christ, the Son of God, had come in the flesh from Gwynvyd, further knowledge of God, and His will, was obtained, as is seen in St Paul's sermon. And when we, the Cymry, were converted to the faith in Christ, our bards obtained a more clear Awen from God, and knowledge about all things divine beyond what had been seen before, and they prophesied improving Awen and knowledge. Hence is all knowledge concerning things divine and what appertains to God.

Q  How is Awen to be obtained, where it is not, so that a bard may be made of him who would be a bard?

A  By habituating oneself to a holy life, and all love towards God and man, and all justice, and all mercy, and all generosity, and all endurance, and all peace, and practising good sciences, and avoiding pride and cruelty and adultery, and all injustice, that is, the things that will corrupt and destroy Awen, where it exists, and will prevent the obtaining it, where it does not exist.

Q  Is it in the way it was first obtained, that Awen from God is still obtainable?

A  It is in this way that Awen is obtained, that the truth may be known and believed. Some, however, are of opinion that the way in which the truth was first known was that the divinities, or holy angels, and the saints, or godly men, who went to heaven, and especially Jesus Christ, the Son of God, came down from Gwynvyd to the Little World in the condition of man, in order to teach, warn, direct, and inform those who seek to be divine. That is, they came in the capacity of messengers sent by God in His infinite love, and in virtue of their own great love co-operating with the love of God, and as His obedient messengers. And we shall have what of Awen from God is necessary for us, by attaching ourselves to the good and godly with sincerity, and out of pure love for all goodness.

## THE THREE STATES

1  According to the three principal qualities of man shall be his migration in Abred: from indolence and mental blindness he shall fall to Annwn; from dissolute wantonness he shall traverse the circle of Abred, according to his necessity; and from his love for goodness he shall ascend to the circle of Gwynvyd. As one or the other of the principal qualities of man predominates shall the state of the man be; hence his three states, Annwn, Abred, and Gwynvyd.

2  The three states of living beings: Annwn, whence the beginning; Abred, in which is the increase of knowledge, and hence goodness; and Gwynvyd, in which is the plenitude of all goodness, knowledge, truth, love, and endless life.

## ANNWN — LIFE — DEATH

**Q**  In what place is Annwn?

**A**  Where there is the least possible of animation and life, and the greatest of death, without other condition.

**Q**  What are the characteristics of life?

**A**  Lightness, light, heat and incorruption, that is, unchangeableness.

**Q**  What are the characteristic marks of death?

**A**  Heaviness, cold, darkness and corruption, that is, changeableness.

**Q**  In what does the nature of death and mortality consist?

**A**  In its characteristics, where one is the cause of another, as heaviness is the cause of darkness, and both the cause of corruption, and corruption the cause of both.

**Q**  In what does the necessity of animation and life consist?

**A**  In its characteristics, that is, brightness, and light, and lightness, and incorruption, one being the cause of another — hence God and life.

## ABRED

To consociate with evil will make one the lowest and meanest of all animated beings; therefore a wicked man, when he dies, and his soul enters the meanest worm in existence, becomes better, and ascends in the migration of Abred. From this has arisen the saying, 'Trample not on thy better', addressed to one who tramples on a worm voluntarily, and without a cause.

## THE ORIGIN OF MAN — JESUS CHRIST — CREATION

Here are Questions and Answers from another book.

**Teacher**  Dost thou know what thou art?

**Disciple**  I am a man by the grace of God the Father.

**T**  Whence camest thou?

**D**  From the extremities of the depth of Annwn, where is every beginning in the division of the fundamental light and darkness.

**T**  How camest thou here from Annwn?

**D**  I came, having traversed about from state to state, as God brought me through dissolutions and deaths, until I was born a man by the gift of God and His goodness.

**T**  Who conducted that migration?

**D**  The Son of God, that is, the Son of man.

**T**  Who is He, and what is His name?

**D**  His name is Jesus Crhist, and He is none other than God the Father incarnate in the form and species of man, and manifesting visible and apparent finiteness for the good and comprehension of man, since infinitude cannot be exhibited to the sight and hearing, nor can there, on that account, be any correct and just apprehension thereof. God the Father, of His great goodness, appeared in the form and substance of man, that He might be seen and comprehended by men.

**T**  Why is He called the Son of God?

**D**  Because He is from God in His essential works, and not from His uncreated pre-existence, that is, He is second to God, and every Second is a son to the primary First, in respect of existence and nature. That is to say, Jesus

Christ is a manifestation of God in a peculiar manner, and everyone is a son to another, who is primary, and the manifested is a son to him who manifests. And where God is seen or comprehended otherwise than as a species and existence beyond all knowledge and comprehension, such cannot take place except in what is seen differently to the attribute of God, in respect of the non-commencement and unchangeableness of His being, His nature, and His quality.

**T** Did man, and other intelligent beings, know anything of God before He was manifested and made comprehensible in Jesus Christ?

**D** They knew that He existed by the creation of the world, and the whole being for good, because there can be no creation without a maker; and that would not be an act but a chance, which should not be thoroughly for good, as a heap of stones occurs by chance, whereas a house or a church is not built by chance.

**T** How may what is made be known?

**D** By unmaking what is possible of it, for where anything can be unmade there must of necessity be a maker to what is thus unmade. For things which were never made, as place and space, without length and without breadth, cannot be unmade. In the same way, time cannot be undone, because it was never made, and it is said in St Paul's sermon that it is impossible to make without a maker.

**T** What is creation?

**D** Everything which can be otherwise, in respect of form and substance and essence, than what it seems. That is to say, it may be annihilated, in respect of what is seen or comprehended of it now; and its non-existence may be conceived. And nothing is made of which its decomposition and non-existence cannot be conceived, as in the case of incorporeal length and breadth and depth, and immeasurable time, for it is impossible that they should not have existed always without a beginning, and it cannot be but that they shall always exist without end and without change. It cannot be judged differently of God, and His existence, because He is spiritual and not corporeal life, wherefore His spirituality can neither change nor end. Everything changeable is made, in respect of what is capable of change and non-existence, as there is a change through burning and rottenness, and melting and hardness, and cold and warmth. That is, there can be non-existence in the change, but there can be no non-existence in the matter and mode, neither loss, except only in its changes.

**T** What is imperishable matter?

**D** There are two kinds: the one dead and lifeless, that is, the elements of the fundamental darkness, whence proceed all inanimation and dead corporeity; and the atoms or elements of light, whence proceed all living corporeity, and all intellect, and all spirituality and life, and all sensibility. For everything dead is cold — everything living is warm.

**T** Why is it requisite to traverse Abred?

**D** Because where there is a beginning there must needs be an increase and an improvement. And in order to magnify man in respect of vital goodness, and to improve and prepare him for Gwynvyd, God arranged it so. And this cannot occur to anything in existence without traversing the middle and intermediate space between the smallest small, and the greatest great. Nor can there be either good or evil, except by chance, in any immutable creation, nor can there be better or worse in what does not circulate, nor better in what cannot be worse, nor worse in what cannot be better. And where one enters upon evil, he cannot become worse by remaining in it for ever and ever; and it is the same with the better, where it cannot be better.

## THE CREATION — THE FIRST MAN — THE PRIMARY LETTERS

### Disciple and his Teacher

**Disciple** Tell me, my kind and discreet Master, whence originated the world, and all visible, all audible, all sensible, and all intelligible things, and whence did they come, and were made?

**Teacher** God the Father made them by pronouncing His Name, and manifesting existence. In the same instant, co-simultaneously, lo! the world, and all that appertains to it, sprang together into being, and together celebrated their existence with a very loud and melodious shout of joy; even as we see them to be now, and as they shall exist whilst God the Father lives, Who is not subject to dissolution and death.

**D** Of what, in respect of materials, were formed living and dead beings, which are cognizable to the human sight, hearing, feeling, understanding, perception and the creation of the imagination?

**T** They were made of the *manred*, that is, of the elements in the extremities of their particles and smallest atoms, every particle being alive, because God was in every particle, a complete Unity, so as not to be exceeded, even in all the multiform space of Ceugant, or the infinite expanse. God was in each of the particles of the manred, and in the same manner in them collectively in their conjoined aggregation; wherefore, the voice of God is the voice of every particle of the manred, as far as their numbers or qualities may be counted or comprehended, and the voice of every particle is the voice of God — God being in the particle as its life, and every particle or atom being in God and His life. On account of this view of the subject, God is figuratively represented as being born of the manred, without beginning, without end.

**D** Was existence good or bad before God pronounced His Name?

**T** All things were thoroughly good, without beginning, without end, as they are now, and ever shall be; though in Abred neither the mode, nor the thing that exists, is seen, except from learning by means of demonstrative hearing and seeing, or by means of reason making it comprehensible, namely, God and His peace in everything, and nothing existing without God and His peace. Therefore, there was good in everything — a blissful world, and a blissful deliverance from every evil, as an unconquerable predominance. And where God exists in every atom of manred, evil is impossible; because there neither is, nor can be room for it, since God and all goodness fill the infinitude, which is without beginning and without end, in respect of place and duration of time. Therefore evil or its like cannot exist, nor the least approximation to it.

**D** What judgment is formed concerning the act of God in giving existence to the world, that is, heaven and earth, and all that are in and from them?

**T** God, with a view to every goodness of which He is capable, branched Himself out of His majesty, incomprehensible to man further it was so. And from this there was an increase of all finite goodness, and all goodness cannot be had, without finite goodness in infinite space.

**D** Who was the first man?

**T** Menyw the Aged, son of the Three Shouts, who was so called because God gave and placed the word in his mouth, namely, the vocalization of the three letters, by which make the unutterable Name of God, that is, by means of the good sense of the Name and Word. And, co-instantaneously with the pronunciation of God's Name, Menyw saw three rays of light, and inscribed on them figure and form, and it was from those forms and their different collocations that Menyw made ten letters, and it was from them, variously placed that he invested the Cymraeg with figure and form, and it is from understanding the combination of the ten letters that one is able to read.

**D** My beloved Teacher, show me the power and mysteries of the three primitive letters, and the forms of the ten letters, which Menyw made from the varied combination of the three.

**T** This is not allowed and permitted to me, for the ten letters are a secret, being one of the three pillars of the mystery of the bards of the Isle of Britain. And before the disciple is brought under the obligation and power of a vow, the mystery may not be revealed to him. And even then it can only be displayed to the eye, without utterance, without voice. It can only take place when the disciple shall have gone through all the cycle and course of his pupillage. Nevertheless, the sixteen letters are formed very differently, and I am at liberty to show and declare their names and their powers, before the cycle of the vow of pupillage shall have been traversed; and thus are the sixteen symbols, and the way in which they are enforced by usage.

## THE DISCIPLINE OF BARDISM

### The Creation

**Disciple** With what material did God make all corporal things, endued with life?

**Master** With the particles of light, which are the smallest of all small things; and yet one particle of light is the greatest of all great things, being no less than material for all materiality that can be understood and perceived as within the grasp of the power of God. And in every particle there is a place wholly commensurate with God, for there is not and cannot be less than God in every particle of light and God in every particle; nevertheless, God is only one in number. On that account, every light is one, and nothing is one in perfect co-existence but what cannot be two, either in or out of itself.

**D** How long was God in making all corporal things?

**M** The twinkling of an eye; when existence and life, light and vision occurred, that is to say, God and all goodness in the act of condemning evil.

### The Creation

**Question** Of what materials did God make the worlds?

**Answer** Of Himself, for existence having a beginning does not otherwise take place.

**Q** How were animation and life obtained?

**A** From God, and in God were they found, that is, from the fundamental and absolute life, that is, from God uniting Himself to the dead, or earthliness

— hence motion and mind, that is, soul. And every animation and soul are from God, and their existence is in God, both their pre-existence and derived existence; for there is no pre-existence except in God, no co-existence except in God, and no derived existence except in God, and from God.

## THE CREATION — WORSHIP — VOCAL SONG — GWYDDONIAID

**Disciple** From what did God make the world and living beings?

**Master** From the particles which He collected out of the infinite expanse in the circle of Ceugant, and collocated in order and just arrangement in the circle of Gwynvyd, as worlds, and lives, and natures, without number, weight or measure, which any mind or intellect but Himself could possibly foresee or devise, even if it possessed the endless ages of the circle of Ceugant.

**D** By what instrumentality or agency did God make these things?

**M** By the voice of His mighty energy, that is, by its melodious sweetness, which was scarcely heard, when, lo! the dead gleamed into life, and the nonentity, which had neither place nor existence, flashed like lightning into elementation, and rejoiced into life, and the congealed, motionless shiver warmed into living existence — the destitute nothing rejoiced into being a thousand times more quickly than the lightning reaches its home.

**D** Did any living being hear that melodious voice?

**M** Yes; and co-instantaneously with the voice were seen all sciences and all things cognitive, in the imperishable and endless stability of their existence and life. For the first that existed, and the first that lived, the first that obtained knowledge, and the first that knew it, was the first that practised it. And the first sage was Huon, the son of Nudd, who is called Gwynn, the son of Nudd, and Enniged the Giant; it was he who first made demonstration visible and inceptive to the inferences of men.

**D** Who was the first that instituted the worship and adoration of God?

**M** Seth, the son of Adam; that is, he first made a retreat for worship in the woods of the Vale of Hebron, having first searched and investigated the trees, until he found a large oak, being the king of trees, branching, wide-spreading, thick-topped, and shady, under which he formed a choir and a place of worship. This was called Gorsedd, and hence originated the name Gorsedd, which was given to every place of worship; and it was in that choir that Enos, the son of Seth, composed vocal song to God.

**D** Who was the first that made a vocal song?

**M** Enos, the son of Seth, the son of Adam, was the first that made a vocal song, and praised God first in just poetry, and it was in his father's Gorsedd that he first obtained Awen, which was Awen from God; hence has arisen the usage of holding the Gorsedd of vocal song in the resort and Gorsedd of worship.

**D** For what honourable purposes did Enos, the son of Seth, invent vocal song?

**M** In the first place, for the purpose of praising God and all goodness; secondly, to commemorate good qualities, incidents and knowledge; thirdly, to convey instruction relative to praiseworthy sciences in respect of God and man, that is, in such a way as would be easiest to learn, and remember, and most pleasant to listen to.

**D** What was the name that the wise men first had, whose employment was vocal song and laudable sciences?

**M** One was called Gwyddon, and many Gwyddoniaid; and they were so called because they followed their art in woods, and under trees, in retired and inaccessible places, for the sake of quietness, and the meditation of Awenic learning and sciences from God, and for the sake of quietness to teach the sciences to such as sought them, and desired wisdom by means of reason and Awen from God.

## THE MATERIAL OF THE WORLD

**Question** What material did God use in the formation of the world, namely, the heaven and the earth, and other things known and conceived?

**Answer** The manred, that is, the smallest of all the small, so that a smaller could not be, which flowed in one sea through all the Ceugant — God being its life, and pervading each atom, and God moving in it, and changing the condition of the manred, without undergoing a change in Himself. For life is unchangeable in all its motions, but the condition of that which is moved is not one and the same. Therefore, because God is in every motion (ymmod) one of God's Names is Modur, and the condition that is moved is called *Moduransawdd*.

## THE FALL IN ABRED

God made all living beings in the circle of Gwynvyd at one breath, but they would be gods and attempted to traverse the Ceugant. This, however, they could not do, wherefore they fell down to Annwn, which unites with death and the earth, where is the beginning of all living owners of terrestrial bodies.

**Q** What is Annwn?

**A** In the extreme limits of the circle of Gwynvyd. That is, living beings knew not how to distinguish evil from good, and therefore they fell into evil, and went into Abred, which they traversed until they came back into the circle of Gwynvyd.

**Q** What ignorance did they commit?

**A** They would venture on the circle of Ceugant, and hence became proud; but they could not traverse it, consequently they fell into the circle of Abred.

## GOD IN THE SUN

**Q** Why is the face turned towards the sun in every asseveration and prayer?

**A** Because God is in every light, and the chief of every light is the sun. It is through fire that God brings back to Himself all things that have emanated from Him; therefore it is not right to ally oneself to God, but in the light. There are three kinds of light, namely: that of the sun, and hence fire; that which is obtained in the sciences of teachers; and that which is possessed in the understanding of the head and heart, that is, in the soul. On that account, every vow is made in the face of the three lights, that is, in the light of the sun is seen the light of a teacher, or demonstration; and from both of these is the light of the intellect, or that of the soul.

## GOD IN THE LIGHT

Q   Why do we say, heaven above, and hell beneath, where there can be no highest in respect of any being, or lowest in respect of any existence? And why God in the highest, and Cythraul in the lowest?

A   Because the light is always highest, and above our heads, and it is in the light that God is found, and there can be no heaven, except in the light; and God and heaven always go together with light. And the darkness is always the lowest, and Cythraul and all go together with it.

## TRIADS OF BARDISM

1   God made the world of three substances: fire; nature; and finiteness.
2   The three instrumentalities of God in making the world: will; wisdom; and love.
3   The three principal occupations of God: to enlighten the darkness; to give a body to nonentity; and to animate the dead.
4   Three things which God cannot be: unskilful; unjust; and unmerciful.
5   Three things required by God of man: firm belief, that is, faith; religious obedience; and to do justice.
6   The three principal temperaments of life: strength; vigour; and perception.
7   The three principal properties of life: temper; motion and light.

## GOD, AND THE FACULTIES OF THE SOUL

Q   What is conscience?
A   The eye of God in the heart of man, which sees everything that is perceptible, in its right form, place, time, cause, and purpose.
Q   What is reason?
A   The revolving of the conscience, whilst it contemplates by means of sight, hearing, and experience, whatever comes before it.
Q   What is understanding?
A   The working of the conscience, whilst it exercises its energies and might for the purpose of acquiring and improving good sciences.
Q   What is wisdom?
A   Sciences acquired by the revolving of the reason, and the powerful working of the intellect, which obtain sciences from God and goodness — and by success in the improvement of them.
Q   What is sense?
A   The exercise and rectification of wisdom, by studying the manner in which it has been obtained, and tasting the counsels of other wise men.
Thus thou knowest the correct saying of wisdom, 'Take as an answer, I know, and I do not know, and try to understand it. He who possesses wisdom, will correct himself, and will not stand in need of another.'
Q   Didst thou not say that wisdom may be rectified by the counsel of wise men?
A   Yes; for trying the advice of wise men, and tasting that which is wise, causes one to improve in wisdom, that is, not by the acquisition of counsel and instruction, but by applying them to the taste, as if bodily food were given to the wretch that asked it. It is not the giver that feeds the body but he that takes what is proper for him, omitting what is otherwise.

**Q** What is God?
**A** The life of all lives.
**Q** What is the spirit of God?
**A** The power of all powers.
**Q** What is the providence of God?
**A** The order of orders, and the system of systems.
**Q** What is the power of God?
**A** The knowledge of all knowledge, the art of all arts, and the agent of all agents.
**Q** What is truth?
**A** The sciences of wisdom preserved in memory by conscience.
**Q** What is justice?
**A** The art and office of conscience, regulated by reason, understanding and wisdom, considering and acting accordingly.
**Q** What is judgement?
**A** God co-reasoning with man in his conscience, in respect of the knowledge which he possesses, after he has revolved in his mind what has been demonstrated.
**Q** What is the soul?
**A** The breath of God in a carnal body.
**Q** What is life?
**A** The might of God.


1. Original published in *Barddas: The Bardo-Druidic System of the Isle of Britain*, for the Welsh Manuscript Society, by Longman & Co., 1862 [Ed.].
2. The Otherworld [Ed.].
3. The Midworld [Ed.].
4. The Overworld [Ed.].
5. The Underworld [Ed.].
6. Roughly equivalent to Purgatory [Ed.].
7. Inspiration [Ed.].

# PART FIVE:
# THE ARTHURIAN DIMENSION

The Arthurian and Celtic traditions are so inseparable that I am glad of the opportunity to include some of the material which falls into this category and which was omitted for reasons of space from *An Arthurian Reader*. Notable is 'The Dialogue of Arthur and Eliwlod' which, after searching nearly 10 years for a translation, I finally ran to earth in Algernon Herbert's fascinating *Britannia After the Romans*. It takes the form of a mystical exchange between Arthur and his nephew Ewilodd, who has been transformed into the shape of an eagle, and contains some of the most interesting concepts I have encountered for many years.

'A Story of Trystan' is perhaps the earliest and most primitive version of the famous love story of Trystan and Esyllt. It takes the form of interspersed prose and poetry, a technique much used by the early bards and story-tellers.

In 'King Arthur and Conghal Cláiringhneach' we return to the curiously different world of the Irish Arthurian tales, for a section from a longer romance dealing with the adventures of the famous hero Conghal. A very different picture of Arthur is to be found herein than we are used to, but nearer, for all that, to the possibly Celtic origin of the greatest of all heroes.

Here are the shadowy traces of a different Arthur to the famous medieval king with his shining Knights of the Round Table, at once a fresher and more savage world, where the concepts of chivalry are as yet unknown, but where the heroic values of the *Mabinogion* and the Triads already obtain.

# Chapter 13
# Dialogue of Arthur and Eliwlod[1]

### Arthur

I wonder, seeing I am a bard,
On the top of the oak and its branches on high
What the vision of an eagle, what the illusion.

### Eagle

Arthur, who hast attained distant fame;
Joy and advantage of thine host,
The eagle heretofore hast thou seen.

### Arthur

I wonder at thy station by the side of the wall,
And I will ask of thee in metre
What the illusion, what the vision, of an eagle.

### Eagle

Arthur whose fame hath travelled far,
And whose host is of gladsome aspect,
The eagle hast thou seen heretofore.

### Arthur

Eagle, being on the top of the oak,
If thou beest of the race of birds,
Thou canst not be either domestic or tame.

### Eagle

Arthur, gladial portent,
Before whose onset nothing stands,
I am the son of Madoc son of Uthyr.

### Arthur

I know not the kind of the eagle
[As one] that frequents the vales of Cornwall.
The son of Madoc ap Uthyr liveth not.

## Eagle

Arthur of speech both subtle and fierce,
Whose host is of unreproached wrath,
Eliwlod erewhile was I called.

## Arthur

Eagle of blameless aspect
And whose discourse is not evil,
Art thou Eliwlod my nephew?

## Eagle

Arthur audacious in the onset,
If I be Eliwlod
Am I a good connection of thine?

## Arthur

Eagle, untreacherous in discourse,
If thou art Eliwlod,
Was the battle-slaughter good around thee?

## Eagle

Arthur, audacious in answering,
Before whose face no enemy standeth,
From death there is no escape.

## Arthur

Eagle, undisguised of speech,
No one could through war
Bring thee to life again.

## Eagle

Arthur, dignitary among the generous,
If the words of the canon shall be believed.
With God contention is not good.

## Arthur

Eagle clear of speech,
Wilt thou say unto Arthur
What thing is evil for him to do?

## Eagle

To purpose evil with premeditation,
And to abide long in the purpose,
Is called sin and failure.

## Arthur

Eagle, most wise in discourse,
Of thyself will I enquire,
How shall I attain to God's approbation?

## Eagle

To love God with righteous mind,
And ask upright requests,
Procures heaven and the mundane gift.

## Arthur

Eagle, veracious in declaring,
If it be correct, I will ask thee,
Is the praising of him good in Christ's sight?

## Eagle

Arthur, thou art the most mighty.
On the tower I will expect the excellent hero.
Let every spirit praise its Lord.

## Arthur

Eagle of serene existence,
Without intrusion I will ask thee.
Who doth the spirit say is nearest?

## Eagle

Arthur, restless with blades,
Who has fallen by the pain of thy blood-sheddings,
Christ it is, whose faith is not concerning falsehoods.

## Arthur

Eagle speaking words of acknowledgment
I will ask, the while I cry out,
What is the course to seek for heaven?

## Eagle

Repentance for perverseness,
And to hope for mercy,
This procureth peace.

## Arthur

Eagle not ungracious in speech,
Declare thou with clearness
What thing it is evil to do.

*Figure 10*: 'Fionn receives the spear of Birgha' by *Vera Bock*.

## Eagle

To meditate unrighteous treason
And conceal your purpose long
Is called complete sin.

## Arthur

Eagle, gentle in discourse,
Speak thou without reserve,
What shall enable me to escape?

## Eagle

Praying God at every dawn,
And seeking to obtain remission,
And asking the aid of the saints.

## Arthur

Eagle, not poor of speech,
I will question thee on thy discourse,
Of what sort is the worst that happens to sin.

## Eagle

Arthur of the elevated language of wisdom,
After experiencing every law,
The worst is to be judged without hope.

## Arthur

Eagle, with the speech of a teacher,
Declare in mystic lore,
Of the hopeless what shall become.

## Eagle

To obtain the long penance infernal,
And get an irrecoverable fell,
And lose God to eternity.

## Arthur

Eagle of speech about to depart,
I will ask of thee previously,
Is there a course devoid of hope?

## Eagle

Arthur of exalted elocution,
If thou wouldest obtain a share of the world,
With the mighty hope is weak.

## Arthur

Eagle, sincere of speech,
Of thyself it shall be asked,
When is not the mighty possessor of the earth?

## Eagle

Arthur, exalted gwyddva,
Not to lose God or the Alpha
Is the summit of mightiness.

## Arthur

Eagle, certain in thy speech,
I will question thee on thy words:
Except that I myself am mighty.

## Eagle

Arthur, head of the battles of Cornwall,
Exalted one, acute-edged of shape,
None is mighty excepting God.

## Arthur

Eagle of intricate speech,
I will ask thee without trifling,
What doeth God with [my] retinue?

## Eagle

If the retinue be sincere to worship,
If upright in praying together,
God will not give hell to them.

## Arthur

Eagle of speech, dismal as the grave,
I will ask thee in my mightiness,
Who shall give judgment in the doomsday?

## Eagle

Arthur, exalted gwyddva.
Sacred enigma of the divided-place,
God himself shall judge.

## Arthur

Eagle of celestial destiny,
Hast thou not obtained to see
What Christ doeth to those who believe?

## Eagle

Arthur, gwyddva of gladness,
With thy host thou wert a complete huntsman,
Thy self shall know the judgment-day.

## Arthur

Eagle, with the speech of . . . . . ..
I will ask of thee the owner of hosts,
What shall the judgment-day do to the Gentiles?

## Eagle

Arthur, exalted swifly-moving lamp,
Whose pure innocency is gash-extinguish'd,
There shall each one know his place.

## Arthur

Eagle, *not fitter* in discourse,
I will ask of thee without offence,
Is it good for the sun to obtain service?

## Eagle

If thou seekest to have the service of the sun,
And favour with God afterwards,
Blessed art thou by reason thereof.

## Arthur

Eagle condescending in discourse,
By the Concealed-God I will ask thee,
What shall be mine, if I shall be without it?

## Eagle

If thou wilt have unveiled discourse,
Thou art the sun, saith Necessity, saith Destiny,
Until the other sun of no illusory lustre.

## Arthur

Eagle of very notable discourse,
I will ask thee in all security,
What is the course for the soul?

## Eagle

The Pater and prayers,
And fasting and charities,
And calmness of the soul until death.

1. Originally appeared in *Britannia After the Romans* by Algernon Herbert (Henry Bohn, 1836) [Ed.].

# Chapter 14
# Trystan and Esyllt[1]

*Figure 11:* 'Trystan and Esyllt with King March' by *Evelyn Paul.*

In the interim Trystan ap Tallwch and Esyllt, the wife of March y Meirchion, fled into the forest of Clyddon (Kelyddon), Golwg Hafddydd (Summer Day Aspect), her handmaiden, and Back Bychan (Little Small), his page, carrying pasties and wine with them. A couch of leaves was made for them.

And then March y Meirchion went to complain to Arthur against Trystan, and to entreat him to avenge upon Trystan the insult offered him, because he was nearer of kindred to him (Arthur) than Trystan was, for March y Meirchion was first cousin to Arthur and Trystan was but the nephew-son of a first cousin to Arthur. 'I will go, I and my family,' said Arthur, 'to seek either satisfaction or bloodshed(?)' And then they surrounded the wood of Kelyddon.

One of the peculiarities of Trystan was that whoever drew blood upon him died, and whoever Trystan drew blood upon died also.

When Esyllt heard the talking around the wood, she trembled against the two hands of Trystan. And then Trystan asked her why she trembled, and she said it was because of fear for him. Then Trystan sang this *englyn*:

> Fair Esyllt, be not fearful;
> while I am protecting thee,
> three hundred knights will not succeed in carrying thee off,
> nor three hundred armed men.

And then Trystan rose up and hastily took his sword in his hand, and approached the first battalion as quickly as he could until he met March y Meirchion. And then March y Meirchion said, 'I will kill myself in order to kill him.' And then the other men all said, 'Shame upon us if we interfere with him.' Thereupon Trystan went through the three battalions uninjured.

Kae Hir (K. the Long) was in love with Golwg Hafddydd. Thus he did: he [went to] the place where Esyllt was and spoke, singing this *englyn*:

> Blessed Esyllt, loving seagull,
> Speaking in conversation, [I say that]
> Trystan has escaped.

Esyllt:
> Blessed Kae, if it is true what thou sayest,
> in conversation with me,
> thou wilt obtain a precious (lit. golden) mistress.

Kae:
> A golden mistress I desire not
> because of what I have said . . . (?)
> Golwg Hafddydd I seek.

Esyllt:
> If it is true the tale
> thou has just told me with thy mouth,
> Golwg Hafddydd will be thine.

And then March y Meirchion went a second time to Arthur and lamented to him because he obtained neither satisfaction nor blood for his wife. And Arthur said, 'I know no counsel to give thee except to send instrumental musicians to sound toward him from afar, and after that to send vocal musicians with *englynion* (epigrams) of praise.' So they did. Thereupon Trystan called to him the artists and gave them handfuls of gold and silver. After that some one was sent to him concerning peace; namely, Gwalchmai. And Gwalchmai sang this *englyn*:

> Heavy is the immense wave
> when the sea is at the centre [of its course];
> who art thou, impetuous warrior?

Trystan:
> Heavy are the wave and the thunder (together),
> though their separation be unwieldy (?);
> in the day of battle I am Trystan.

Gwalchmai:   Trystan of irreprovable qualities,
             I find no fault with thy discourse;
             Gwalchmai was thy companion.

Trystan:     I should perform for Gwalchmai, on the day
             he should have on hand the bloody work,
             what brother would not do for brother.

Gwalchmai:   Trystan, noble (lit. bright) chieftain,
             Heavy [the blows] thy effort has struck (lit. threshed) (?);
             I am Gwalchmai, nephew of Arthur.

Trystan:     Quicker than an instant, O Gwalchmai (?),
             if thou shouldst have on hand the work of combat,
             I would make gore up to the two knees (blood knee-deep?).

Gwalchmai:   Trystan of perfect qualities,
             if *Archgrwn* did not refuse [service],
             I would do the best I could.

Trystan:     I ask in order to pacify,
             I ask not out of asperity;
             what is the number which is before [me]?

Gwalchmai:   Trystan of noble qualities,
             they do not know thee;
             it is the family of Arthur which is ambushing thee.

Trystan:     Because of Arthur I do not threaten;
             nine hundred battalions I shall provoke;
             unless I am slain, I shall slay.

Gwalchmai:   Trystan, friend of women,
             before entering upon the bloody work,
             the best thing is peace.

Trystan:     If I have my sword on my hip,
             and my right hand to defend me,
             am I worse off than they?

Gwalchmai:   Trystan of shining qualities,
             who breakest the [lance-] shaft with thy effort,
             do not reject Arthur as a kinsman.

Trystan:     Gwalchmai of pre-eminent qualities,
             the shower has over-drenched a hundred hosts;
             as he may love me, I shall love him.

Gwalchmai:   Trystan, whose habit is to be foremost,
             The shower has over-drenched a hundred oaks;
             Come and converse with thy kinsman.

Trystan:     Gwalchmai of crossgrained (?) qualities,
             the shower over-drenches a hundred furrows;
             I will go wherever thou mayest wish.

Then Trystan went with Gwalchmai to Arthur, and Gwalchmai sang this *englyn*:

             Arthur of courteous habits,
             the shower has over-drenched a hundred trees;
             here is Trystan, be joyful.

Then Arthur sang this *englyn*:

> Gwalchmai of faultless manners,
> who wast not wont to conceal thyself on the day of battle;
> [I bid] welcome to Trystan my nephew.

Notwithstanding that, Trystan said nothing; and Arthur sang the second *englyn*:

> Blessed Trystan, army chieftain,
> Love thy kindred as well as thyself,
> and me as head of the tribe.

And notwithstanding that, Trystan said nothing; and Arthur sang the third *englyn*:

> Trystan, chief of battles,
> Take as much as the best,
> and love me sincerely.

In spite of that, Trystan said nothing; and Arthur sang the fourth *englyn*:

> Trystan of exceedingly prudent manners,
> love thy kindred, it will not bring thee loss;
> coldness grows not between one kinsman and another.

Then answered Trystan and sang this *englyn* to Arthur, his uncle:

> Arthur, I will consider of what thou sayest,
> and thee first will I adorn [with praise];
> whatever thou mayest wish, I will do.

And then peace was made by Arthur between Trystan and March y Meirchion, and Arthur conversed with the two of them in turn, and neither of them was willing to be without Esyllt. Then Arthur adjudged her to one while the leaves should be on the wood, and to the other during the time that the leaves should not be on the wood, the husband to have the choice. And the latter chose the time when the leaves should not be on the wood, because the night is longest during that season. And Arthur announced that to Esyllt, and she said, 'Blessed be the judgment and he who gave it!' And Esyllt sang this *englyn*:

> Three trees are good in nature:
> the holly, the ivy and the yew,
> which keep their leaves throughout their lives:
> I am Trystan's as long as he lives!

And in this way March y Meirchion lost his wife forever. And so ends the story.

1. Originally appeared as 'A Welsh Trystan Episode' by T.P. Cross, *Studies in Philology*, vol. 17 (1912) [Ed.].

# Chapter 15

# King Arthur and
# Conghal Cláiringhneach [1]

The king of Britain at that time was Arthur the Great, son of Iubhar, [2] and the king of the Saxons was Torna mac Tinne. Arthur, son of Iubhar, sent messengers to Conghal to tell him that he himself would give the kingship of Britain to him; 'and let him not bring his fleet to harry this territory,' said he, 'but let him go against the king of the Saxons, for he is an enemy to me.' The messengers came to seek Conghal from the British shore into the district of Scotland; and Conghal asked: 'Whence have come yonder messengers?' said he. 'From Arthur, son of Iubhar, the king of Britain, we have come in order to hand over to you the kingship of Britain from Arthur,' said they, 'and to tell you to lead your hosts into the territories of the Saxons against Torna mac Tinne, for he is your enemy and his [Arthur's], and he says he will attack you.' 'Proceed,' said Conghal to the messengers, 'and let the king of Britain have a feast ready for me'; and he gave jewels and rich store to the messengers, and they went off right thankful.

As to Conghal, he did not leave that district till the Scots gave pledges to him, and they came to the British shore every night; and Fachtna Finn File said to Conghal: 'Well, O king,' said he, 'it is time for you to go to take the kingship of Scotland and the Isles.' 'As the great king, Fergus, shall say, so shall we do,' said Conghal. 'I say to you,' said Fergus, 'abide in your own encampment, and I shall give battle to the kings of the Saxons till I shall seize his kingship for you.' 'Success and blessing, O great king,' said Conghal, 'and we shall all go there.'

A very great multitude went on one expedition into the territories of the Saxons, and the chiefs of the Saxons were gathered round their king; and when they saw Conghal and his battalions coming towards them, great fear and dread seized them at the sight of him. 'Rise, O men,' said the king of the Saxons, 'and draw up your battalions against Conghal.' 'Say not so, O king!' said the chiefs of the Saxons, 'for we are not a match in numbers for Conghal, for, to judge from appearance, it is he is strongest; and the warriors of Lochlann did not offer him battle; and we shall give the kingship to him, and we shall drive you out of the kingship.' 'I shall arrange with him, if that be so,' said the king of the Saxons — for he refused no warrior who came into his house, even though he had a spite against him. The king moved forward, till he reached the rock that was above the harbour into which the fleet of Conghal came; and these had the decks of their ships bound together, and a naval platform made of them. The king of the Saxons spoke to them from the rock, and said: 'O Conghal!' said he, 'it is in order to grant you your own terms I have come, and let your men of science come before me'; and they came before the king, and they brought him to Conghal. 'To offer submission to you I came on this occasion,' said the king, 'for the sake of my territory and land; and it is better for you to have me in submission to you, and to have me go with you to devastate some other island than for you to devastate this land of mine.' 'That is true,' said Conghal; and he kept conversing with them; and they recited the following poem —

> O fleet of the active sea!
> What do you seek?
> Is it devastation or [war] you seek,
> Or shall you take peace without deceit?
> We prefer peace to harsh fighting;
> After having searched south and north
> A wall was raised . . .
> So that our followers would be the greater thereby;
> I shall go with you gladly
> With fifty ships' crews of heroes
> To devastate territory, thunder of wars!
> If you prefer my voyaging.

'Take the kingship of my own land, O Conghal,' said the king of the Saxons. That was given to him, and an alliance and friendship were made between them. 'Come to land forthwith,' said Torna. It is then that Conghal and his followers came to land. They then went into the broad-armed port, and a great feast was given to Conghal and his fleet by the king of the Saxons; and the king was with Conghal every day. A strong, very handsome young warrior came from the hosts of the Saxons towards them; and what he was engaged in doing was performing a feat, viz., running from the deck of one ship to another of the whole fleet, like the movement of a swallow or a roe-deer, without halting in his running; and the chiefs of the whole host were watching him. 'Who is the little fellow yonder, performing feats of valorous cunning on the ships?' said Conghal. 'He is my own son,' said the king and he reddened as he said it. 'What is his name?' said Conghal. 'Arthur Aoinfhear,' said the king of the Saxons. 'Let him be called hither to us,' said Conghal. He was called, and he sat down before Conghal; and Conghal commenced questioning him, and the youth answered in clever fashion. A feast was got ready by the king of the Saxons, and Conghal and his followers were entertained at it till night came. Here belongs a portion of another story in the martial exploits of Conghal Cláiringhneach.

As to Arthur the Great, the son of Iubhar, the king of Britain; when Torna mac Tinne first seized by force the sovereignty of Saxondom, he made a foray on Arthur, son of Iubhar, the king of Britain, and he devastated the fortress in which the king was, and he slew his people, and a woman died in it; and the cause of her death was that she was pregnant, and the time of childbirth had come to her there; and she and her maid-attendant came out of the house to the side of the strand, and the pangs of childbirth came upon her there, and as she heard the shout of the host devastating the place, she gave birth to the child in her womb, viz., a son; and the handmaid helped her. When the 'cathair' was devastated, the hosts of the Saxons separated to seek booty, and a warrior from the followers of the king of the Saxons happened upon the queen and the handmaid, and slew them both: and he saw the little baby fall from the lap of the handmaid. Disgust seized him at the idea of destroying it, and he took it in his arms to where the king was, and he showed it to him. 'Here is, O king!' said he, 'a waif I found'; and he told him how he had found it. 'Cover and care it well,' said the king of the Saxons, 'and let it be reared for me, for I have no son.' Thereafter it was reared for the king, and that is the lad Conghal saw running across the ships; and he told the king of the Saxons that the young fellow was not his son.

As to Arthur, son of Iubhar, the king of Britain, he was very unwell through grief for his wife, and he had neither a son nor a daughter, and he was greatly put out at not having any children — someone who should take his place after him; and it was heard in the neighbouring territories to him that the king of Britain had no children. There was a hosteller in the district of Scotland, and he had three sons, active in deeds of valour; and they considered the father they had as no honour to them, and they heard that the king of Britain had no children. 'We regret not having some kingly inheritance of our own,' said they, 'since we have the deeds and the valour and the bravery to defend it, and what better could we do than to go to the king of Britain and tell him that we are his sons?' That is the resolution they adopted, and they gathered together hosts and multitudes, and they came to the king of Britain; and when they reached him, they were well served and entertained, and they were there till the end of seven days. Arthur then asked them who they were. 'We are, we believe, your own sons,' said they. 'Where were you begotten?' said he. 'When you were in banishment from the territories of Britain, you begot us there.' 'I had more wives than one,' said the king, 'and I do not know which of them was your mother; and I have a sign by which I recognize my own sons,' said he, 'and he who is not kin to me shall not receive it from me, though I am without children. Let an apple-stone be brought us,' said he, 'and I have an iron apple, and do you cast that stone, and whichever of you shall break the stone at the first throw is my own son without a doubt, for the race to which I belong have this peculiar to them, that none of them gives a false throw.' 'Let that stone be given us,' said they, 'and the iron apple, so that each of us may give a cast of it'; and they were given to them, and they threw a cast each, and they missed. 'It is certain,' said Arthur, 'that you are not my sons, and I should prefer that you were, and you had no right to tell me a lie'; and he recited the poem —

> I have a question for you every day,
> O youths who uttered the falsehood!
> There is not one of you, floods of valour!
> To whom is due the kingdom of Britain.
> Were you sons of the excellent woman,
> Of the daughter of Edersceol, the very good,
> You would be dear to my heart,
> O youths of great activity!
> I was left alone
> That my danger might be the greater;
> I have not found a son,
> Farther off from me is his protection (?).

'Go away,' said he, 'and though I am without children, I shall not receive you.' The sons of the hosteller then left him.

It is then that Conghal finished feasting in the house of the king of the Saxons; and they all went thence to the house of the king of Britain, and they received a hearty welcome in it, and they kept up the feasting there till the end of a fortnight and a month; and the young fellow, Art Aoinfhear, was with Conghal during that time, and it was a characteristic of Conghal's that he had a judicial sense and the skill of a king. He saw that the habits that served the king of Britain served the youth; and Conghal was so situated as to have the king of Britain on his right hand and the king of the Saxons on his left hand, and Conghal said: 'Well, O Arthur!' said he, 'have you children or posterity?' 'I have not, indeed,' said he. 'It is hard to be in that plight,' said Conghal; and so they passed that night. Conghal took the king of the Saxons into secret council and consultation in the morning. 'Well, O king of the Saxons,' said Conghal, 'tell me the truth about yonder youth that I see with you,' said he, 'for he is not your son indeed, and his habits and his speech are like the king of Britain's.' 'I shall tell you the truth about it,' said the king of the Saxons; and he told the whole story as it happened from beginning to end. Their drinking-hall was then set up as it was always done, and Conghal said. 'Well, Arthur!' said he, 'what reward would be given to me if I find you a worthy son?' 'There is not anything in the world I have that I would not give you,' said Arthur, 'were he but a real son.' Conghal told him the whole true story, and judgment was given them; and the king of the Saxons told them the truth; and they brought his own son to Arthur to be judged there, and Conghal said: 'Make a fosterage and friendship with the king of the Saxons, O Arthur, and be friends to one another.'

Conghal was there till the feast was ended; and they were all in good spirits then, since they had seized the kingship of the Saxons, of Britain, and of the Isles; and Conghal said, 'A blessing on you, O Arthur!' said he, 'we have received much of good and honour at your hands'; and he commenced bidding him farewell, and he spoke these words there —

> Time for us to go over the sea,
> O Great Arthur, son of Iubhar!
> We received of thy wealth, I speak the truth!
> Good is the prince from whom we got it;
> We partook of thy feast truly,
> And of thy welcome without anxiety,
> And of thy riches, true it is!
> And of the household of your house;
> Though we partook of all that
> From you, O king and O noble man!
> As we have come over the sea of the son of Lir,
> It is time to bid you farewell.

1. Originally published in *The Martial Career of Conghal Cláiringhneach*, ed. and tr. by P.M. Macsweeney (Irish Text Society, 1904) [Ed.].
2. Uther Pendragon [Ed.].

# PART SIX: CELTIC MYSTERY — THE ONGOING TRADITION

The final part of this collection is drawn from three periods in which the Celtic Tradition has remained active. The first period, represented by 'Cormac's Adventures in the Land of Promise' looks back to a primitive, pre-Christian Ireland, where the borders of the Otherworld were always close. The second period is a little before the so-called 'Celtic Revival' and takes us back to the eighteenth century and to our old friend Iolo Morgannwg. Once again there are precise references to sources which, however, we must be careful of accepting at their face value. It may well be that Iolo, in his wanderings throughout Wales, did indeed discover and copy ancient MSS, though these may in fact have been no older than the previous century — or invented by Iolo himself. Looked at as stories or fables in their own right they stand up well to comparison with genuinely early texts. They add an interesting dimension to the continuing tradition of the Celtic peoples.

The next piece, 'Taliesin' by Thomas Samuel Jones, is one of my own personal favourites. Despite one or two nineteenth-century turns of phrase, the story is a gem of precise poetic evocation. It came into my hands quite by chance a number of years ago, and details of its author remain unknown to me. It is one of the best examples of modern adaptations of an ancient myth that I know.

'The Cosmic Legend' by Ross Nichols is one of the most fascinating glimpses of the way in which ancient themes can be taken up and utilized by modern writers. Nichols was the chief of one of the more recent Neo-Druidic revivals, The Order of Bards, Ovates and Druids (recently revived once again after a gap following Nichols's death). He spent a lifetime studying the magical and mystic systems of the Druids, and much of this knowledge is contained, in compressed form, within this poetic work. [1]

'A Dream of Angus Oge' by 'A.E.' (George William Russell) is one of many stories by this prolific and visionary writer which open a window into the remarkable world of Celtic mysticism. Russell, who lived into the troubled years of the Irish struggle for independence, saw beyond the politics of the age into a world where the magical could be experienced by all and where the hero in man could function in ways other than the bloody revolutions of the time.

It seems fitting to end thus with something which has never really been absent from our journey through the Celtic realms. It is my hope that you have found things that will inspire you to look further, and in the next few pages you will find lists to help you explore the magical world of the Celts for yourself. Here is an ancient Celtic blessing to send you upon your way:

> The peace of joys,
> The peace of lights,
> The peace of consolations.

The peace of souls,
The peace of heaven,
The peace of virgins.

The peace of fairy bowers,
The peace of peacefulness,
The peace of everlasting.[2]

1. *The Book of Druidry*, by Ross Nichols (Aquarian Press, 1990).
2. From the *Carmina Gadelica* tr. Alexander Carmichael (Edinburgh, Scottish Academic Press, 1972).

# Chapter 16
# Cormac's Adventures in the Land of Promise[1]

King Cormac, the hero of the present narrative, was the son of Art, who figures in the preceding selection. The piece is not a single unified story; it is a collection of narratives based on an ancient account of various legal ordeals, and later expanded into a story of a visit to the fairy world. Here, as in the preceding story, we see illustrated the strong tendency toward moralizing and social criticism exhibited by Irish literature of the middle period. These stories, of course, are not told entirely for the purpose of expounding the legal or social ideas to which they refer; they merely capitalize upon an already established interest and follow the usual Irish literary habit of furnishing a narrative to explain very well-known fact.

Cormac's Cup was a cup of gold which he had. The way in which it was found was thus:

One day, at dawn in Maytime, Cormac son of Art son of Conn the Hundred-Fighter was alone on Mur Tea in Tara. He saw coming towards him a calm, grey-haired warrior, with a purple, fringed mantle around him, a ribbed, gold-threaded shirt next his skin, and two blunt shoes of white bronze between his feet and the earth. A branch of silver with three golden apples was on his shoulder. Delight and amusement enough it was to listen to the music made by the branch, for men sore-wounded, or women in child-bed, or folk in sickness would fall asleep at the melody which was made when that branch was shaken. The warrior saluted Cormac. Cormac saluted him. 'Whence has thou come, O warrior?' said Cormac.

'From a land,' he replied, 'wherein there is nought save truth, and there is neither age nor decay nor gloom nor sadness nor envy nor jealousy nor hatred nor haughtiness.'

'It is not so with us,' said Cormac. 'A question, O warrior: shall we make an alliance?'

'I am well pleased to make it.' So they became allies.

'Give me the branch!' said Cormac.

'I will give it,' said the warrior, 'provided the three boons which I shall ask in Tara be granted to me in return.'

'They shall be granted,' said Cormac.

Then the warrior bound Cormac to his promise, and left the branch and went away; and Cormac knew not whither he had gone. Cormac returned to the

*Figure 12:* 'A vision of the children of Dana' by *Beatrice Elvery*.

palace, and the household marvelled at the branch. Cormac shook it at them, and cast them into slumber from that hour to the same time on the following day.

At the end of a year the warrior came and asked of Cormac the consideration agreed upon for his branch. 'It shall be given,' said Cormac.

'I will take thy daughter Ailbe today,' said the warrior. So he took the girl with him. The women of Tara uttered three loud cries after the daughter of the king of Erin. But Cormac shook the branch at them, so that he banished grief from them all and cast them into sleep.

A month later the warrior returned and took with him Cairbre Liffecair the son of Cormac. Weeping and sorrow ceased not in Tara at the loss of the boy, and that night no one ate or slept, and they were in grief and exceeding gloom. But Cormac shook the branch at them, and their sorrow left them.

The same warrior came a third time.

What askest thou today?' said Cormac.

'Thy wife,' said he, 'even Ethne Taebfada daughter of Dunlang king of Leinster.' Then he took the woman away with him.

That thing Cormac could not endure. He went after them, and everyone followed him. A great mist was brought upon them in the midst of the plain, and Cormac found himself alone. There was a large fortress in the midst of the plain with a wall of bronze around it. In the fortress was a house of white silver, and it was half-thatched with the wings of white birds. A fairy host of horsemen were at the house, with lapfuls of the wings of white birds in their bosoms to thatch the house. A gust of wind would blow and would carry away all of it that had been thatched. Cormac saw a man kindling a fire, and the thick-boled oak was cast upon it, top and butt. When the man came again with another oak, the burning of the first oak had ended. Then he saw another royal stronghold, and another wall of bronze around it. There were four palaces therein. He entered the fortress and saw the vast palace with its beams of bronze, its wattling of silver, and its thatch of the wings of white birds. Then he saw in the enclosure a shining fountain, with five streams flowing out of it, and the hosts in turn drinking its water. Nine hazels of Buan grew over the well. The purple hazels dropped their nuts into the fountain, and the five salmon which were in the fountain severed them and sent their husks floating down the streams. Now the sound of the falling of those streams was more melodious than any music that men sing.

He entered the palace. There was one couple inside awaiting him. The warrior's figure was distinguished owing to the beauty of his shape, the comeliness of his form, and the wonder of his countenance. The girl along with him, mature, yellow-haired, with a golden headdress, was the loveliest of the world's women. Cormac's feet were washed by invisible hands. There was bathing in a pool without the need of attendance. The heated stones of themselves went into and came out of the water.

As they were there after the hour of nine they saw a man coming into the house. A wood-axe was in his right hand, and a log in his left hand, and a pig behind him. ''Tis time to make ready within,' said the warrior 'because a noble guest is here.'

The man struck the pig and killed it. And he cleft his log so that he had three sets of part-cleavings. The pig was cast into the cauldron.

'It is time for you to turn it,' said the warrior.

'That would be useless,' said the kitchener; 'for never, never will the pig be boiled until a truth is told for each quarter of it.'

'Then,' said the warrior, 'do thou tell us the first truth.'

'One day,' said he, 'when I was going round the land, I found another man's cows on my property, and I brought them with me into a cattle-pound. The owner of the cows followed me and said that he would give me a reward for letting his cows go free. I gave him his cows. He gave me a pig and an axe and a log, the pig to be killed with the axe every night, and the log to be cleft by it, and there would then be enough firewood to boil the pig, and enough for the palace besides. And, moreover, the pig would be alive the next morning and the log be whole. And from then till today they have been like that.'

'True, indeed, is that tale,' said the warrior.

The pig was turned in the cauldron and only one quarter of it was found boiled.

'Let us have another tale of truth,' said they.

'I will tell one,' said the warrior. 'Ploughing-time had come. When we desired to plough that field outside, it was found ploughed, harrowed and sown with wheat. When we desired to draw it into that side out there, it was found in the enclosure all in one thatched rick. We have been eating it from then till today; but it is no whit greater nor less.'

Then the pig was turned in the cauldron, and another quarter was found to be cooked.

'It is now my turn,' said the woman. 'I have seven cows and seven sheep. The milk of the seven cows is enough for the people of the Land of Promise. From the wool of the seven sheep comes all the clothing they require.'

At this story the third quarter of the pig was boiled.

'It is now thy turn,' they said to Cormac.

So Cormac related how his wife and his son and his daughter had been taken from him, and how he himself had pursued them until he arrived at that house.

So with that the whole pig was boiled.

Then they carved the pig, and his portion was placed before Cormac. 'I never eat a meal,' said Cormac, 'without fifty in my company.' The warrior sang a song to him and put him asleep. After this he awoke and saw fifty warriors, and his son and his wife and his daughter, along with him. Thereupon his spirit was strengthened. Then ale and food were dealt out to them, and they became happy and joyous. A cup of gold was placed in the warrior's hand. Cormac was marvelling at the cup, for the numbers of the forms upon it and the strangeness of its workmanship. 'There is something about it still more strange,' said the warrior. 'Let three falsehoods be spoken under it, and it will break into three. Then let three true declarations be made under it, and it will unite again as it was before.' The warrior spoke under it three falsehoods, and it broke into three parts. 'It would be well to utter truth,' said the warrior, 'for the sake of restoring the cup. I declare, O Cormac,' said he, 'that until today neither thy wife nor thy daughter has seen the face of a man since they were taken from thee out of Tara, and that thy son has not seen a woman's face.' The cup thereupon became whole.

'Take thy family now,' said the warrior, 'and take the cup that thou mayst have it for discerning between truth and falsehood. And thou shalt have the branch for music and delight. And on the day that thou shalt die they all will be taken from thee. I am Manannan son of Lir,' said he, 'king of the Land of Promise;

and to see the Land of Promise was the reason I brought thee hither. The host of horsemen which thou beheldest thatching the house are the men of art in Ireland, collecting cattle and wealth which passes away into nothing. The man whom thou sawest kindling the fire is a thriftless young chief, and out of his housekeeping he pays for everything he consumes. The fountain which thou sawest, with the five streams out of it, is the Fountain of Knowledge, and the streams are the five senses through which knowledge is obtained. And no one will have knowledge who drinks not a draught out of the fountain itself and out of the streams. The folk of many arts are those who drink of them both.'

Now on the morrow morning, when Cormac arose, he found himself on the green of Tara, with his wife and his son and daughter, and having his Branch and Cup.

1. Originally published in *Ancient Irish Tales* by Tom Peete Cross and Clark Harris Slover (Dublin, Figgis, 1936) [Ed.]

# Chapter 17

# Ancient Fables[1]

## by Iolo Morgannwg

### ENVY BURNING ITSELF

Talhaiarn was a bard; and a learned, wise, and good man was he, and he had a son named Tanwyn. And after having given learning to that son, together with the means of promoting talent and genius, until he became acquainted with art and science, and possessed of every wisdom and praiseworthy knowledge, together with conscienciousness and piety, and adorned by every propriety of conduct towards God and man, one day Talhaiarn called his son to him, and spoke to him thus. 'My son Tanwyn, my only and beloved son art thou, I have loved thee, and reared thee, as a father should do towards a son he dearly loved. I have instructed thee in every science, and useful learning, and in every becoming conduct, that would make thee, as I thought, a man capable of good and of service to thy country and race, and to every living being of the world, and that would make thee one that every upright man would rejoice in finding ready in the service of thy race and country; and above all, one who should enjoy the favour of God in this world and in the world to come. Thou seest, therefore, that I have performed my share, and fulfilled my duty towards thee. And now my beloved son, I have neither houses nor land for thee, nor gold nor silver, nor sumptuous apparel, nor horses, nor jewels of any kind whatever; therefore, my son, I am necessitated, contrary to my affection for thee, to cause thee to leave thy father and his house, and to go wherever thou mayest be led by God and thy destiny, to follow thy fortunes and earn thy livelihood. There is neither possibility nor need for giving thee instruction and counsel further than I have done, excepting in that which I now say to thee, namely: travel not on a new road where there is no broken bridge on the old road, seek not power where thou canst have love in its stead; and pass not by the place where there is a wise and pious man teaching and declaring God's word and commandment, without stopping to listen to him.'

Then Tanwyn took his departure from his father's house, after receiving his blessing, and prayer to God for him. And he knew not where he should go, excepting that he went under the guidance of God, and his destiny, until he came to a long and even strand, by the seaside, a road leading across it, and the strand was level and smooth; and Tanwyn wrote with the point of the staff which was in his hand these words, namely: 'Whoso wishes evil to his neighbour, to himself will it come.' And a wealthy and powerful nobleman chanced to see him from a distance as he rode to meet him. And after they had passed each other with a civil and friendly salutation, the nobleman saw the writing on the sand; and after observing its elegance and correctness, he turned his horse round, and rode hastily, until he overtook Tanwyn. 'Was it thou,' said the nobleman, 'that didst write on the sand?' 'Yes,' answered

Tanwyn. 'Let me,' said the nobleman, 'see thee writing again.' 'I will do so,' said Tanwyn. And he wrote, more elegantly than before, these words, 'Man's best candle is discretion.' 'Whither art thou going?' said the nobleman. 'Into the world to earn my livelihood,' said Tanwyn, 'wheresoever and howsoever God wills, and myself am able.' 'Thou,' said the nobleman, 'art the man I want; wilt thou come with me, and be my steward, to manage my property and my household, and thou shalt have what remuneration thou demandest?' 'I will,' said Tanwyn. 'What wages dost thou ask?' said the nobleman. 'Whatsoever my service is worth,' said Tanwyn, 'in the judgment of the skilful and honest, after it has been performed.' 'Very well,' said the nobleman. 'That is the fairest arrangement I ever heard of.' So Tanwyn went along with the nobleman, and was appointed steward of his property and household. And Tanwyn managed everything so prudently, and conducted himself so uprightly, and answered all enquiries so correctly, that he was beloved by the nobleman, and by all his household. And when the time came to pay his wages, the nobleman left the matter to each of his attendants as were skilful and upright men. And they awarded to Tanwyn twice as much wage as any other person anywhere gave to the best in his service. And when the nobleman heard of the award, he made the wage twice as great as the award. And in the course of time, Tanwyn's fame became so great for wisdom, and benevolence, and justice, and for all useful and valuable knowledge, that he would not exercise power over anyone, but retain the love of all; practising kindness and justice and teaching wisdom and justice wheresoever he went, upon every occasion and at every leisure he possessed, according to the advice his father had given him.

The nobleman was a wise and prudent man, and knowing, and discreet; but when he saw that Tanwyn's fame was higher than his own, for all honourable actions and knowledge, he became envious of him. And observing day by day the fame of his servant increasing, and his own fame diminishing, he had recourse to stratagems, and found persons to accuse Tanwyn of treachery, and injustice, and dishonesty. But Tanwyn, by mere discretion and wisdom, brought the perjuries to light, so that the perjurers were by the judgment of the land and the law condemned, and all of them hanged.

After this the nobleman became more and more angry with Tanwyn, though with so little cause, and meditated his death. He at that time had a lime-kiln at work, and he went early in the morning to the lime-burners and said to them thus: 'There is a man,' said he, 'who is my enemy, and purposes to bring a foreign chieftain in a hostile manner into my dominion, and to dispossess me of my land and property, and my friends and faithful servants, and to carry away captive all of you together with myself, and to make numbers of us objects of vengeance before the country, especially you and others of my faithful people, whom I love best of all. He is at this time on a visit to me; and if he could be put to death, it would be a good thing, and safety to us all.' Upon which the lime-burners swore they would burn him in the kiln, if they knew who he was. 'You shall know that,' said the nobleman, 'by this token, namely, the first that comes to you, after I leave you, along the road I came from my house here, and makes you presents, that will be the person. Throw him into the kiln, and after that I will bring you more presents in my hands to reward you.' And this was agreed upon.

Then the nobleman went to his house, and called Tanwyn to him, and said to him thus. 'I have,' said he, 'men burning lime at the kiln, at the head of the new road. Go along that road and to them, and pay them their hire in gold and silver; and give them over and above their demands, in liberality according as thou art disposed. And give them ale and mead as much as they like; and go along the new road.' Tanwyn was silent, thinking of the advice of his father, Talhaiarn; and he took in his hands some silver and a vessel of mead, and that to a liberal amount according to his lord's instructions. And he went towards the lime-kiln, but along the old road, according to his father's injunction.

And whilst on his way, he heard in a house, near the road, a wise and pious man, preaching the word of God, and his wisdom. And Tanwyn turned in to listen to him, and remained there some time, where he heard the voice of godliness and wisdom. Meanwhile, the nobleman, concluding that by that time it was not possible but that Tanwyn must be reduced to ashes, bethought him of going to the kiln, to see and hear how it befell. At this time there were none but strange workmen placed by order of the lime-burners at the kiln, who were not acquainted with the nobleman, and they having received orders and injunctions from their employers; and as the nobleman was behaving liberally to them, and had come along the new road, they without one word from either of them threw him into the kiln, and burnt him to ashes. And in the course of a short time, behold Tanwyn came to the kiln with his gold and silver, and his vessel of mead.

## KING ARTHUR AND THE HANNER DYN[2]
### [By Taliesin, says Iolo Morganwg]

As King Arthur was walking in the early part of the day, on the first day of summer, along meadows clad in green and covered with sweet-scented trefoils, the trees being in full blossom, and every flower of wood and mead in full beauty around him, and tuneful birds in every grove, and on every leafy branch in every glade, within three arrow flights of the royal city of Caerlleon upon Usk; he being rejoiced in heart, to feel the softness and sweetness of the air, and the calm of early radiance of the brilliant summer's day, King Arthur perceived some distant object approaching with weak and feeble efforts, so that it might be supposed he would not advance as much as three steps of a wren within a year and a day. But King Arthur, casting his eyes around him in the midst of his enjoyment, did not the least regard the feeble creature he had seen afar, and which appeared to be on the point of death. However, in a short time afterwards, directing his attention to a turn in the vale, he again perceived the object which had before attracted his notice approaching nearer and nearer towards him by nine parts of the way, and more rapidly, although still weak and feeble. King Arthur looked around, but continued meditating revenge upon the Saxons and their utter extermination, when again looking about he perceived the abortive form of the Hanner Dyn coming to meet him. There was nothing in his appearance that could intimidate King Arthur, who continued to listen to the songs of the birds, until the Hanner Dyn was close to him and in his presence and saluted him, 'Good day to thee, King Arthur.' 'Good day to thee also, Hanner Dyn; what wilt thou?' 'I would wrestle a fall with thee.' 'What glory should I gain by wrestling with thee?' And King Arthur looked down again on the flower-bearing greensward. 'Thou wilt repent,' said the misshapen figure, and returned. And on the morrow King Arthur repaired to the same spot, and with him Trystan, the son of Tallwch, and Taliesin, chief of the bards, and the deformed Hanner Dyn came there as before, and saluted and derided Arthur. 'Do contend with him,' said Taliesin, 'that he may be subdued ere he becomes a perfect man.' 'I shall derive no glory whatever, by contending with such an unformed object,' replied King Arthur, who walked away along the meadows. And the shapeless being challenged Trystan; and Trystan, by the counsel of Taliesin, approached him, and said, 'Why should I contend with thee, and for what?' 'For thy head, Trystan,' said the misshapen figure. Then Trystan by Taliesin's advice wrestled with him and threw him down. 'Thou hast won my head,' said the misshapen figure. 'Yes,' replied Trystan, 'but what good do I gain by that?' 'If thou wilt let me have it at a price, thou shalt receive a ransom.' 'I desire no one's head,' replied Trystan, 'but to lame the foot of him that is more swift than just.'

## THE MOUSE AND THE CAT [3]

A Mouse of old, as he was taking a walk in a wine tavern, happened by an unlucky accident to fall into a reservoir of wine that was in front of the vats, and there he cried out with all his might for help. The Cat in consequence of the cries hastened to the spot, and asked what was the cause; the Mouse replied, 'Because I am in danger of my life, and I cannot extricate myself without assistance.' Then asked the Cat, 'What wilt thou give me for thy release, provided I draw thee out?' 'I will accede,' replied the Mouse, 'to whatever terms thou mayest propose.' Then said the Cat, 'If thou wilt that I should assist thee, it must be on the condition that thou wilt come to me the very first time that I shall call thee.' 'I will do it cheerfully,' replied the Mouse. 'Give me thy pledge,' said the Cat; and the Mouse vowed he would do whatever the Cat wished. Then the Cat stretched down his paw and drew the Mouse out of the pool, and let him have his liberty to run away. Now it happened some time after that as the Cat was strolling about, and being exceedingly hungry, the agreement between him and the Mouse came to his recollection; and he hastened to the spot where he knew the Mouse's hiding place was, and standing outside he called out to the utmost extent of his voice, and said, 'Mouse come here to me upon business.' 'Who art thou?' asked the Mouse. 'I am the Cat,' replied he. 'Didst not thou pledge me thy vow, that thou wouldest come to me the very first time I should call for thee?' 'Yes,' said the Mouse, 'but I was then drunk, and I will not therefore now fulfil my agreement.' Thus many people, when overcome by sickness or exposed to danger, promise faithfully to amend and that they will not again transgress, but when they escape from their trouble they will not fulfil any of their promises, saying, 'Yes, we were in danger then.' And so they do not perform their promises; as is related of a mariner, who was overtaken by a tempest and, being in great danger of his life, made a solemn vow that if he was delivered he would be a good manager after as long as he lived, but no sooner had the vessel been brought to shore, and he himself safely landed than he exclaimed, 'Aha, I have indeed cheated this time, I will not be a good man yet.'

## REVENGE

When Cynlas, the son of [Glywys], was lord of Glamorgan, he had a son named Cadoc, an exceeding pious man, and a saint of the college of Illtyd. One day

*Figure 13*: 'The hero Dairmuid brings forth a magical cat' by *Vera Bock*.

as he was in his father's house, a tinker came by and requested to be allowed to burnish the gold and silver jewels of the Lord Cynlas. And after finishing his work, his pack being open, a young woman, a servant there, took a silver cup and put it in the tinker's pack, concealed beneath his tools; and so the tinker shut up his pack and departed. Cadoc chanced to see all that was done. After missing the cup, the tinker was pursued, and the cup was found in his pack, and he was put in prison. But Cadoc thought within himself thus, that God who is altogether just would not permit the innocent and unoffending tinker to be punished, but would cause him to be delivered from the punishment and the disgrace. However the time of trial came, and the tinker was found guilty, and hanged. And when Cadoc saw this he thought that there was no God, or else that he was not just, for allowing the innocent and guiltless tinker to be wrongfully hanged. Therefore he fell into unbelief respecting God and goodness, and he set his mind upon the pleasures and enjoyments of the world in every way it could be obtained, without regarding either religion or law.

And after all his property was spent he took a horse and arms, and went into a wood through which there was a highway along which wealthy persons often travelled, with the intention of robbing all who should come that way. And after taking up his station in the wood, he saw, as it were, an aged and wealthy nobleman coming armed along the road. But Cadoc being a daring man, in the prime of manhood, went to meet the nobleman and demanded his gold and silver without delay or refusal. 'Thou shalt not have them,' said the nobleman, 'although thou art young and I old, I will contend with thee for my property, by force of arms and courage.' 'Very well,' said Cadoc, 'I am ready.' 'But,' said the old man, 'first of all let us dig each his grave, in order that there may be a place ready to bury the one that is slain, so that there may be nothing more heard of him.' 'With all my heart,' said Cadoc. So they set about digging, each his grave. And by digging there were found in each of the graves a man's bones. 'Behold,' said the old man, 'these are the bones of two men who were murdered for their property by the tinker who stole thy father's cup; and one of them was the father of the girl who put the cup in the pack; and by this see that God is just, and that he will not suffer the wicked to escape unpunished. But the most tardy vengeance is that of God, and the completest vengeance is that of God. Thou didst see the putting of the cup in the pack; but thou didst not receive power and permission of God to mention it, because it was his will to punish the tinker. And henceforth understand this instruction, namely, that thou canst not perceive the manner in which God brings into operation his justice, nor his wisdom, nor his mercy; leave God to his own wisdom, for it is not for man to judge him in the exalted wisdom of his arrangements, and his incomprehensible knowledge; and behold his mercy in saving thee from punishment, by sending me to rescue thee, and to teach thee when thou didst deserve nothing but the gallows on which the tinker was hanged. God is too bright for man to look upon him and see him; and so are his works and providence.' And with these words, Cadoc could see him as a young man of most comely aspect, and the most beautiful he had ever seen, and by that he knew that he was an angel from heaven.

He then returned home; and after becoming possessed of wealth, he made compensation to all for the wrong he had done them, and gave liberally to the poor, and relinquished the lordship, and built a college in Llanearvan for three

hundred saints, and they were greatly celebrated for their piety and alms-
giving, choosing the service of God before all worldly happiness and enjoyment, counting the wealth and honour of the world as nothing in comparison
with God and godliness.

## THE OWL, THE DOVE, AND THE BAT

As the Dove and the Owl were once on a journey together, they came towards
the dusk of night to an old barn, where they determined to lodge that night.
In that old barn was the chief of a tribe of Bats with his family residing, and
after seeing these strangers he invited them to sup with him. And after eating
and drinking sufficiently of choice viands, and strong drinks, the Owl arose
and began to laud the chief in this manner, saying: 'O most noble Bat, vast is
thy liberality; thy fame is unutterable. I do not consider any to be equal to thee,
and thy splendid family. Nor do I know thy compeer in learning and literary
knowledge. Thou art more valiant than the eagle, and more handsome and
beautiful than the peacock, and thy voice is more melodious than that of the
nightingale.' The Bat was exceeding proud of the encomium. And now he
expected that the Dove should address him in a similar manner, but the Dove
sat at the table in silence, without taking any notice of, or making any remark
upon, what was said by the Owl. But by-and-by she turned and courteously
thanked the chief of the Bats for his hospitality and his liberality, without
giving any further commendation. Upon this, lo, the whole family looked
angrily on the Dove, and cast a frown upon her, and blamed her unman-
nerliness, and taunted her with her want of good breeding, and her boorish-
ness, in not lauding the chief of the family in a genteel and courteous manner,
as the Owl had done; and all that the Dove said was that she hated flattery.
And all the party became enraged, and they beat and wounded her, and turned
her out in the depth of a dark and stormy night, to starve and shiver till the
dawn broke. And then she flew to the eagle, and complained of the Bats and
the Owl. Upon which the eagle swore that if the Bat and the Owl should ever
after show themselves by day, all the birds of the world should maltreat and
disrespect them; and he granted the Doves for ever after that they should
aggregate together, and he loved and respected them greatly from thenceforward, on account of their sincerity and truth, but a flock of bats or of Owls
was never seen since then. Here is respect crowning undeceiving truth and
disrespect and disgrace fettering adulation.

## EINION AP GWALCHMAI AND THE LADY
## OF THE GREENWOOD

Einion, the son of Gwalchmai, the son of Meilir, of Treveilir in Anglesey,
married Angharad, the daughter of Ednyved Vychan. And as he was one fine
summer morning walking in the woods of Treveilir, he beheld a graceful,
slender lady of elegant growth and delicate feature, and her complexion
surpassing every white and red in the morning dawn, and the mountain snow,
and every beautiful colour in the blossoms of wood, field and hill. And then
he felt in his heart an inconceivable commotion of affection, and he
approached her in a courteous manner, and she also approached him in the
same manner; and he saluted her, and she returned his salutation; and by these

mutual salutations he perceived that his society was not disagreeable to her. He then chanced to cast his eye upon her foot, and he saw that she had hooves instead of feet, and he became exceedingly dissatisfied. But she told him that his dissatisfaction was all in vain. 'Thou must,' said she, 'follow me wheresoever I go, as long as I continue in my beauty, for this is the consequence of our mutual affection.' Then he requested of her permission to go to his house to take leave of and say farewell to his wife, Angharad, and his son Einion. 'I,' said she, 'shall be with thee, invisible to all but to thyself; go visit thy wife and thy son.'

So he went, and the goblin went with him; and when he saw Angharad, his wife, he saw her a haglike one grown old, but he retained the recollection of days past, and still felt extreme affection for her, but he was not able to loose himself from the bond in which he was. 'It is necessary for me,' said he, 'to part for a time, I know not how long, from thee Angharad, and from thee my son Einion.' And they wept together, and broke a gold ring between them; he kept one half, and Angharad the other. And they took their leave of each other, and he went with the Lady of the Wood, and knew not where, for a powerful illusion was upon him, and he saw not any place, or person, or object, under its true and proper appearance, excepting the half of the ring alone.

And after being a long time, he knew not how long, with the goblin, the Lady of the Wood, he looked one morning as the sun was rising upon the half of the ring. And he bethought him to place it in the most precious place he could, and he resolved to put it under his eyelid, and as he was endeavouring to do so, he could see a man in white apparel, and mounted on a snow-white horse, coming towards him. And that person asked him what he did there, and he told him that he was cherishing an afflicting remembrance of his wife Angharad. 'Dost thou desire to see her?' said the man in white. 'I do,' said Eionion, 'above all things, and all happiness of the world.' 'If so,' said the man in white, 'get up on this horse, behind me.' And that Einion did, and looking around he could not see any appearance of the Lady of the Wood, the goblin, excepting the track of hooves of marvellous and monstrous size, as if journeying towards the north. 'What delusion art thou under?' said the man in white. Then Einion answered him and told everything, how it occurred betwixt him and the goblin. 'Take this white staff in thy hand,' said the man in white; and Einion took it. And the man in white told him to desire whatever he wished for. The first thing he desired was to see the Lady of the Wood, for he was not yet completely delivered from the illusion. And then she appeared to him in size a hideous and monstrous witch, a thousand times more repulsive of aspect than the most frightful things seen upon earth. And Einion uttered a cry from terror; and the man in white cast his cloak over Einion, and in less than a twinkling Einion alighted as he wished on the hill of Treveilir, by his own house, where he knew scarcely anyone, nor did anyone know him.

After the goblin had left Einion, the son of Gwalchmai, she went to Treveilir in the form of an honourable and powerful nobleman, elegantly and sumptuously apparelled, and possessed of an incalculable amount of gold and silver; and also in the prime of life, that is thirty years of age. And he placed a letter in Angharad's hand, in which it was stated that Einion had died in Norway, more than nine years before, and he then exhibited his gold and wealth to Angharad; and she, having in the course of time lost much of her regret, listened to his affectionate address. And the illusion fell upon her; and seeing that she should become a noble lady, higher than any in Wales, she named a day for her marriage with him. And there was a great preparation of every elegant and sumptuous kind of apparel, and of meats and drinks, and of every honourable guest, and every excellence of song and string, and every preparation of banquet and festive entertainment. And when the honourable nobleman saw a particularly beautiful harp in Angharad's room, he wished to have it played on; and the harpers present, the best in Wales, tried to put it in tune, and were not able. And when everything was made ready for to proceed to church to be married, Einion came into the house, and Angharad saw him as an old decrepit, withered, grey-haired man, stooping with age, and dressed in rags, and she asked him if he would turn the spit whilst the meat was roasting. 'I will,' said he and went about the work with his white staff in his hand after the manner of a man carrying a pilgrim's staff. And after dinner had been prepared, and all the minstrels failing to put the harp in tune for Angharad, Einion got up and took it in his hand, and tuned it, and played on it the air which Angharad loved. And she marvelled exceedingly, and asked him who he was. And he answered in song and stanza thus:

> Einion the golden-hearted am I called by all around,
> The son of Gwalchmai, ap Meilir;
> My fond illusion continued long,
> Evil thought of for my lengthened stay.

Where hast thou been?

> In Kent, in Gwent, in the Wood, in Monmouth,
> In Maenol Gorwenydd;
> And in the valley of Gwyn, the son of Nudd,
> See the bright gold is the token.

And he gave her the ring.

> Look not on the whitened hue of the hair,
> Where once my aspect was spirited and bold;
> Now, grey, without disguise, where once it was yellow;
> The blossoms of the grave — the end of all men.

> The fate that so long afflicted me, it was time
> That it should alter me;
> Never was Angharad out of my remembrance —
> Einion was by thee forgotten.

And she could not bring him to her recollection. Then said he to the guests —

> If I have lost her whom I loved, the fair one of polished mind,
> The daughter of Ednyved Vychan;
> I have not lost (so get you out)
> Either my bed, or my house, or my fire.

And upon that he placed the white staff in Angharad's hand, and instantly the goblin which she had hitherto seen as a handsome and honourable nobleman, appeared to her as a monster, inconceivably hideous; and she fainted from fear, and Einion supported her until she revived. And when she opened her eyes, she saw there neither the goblin nor any of the guests, or of the minstrels, nor anything whatever except Einion, and her son, and the harp, and the house in its domestic arrangement, and the dinner on the table, casting its savoury odour around. And they sat down to eat; Einion and Angharad, and Einion their son; and exceeding great was their enjoyment. And they saw the illusion which the demoniacal goblin had cast over them. And by this perchance may be seen that love of female beauty and gentleness is the greatest fascination of man; and the love of honours with their vanities, and riches, is the greatest fascination of woman. No man will forget his wife, unless he sets his heart on the beauty of another; nor a woman her husband, unless she sets her heart on the riches and honour of lordly vaingloriousness, and the pomp of pride. And thus it ends.

Hopkin, the son of Thomas, of Gower, composed it.

## THE TALE OF RHITTA GAWR [THE GIANT]

There were formerly two kings in the Island of Britain, and their names were Nynniaw and Peibiaw; and as these two were walking in the fields one light star-light night, said Nynniaw, 'See what an extensive and fair plain I have.' 'Where is it?' said Peibiaw. 'The whole firmament,' said Nynniaw, 'as far as the eye reaches.' 'See thou also,' said Peibiaw, 'what a number of cows and sheep I have grazing upon thy field.' 'Where are they?' said Nynniaw. 'All the stars thou seest,' said Peibiaw, 'fiery coloured gold every one of them, with the moon a shepherd watching them.' 'They shall not remain on my field,' said Nynniaw. 'They shall,' said Peibiaw. 'They shall not,' said the one. 'They shall,' said the other, sentence for sentence, till there arose a wild contention and tumult between them; and at last from contention they went to furious war, until almost all the troops of either country were killed in the battles. And Rhitta Gawr, king of Cymru, heard what slaughter had been committed by these two unreasonable kings, and he determined to conduct an expedition against them. And after proceeding according to the laws of his country, with his armies they assembled and went against the two impetuous kings, who had run as had been mentioned into lawlessness and wrong, being led away by their own insane imaginations; and they defeated them, and Rhitta cut off their beards. And when the rest of the twenty-eight kings of the Island of Britain heard these things, they collected their armies to revenge the insult of the other two kings who were deprived of their beards; and they made an expedition against Rhitta Gawr and his men, and there was hard fighting on all sides, but Rhitta Gawr and his army carried the field. 'Here is *my* pasture,' said Rhitta, and then he and his men cut off the beards of all the other kings. And when the kings of all the surrounding countries heard that, they armed themselves against Rhitta Gawr and his men, and hard and fierce was the fighting, but Rhitta and his men carried the field, with dry heads. 'Here then is our fair and extensive field,' said Rhitta; and he and his men cut off the beards of all those kings. 'Here are the beasts that grazed my field,' said Rhitta to the imprudent kings, 'and I have driven them all out, they shall not graze my field.' And after that Rhitta took their beards, and made of them an ample robe from his head to his heels; and Rhitta was a man as large as the biggest man that ever was seen. And after that he and his country did the first thing of this kind which was ever seen. Order and law according to justice and reason between king and king, and between nation and nation, in all the Island of Britain, and Norway, and Germany, and Gaul, and Spain, and Italy. And may that order and law be for ever preserved, for the opposing of such things as have been mentioned, lest they should again go to war where there is neither necessity nor just cause. Amen, so be it for ever more. And thus ends the Tale of Rhitta Gawr.

# THE ANCIENTS OF THE WORLD

There was formerly an Eagle living in the woods of Gwernabwy, in Scotland, and he was the first of his kind and of his name ever known there. And after he and his mate had had progeny till the ninth generation, and far beyond that, and had seen his race and progeny in countless numbers, and possessing all the woods and rocks of the Island of Britain, the old mother Eagle died, leaving her grey old Eagle a lonely widower, and destitute of friends, without any person to console and cheer him in his old age. Then through depression of spirits, and sadness of heart, he thought it would be better for him to marry an old widow of his own age; and after having heard of the old Owl of Cwmeawlwyd, in North Britain, he took it into his head that she could be affianced to him, and be his second wife. But he did not wish to deteriorate and debase his blood, and to degrade his race by having children by her, and bringing contempt upon his descendants. 'Better therefore,' said he to himself, 'for me to enquire of those who are older than I concerning the age of the Owl, in order to know whether or not she is past the age of child-bearing.' He had an old friend, older than himself, and this was the Stag of Rhedynvre, in Gwent, and he went to him, and asked the age of the old Owl. And the Stag answered him thus: 'Thou seest, my friend and companion, this oak by which I lie. It is at present no more than an old withered stump, without leaves or branches, but I remember seeing it an acorn on the top of the chief tree of this forest, and it grew into an oak, and an oak is three hundred years in growing, and after that three hundred years in its strength and prime, and after that three hundred years decaying before death, and after death three hundred years returning into earth, and upwards of sixty years of the last hundred of this oak are passed, and the Owl has been old since I first remember her, without my being acquainted with any of my own kindred, who knew her age, or to whom she had appeared younger than she does now. But there is an old friend of mine, who is much older than myself, the Salmon of Llyn Llivon. Go to him. It is a chance if he does not know something of the age and history of the old Owl.' The Eagle went to him and asked information concerning the Owl, and the Salmon answered him thus, 'The number of the scales and the spots upon me, and added to these the number of grains of spawn which I contain, are the number of years of my age, and to the utmost of my recollection, an old spectre was the Owl; and none of my friends, who were of full age when I was young, either remembered or ever heard anything of the youth of the Owl, nor moreover of her having any children. But there is a companion of mine, who is much older than I, the Ousel of Cilgwri. Go to him. It is a chance if he does not know something beyond the knowledge and recollection I have of her. Go to him and ask.' The Eagle went and found the Ousel sitting on a small bit of hard flint, and he asked him the age and history of the Owl.

And the Ousel answered him thus: 'See here how small this little stone is under me; it is not more than a child of seven years old could take up in his hand, and I have seen it a load for three hundred yoke of the largest oxen, and it never was worn at all, excepting by my cleaning my beak upon it once every night before going to sleep, and striking the point of my wings upon it every morning, after alighting upon it from the midst of a thorn-bush, and the number of the years of my age are entirely beyond my recollection and notwithstanding that, I never knew the Owl younger to my judgement and observation, according to her appearance, than she is at this day, and I never heard from any of my friends the slightest report of any recollection of her having children. But there is one a great deal older than I, or, for all I ever heard, older than my father, and this is the Toad of Cors Vochno, in Ceredigion [Cardiganshire]. Go and ask him, and if he knows not, I know of none who does.' The Eagle went to Cors Vochno, and met the Toad there, and asked him the age of the Owl, and the Toad answered him, 'I never eat any food save the dust of the earth, and I never eat half enough to satisfy me; see thou those large hills around this bog; where they stand I have seen plain ground; and I have eaten as much earth as they contain, though I eat so little lest the mould of the earth should be consumed before my death. Beyond all memory of mine are the years since I was born, and even the first subject of my recollection; nevertheless, much older than I am is the Owl, without the slightest appearance of youth belonging to her, but an old grey hag crying, *Ty hict, ty hic*, in the woods in the long winter nights, frightening the children, and disturbing everybody; and I have no recollection, nor did I ever hear of her bearing children, but what I saw myself, old hags far beyond the age of bearing children were the youngest of her daughters, and her granddaughters, and her great-granddaughters.' Then the Eagle saw he could marry her, and take her for a mate, without bringing on his tribe debasement or disgrace, degradation or degeneration. And so it was from the courtship of the old Eagle it was known which were the oldest creatures in the world; and they are the Eagle of Gwernabwy, the Stag of Rhedynvre, the Salmon of Llyn Llivon, the Ousel of Cilgwri, the Toad of Cros Vochno, and the Owl of Cwmeawlwyd, and there is not save the ridge of land older than they of the things that had their beginning in the age of this world. And thus it ends.

## HERE IS THE ACCOUNT OF CARADOC

[Caractacus], the son of Bran, the son of Llyr, and of Manawyddan, the son of Llyr, his uncle, and of the prison of Oeth and Annoeth

When Caradoc, the son of Bran, the son of Llyr Llediaith, was warring with the Romans, and slaughtering them terribly, some of those who had escaped told their emperor that there was neither chance nor hope of overcoming Caradoc, the son of Bran, as long as the woods and thickets remained in the territories of Caradoc and his Cymry, viz., in the dominion of Essyllwg [Siluria], inasmuch as, they said, that in the woods and forests they conceal themselves like wild beasts, and it is impossible to obtain a sight or a glance of them, in order to slay them, so that they come upon us Caesareans unawares, as numerous as bees out of a hive in a long hot summer's day, and slaughter us in heaps; upon which the emperor answered, 'By my great name and destiny, the woods in the territory of Caradoc and his Cymry shall not long stand; I will dispatch to that territory one hundred legions of my best warriors with fire instead of weapons, and I will set on fire all the woods in the territories of Caradoc, and his race of Cymry and their tribes.' These words came to the hearing of Caradoc, the son of Bran, and his men, upon which they said as with one voice and one mouth, 'It is a small thing for us to defend our country, otherwise than through strength of body and heart. Therefore let us burn our woods, as broad and as far as there is seen a leaf of their growth, so that there may not be found a sprig to hang a flca from the shore of Severn to the river Towy, as broad and as long as the territories of Siluria extend, throughout all the countries in our possession, and under our name; then let us invite the Caesarians to our country, and meet them army against army, upon the plain and open ground, the same as we did on the covert ground, and on the wilds.' Then they burned all the woods from the shore of the Severn to the extremities of the vale of Towy, as far as the territories of Caradoc and his Cymry extended, without leaving a sprig upon which the smallest gnat could alight, to rest from the heat on a long summer day. Then they sent messengers to the emperor of Rome, and when they came to the emperor's court, they addressed him courteously in this manner: 'We are the men of Caradoc, the son of Bran, the son of Llyr Llediaith. Greatly would our king and race prefer tranquillity and peace to war; more gladly would they have fed milch kine and wool-bearing sheep than their war horses; more desirable to them the entertainment of their friends than the slaughtering of their enemies. If thou dost find fault, it lies not on the race of the Cymry, nor their kings; search elsewhere for it, narrowly observing that which is done under thy hand and eye. We have met them army to army in the wilds, and thou knowest what occurred, but our lands are no longer in thicket, inasmuch as the burning has not left either tree or sprig alive upon the face of our country, and now all the territories of Caradoc, the son of Bran, are open land. Keep at home, therefore, thy wild fire; there is not cause or work for it upon the face of Wales. Let thy men meet us army to army on open ground, two foreigners for one Cymro on plain land, and try to win back the honour thou hast lost in the wilds. One wide plain is our country, without any spot in which it is possible to hide or lurk. Thus we greet thee; stamp this deep on thy memory and be manful: Caradoc, the son of Bran, he himself, it is true, addresses thee, and no other.' Strange and astounding was this address to the emperor, and grievous to his mind was the recollection of the protection the Cymry received from him, by the privilege of ambassadors from a foreign country, when he understood that it was no other than Caradoc himself who addressed him. The ambassadors returned to their own country, and the Romans brought their armies into the field, wheresoever the wind blew from the four quarters of the world. And Caradoc and his Cymry came against them valiantly, slaying them in heaps wheresoever they turned their faces towards them. And equal were Caradoc and his Cymry on open ground to what they before were found in the woods, as good on the plain as in the covert; and then it became one of the proverbs of the country, when they would say, 'Equal in the wild as in the open ground' — 'The same to him Oeth as Anoeth [open or concealed].'

After burning the woods, as above mentioned, in the territories of Bran and his Cymry, there was such a scarcity of timber that they had not materials for building houses; and from that arose the proverb, 'It is easier to find a carpenter than materials.' And also, 'Few the carpenters, but fewer the materials,' in consequence of which the Cymry were obliged to build their houses of stone, and those houses were constructed in the form of a stack of corn or hay, or the form of a beehive, being round, gathered together at the top, instead of a wooden roof, with a hole for the smoke in the centre overhead, as may be seen in the ruins of those houses that are to be found to this day on the mountains, and in uncultivated places. Then they sought to make lime, to impart strength to those stone houses; and in those times they began in Wales to build houses with lime, and to arrange houses in villages, in order that it might be easier to protect each other from enemies and foreigners, and render mutual assistance, and herd their sheep and milch kine, and defend their arable and hay land. After those wars, when so many of the Caesarians had been killed, their bones, which had been left by the wolves, and dogs, and ravens, like a white sheet of snow in many places covered the face of the earth, and in the Maesmawr in Wales, namely, the country where now is the mon-astery of Margam, were found the greatest quantity of bones, on account of the great battle on the open ground, which was fought with the Romans, who were there slain. And Manawyddan, the son of Llyr, seeing that, caused the bones to be collected together into one heap, and to put others also there, which were found throughout his dominion, so that the heap became of a marvellous magnitude. Then it came to his mind to make lime and to form a prison of those bones, in which to confine such enemies and foreigners as might be taken in war; and they set about the work, and constructed a large edifice with exceeding strong walls, of those bones mixed with lime. It was of a circular form and wonderful magnitude, and the larger bones were on the outer face of the walls, and within the circle many prisons of lesser bones, and other cells under the ground, as places for traitors to their country. This was called the prison of Oeth and Annoeth, in memorial of what the Cymry and Caradoc, their king, had done for their country and race, as well in the open ground as in the covert. And in that prison were confined those, who were taken in war as enemies to the race of the Cymry, until the judgment of a court should be obtained upon them; and if it should be found that any one of those foreigners was taken practising treachery, he would be burned; if he was taken in open battle, and it should be found true by the judgment of the court, he would be returned to his country in exchange for a Briton. And after that they imprisoned there everyone who should be found a traitor to his country, and were not burned by judgment of the court, they were kept there during their lives. And that prison was demolished several times by the Caesarians, and the Cymry would afterwards reconstruct it stronger than before. And in the course of a long time, the bones becamed decayed, so that there was no strength in them, and they were reduced to dust. Then they carried the remains and put it on the surface of the ploughed land; and from that time they had astonishing crops of wheat and barley, and of every other grain for many years. Thus it ends.

## THE HISTORY OF THE THREE BIRDS OF LLWCH GWYN

Drutwas, the son of Trephin, received from his wife three birds of Llwch Gwyn, and they would do whatsoever their master bid them, and a combat was appointed between Arthur and Drutwas, and no one should come to the field but they two; and Drutwas sent his birds forth, saying to them, slay the first that comes into the field. And as Arthur went into the field, the sister of

Drutwas, who was Arthur's friend, came and prevented Arthur going to the field, out of affection to each of them; and at last Drutwas came into the field, thinking the birds had slain Arthur, and the birds caught him up and killed him, and when high in the air, they knew him, and fell to the ground with most doleful lamentations, for having slain Drutwas, their master. And the song of the birds of Llwch Gwyn still exists on the strings, which was made at that time to record the event. And from that Llywnch Hên had the subject on which he composed the following *englyn* —

> Drutwas, the son of Trephin, on the day of combat,
>    With toil and exertion,
> A breach of compact committed, formerly,
>    And was slain by the birds of Llwch Gwyn.

1. Originally published in Iolo MSS, ed. Taliesin Williams (Llandovery, 1848) [Ed.].
2. 'Half-man'.
3. This Fable was taken from a MS in the handwriting of Iolo Morganwg, who transcribed it from Owain Myvyr's *Collection of Proverbs*, which was extracted from an ancient MS on parchment, written about the year 1300.

# Chapter 18
# Taliesin [1]
## by Thomas Samuel Jones

## I

Only the harpers who chanced to pass the turfed hut on the spur of the hills sang of days so long ago that no one remembered them, when Hu with his team of gigantic oxen dragged forth the ancient lake monster, and with his shining plough tamed the wild earth and caused it to yield man yellow grain, until the Midlands became a pleasant pasture for the herds of a peaceful tribe. Their songs brought back that time of simple innocence when the secret places of the gods were plain: the black vale of Ked, misted with pale moonlight; the windswept crests of Beli, where May Fire roared into the lonely dawn. The old men sang, too, of the coming of the sea eagles; of banners advancing over the green wastes of the fen. Once more the woad-stained chieftains rallied on the river bank and trampled plain, and the fierce queen of the Brythons drove her roaring chariot against the might of Rome.

Again the island of mystery lay reddening beneath the dark water and the darker sky, while smoking torches striped the sacred groves, harsh spears beat back the magic wands of willow-wood, and the mail-clad warriors triumphed over the white wizards in the awful circle of the god. Of the strong cities afterward built where the grey wolf had shambled, loftily towered as the greater citadel, that Rose of the World whose wonder drew a swarm of howling barbarians to spoil her beauty as a cloud of savage bees, there was no need to remind men. Strange temples of Mithras gleamed in the Druid woodlands; broad highways carried the riches of the rainless countries into the deeps of the wilderness, making the heart of the hero mild as a milch cow, so that the shadow of a mighty wall was needful to shield him from the naked hordes of Caledonia.

But although the lords of the South brought a deeper understanding to the wizards of the North, neither the wise laws nor the cunning that gave such beauty to the simple uses of life could charm the hardier chieftains from the moors and rocky gorges of the West. Long before Gratian perished in the purple of a lost empire, raven-plumed pirates had harried the watchers on the Saxon shore, and the black coracles of Iberia had borne away the defenceless Britain into captivity. Then when no help could come from the fallen city, these wild kings of the mountain, beloved of the bardic men, sounding their war horns, gathered the host from the hills to make a last stand before the foemen of Frisia: Cunedda, now asleep in battered armour beneath a forgotten mound, Arthur, who on stormy nights still haunts the Valley of Usk, riding towards unknown Caers in quest of the mystical Cauldron; and Urien of Powysland, whose bard Taliesin, a little lad listening to a wanderer's harp-strings, felt in his soul the stirring of a mightier music.

## II

Not many years before Taliesin was found near the hut of Elphin's swineherd, a wood-woman, home-faring to her yellow thatch beside the lonely waters of Tegid, had seen a strange warrior shining through the forest. It was a stormy night hard upon the close of autumn, and although a wan moonlight glanced from the silvered mail and the enamelled trappings of the war-horse, she could see that the chieftain sheltered within the hollow of his shield arm a crimson cloak carefully folded. Then a wintry gust blew out all the stars, as the frosted breath of a warder extinguishes the candles of the king's hall, and the great steed went plunging by toward the dark lake shore. When at length the woman, beaten and wind-weary, reached her threshold, the door was wide open and by the ashes of the peat fire lay a sleeping child very young and fair, wrapped in a scarlet cloth. There was no trace of the rider, but looking out into the heart of the storm she beheld a huge mare, foaled in no earthly meadow, the black mare with hooves of fire, while from the island in the midst of the waves came the fragrance of summer and the sound of most sweet music.

The savage priestess of the valley soon divined a part of the mystery of that midnight. In her horn of magic smoke, slowly arose the mighty forms of the past. Again the lances of the Northern horde smote the battling host at Camlan; kite and raven wheeled above the bleeding dragon of the Brythons, and the cloud-swept pinnacle of Caerleon flamed and fell forever from the sky; and the wounded emperor was borne toward the gloomy regions of Gwyn-ap-Nudd, where a strange God now called men over the desolate marshes. So, fearful of the heroes beyond the mountain, Ceridwen nursled the stranger with her own fierce whelps. Here he seemed like a milk-white faun doomed by enchantment to wander among a shaggy, uncouth brood. Because of this, and for reason of his wistful singing upon gentle days, she waxed jealous; yet his fate was written in the witch fires, and she knew that he could not be destroyed.

Now it chanced one morning, when all the woods were wild with April, that the wood-woman turned the dark hull of her coracle from the strand, and left the child to tend a mystical cauldron filled with speckled herbs gathered in dank dews from the side of the ravine where sunlight never came. As he watched, three drops of the liquor spurted up from the seething depths and burned his hand. Immediately he began to dream with eyes open. In changing shape he fled, circling earth, air, and water, pursued by a nameless fury. Yet through his flight he could understand the twittering of the birds in the coppice, the thoughts of the little snakes darting from the brushwood, and the stir of life in the hidden centres of the ground. Just as he was about to fall into the abyss beyond the edge of the world, he heard the priestess howling over her broken vessel, whose brown juices were creeping across the clear lake tides. (The harpers say that they poisoned the Pool of the Shepherds and the weedy marsh where the young stallions go down to drink in the spring twilight.) Turning upon him she would have slain him with the knife of sacrifice, save that he was so little and innocent. Instead she thrust him into a bag of dappled deerskin, which she dropped in the coracle afloat upon the white mouth of the mere.

## III

On green May Eve the light coracle drifted down a valley of faery loveliness; now tangled in the fleeces of wool floating on the water, an offering to Arianrod, whose radiant body rose from a meadow of spring flowers; now passing heedlessly over a treasure of sunken gold, the sacred spoils of Hu, or Gwydion of the Rainbow Girdle. Far away, beyond the soft gleam of budding ash and alder, stretched the windy moors and rolling hills horned with Beal Fire where the men of wood-wisdom gathered to foretell the fate of unknown kingdoms. At length the boat of skins, whirled about by the brawling river, overturned, and the bag of red deerhide leapt like a salmon into a pool that lay broad and glistening beneath a wizard moon.

Upon the reedy bank stood wild Elphin, a king's son wrapped in a mantle worn and faded as a beggar's cloak that knows all weathers. For the ocean had crept over his orchards and woodlands, the gables of many a dwelling, and the sea-sweet pasture where a hundred cows moved lowing at milking time. Because of the lost cantrev[2] he now hunted with fierce dalesmen, or sought the black bread of a swineherd instead of the wine and spiced collops served in the rush-strewn hall of Gwyddno. And he was come to draw a rich yield of the fish that spawned in the shadow of a huge rock. But when his man had drawn the snow-cooled waters, only a heavy leathern bag lay in the pull of the dam, and bewailing the evil luck he cut the tough thongs to find within a young child whose white and noble brow shone under a thatch of gorse-yellow hair. Instantly the prince loved him of that shining forehead, nor mourned the loss of perch and trout because the gods had sent him such a Falcon of May. Thus Gwion the Little was gathered by the woodward from the depths of Elphin's weir. The singing of Taliesin so pleased his master that he boasted throughout Powysland that his ill fortunes would soon be mended by the enchantment of a magic bard. And the herdsman of the prince carefully tended the boy, until he was old enough to roam with the swine in the vast wood behind the turfed hut. Then he would run through footless thickets, following a wilder music than his own; or he would lie for hours in a leafy dingle, hearing the talk of the faery folk, from the eerie whispers of the fishes in the tarn to the savage snarl of the mountain monster. Sometimes upon calm nights when the north trembled with light, he could see majestic shapes wandering across the sky through a maze of stars to the Golden Court of Don sung by the harpers. Once he had seen the dark hunter ride into the Sunsetland with a flight of souls that soared above him in the form of swans. Then, when a lad almost as tall as the twisted thorn-tree, he chanced one dawn upon a valley of strange stones, haunted by the sound of rushing water. Like snow upon the coarse moor-grass, a company of white-bearded men waited outside a circle of twelve great rocks. The blue-robed priest beside the central stone, which bore the naked sword of the Gorsedd, touched the Crwth and Taliesin, hidden in a craggy pinnacle, listened to a chanted mystery so hauntingly beautiful that it seemed like the echo of a forgotten dream. Slowly the sky changed from grey to crimson, the harp-strings quivered and were still, while the Druids knelt silently in the eye of the rising sun.

## IV

All that winter a one-eyed bardsman lay beneath the thatch of the weirward, and while the brindled wolf and the brown hare grew lean in the leafless woods, the boy, stretched on an otter skin beside the hearth flame, heard the harp-strings tell the deeds of heroes and the wisdom of the world-making gods. Within his heart, shaken by the strange tales, stirred deeper harmonies than the wild wood songs that so charmed his master. When he asked the harper the mystery of the hidden valley, the old man bade him find a lake high in the hills, upon whose waves no waterfowl would rest. There, the first man had heard the lonely echo of God's Name breathed by the Eternal Spirit and thrice thundered by Creation in a wild dawn. And now, on the three feast days that mark the wandering of the Bull of Fire among the heavenly Stalls, beautiful coracles ever seek a mist-folded vanishing shore where the children of evening sing in the golden and silver light. But it was not until the hush of brooding summer that Taliesin found the unknown mere all creatures hold in awe, girdled by mountains that rose upon mountain as when the earth shook with that First Great Cry.

The Druids who dwelt in the holy wood welcomed the lad as one rent from the Starry Caers to bring a brighter dreaming to the sons of man. For through the vision of the oldest, which was clear as morning dew, they had watched the life of the Radiant Child and followed his quest of them beyond the savage dales. It was the feast of midsummer, so he entered into their mystic barque and sailed to the island grove of Ceridwen, whose empty chariot with poles of gleaming Findrinny waited, yoked to three snow-white heifers. A veil woven with many coloured threads trailed over the bronze wheels and lay rippling like water in the green bracken. Near the altar of the willow thicket, throughout the silent hours of darkness, the wizard harps swelled with such an unearthly music that the spirits of the dead returned from the Sunset Meadows and the living tasted the peace of death. Then Taliesin beheld a blinding Presence. A bridge of sword-blue lightenings quivered above the tarn, and the silver-shod heifers, trampling the windless air, bore the goddess to purpling vineyard and yellowing harvest-field.

Now a time came after the ordeal of the Forest Faith, when the shadow of the world crept over the serene valley of the Oracles. Red winds of battle carried the sound of clashing barge and screaming bow-string, as the sea men marched in flames upon the tawny moors and the hilly wilderness of the West. Unable to keep back the burning songs that leapt in his breast, the young bard bade farewell to the venerable Priests of the Cauldron and turned his face toward the realm of Rheged that lies between the day and the night. Black against an ice-green sky towered the Castle of Urien. Yet the lad, fresh from the russet plains and gaunt flanks of woody ravines, was not dismayed by the barbarous turrets, or by the jewelled crown of the mightiest prince of the Northland and the golden tongues of his chieftains as they sat in the circle of foaming horns. Instead, when bidden, he sang the wars of the Dragon Kings, until the heroes of the Cymru gripped their spear-shafts and a shout arose that blew the smoky torches to a flare and shook the shields upon the massive walls. And dark Morvudd, robed in apple-crimson, entered with her mead-bearing maidens to look upon the stranger. Nor did she rest that night because of him, but long before the riding of the host she walked at sunrise through her fragrant gardens overlooking the sea.

## V

The wizard harps that rippled through the wood dreams had not held the wandering bard in a Druid peace, content to watch the changes of a troubled world shadowed in the depth of the magic tarn. Nor could the beauty of a king's daughter charm him from battles trumpeted among the bellowing hills, where the princes of Deira and Bernicia harrowed the blood-drenched plains in their clashing cars. But beside the chieftain of the ruddy West Taliesin rode at the forefront of the armies, upon a stallion foaled on May Eve by the demon mare of Teynon. Banners of purple and crimson, splended as the evening sky above the savage battlements of Rheged, fluttered about him. And gay, triumphant, exultant, rang the war songs that were never to fail the men of Powys. Along the dangerous pass, through the terrible forest of spears, under the arc of swinging axes, and in the falling flame of the high-hurled brands, the brave notes sounded, ever driving the lost over the fallen foemen, as the belling of the stag leads the thirsty deer over the young water-grass. Moreover, the Saxons say that once upon a field of flight so madly shrilled his singing that a wildwood copse moved from a hillcrest — tall stalwart warriors, clad in green armour, who rushed upon the fighting heath with levelled lances. Yet surpassing the battle triumph was the perilous riding in search of a mystery beyond the oracles of the quivering stone: now on a roadstead, in whose eerie hollows suddenly gleamed a girl lovely as Arianrod, who flitted a moon mist over marsh and mere, luring the stranger on the leaf-hidden way to a vanished kingdom; now where the horns of an enchanted Caer rose above the spume of a wild sea. Within, the undaunted adventurer could find the Golden Bowl which fell like a star from the Feasting Hall of Heaven, the pearl-rimmed Cauldron that yields its divine draught only to the pure lips of a hero. Then among the ancient bards he contended in the mysterious circle until flames sprang from the Crwth's brazen strings and the cry of a god came from the mouth of a harpsman, uttering in a word-woven melody secrets older than night or the wind. Truly a difficult seat in Caer Sidde!

It later befell thus with the bard as he journeyed in a swampy wilderness, near the grassy valley whence a coracle of glass sped into the twilight of the West with the wounded King of the Cymry, beneath the burning sail. He had long been aware of a radiant arch above the distant oaks and of a low vibrant hum that drowned the boom of the bittern and the heron's thunderous wings. Eager to discover a river of prophecy or the unknown source of the Stream of Sorrow, he urged his war steed past bog and bracken, until he was come to knoll well outside the willowed pools of the waste. Before him stretched a land of white, fragrant silence, the forgotten garden of a god-like face. A rainbow, as from the centre of a faery sun, woven of many hues unseen by mortals, trembled over the blossoming apple trees and brightened the clear brook that leaves the meadow of Merlin. Innumerable bees clung to the snow-dropping boughs. Sudden birds, sweeter than the Three Singers of Rhiannon, darted on coloured wings down the windless alleys without fear of dragon-scales hidden in the foam of the flowers: for in the middle of the orchard plot stood a beautiful youth, fair as the girdled Gwydion, armoured in silver mail, yet when the harper hailed him Lord of the Caers of Light, the Shining One uttered no word of Don, but bade him seek the pale Master of Death, for whose blood the Mountain Eagles had long thirsted, and who ruled thorn-crowned in Druid

Avalon. There in the blue-grey mist of shaken censers he would find the strange God bound to a quicken rood, promising truth beyond the ancient wisdom of the forest. The warrior ceased, and lifting his sword, passed from sight between the dawn-white branches. The rainbow, a reflection of his ghastly blade, faded on the skyline. And Taliesin, spent and wondering, looked on the desolate border of Avalon's land.

## VI

Long time he searched the green waste for a bough of the delicate apple blossom, in vain he listened for the footfall of Him who guarded the vanished loveliness. But those white trees of morning no longer lightened the leafy gloom, and where the bright Chieftain had stood a crane rose flapping from the sedge. Idly the bard followed its ragged flight across the swamp, until he saw a hive-like hut in the thick of the wood. A wrinkled Druid, grey as the mist of the marshes, wavered between the birch boles worshipping in a maze of subtle movement. With the goat's milk he offered, Taliesin also tasted the honey of his wild wisdom. He learned how Avalloc and his swan-hued daughters passed the wandering stars out of the Valley of the Flaming Bowl, and how a warrior leader of the Winged Hosts that veil the Three in One now watched over Merlin's Orchard of Mercy. There now whispered talk of a wonderous hall built by David, where shaven men knelt at the Table of a God before the lifted Horn of Love. And while the light of day silvered into the ashes of even, the Child of the Sun heard the far off bells of Christ ring through fen and forest.

As he slept upon deerskins in the strange County of the Gods, terrible as a wolf howl at night came a dream of Elphin in danger, not from pirate galleys or the Saxon swords, but from a fettered death in a dark tower. Without waking the Priest of Ceridwen, Taliesin sprang on his horse to follow the glimmering Wheel of Arianrod into the west. The way was full of peril, for pale hounds of darkness padded over the marsh moss and demon eyes glared from black pools among the reeds. Now great mocking voices shook the vale with thunderous laughter, now immense shapes menaced from the cloudy hills. But with the lark song the yellow-haired harper rode past the reaches of the ghastly land, and looking backward saw it turn to fire beneath the dawn.

In Teganwy, beyond the vales of the Severn, a rich arras had been hung on the walls of the fortress, and rushes, freshly plucked for the mead-feast of Maelgwyn, strewed the floor. Around the dais of the crafty king ranked shielded captains, wizards with hazel wands, and fair women clad in webs of coloured raiment. Glorious was the shine of clear stone on golden clasp. Outside the Caer stamped a herd of horses, battle-bold stallions and lusty mares eager for the racing. Inside the bards began their Contention; and Taliesin, true to the best of his master, stood in their midst, an eagle with extended wings, who prophesied the coming of an unknown hero to the Wise Men of the Mountain. As he sang, seven radiant spirits circled in the dome of the pillared hall, and the chains of Elphin fell straightway. Then with fierce eyes, blue as sword-flame, he denounced the coward bards, unfed by the Cauldron, and the evil king, the foe of starry knowledge. The chief trembled under the death-song. All lights darkened, all sounds ceased, while the castle filled with the roar of wind and sea. Suddenly, over each face wandered a chilly breath. And when the sun came forth again, Maelgwyn lay smitten by the savage marsh monster. Never had such harping been heard in Teganwy!

Soon after this a battle fury shook the West. Horned kings with raven banners fought against the armoured prince of the Brythons until the little rivers of the glens were red because of that dreadful heath. That they might shorten the hero line of Cunedda, the Shining Ones of the Sea came and stood on a hillock apart. Through blood and fire their robes shone pure as newly fallen snow; above the crash of warwain and the rattle of shaft on shield, men listened to their songs and died in peace. Then the bull-throated Bretwalda, fearing the white magic, charged them with his bellowing thanes. Nor did the lifted crosses save any, but each fell singing, as the swan falls to die among the puple flag-flowers. Awed by the holy sight, the harper, who knew well the joyous strife of mailed warriors, marvelled that unarmed monks should face death exultantly. And louder than triumph's trumpets or the cry of the captive Cymru sounded the mysterious voice of the God from the shadowy place in distant Avalon.

## VII

Springtime and autumn, long lines of grey geese flew above a wattled cell in the wild heart of the fen. These wanderers over many seas were Bregoret's sole missioners. For although neither war-flame nor battle-axe threatened the peace of Avalon, and the plumed aethelings began to run from Odin to Him of the Sorrowful Bells, yet the Saxons were ever jealous of power among the Cymru and their last Abbot had chosen to dwell in the swampy waste apart. Such was his love that the bear, the otter, the fox and the fawn were become his creatures; the joyous singers of the marsh, his perpetual choirs; and all worshipped together beneath the whirling thuribles of sun and moon.

With eyes quickened by fasting and solitude, he often caught the swift bright Shadow of the World beyond the walls of air. And in the great dim Druid wood, whose warrior once kept May with wimpled queens of faery, archangels now passed in a storm of snowy wings. Thus far mortals had not ventured on those wizard paths, until one day a youth with yellow hair moved like a torch between the lofty trees. He bore no targe or jewel-hilted sword, only a harp that sighed as the winding of the wind over a lonely water. The old man watched this green falcon from the mouth of the hut, wondering if the gods still walked in the meads of the Severn at the greenery of the year. But he had lived alone with love for so long that he feared nothing.

Entering the glade the harper greeted Bregoret as a Druid, and when he learned that the holy one was the servant of the Three in the Valley, he fell at his feet. From dusk to dawn, without breaking fast, Taliesin listened while the monk told of the young hero, the Son of God and a daughter of earth, born before Merlin had seen the Dragon Star of Arthur on the crimson hills. Strangely the Christ story blent with the mysteries of the circle, enriching the forest love as the fresh sweet breath of April draws colour and fragrance from the winter field. And in the White Life, unfolded by the Abbot, the men of morning asleep in cair and burrow, the lion-hearted chieftain who laughed at death, the venerable priests, seekers of deep understanding, lived again, mightier because of Him. Then the hermit brought forth a common silver Chalice, battered and tarnished. A sorry sight was the world-conquering Cup before Urien's golden mead horn or the pearl-rimmed Cauldron of prophecy. Yet as they looked, it began to glow as if it were the very core of light, and all about them broke a dawn of soft blossom-dropping boughs. Overwhelmed, the bard fell upon the reeds in a death-like slumber, while from the strings of his forgotten harp glimmering hands drew an unearthly melody throughout that strange dreaming.

As a bird wings north from the summerland, so the soul of Taliesin crept into his body and guided him to the Vale of the Three Gods. Hidden there in the gloom of a swart-hill he saw no crystal fortress float like moon-disk through the leafy space; instead, in the hollow, stood the royal Christ Caer thatched with pale fire. Long time the Priest of the Sun wandered beneath the stars, hearing the talk of bells and hymns and of Saxon men. Before he turned toward the mountains, it seemed to him that a warrior clad in silver mail, riding a huge white war-horse, guarded the top of the tor. The bosses of his wide blue shield were myriad planets, and from the lifted sword of this Heavenly Hunter a rainbow river flowed down around the Isle of Avalon and the court of the unknown King.

At the Gathering of the Eagles in the West, the harper wove a spell of music so powerful that the print of each bard, passing with him into the ancient dark trod again the mysterious upward way through the ages. Woven in and out the glorious woof of sound range the wars of armoured angels and the lonely tread of the First Kings who taught man the secrets of fire and wheat; the circle was shaken by the trumpets of the conquerors of towered cities, or filled with the psalm of a prophet taming the fierce hearts of the tribe. Now the earth sang with rapture beneath the radiant feet of Arianrod; now a voice whispered to Mary of the Lilies. Then, when the lyre broke with the last cry from the Cross, the red ray touched the stony pinnacles, unseen, unhailed by the druids as they drank the words of the New God, come to lead them to the Dragon City of Light.

## VIII

With the drift of the years, the fiery oracles of the white and the red dragon were made plain. Crested kings in their sea wains, summoned by Vortigern from the ocean-foam, now divided the kingdom of Arthur. And the prophecy of the forest harp was fulfilled as the shadow of the rood fell across the ancient pillar of stones. The new truth brought men a new dreaming, for miracles were done behind the gates of the monasteries that arose throughout Saxonland. A new learning quickened the barbaric courts of Heptarchy, so that the hearts of the heroes yearned after the young Chieftain whose Caer opened to the cry of the warrior lost in the Wood of Death. Yet, in the outlying solitudes were still those who would follow the wild feet of the sun, heedless of the noble reds that flamed in coloured letters from the monkish vellums. These ever found more peace in the laughter of the Flower woman than a prayer chanted to the Mother of God.

In that time when the bards gathered in secret places, a harper wandered throught he land, sheltered in a shepherd's fleece, singing to the moor-wind and the moon, or borne upon a great horse, he was heard like a trumpet in the night by the warders on the watch-towers of a walled city. As he sang, the island folk remembered the strange wars over the herds of magic swine. Once more the lake-isle roared with the battle din of eagles, until the sleeping mere lay like a crimson shield and the helmed host of the West rallied to meet the coming foe. Again watchers upon a savage shore beheld the mystic coracle return from unknown seas, glowing with the Wine Bowl of a God. And the lords of the forest appeared upon their mountain, visions of earth's mysterious forces seen by man in his loneliness. Then the Radiant Brow sang the story of the White Christ, the companion of that loneliness, who waits beyond the wilderness of stars and winds and waters, with a heart like unto man's own.

The strings of the wizard harp are broken now. The hands that touched them have vanished from the world. Gone, too, are the rulers of battlemented Rheged; the arch-Druid veiled with the lonely dawn; the croziered Abbot in the mild shrine of the cloister tapers. Only the simple know how the grey wraith of a harper haunts the desolate gorge at fall of dew, how the armour of a gigantic warrior-prince gleams at midnight through a deserted valley street. But the songs sung under thatch of fern and thatch of gold live on, telling of the forgotten days when God drew nearest to the sons of men.

This tale of Taliesin was completed on the nineteenth day of January, in the year of our Lord one thousand nine hundred and thirty three.

1. Privately printed in New York, 1933 [Ed.].
2. Cantrev (or cantref) = roughly the equivalent of a county [Ed.].

# Chapter 19
# The Cosmic Legend[1]
## by Ross Nichols

## I

Twelve are the starbeams running light about the zenith-pole by night,
twelve the armoured months revolving weave the sword-dance bright:
brother-band of Maruts, youthful nobles, with the god of fire
shining constantly upon the earth with him their one desire
seven rivers bound with ice-chains to unleash and bid the spring.
Indra of the fire and sunrise
for the death of Vrita, cold
dragon coiling manifold,
is dancing with his arms and eyes
speaking very silently
under earth and in the skies.

Here like ascending domes haled from the earth's foundations
crebrant with twittering leaves the great trees come
dim-patterned mushrooms now in a larger than human meadow
misted and wreathed in a most fertile gloom.
The snowdrop and the violet lurk in the year's beginning yet,
the dews are cold the young grass wet, the moon updraws the sap
beneath the tree-bark from the roots' web-fingers and long tap.
Coos the ringdove with incipient domesticity,
fishes dart in water manifold in progeny.
The May-king leads the celandine smiling over field and hill,
Adonis the white hunter tips his arrows for the kill.
On mountain-side the moon Selene loves Endymion's sleep,
monthly in her waxing waning dotes upon his fleece-touched cheek.
Adonis will not Aphrodite, Endymion cares but for his sheep:
yet goodesses of love and death still the young men seek.
Dark the young strength of Arthur's name,
pale as the fatal horse his fame
who Gascoyne took with iron hook (swimming serpent of the night),
fisher of the northern mere and islands scarfed with light.

> The cup is filled the cup has power
>     the waters of new vision flow,
> the crops upstart, and into flower
>     the later grasses glow.
> The deep mist drowns the northern land
>     and channels of the yellow south
> floodwater fills; the lance upstands
>     and pierces the balloons of drought.
> Within the storehouse fill the shelves.
>     The people in the copper throne

intensely burnished, see themselves:
   the people and the king are one.

Legend of the earth's beginning, of the unaccomplished state
innocent of crime and virtue, Isis and her Horus-mate
son and husband, master tale whereon the race-myths variate.

## II

I would not throughout creation see the shadow that deep-grows
past the sunlight down the moonlight in the lichened rocks and shadows.
Now Isis, Magna Mater, Cybel, flies incumbent upon night
as a veil blown billowing outward from a window filled with light.
Stiffly gulls in circles flying crying round the unlit tower
through the omnipresence of a moonlit shade and shower:
these her familiars as in a mist thick-charged and visible
she sits aloof and wave-drifted, dark, concentrated, very still.
Cloudy wreaths creep round and vanish, spectral crowns arise and fail,
anchorless as lantern-lighted mountain swaying in a gale.
Earth-born children of the ages posture their memorial gloom,
heave upon the mouldering spaces marbles to the urn-decked tomb:
silk-heeled squires and swathed penmen gleam enormous white as doom —
solemn light across the pavement from the windows arching high
alternates with silent dusty darkness, stiff and dry.
Isis yet to reconcile with the dust of Horus-son
man and spirit; but the toilers of the world not yet had known
earth and heaven to bridge, or clutch with massive hand unskilled
when the Mother threw her girdle. As magicians Babel build
levering forces turned to evil; with divine pre-aim unfilled
their measureless grey strength miswilled.
Pharaohs, communes, demes and nations weltering perished from some rule
by godhead written and for earth designed
to quench from evil fiery desolate man.
The cruelty that worms the heart of love
feeds upon jealous sad despair; great pain
mingles with every sweetness fleshly grown.

The Cup is dry, the land is blowing with the dust of Horus slain.
The fated Mother hooded cut his stalk of life; she weeps again
lament for Thammuz and Adonis. Death-in-life Osiris reigns
on shadowed earth.

Excalibur is fixed within the magic stone.

Guinevere and her twelve maidens singing weep and weeping moan
in the chapel perilous beside the entranced neophyte;
the cup has floated far away from the questing knight.
See the temples of brown Egypt fill with eyes within, and cool
grows the intent of souls. Habit and air and fire
fall from the spirit.

Isis floated then
in darkened garments, lined with crescent moons, without desire.
Lakes with silver seeded, darkened under trees inverted green
bore her on the cosmic voyage for the Horus-dust divided

when the god betrayed was cut and scattered many-sided
among all men; and she the heavy searcher for the fragment-truth
hid on earth in many temples — quest through lands of age and youth:
Arthur at the close of day by the death-queen rowed away,
Adonis by the boar at bay pierced, lies gory-thighed.
Adonis-Attis gardens planting shallowly, the girls inchanting
weep to the sacred numen-tree in whose laden hollow
the form of carven Attis they may show.

O enwoven in the darkness: so to a faithless century,
ghostly mother, also coming: in the night a breded tree
is domed enormous to the sky with leaves that whisper and branches whine
brushing up among the stars, touching at the zenith's bars,
until they fall sometimes in fire through an arc entranced and fade
burnt for the glamour of earthly tales:
soft mansion of innumerable veils
that shield around from penetrable shade
ancient Isis: so within the night of drought and death
amid harsh breaths a softer breath is met
Weaves a loom of eerie dream,
    woven forms that mime and cry
and empassioned sleepers seem
    bound in weird reality
when the fluttering shape is sent
    charged with meaning's inner gleam
and swathed in moving lineament.

Then are the windows' pale blank overhang
of shifting shades on many a muted way
of that dun empire, glittering from a ray
through frond-lit trees as throbbing hum
touches the sleeping ear. So come
white morning and still pools of truth
showing still image in that vigil, youth.

Isis searches night by night in heaven and earth and stars (they say)
fragments of the ever-living Horus; and from day to day
what is found she joins, but never whole again has she
the child and mate she bore and slew in the land beside the sea.
That is the sorrow eternal, the sorrow of Isis unfree.

And even as your partial forms, O Isis — and even as she —
neither in light nor dark, come terribly
the hours of knowledge clear and dim
that build upon the loom for him,
the watcher, his flax-hearted thought
then with an image closely caught;
and when the intense hour is done
in memory is clearly laid
thought shapely as the informing shade
that lives when life and death are one.

Flows the blood of Mithra's bull, the waters under the moonpull
fall and draw out from the pool, the grain floats far away:
the Graal is vanished from the chapel where the knight lies grey.

I would not throughout creation see this shadow that deep-grows
even in sunlight and in snows:
cursed is this mad and musical mephitic air —
speak then I no more, there is horror in my hair.

# NADIR

The bed of darkness whereinto light bends
where thought begins and toward which it tends:
here round and round the silent stones are rolled
wherewith the caster makes the vital mould:
there constantly the changing clays are poured,
then taken, hard and changeless, to be stored
with all the records of the dead that lie
time past, in barren dull rigidity.

Yet is no past, no future, and no fate
but being, jetting from the increate.
The breath whereon the universe is poised
exhales, indraws, undreaded and unnoised.
So does the large-expanded ocean breathe
in mists that on the silent headlands wreathe.
By forms from this unseeing mould we live;
time here goes meaningless as some old sieve
no longer straining the grey death-dust through.
Simultaneity is the sole view
of the eternal eye that never shone
because it is that which it looks upon.
The eye in matter veiled can only see
the wild destruction danced by Shiva, he
whose traceries are spread before man's face:
not so the gathering in depths of space,
the exhalation germinal and vast
of Brahma's breath sustaining first and last.

# III

*Prose*:
I have made my ceremonies; the crisis
comes. None can reproduce, no water flow,
until the sword is from its sheath pulled.
Only I, the medicine-man Gawain, instructing
at midnight Galahad, the pure one of
spring — I alone can save you, faithless
with the fallen leaf. I prove to you,
O my dead people, once again that
I alone am your strength.

In the first ray beating touching on the centre altar-stone
to the eye prepared at vigil-end, the vessel of the sun,
cup and heart, to Galahad.
            Life runs along the central vein:
on the broadened ray the yellow seeds are floating in a rain:
so the neophytes entranced can move their hands and feet
as from the stone the sword leaps out, as the pulses beat

strongly in the waiting people — rising of the slain,
movement-ripple as the crowd
with smile and speech move each to each.
Now from a deep blue cloud
the oarless barge of sleep
carries again twelve figures from its deep,
surround that fisher king who lives again
his simple folk to greet.

## IV

Horus in Isis can fulfil, man and woman have their will
each of each; the night is still, the secret forces rise.
Glory in the darkness: Isis has the power that prisoned lies
in the search and in the shadow warm, creative, slow and wise
in the night beneath the moon, when the male forces wane
and the woman, white, pervasive, moves in restless joy and pain,
tremulous and flowerlike, with shining knowledge wan.
The face that dances silently through the star-powdered sky
with a yellow mirror, lips that flicker movelessly,
is the vessel of her strength unfolded riding by.
All the silver mazes drawn by Aphrodite orbed at sea
lead but into one deep cavern soft and warm and free
where the man at last at rest his peace extends; the cave is she.
On the sun-filled plain and mountain comes the power to man;
all Adonis flame-ringed chases with a hunter's cry
down the golden frets and clanging corridors of sky.
Engine-muscled implemental on the earth, the man in pain
sweating cuts and cutting binds, threshes heavy grain.
On the weary plain go wending the yoke-cattle dusty grey
beneath the hammers of eternal heat and showering sparks all day
from the sun's colossal forge white-blinding from of old.
Behind the trees at forest-edge in black and crooked fantasy
wave and ripple rich on ripple hangs the sheeted corn in gold.

As Rá in angry pleasure runs along the western rim
man the hard won sheaf is carrying with wasted limb:
nightly then the garnered taking, she transmuting not in vain
shapes conception; Isis blows through her unknowing brain,
every motion hers is filled with thoughtless wisdom, she who is
the urgent lifecup and the circle.

      Horus mangled lies
in a thousand pieces, cut by his ambition (so
mankind is lost in its inventions' curious vain show).
Horus, Isis — rhythm of the aeons in the earth and air;
the careworn and divided one — the brooding and the bare.
Man that taketh woman . . . Horus to the ancient Isis there.

On sanded waste a youth with a maiden oxen-eyed
slowly wandered hand in hand on feet that searched no path, but wide
went, with only footpalms knowing how they walked, for so
enwrapped they were that eye and mind did large and single grow.
Isis hovering sought and muttered in their touches soft and slow.
Crebrant is the land; the throne restored and shining; seasons swing

again beneath twelve signs, the noble youths that dance about the spring
dance to the completed ring.
Persephone sometime is captive, Mithra now shall mediate
knowing life and death; the people comforted endure to wait:
for the circle is fulfilled, life and death have been explored
and deepened summer ripens Attis-Arthur, the wise risen lord.

## PROSE OF THE MYTH FUSION EMPLOYED

*First Movement*:

In the sky and from sky to earth dance the star-beams, a flashing sword-dance
by twelve glorious youths of equal age (Maruts, Korētes, Salii, Knights). They
are fertility daimons dancing eternally for the freeing of the waters, seven rivers
imprisoned by Vrita; the feat is performed by Indra (the god of fire, lightning
and volcano) for the coming of the May King, the spirit of Adonis loved by
Aphrodite, of Endymion loved by the fertility-moon Selene, of all vegetation.
Fishes and doves are symbols of fertility; Arthur the fisher-king catches
Gascoyne the world-fish of reproduction (Sesha, the world-serpent). As Attis
he is loved by the mother-goddess, as king he is loved by Guinevere. The Graal
dwells in the land, by the waters of plenty.

Symbol of the guarded Graal

*Second Movement*:

The god-king is smitten with the Dolorous Stroke, Adonis is wounded in the
thigh, Attis is emasculated by the mother-goddess, Horus is cut up by his
enemies, Arthur's kingdom is desolated, fertility is gone, the Graal vanishes.
Osiris the underworld undersoil death-in-life god reigns. Excalibur is
immovable in the stone.

The eternal mother-lover who is essentially the moon, Isis-Aphrodite, Magna
Mater, Cybele, Anahita, laments for the scattered Horus, for Thammuz, for
Attis-Adonis; Selene watches over Endymion, Guinevere weeps with her
maidens. All nature is waste.

Arthur is rowed away over the death-waters, Horus (who is also the scattered
seed) is dispersed throughout the land. In his death must die also the initiate
in the chapel perilous. The grain is floated away. The sacred Bull bleeds under
the knife of Mithra. It is the indrawing of creation's breath, the darkness of
Brahma, the triumph of Shiva.

The sword-in-stone symbol

*Third Movement*:
Appears the hero, the returning year, the medicine man, Gawain-Galahad, the herb-healer. His is the vigil of the initiate, and with him watch all the initiation-test novices. The dead knight-king is in the chapel perilous; by him the Graal-aspirant awaits the vision. If he fail, if the novices fail, they too die. The proof of the success of the initiation is in the resurrection of the god-king, the new birth of the year, the new flame of spring. Galahad initiated by Gawain alone can draw the symbolic sword from the stone, free the reproductive powers from the chill of death; he rides out with the unconquered lance and to him comes the vision of the Graal, the Cup, the female emblem; and where the Cup is, there is plenty and moisture.

Symbol of the piercing lance and fire

*Fourth Movement*:
Isis collects into a whole her scattered child Horus, Arthur arises from sleep, comes again from the West; the initiation is completed. He is the same yet different; he identifies in his renewed youth with the hero, he is Attis, he is Adonis, loved again by the mother-wife-goddess. He is now the six-months' sojourner on earth, the season of growth and fruition; but Persephone must later spend six months in captivity with Dis of the underworld. The Lord is risen, the seasons revolve again. He is now the mediator, knowing both life and death; he is agent, as Mithra, of the resurrection of all men. The circle is completed.

The four parts of the completed cycle may therefore be summed in the phrases; Spring paean — the trance of death — the efficacious magic — resurrection and fulfilment.

## A NOTE ON VARIANT ELEMENTS

A word is due to the scholar of mythology.
   I am aware that not all the mythical figures quite fit into this generalized myth; the death of the hero remains (probably advantageously) mysterious — whether he is motivelessly sacrificed by the mother-goddess or cut up by enemies: herein therefore it has been left inconsistent. Similarly, the confusion

between Gawain and Galahad — or whether Galahad *is* Gawain, or a risen Arthur; and the confusion between the short seasonal cycle (spring death and late summer life) and the longer yearly cycle (autumn death and spring life); both are unresolved.

More detailed divergences I here merely note, again without attempting to synthesize opposing conceptions. In brief, Attis-Adonis-Thammuz is essentially a youth loved by a goddess; only after tragic death does he become divine. There was for his Phrygian followers a mystic feast in which women also partook. The Attis initiate theoretically died with his hero and rose with him; presumably a western version of well-known Indian mystical initiation methods.

Mithra, however, is from the first a mediator between god and man; he is also the sun (his is a Persian cult) and agent of the resurrection of all men, the sacrificer of the divine bull in whose blood his followers were washed. The ritual was an all-male one, a favourite with soldiers. The Mithra initiate did not die — the bull's death as all-sufficing; but he rose direct to the new life, up seven ladders into heaven.

1. Originally published in *The Cosmic Shape* by Ross Nichols & James Kirkup (The Forge Press, 1946) [Ed.].

# Chapter 20
# A Dream of Angus Oge[1]
## by 'A.E.'

The day had been wet and wild, and the woods looked dim and drenched from the window where Con sat. All the day long his ever restless feet were running to the door in a vain hope of sunshine. His sister, Norah, to quiet him had told him over and over again the tales which delighted him; the delight of hearing which was second only to the delight of living them over himself, when as Cuculain he kept the ford which led to Ulla, his sole hero heart matching the hosts of Meave; or as Fergus he wielded the sword of light the Druids made and gave to the champion, which in its sweep shore away the crests of the moutains; or as Brian, the ill-fated child of Turenn, he went with his brothers in the ocean-sweeping boat further than ever Columbus travelled, winning one by one in dire conflict with kings and enchanters the treasures which would appease the implacable heart of Lu.

He had just died in a corner of the room from his many wounds when Norah came in declaring that all these famous heroes must go to bed. He protested in vain, but indeed he was sleepy, and before he had been carried half way to the room the little soft face drooped with half-closed eyes, while he drowsily rubbed his nose upon her shoulder in an effort to keep awake. For a while she flitted about him, looking, with her dark shadowy hair flickering in the dim, silver light, like one of the beautiful heroines of Gaelic romance, or one of the twilight race of the Sidhe. Before going she sat by his bed and sang to him some verses of a song, set to an old Celtic air whose low intonations were full of a half soundless mystery —

> Over the hill-tops the gay lights are peeping;
> > Down in the vale where the dim fleeces stray
> Ceases the smoke from the hamlet upcreeping:
> > Come, thou, my shepherd, and lead me away.

'Who's the shepherd?' said the boy, suddenly sitting up.
'Hush, alannah: I will tell you another time.' She continued still more softly:

> Lord of the Wand, draw forth from the darkness,
> > Wrap of the silver, and woof of the gold:
> Leave the poor shade there bereft in its starkness:
> > Wrapped in the fleece we will enter the Fold.

> There from the many-orbed heart where the Mother
> > Breathes forth the love on her darlings who roam,
> We will send dreams to their land of another
> > Land of the Shining, their birthplace and home.

He would have asked a hundred questions, but she bent over him, enveloping him with a sudden nightfall of hair, to give him his good-night kiss, and departed. Immediately the boy sat up again, all his sleepiness gone. The pure, gay, delicate spirit of childhood was darting at ideas dimly perceived in the delicious moonlight of romance which silvered his brain, where many airy and beautiful figures were moving: the Fianna with floating locks chasing the flying deer; shapes more solemn, vast, and misty, guarding the avenues to unspeakable secrets; but he steadily pursued his idea.

'I'd guess he's one of the people who take you away to faeryland. Wonder if he'd come to me? Think it's easy going away'; with an intuitive perception of the frailty of the link binding childhood to earth in its dreams. (As a man Con will strive with passionate intensity to regain that free gay motion in the upper airs.) 'Think I'll try if he'll come'; and he sang, with as near an approach as he could make to the glimmering cadences of his sister's voice:

> Come, thou, my shepherd, and lead me away.

He then lay back quite still and waited. He could not say whether hours or minutes had passed, or whether he had slept or not, until he was aware of a tall golden-bearded man standing by his bed. Wonderfully light was this figure, as if the sunlight ran through his limbs; a spiritual beauty was on the face, and those strange eyes of bronze and gold with their subtle intense gaze made Con aware for the first time of the difference between inner and outer in himself.

'Come, Con, come away!' the child seemed to hear utterred silently.

'You're the Shepherd,' said Con, 'I'll go.' Then suddenly; 'I won't come back and be old when they're all dead?' a vivid remembrance of Ossian's fate flashing upon him.

A most beautiful laughter, which again to Con seemed half soundless, came in reply. His fears vanished; the golden-bearded man stretched a hand over him for a moment, and he found himself out in the night, now clear and starlit. Together they moved on as if borne by the wind, past many woods and silver gleaming lakes, and mountains which shone like a range of opals below the purple skies. The Shepherd stood still for a moment by one of these hills, and there flew out riverlike a melody mingled with a tinkling as of innumerable elfin hammers, and there was a sound of many gay voices where an unseen people were holding festival, or enraptured hosts who were let loose for the awakening, the new day which was to dawn, for the delighted child felt that faeryland was come over again with its heroes and battles.

'Our brothers rejoice,' said the Shepherd of Con.

'Who are they?' asked the boy.

'They are the thoughts of our Father.'

'May we go in?' Con asked, for he was fascinated by the melody, mystery and flashing lights.

'Not now. We are going to my home where I lived in the days past when there came to me many kings and queens of ancient Eiré, many heroes and beautiful women, who longed for the Druid wisdom we taught.'

'And did you fight like Finn, and carry spears as tall as trees, and chase the deer through the wood, and have feasting and singing?'

'No, we, the Dananns, did none of those things; but those who were weary of battle, and to whom feast and song brought no pleasure, came to us and passed hence to a more wonderful land, a more immortal land than this.'

As he spoke, he paused before a great mound grown over with trees, and around it silver clear in the moonlight were immense stones piled, the remains of an original circle, and there was a dark, low, narrow entrance leading within. He took Con by the hand, and in an instant they were standing in a lofty, cross-shaped cave built roughly of huge stones.

'This was my palace. In days past many a one plucked here the purple flower of magic and the fruit of the tree of life.'

'It is very dark,' said the child disconsolately. He had expected something different.

'Nay, but look: you will see it is the palace of a god.' And even as he spoke a light began to glow and to pervade the cave, and to obliterate the stone walls and the antique hieroglyphs engraven thereon, and to melt the earthen floor into itself like a fiery sun suddenly uprisen within the world, and there was everywhere a wandering ecstasy of sound: light and sound were one; light had a voice, and the music hung glittering in the air.

'Look, how the sun is dawning for us, ever dawning; in the earth, in our hearts, with ever youthful and triumphant voices. Your sun is but a smoky shadow, ours the ruddy and eternal glow; yours is far away, ours is heart and hearth and home; yours is a light without, ours a fire within in rock, in river, in plain, everywhere living, everywhere dawning, whence also it cometh that the mountains emit their wondrous rays.'

As he spoke he seemed to breathe the brilliance of that mystical sunlight and to dilate and tower, so that the child looked up to a giant pillar of light having in his heart a sun of ruddy gold which shed its blinding rays about him, and over his head there was a waving of fiery plumage, and on his face an ecstasy of beauty and immortal youth.

'I am Angus,' Con heard; 'men call me the Young. I am the sunlight in the heart, the moonlight in the mind; I am the light at the end of every dream, the voice for ever calling to come away; I am desire beyond joy or tears. Come with me, come with me: I will make you immortal; for my palace opens into the Gardens of the Sun, and there are the fire-fountains which quench the heart's desire in rapture.' And in the child's dream he was in a palace high as the stars, with dazzling pillars jewelled like the dawn and all fashioned out of living and trembling opal. And upon their thrones sat the Danann gods with their sceptres and diadems of rainbow light, and upon their faces infinite wisdom and imperishable youth. In the turmoil and growing chaos of his dream he heard a voice crying out, 'You remember, Con, Con, Conaire Mor, you remember!' and in an instant he was torn from himself and had grown vaster, and was with the Immortals, seated upon their thrones, they looking upon him as a brother, and he was flying away with them into the heart of the gold when he awoke, the spirit of childhood dazzled with the vision which is too lofty for princes.

1.  Originally published in *Imaginations and Reveries* (Maunsel & Co., 1915) [Ed.].

# Bibliography of Further Reading

All books are published in London, unless otherwise stated.

## TEXTS

Allchin, A.M. and De Waal, Esther (eds.), *Threshold of Light: Prayers and Praises from the Celtic Tradition* (Darton, Longman & Todd, 1986).

Cross, T.P. and Slover, C.H., *Ancient Irish Tales* (Dublin, Figgis, 1936).

Dillon, Miles, *Cycles of the Irish Kings* (Geoffrey Cumberledge/Oxford University Press, 1946).

Gantz, Jeffrey, *Early Irish Myths and Sagas* (Harmondsworth, Penguin, 1981).

Geoffrey of Monmouth, *History of the Kings of Britain* (Harmondsworth, Penguin, 1966).

——, *Vita Merlini*, tr. J.J. Parry (Illinois, University of Illinois Press, 1925).

Gerald of Wales, *The History and Topography of Ireland*, tr. John O'Meara (Harmondsworth, Penguin, 1982).

——, *The Journey Through Wales*, tr. Lewis Thorpe (Harmondsworth, Penguin, 1978).

Jackson, Kenneth Hurstone, *A Celtic Miscellany* (Routledge & Kegan Paul, 1951).

Joyce, P.W., *Old Celtic Romances* (C. Kegan Paul, 1879).

*Lebor Gabala Erenn* (The Book of the Taking of Ireland) (5 vols.), tr. R.A. Stewart Macalister (Dublin, Irish Texts Society, 1938, 1939, 1940, 1941, 1956).

*The Mabinogion*, tr. Lady Charlotte Guest (Ballantyne Press, 1910).

*The Metrical Dindsenchas* (5 parts), tr. Edward Gwynn (Dublin, Hodges, Figgis & Co., 1903–35).

Meyer, Kuno, *Ancient Irish Poetry* (Constable, 1913).

——, 'Death Tales of the Ulster Heroes', in *Royal Irish Academy Todd Lecture Series*, xiv (Dublin, Hodges, 1906).

——, *The Voyage of Bran Son of Febal* (David Nutt, 1895).

'The Prose Tales in the Rennes Dindsenchas', ed. and tr. Whitley Stokes, in *Revue Celtique*, 15, 272–336, 418–84; 16, 31–83, 135–167, 269–312.

*Sanas Chormaic* (Cormac's Glossary), tr. John O'Donovan, ed. Whitley Stokes, (Calcutta, O.T. Cutter, 1868).

'The Colloquy of the Two Sages', tr. Whitley Stokes, *Revue Celtique*, 26 (1905), 4–64.

*Tain Bo Cuailnge* (The Cattle Raid of Cooley), tr. Thomas Kinsella (Dublin, Dolmen Press, 1970).

*Trioedd Ynys Prydein* (The Welsh Triads), ed. and tr. Rachel Bromwich (Cardiff, University of Wales Press, 1961).

# THE CELTS IN FOLK TRADITION

Campbell, J.F., *Popular Tales of the West Highlands* (4 vols.) (Wildwood Press, 1983–4).

*Carmina Gadelica* (6 vols.), tr. Alexander Carmichael (Edinburgh, Scottish Academic Press, 1972).

Curtin, Jeremiah, *Hero Tales of Ireland* (Macmillan, 1894).

Mackenzie, Donald A., *Wonder Tales from Scottish Myth and Legend* (Glasgow, Blackie and Son, 1917).

Wimberley, Lowry Charles, *Folklore in the English and Scottish Ballads* (Chicago, University of Chicago Press, 1928).

Young, Ella, *Celtic Wonder Tales* (Edinburgh, Floris Books, 1985).

# GENERAL BOOKS

Bamford, Christopher and Marsh, William Price, *Celtic Christianity* (Edinburgh, Floris Books, 1986).

Byrne, F.J., *Irish Kings and High Kings* (Batsford, 1973).

Carney, James and Green, David (eds.), *Celtic Studies* (Routledge & Kegan Paul, 1968).

Corkery, Daniel, *The Hidden Ireland* (Dublin, Gill & Macmillan, 1967).

Cunliffe, Barry, *The Celtic World* (Bodley Head, 1979).

De Jubainville, H. D'Arbois, *The Irish Mythological Cycle* tr. Richard Irvine (Dublin, O'Donoghue and Co., 1903).

Delaney, Frank, *A Walk in the Dark Ages* (Collins, 1988).

Dillon, Myles and Chadwick, Nora, *The Celtic Realms* (New York, New American Library, 1967).

Finlay, Ian, *Columba* (Gollancz, 1979).

Gregory, Lady, *The Voyage of St Brendan the Navigator and Stories of the Saints of Ireland* (Gerrard's Cross, Colin Smythe, 1973).

Guyonvarc'h, Christian-J., *Textes Mythologiques Irlandais*, I, (Rennes, Ogam-Celticum, 1980).

Guyot, Charles, *The Legend of the City of Ys* (Amherst, University of Massachusetts Press, 1979).

Herm, Gerhard, *The Celts* (Weidenfeld & Nicholson, 1976).

Hubert, H., *The Rise of the Celts* (Constable, 1987).

——, *The Greatness and Decline of the Celts* (Constable, 1987).

Humphries, Emyr, *The Taliesin Tradition* (Black Raven Press, 1983).

Joyce, P.W., *A Social History of Ancient Ireland* (Longmans, Green & Co., 1903).

Keating, Geoffrey, *The History of Ireland* (4 vols.), (Irish Texts Society, 1902, 1908, 1914).

Le Roux, Françoise and Guyonvarc'h, Christian-J., *Les Druides* (Rennes, Ouest-France, 1986).

66. Löffer, Christa Maria, *The Voyage to the Otherworld Island in Early Irish Literature* (Doctoral dissertation in 2 parts) (Salzburg, Institut für Anglistik und Amerikanistik, Universität Salzburg, 1983).

Logan, J., *The Scottish Gael* (2 vols.), (John Donald, Edinburgh, 1976).

Mac Cana, Proinsias, *The Learned Tales of Medieval Ireland* (Dublin, Dublin Institute for Advanced Studies, 1980).

Macleod, Fiona (William Sharp), *The Winged Destiny* (New York, Lemma Pub. Corp., 1974).

Macneill, John T., *The Celtic Churches: a History* AD *200–1200* (Chicago, University of Chicago Press, 1974).

Mallory, J.P., *In Search of the Indo-Europeans* (Thames & Hudson, 1989).

Markale, Jean, *Celtic Civilization* (Gordon Cremonesi, 1978).

Matthews, Caitlín, *Arthur and the Sovereignty of Britain* (Arkana, 1989).

——, *Mabon and the Mysteries of Britain* (Arkana, 1987).

Matthews, Caitlín and John, *The Western Way* (2 vols.) (Arkana, 1985, 1986).

Matthews, John, *The Elements of the Arthurian Tradition* (Shaftesbury, Element Books, 1989).

——, *The Elements of the Grail Tradition* (Shaftesbury, Element Books, 1990).

——, *Gawain, Knight of the Goddess* (Wellingborough, Aquarian Press, 1990).

——, *Taliesin: Shamanic Mysteries of Britain and Ireland* (Unwin Hyman, 1990).

Merry, E.C., *The Flaming Door: The Mission of the Celtic Folk-Soul* (Edinburgh, Floris Books, 1983).

Montague, John (ed.), *The Faber Book of Irish Verse* (Faber, 1974).

Naddair, Kaledon, *Keltic Folk and Faerie Tales* (Century, 1987).

O'Curry, Eugene, *On the Manners and Customs of the Ancient Irish* (Williams & Norgate, 1873).

O'Hogain, Dáithi, *Fionn Mac Cumhail* (Dublin, Gill & Macmillan, 1988).

——, *The Hero in Irish Folk History* (Dublin, Gill & Macmillan, 1986).

Rees, Alwyn and Brinley, *Celtic Heritage* (Thames & Hudson, 1961).

Renfrew, Colin, *Archaeology and Language: The Puzzle of Indo-European Origins* (Cape, 1987).

Rhys, J., *The Hibbert Lectures on the Growth of Religion as Illustrated by Celtic Heathendom* (Williams & Norgate, 1888).

Ross, Anne, *Pagan Celtic Britain* (Routledge & Kegan Paul, 1967).

Sjoestedt, Maie-Louise, *Gods and Heroes of the Celts* (Berkeley, Turtle Island Foundation, 1982).

Stover, Leon E. and Kraig, Brian, *Stonehenge: The Indo-European Tradition* (Chicago, Nelson-Hall, 1978).

# Discography

The following records and tapes are recommended for capturing the spirit of the Celtic world.

## The Celtic Tribe

Aberjaber, *Cerddoriaeth o'r Gweledydd Celtaidd* (Sain/Cambrian 1340M).
Davey, Sean, *The Pilgrim* (TARA 3011).
Williamson, Robin, *Music for the Mabinogion* (Ceirnini Cladaigh CCF10).

## The Otherworld

Davey, Sean, *The Brendan Voyage* (Tara 3006).
Matthews, Caitlín and John, *Walking the Western Way* (meditation tape) (Sulis Music and Tapes, BCM Box 3721, London WC1N 3XX).
Stewart, Bob, *The Unique Sound of the Psaltery*, (Sulis Music and Tapes, BCM Box 3721, London WC1N 3XX).
Stivell, Alan, *Légende* (AZ/475).

## The Celtic Church

Ni Riain, Noirin and the Monks of Glenstal, *Caoineadh na Maighdine* (Gael-Linn CEF084).
Ni Riain, Noirin and the Monks of Glenstal, *Good People All* (Glenstal GR01).
Reznikoff, Iegor, *Alleluias et Offertoires des Gaules* (Harmonia Mundi HM 40.1044).

# Journals

*Cambridge Medieval Celtic Studies*, Dept of Anglo-Saxon, Norse and Celtic, 9 West Road, Cambridge CB3 9DP (2 issues a year).

*Seanchas*, The Journal of the Celtic Research and Folklore Society, Ivy Cottage, Glenasdale, Whiting Bay, Isle of Arran, Scotland. (This is is one of the most accessible of the scholarly journals where recent Celtic scholarship is aired.)

# Useful Addresses

When writing to any of these addresses, please remember an SAE or international reply-paid coupons for a response.

**Keltia Publications,** P.O. Box 307, Edinburgh EH9 1XA. Kaledon Naddair publishes numerous books and magazines in the Celtic and Pictish spirit, as well as selling other artifacts. He also runs a college of Druidism.

**Order of Bards, Ovates and Druids,** 260 Kew Road, Richmond, Surrey TW9 3EG. The Order runs a correspondence course and numerous other activities in the spirit of the Celtic Mysteries, combining concern for the planet earth. It also runs a tree-planting programme.

**Sulis Music and Tapes,** BCM 3721, London WC1N 3XX. Issues many musical, magical and meditation tapes of Celtic interest.

**Robin Williamson Productions,** P.O. Box 27522, Los Angeles, Calif. 90027, U.S.A. Issue many tapes of Celtic story-telling and song, arranged and performed by a modern bard.

**Domus Sophiae Terrae et Sancte Gradalae,** BCM-HALLOWQUEST, London WC1N 3XX. For more information about courses and workshops led by Caitlín and John Matthews, please send four first class stamps or two international reply-paid coupons to the above address.